About the author

Violet Barungi was born in Mbarara, westei
Bweranyangi Girls School, Gayaza High Schoc
Kampala, where she graduated with a BA (Honou
married and has six children.

Violet Barungi's first novel, *The Shadow and The Substance,* was published by Lake Publishers, Kenya, in 1998 and her play, *Over My Dead Body,* won the British Council International New Playwriting Award for Africa and The Middle East, 1997. She has also published a number of short stories in magazines and short story anthologies. She also writes short stories for children.

Violet Barungi is currently working with **FEMRITE** (Uganda Women Writers Assocition).

CASSANDRA

Violet Barungi

FEMRITE PUBLICATIONS LIMITED
KAMPALA

FEMRITE PUBLICATIONS LIMITED
P. O. Box 705, KAMPALA
Tel: 256-041-543943/256-077 743943
Email: femrite@infocom.co.ug

Printed in Uganda by **The New Vision**

ISBN 9970 9010 4 4

Ever let Fancy Roam,
Pleasure never is at home:
At a touch sweet Pleasure Melteth,
Then let Winged Fancy Wander
Through the thought still spread beyond her:
Open wide the mind's cage-door,
She'll dart forth, and cloudward soar.

John Keats

Chapter One

Cassandra was walking home one evening when a car screeched to a stop, missing her by a hair's breadth. She jumped clear before turning to glare at the homicidal driver.

"Well, well, if it isn't Cassandra Tibwita!" the man behind the wheel drawled, thrusting his head out of the car window.

It took Cassandra only a fraction of a second to recognise the laconic voice. She bent slightly towards the car and received full-blast the effect of the mesmeric eyes of Raymond Agutamba. She had met him at a party and the two had quickly developed a rapport between them, the dark beguiling eyes in the handsome face making an indelible mark on her heart. It gave her quite a jolt, though, to feel her heart thundering away at the mere sound of his voice.

"It's you!" she said inanely, momentarily deprived of her faculties.

"Yes, it's me," he confirmed in his lazy voice. His mouth opened slightly in a kind of smile, revealing snow-white teeth neatly set in dark gums.

"Hop in and I'll take you the rest of the way," he added, holding the passenger's door invitingly open.

"Thank you, Mr . . . eh . . . Agutamba, isn't it?"

The hesitation was for effect, of course, since his name had been sculpted on her memory right from their first meeting, and since he also shared it with his brother, Bevis, a great friend of her own brother, Gavin.

"Yes, Raymond Agutamba. I'm flattered you still remember my name," he added mocking her.

"What I was endeavouring to say, Mr Agutamba, is that I'm only a short distance away from my destination. But thank you all the same," she said, managing an inflexion of brusqueness in her voice and turning to walk on.

"Wait a minute please," Raymond pleaded, all signs of indolence gone.

"Look, Cassandra . . . Miss Tibwita, if you prefer, I'd like to buy you a soda, or a cup of coffee if you're not in too much of a hurry. I'm not a dirty old man, honestly. And in any case, you look quite capable of defending yourself in the unlikely event of such a situation arising."

1

Little do you know, Cassandra thought grimly. Aloud she said, "Okay, I accept. It's getting rather chilly and the prospect of a hot cup of coffee sounds tempting."

"So how have you been, Cassandra, since we last met three months ago, isn't it?" he asked when they were seated and had both been served with steaming mugs of insant coffee. He was leaning back in his chair, his eyes studying her with a trance-inducing gaze.

"Three months? So long?" she remarked for lack of something better to say.

"Does it seem as if we just met recently to you too? Didn't you ever wonder whether we'd meet again?" he asked.

"I've been rather busy," she replied, avoiding a direct answer.

"Ah, yes, I remember you said you worked for a publishing firm. Tell me, what do you exactly do?"

"Well, I work in the editorial section, reviewing and preparing manuscripts for publication," she explained, glad to be on home ground.

"That sounds like an interesting job. You get to read all that stuff free while we have to pay enormous sums of money for the procurement of a single copy. Aren't you the lucky ones!"

"It's not all that interesting really. Reading for pleasure and reading with the object of assessing and correcting are two different things. Besides, we don't deal with works of an entertaining nature only. We get quite a lot of technical stuff too. Of course we usually refer highly specialised material to experts in the field for vetting and recommendation. That reminds me, would you mind if I included your name on our readers' list? Someone might venture to write a book on architecture one of these days. Or better still, we could commission you to write one. Would it sell, do you think?" she asked.

"Firstly, I'm afraid I 'd not accept your commission. That kind of work entails a lot of research which is time-consuming. As for the marketability of the book, I would not bet on it."

"Why's that? What about the school of architecture which has just opened at the University? How about all the polytechnics? Surely they need reference books."

"And they already have them in plenty in the libraries, courtesy of our donors. Shall we order another round of coffee?" he asked, glancing at her empty cup.

"No, thanks. For coffee, one's my limit."

"Perhaps we could change to something more heat-generating. What do you say to that?"

"It's still no, thank you. I must be getting home now. I stay with my

2

brother and have to see to things, you know," she added vaguely, searching for an avenue of escape.

Her instinct told her that a liaison with this man could be fatal. It could lead to a situation that could prove too big for her to handle and interfere with her carefully laid out plans. Already her heart was clamouring for a closer relationship after only two meetings. If that was not a danger warning, then she did not know what danger warnings were like. She was committed to making something worthwhile of her life and if she allowed anybody or anything to interfere with that commitment, she would end up like thousands of other women, behind a kitchen sink and a line of dripping nappies. Men were the reason why the majority of women were still lagging behind in social, economic and political development. Once you let a man into your life, it was good-bye to ambitions of meaningful existence.

"A penny for them?" her companion broke into her thoughts.

"A penny? I'll have you know, sir, my thoughts are worth more than a penny."

"A pound then," he suggested, smiling pleasurably at her.

"Make it a dollar. An American dollar."

"Oh dear," he sighed, putting on an expression of utter gravity as he dramatically searched his pockets. "I'm sorry, I carry only local." He displayed twenty and fifty Uganda shilling notes.

Cassandra looked at them despairingly and with a sigh said, "I suppose I'll have to forgo the dollar and let them go for free."

"Wait a minute, do you have a piece of writing paper? A notebook, perhaps?"

Puzzled by his request but nonetheless willing to humour him, Cassandra fished in her spacious shoulder bag and produced a diary. "Will this do?"

"Perfectly," he said but made no move to take it. "Might I trouble you further and ask you to select a suitable page for me? I don't want to pry into your maidenly secrets," he added.

"Oh you," Cassandra said, laughing infectiously. "I have no secrets from a stranger. Here you are," she added, pointing to a blank 'Notes' page at the back.

"Thank you," he murmured as he pushed his cup aside and, extracting a pen from his jacket pocket, started to write with studied gravity, enunciating loudly thus, "I Raymond, owe you, Cassandra, 1 US dollar." He signed with a flourish and held it out to her to see. "My IOU clearly written and signed but, unfortunately, not witnessed. Still, legal and binding, I think. What do you say to that?"

"I say you're a very funny man, Mr Agutamba," Cassandra replied, trying hard not to laugh at his antics. She accepted her diary back and, when he suggested that they drink to the beginning of their new relationship, she did not demur.

"Just a little one and I must be on my way, Mr Agutamba."

"I call you Cassandra, why don't you call me Raymond, or Ray for short?"

"Ray," she rolled the name on her tongue huskily, and raised her eyes to his face but her gaze suddenly wavered and she turned away, studying other patrons of the place to see whether the world was still the same and people were still walking on two feet or whether they had grown wings. She felt positively ethereal herself. She turned back to Raymond and found his gaze steadfast on her.

"Shall we go?" he asked, forgetting their proposed toast.

Cassandra silently got up and shouldered her bag.

Outside the gate to her brother's house, Raymond stopped the car and switched off the engine. "Thank you, Cassandra," he said softly. She did not answer. She did not understand why he was thanking her. Her emotions were in chaos and she was wondering how to end the evening with minimum damage to herself. "Cassandra?"

When she turned her face in his direction, he cupped it in his hands and looked deep into her almond eyes. "I always kiss my dates goodnight, do you mind?" he said as he brought his mouth down on hers, at first in a gentle, exploratory kiss, which, as time progressed, turned perilously to agonising intensity. "Goodnight, Cassandra," he said, releasing her. He leaned across and opened the door for her and she tottered out.

She had taken only a few steps when he halted her with, "By the way, 'Tibwita', what does it mean – *obusasi ninga oburungi?*"

She turned and stared at him blankly at first. When she finally got the meaning of his question, she said shortly, "Both," and stalked away towards the gate, feeling strangely disappointed that he had not suggested they meet again.

Raymond did not drive away immediately she left him but sat still in the gathering dusk, trying to make sense of his strange behaviour of the evening. Cassandra was, without doubt, a wonderful girl; not the type for casual affairs, and casual affairs were all that were left him. With a grimace, he put the car in gear and let out the clutch. But all the way to his lonely house in Muyenga, his thoughts kept returning again and again to the girl with the almond eyes and the rhythmic swing to her body. She was as refreshing as a cold morning breeze after a hot, sweltering night. So different from the insipid, flirtatious females he came across at every turn.

The state of euphoria stayed with him for a long time afterwards. He knew he should not have engineered a second meeting, the warnings had been loud and clear the first time they met. So he resolved that he would not give in to the dictates of his heart again, although it was nice to dream again, pleasant dreams.

* * *

Mellinda opened the kitchen door to Cassandra's knock and immediately noticed how upset the latter looked. "What's the matter, Cassandra?" she asked sharply but Cassandra walked past without answering.

"Is something wrong?" Mellinda asked again. "You look ghastly. Did somebody try to mug you?"

"Mug?" Cassandra laughed uproariously. "I suppose you could call it that."

"What do you mean?" Mellinda exclaimed, alarmed by her manner.

"What do I mean?" Cassandra sighed, sobering up immediately. "I wish I knew." She threw her bag on the chair and followed it with a plonk as her body sagged in. For some time, she sat hunched forward, cheek in hand, seemingly lost in a world of her own. "What do you know about Raymond Agutamba, Mellie?" she finally asked.

"So that's it!" her sister exclaimed. "Every woman in town below the age of seventy knows about Raymond Agutamba."

"Umm, as bad as that? I thought so," Cassandra remarked, getting up and wandering listlessly around the room until she found herself standing below a water colour of indeterminate age and origin.

The picture depicted a group of village girls emerging from a forest with water pots balanced expertly on their heads. The artist, although not one of the masters in the field, had managed to capture skilfully the admixture of eeriness and vibrancy of a tropical evening in the countryside. Cassandra had chosen the picture herself out of many, not for its artistic merit, but rather for its decorative value. She knew nothing about art, especially contemporary art, which in her opinion, inclined to the obscure. She judged a painting by its colour scheme and decipherability. How long ago was it when she had bought this painting, with her first salary, as a contribution to the furnishing of her brother's house? Could it be only one year? It seems like a century has gone by, she thought. So much seems to have happened to me.

She went back to her chair and leaned back, raising her eyes to the ceiling, as she conjured up, in detail, her first meeting with Raymond Agutamba. What was it about him that had attracted her to him, she wondered? It was not his handsome face, for handsome men were a dime a dozen. It must have been his

5

eyes, the way they looked at you and seemed to bore a hole right into the centre of your very being.

She had gone with her brother to a Christmas party given by one of his clients. After introducing her to some nebulous figures, Gavin had drifted off, leaving her to her own devices. At that particular moment of Raymond's entry into her life, Cassandra was in a group of people, trying, without success, to listen intelligently to some pompous gentleman discoursing volubly on the shortcomings of the IMF and the fatalities resulting from the so-called structural adjustment policies in developing countries.

"How can a man in Paris or New York, in his de luxe surroundings, perceive the plight of a Third World peasant, whose annual income cannot even guarantee him a square meal a day?" he expostulated, and looked around.

Some other gasbag jumped in and started to give his own views. At this juncture, Cassandra felt somebody touch her elbow gently and turned to see a man standing behind her, smiling. He detached her from the group and said, "Trade names with you? I'm Raymond Agutamba."

"I'm Cassandra Tibwita."

They shook hands solemnly, and then she asked, "Would you be Bevis Agutamba's brother?"

He pretended to consider the question while she studied him covertly, thinking that her question was actually superfluous since the resemblance between the two men was unmistakable. It was clearly manifest in their imposing stature and handsome features. Of the two, Bevis is the more good looking, with more sinew to his frame and more clear-cut features, she thought dispassionately. But he is morose and arrogant. Obviously his brother has the more sanguine nature.

"I wasn't consulted in the matter," he said, his mouth twitching with the suspicion of a smile, "but since he stopped pinching my clean socks and filling my shoes with water, yes, I think I would."

Cassandra smiled, enjoying his wry humour. "He doesn't look the type."

"No, he doesn't, does he? The old sham! So, Cassandra, how do you like the party?" His voice seemed to caress her name but when she looked up sharply, the eloquence in his eyes stopped her in her tracks.

Affecting nonchalance, she shrugged and said, "It's a good party as parties of this nature go."

"That tells me two things. One, that you're not enjoying yourself and two, that you don't normally go in for this kind of entertainment. Am I right?"

"Yes. I don't have much time for this kind of frivolity."

"What kind of serious activity do you have time for?"

Cassandra glanced at him before she replied, suspecting mockery but his

6

expression was grave enough; a shade too grave perhaps but that did not deter her from answering with equal gravity.

"I work with a publishing firm and as I'm new on the job, I find that I have a lot to learn. I usually carry home some extra work to do in the evenings and during the weekends."

"And tonight?"

"My brother bullied me into coming and as it's Christmas time, well . . . he has the mistaken notion that I'm becoming a workaholic and the sooner I'm stopped the better for me. Farfetched of course. All I want is to get on in my chosen field and I believe anything worth doing is worth doing well, don't you agree?"

"Absolutely. It's the shoddiness that's behind the wreck and ruin of our country."

"Are you laughing at me, Mr Agutamba?" she asked. His studied seriousness made her feel like a child trying hard to impress a grown-up.

"Mr Agutamba, why so formal? But to answer your question, no, I was not laughing at you. In my kind of business, accuracy and precision are the guiding principles too," he replied, adapting himself to her serious manner.

"What's your line of business, if you don't mind my asking?"

"I don't mind at all although I'm afraid I can't match your glamour. I belong to the oldest and dullest profession, architecture."

"That's one of the finest and most respectable of the creative arts. What would man do without his shelter from sun and rain, blitz and thunderstorm? Modern man, that is."

"Yes, modern man. They managed very well in their trees and caves during the Stone-Age, but each civilisation brings with it new and better inventions which accord man more and more physical comforts, thereby eroding his stamina to withstand natural elements."

"I guess that's nature's way of keeping the balance. Tell me about your work, please. Do you supervise the construction of buildings or do you work your plans on paper and have them translated into fact and form?"

"Actually, as you've guessed, ours is a 'behind-the-desk' job. I get a commission to build, prepare specifications of the building or buildings and contract it out to a builder or a mason. Of course as far as the client's concerned, I'm wholly responsible for what develops. So I have to keep sight of whatever's going on to ensure that the details of the plan are adhered to. But by and large, the contractor and his team of experts do the laying of brick and mortar."

"Are you working on something currently?"

"I'm always working or the bread would stop coming in. Currently I'm working on the projected extension to 'All Souls Church'. As a matter of fact, I arranged to meet with the contractor here tonight. You can listen in to the gab if you like but I promise not to prolong it. Oh, I say," he added, squinting at her glass, "that drink of yours seems to possess remarkable undiminishing powers. Don't you like it? Let me see," he said as he took the glass from her and sniffed it. "Whisky, ugh! Allow me to get you something else more suited to your . . . " he searched for the right word, not wishing to offend her by alluding to her tender age "... to your disposition," he ended triumphantly.

"You cannot know my disposition; we just met," Cassandra pointed out.

"You'd be surprised at how much I can glean about somebody from a few words of conversation. What would you like, something sweet and addictive like your name?"

"A soda'll do fine, thank you."

He left her, adjuring her to stay put. She followed his broad back thoughtfully as he snaked his way through knots of people, shouting his greetings and raising his glass in salute here and there.

Extraordinary man, she thought. And so attractive if you were the type easily swayed by the obvious. For her part, Cassandra mistrusted men as handsome as that one. It was, in her opinion, a camouflage intended by nature to hide a multitude of defects. But even as she thought that, she knew she was deceiving nobody, least of all herself. Those deep, dark brown eyes, she knew, would haunt her for a long time.

"Excuse me, ma'am," a voice dripping with honey said at her side, making her start a little. She turned and saw a short, stocky man with graying hair regarding her. He had bold lively eyes which he was using as a searchlight on her, as he asked, "I thought I saw Mr Agutamba here with you a minute ago?"

"He has gone for more refreshments," Cassandra answered briefly.

"Mind if I stick around until he returns? I'm Jack Mwezi," he added, proffering his hand.

Cassandra rudely gave him the tips of her fingers murmuring, "Cassandra."

"Well, how do you like the party, Cassandra?" The usual opening gambit.

"It's okay. How do you like it yourself?"

"Actually I'm not in a position to judge yet as I've just come. But judging by the crowd, I'd say the turnout is gratifying, especially in view of yesterday's bombing scare."

"Yes, quite remarkable really. But then where are people safe nowadays? Not in their homes any more or even the supposedly holy places," Cassandra said, alluding to the recent bombing of a church, full of worshippers, one Sunday morning. Many of them had been killed on the spot and the survivors mortally wounded or left with crippling injuries. The incident had taken place less than a hundred kilometres away from the city, and as usual, had been attributed to rebel activities.

Cassandra felt strongly about the indiscriminate killings of innocent people, whether by rebels or government soldiers. It was evil, inhuman, barbaric. She turned her full attention to her fellow guest, anticipating a lively debate but Mr Mwezi, in spite of his bold appearance, was cautious and noncommittal in his views. But in his defence, one could not be too careful. These were dangerous times and government agents were everywhere.

Bored by the usual generalities, Cassandra turned her attention to her surroundings. The Banqueting Hall of the Grand in which the party was taking place was decorated with Christmas trinkets. A huge Christmas tree winked and twinkled in one corner, while muted music filtered through the buzz of voices, giving the place a festive air. She let her gaze sweep over the sea of people, considering them en masse. It was a cosmopolitan gathering, embracing people from the upper and middle echelons of society.

The men wore sombre greys and blacks while the women, in contrast, sported gay and colourful designs for their party gowns. This was the time when people could still afford to indulge their extravagant tastes in the good things of life: when money was still money and not useless pieces of paper.

Mr Mwezi was not offended by Cassandra's deliberate rudeness. He knew that at his age, most young women found him uninteresting. Besides, her neglect gave him a chance to study her at his own leisure. He was still a connoisseur of feminine beauty and awarded Cassandra full marks as his eyes dwelt on her beautiful oval face, with slightly slanting eyes and a determined chin, with a proud tilt to it. Her hair, which still retained its natural look, grew upward in a widow's peak, and was abundant and luxuriantly long. His gaze shifted down to her shapely legs, and was roving upwards, past her tiny waist to her provocatively full bust when Raymond hailed him with, "Chatting up Miss Tibwita, I see, you old charlatan. Try this," he added, handing Cassandra a glass of amber liquid. "I hope you like it. They're not serving soda for love or money."

Cassandra took a sip of her drink and said that she liked it very much. The two men then turned to business. But true to his word, Raymond quickly concluded the discussion and shook hands with Mr Mwezi, after arranging to meet him on the site the following day.

"It has been a pleasure meeting you, Cassandra," Mr Mwezi murmured, drooling over her hand, imprisoned in both his. "A great pleasure indeed," he repeated, leering sideways at Raymond.

"Right, Jack, till tomorrow," Raymond said in a bid to speed up the leave-taking.

"Is that your contractor?" Cassandra remarked, looking at him obliquely.

"That is the contractor," Raymond confirmed, raising his eyebrows a

9

fraction. "I don't have to love or even like them, you know. But that particular man has a very high reputation in his field and is quite reliable. Unfortunately, we don't have many of his kind left, most of them having gone away in the exodus of the seventies."

"I'm sorry, I didn't imply criticism."

"And I did not detect any. How do you find your drink?"

"Delightful."

"Good. Shall we circulate, meet a few more people? I don't want to be accused of monopolising you."

They wandered around, always together and the evening miraculously turned out to be very enjoyable for Cassandra.

* * *

"In conclusion, I'd like to thank you all for your contributions and I hope that when we next meet, we will have more concrete ideas for the accomplishment of our programme for this year. The problems are immense but they are not insurmountable if we synergise and work as a team. This kind of business calls for boldness and dynamism. So let's stop shilly-shallying and give it all we're worth. Any comments... no? Anything else we might have overlooked... no? Good. Date for the next meeting . . . Mr Secretary?"

"Friday, 20th."

"Right. Thank you, ladies and gentlemen. Meeting adjourned."

Suddenly there was a burst of voices and scraping of chairs in the room as a group of ten men and four women prepared to leave.

"Eh . . . Cassandra, a minute before you go," Mr Wakilo said, arresting her advance to the door. "Just give me a minute and I'll be with you," the chief said, his head bent over his notes as he added some last minute scribbles.

Cassandra silently resumed her seat and studied the bent bald head of the Chief Editor. He was a massive man, with a build reminiscent of the fairy tale gorilla. But his kindly face and soft voice compensated for his unprepossessing appearance. He looked fiftish and Cassandra found it difficult to credit the rumours of his notoriety as a womaniser. But that he was having an affair with Juliet, her officemate and fellow assistant editor, was true enough. Juliet belongs to the class of females whose ambition does not go beyond being the boss' pet, mistakenly equating a pat on the head with a badge of success, Cassandra thought disparagingly.

When she first joined Lotus International, commonly referred to as LI, and discovered that her officemate was a girl of about her own age, she had been delighted and looked forward to a stimulating and pleasant relationship.

10

But her hopes were dashed the minute the two of them took measure of each other and conceived a mutual dislike. To Cassandra, Juliet appeared shallow, vulgar, with no self-esteem at all. She gossiped incessantly and men seemed to be her only hobby. Juliet was no more enamoured of the newcomer, regarding her as a potential rival not only professionally but also for the affections of the head of the department. She also thought her arrogant and her pretensions to intellectual superiority distasteful. In the course of time, Juliet also discovered that Cassandra was extremely ambitious, the overachiever type, and, therefore, a great threat to her own aspirations. Brutally and viciously she set about isolating her from the rest of the staff by pointing out and exaggerating the flaws in her character. This task was rendered easy by Cassandra's indifference to what was being said or thought about her.

"Ah, sorry to keep you waiting, Cassandra," the chief said, raising his head from the file and putting his pen down. "Let me see. Yes, two things: I'm meeting the printer this afternoon and hope that you can have the proofs of Okech's book ready for me before two."

Cassandra assured him that they would be on his desk by noon. "I only have a few pages left to go through."

"Good. I know I can always rely on your word. Tell Sharp to bring the prelims too, at the same time even if they are not ready. I'll need them for the meeting. Now, about the trip to the seminar in Nairobi, I'm putting you in charge of the preparations; coordinate with the transport officer and make sure that nothing's left to chance. And also remind everybody going to see to their travel documents. Do you have a passport yourself?"

"Yes. Got it a few months ago."

"That's fine then. Umm, how do you and Juliet get on?"

Cassandra, caught unprepared by the direct question, hesitated, unsure of the reason behind it.

"You see, I'm thinking of shuffling you around a bit and I wondered whether you'd mind sharing the office with somebody else?" he explained, his shrewd eyes studying her.

"I don't really mind with whom I share an office, Mr Wakilo, provided I'm allowed to do my work in peace," Cassandra replied.

"Of course. Isn't that what we all want? I have a feeling you'll go far in this business if you keep your single-mindedness and creditable dedication to your job."

"Thank you, sir," Cassandra said, glowing with gratification. She wished Juliet was around to hear for herself. Part of Juliet's problem was the mistaken belief that she, Cassandra, was vying for Mr Wakilo's favours. But nothing could be further from the truth. She, as a matter of principle, disapproved of men who used their privileged positions to exploit women.

"Word of caution though," the chief went on ponderously. "In life, we come across all sorts of situations to which we very often react differently. It doesn't always follow a different approach from ours is necessarily wrong, do you follow me?"

Cassandra looked at him blankly.

"I guess what I'm trying to say is that however praiseworthy our own views are, we can't always afford to be too rigid about them. We have to try and understand and respect other people's opinions and judgements."

"Mr Wakilo, has somebody been complaining . . . "she started to say but he waved her to silence. "Don't look agitated, my dear, we old men like to pass on these useless pieces of advice. I personally have every confidence in you as I've just said. Keep doing your job and you and I will get on very well."

"I don't understand, has somebody else complained to you about my work?" Cassandra persisted.

"Nobody has complained about you to my knowledge," Mr Wakilo assured her. "I was talking randomly. Now off with you," he added brusquely, glancing at his wristwatch as if to suggest that her time was up.

Still mystified, Cassandra left his office.

When she returned to her office, the atmosphere was chilly between her and Juliet, who probably thought she had been having a tete-a-tete with the chief. After a prolonged silence, the latter got up and left the room. Cassandra drew a deep breath and tried to empty her mind of all the irritating thoughts before settling down to her work. She found Juliet's hostile attitude too unsettling although she always endeavoured to assume an air of indifference. The best thing that could happen was for one of them to be transferred to another office as the chief had hinted. With that comforting thought, she resolutely turned her attention to her work until the intercom interrupted her thirty minutes later.

"Let's meet for lunch," her friend, Marie Nalubega from Production suggested. "You can then tell me all about your pow-pow with the chief."

"Where're we going?" Cassandra asked unenthusiastically. She preferred a canteen lunch in the building which she could afford and eat at her own pace.

"I thought we'd try the *Step-In*. Now wait a minute, we're not paying, Dan is."

"That's what I was afraid of."

"Why? He can afford it."

"I know he's loaded but I prefer to pay for my own meals."

"And what does that prove for heaven's sake?" Marie cried with irritation at the other end of the wire. "That you're a superior being to us poor simple females who sponge on men? Have you ever heard of rights, privileges and prerogatives? I think you need a course in Natural Law and the History of Creation. Men're not women's enemies, Cassandra, they're their allies. The two're meant to complement each other, not to collide or counteract each other's moves. We cook for them and bear their children, and boost their egos and they pamper us and sweeten us up by spending on us. Wisen up, girl, and take what's your due or you'll end up an embittered old maid."

"I can't help what I feel, Marie, and what I feel is that my values and principles'll be compromised once I become beholden to men. So let's not argue about it."

"Who's arguing? See you at one," Marie said and quickly replaced the receiver.

Marie's boyfriend, Dan Kizito, was a young man of about thirty whose family had benefited a lot from the expulsion of Asians by the dictator, Idi Amin, in the early seventies. After his father's death some years back, Dan had found himself the proprietor of a successful industrial concern which dealt in plastics, among other things. He worked hard to modernise, innovate and diversify until his efforts earned him a place among the ten richest industrialists in the country. He was a soft-spoken, ordinary-looking guy and quite besotted with Marie. The two had hinted at a wedding in the not too distant future but the plans had yet to crystallise.

When he dropped the two girls at the office after lunch, Marie asked him to collect her at six instead of the usual time and Dan calmly said, "Whatever you say, my dear."

"Don't you ever feel irritated by Dan's placid manner?" Cassandra asked as soon as they were out of earshot. "I know I would be."

"What do you want, a tiger?" Marie retorted defensively. "I like a man who panders to my whims. Anyway, he's not all that tame really. He can be as stubborn as a mule when he chooses. Don't let 'the butter can't melt in my mouth' look deceive you. Why, look at that wiggly-waggly behind," she added pointing at Juliet ahead of them. "I wonder what's biting her these days. When I ventured to salute her this morning, she as good as told me to get lost."

"Juliet carries a perpetual chip on her shoulder. She refuses to accept what she is but will insist on blaming her inadequacies on other people," Cassandra told her with a shrug.

"And what is she, if I may ask?" Marie asked in a serious voice.

"She's cheap and vulgar and thinks everybody else's like her."

"Obviously by 'everybody' you mean yourself?"

"I do," Cassandra arrogantly confirmed, failing to notice the narrowed look with which her friend regarded her.

"Have you been tussling over the Nairobi trip?"

13

"I don't tussle: I leave that to the puerile. I'm going, she's not, period. What else's there to say?"

"There are rumours, you know," Marie said cautiously.

"So? Surely you don't believe such rubbish too, do you?"

"What I believe or don't believe's immaterial, Cassandra. You've got to be very careful because one, the old man has a reputation and up to now, he's been Juliet's entire preserve. So you can see how your being included in the exclusively male group instead of her, can be perceived not only by her but by other people too. Also keep in mind the fact that she's your officemate and can make life generally uncomfortable for you if she chooses to."

"She doesn't scare me," Cassandra scoffed. "Tell me, though, are men and sordid love affairs the only subjects of interest around here?"

"What else?"

"There are a number of more elevating subjects, in my opinion, which don't always revolve around men."

"Such as?" Marie asked in the same flat tone.

"Well, work goals, ambitions, things like that. But drivelling about men all the time's sickening."

"You make it sound like an obsession," Marie mildly objected. "Come into my office," she invited, inserting her key in the lock. "There's something I want to discuss with you." Cassandra followed her inside the small compacted room smelling a little of paint and turpentine. Marie, whose usually vivacious face was looking grave, lifted herself up on her stool, and fidgeting with her drawing pencil said, "I hope you won't mind if I give you a piece of unsolicited advice, regarding this trip to Nairobi and the rumours it has generated. If I were you, I would get myself attached to one of the many young men who're pining for you," she hurried on at the chilling look from her friend. "At least I'd appear to."

"And pray for what reason would I be taking such a preposterous step?"

"It would kill these rumours circulating about you. And at the same time, it would remove you from Wakilo's sphere of interest."

"Don't you think this whole thing's being blown out of all proportion? The man has not so much as made a single step that could be interpreted as inappropriate, for heaven's sake."

"He will soon, when he deems it the right moment. Ask yourself why you should be included in the team going for the seminar when there're already two members from Editorial going. Doesn't it strike you as odd especially when you go as a replacement for Juliet?"

"Hardly a replacement unless you think I don't qualify in my own right," Cassandra told her in a chilly voice.

"Oh I didn't mean that and you know it, Cassandra. But merit has never

14

been the criterion before and nobody is going to believe that it is now. Take my advice and don't wait until you're forced to make a choice."

"A choice between what?"

"Your job and your integrity."

"And so, according to you, in order to avert this calamity, I'm to approach some unsuspecting poor fool and invite him to play Romeo in the scenario. Is that how you have it in your script?" Cassandra asked sarcastically.

"There's no need to jump on your high horse, Cassandra, I'm only trying to help," Marie responded stiffly. "Actually," she went on, brightening up a second later, "we already have the perfect candidate for the role. George."

"George?" Cassandra raised her eyebrows.

"Yes, George. There's some kind of rapport between you two already and the man worships the ground you walk on."

"Hey, hey, wait a minute. Are we talking about acting a part or starting a relationship with George or whoever auditions for the part?"

"Well, would that be such a disaster? George has what it takes."

"That's not the point. Anyway, I've made up my mind: I'm not going on this trip," Cassandra told her firmly.

"Don't be hasty, please. I'd feel rotten knowing you've based your decision on what I've told you. I know you're looking forward to this trip. Besides, that will not solve the problem between you and the chief. It will just postpone it. If the man has set his eye on you, nothing short of what I've suggested will deter him."

"But I like George. I don't want to use him. Besides, my mind's made up: I'm not going to Nairobi. In any case, it takes two, doesn't it? If I say no, I'm sure he'll respect my feelings."

"Oh grow up, Cassandra! He may not exactly force you to reciprocate but he can make life dashed difficult for you. That's what I meant by being forced to make a choice."

"He wouldn't dare! We live in a civilised society, for heaven's sake, not in a jungle where might's right."

"That shows how innocent you still are about the world we live in. These office intrigues go on every day, everywhere in the country, if not in the world, and there isn't the slightest thing you can do about them. You can make noise of course, and attract a lot of publicity but why set yourself up for martyrdom when you can find an easier way out of the problem?" Marie counselled.

"That's the trouble with women, always looking for the line of least resistance. Is it any wonder men treat us the way they do if we're not prepared to stand up for our own rights? How can we ever hope to achieve total liberation from all forms of injustices unless we fight for them?" Cassandra shot back.

"So you go ahead and fight, I have some work to do. Besides, you're wasting your time if you still think you can convert me to your way of thinking. I have only one life and I don't intend to spend it fighting battles I can't win," Marie told her.

"How do you know you can't win if you've never tried?"

"Look, Cassandra, we don't have time to discuss gender issues now. Whether you believe it or not, you have a problem on your hands which, in my opinion, needs to be tackled now. I've given my advice, such as it is, and if you don't feel inclined to take it, you don't have to. You can find your way out. But don't pretend there's no problem because it is evidently there."

"I've already said that I'm withdrawing from the trip."

"And I've already pointed out that that's not a permanent solution. Besides, what possible excuse could you give for doing so?"

"A death in the family?"

"A bit drastic but that's one ruse that never fails to deliver. So who are you going to 'kill'?"

"I'll think of somebody – fictitious of course," Cassandra said as she checked her watch. "I better get going, it's two-thirty already. Pray Juliet does not engage me in hand-to-hand combat. She was working herself up to it this morning if George had not come in at the right time."

"He can save you from another impending one if you give him the chance."

"George's a decent guy, I think he deserves better. See you later and thanks for your advice," Cassandra said, letting herself out of the room and feeling her friend's eyes on her back.

That's two people who have ventured to advise me on my outlook on life in one day, she thought wryly.

* * *

Cassandra's plan succeeded better than she had envisaged. Her moment of unease came when coincidently a cousin of hers, a newly married young woman, died of a mysterious debilitating disease. Inevitably her death was attributed to witchcraft by her ill-wishers. But when her husband followed her not long after from the same disease, people were confounded beyond measure. No amount of medical investigations, or consultations with medicine men could establish the cause or nature of the disease. But in Europe and America, researchers and doctors were already grappling with the newly discovered disease known as AIDS (Acquired Immune Deficiency Syndrome), gathering all the data they could about it. In Uganda too, people were gradually awakening to the fact that there was a new disease of an infectious nature that they

16

nicknamed 'slim' because of the weight-loss effect it had on the victims. A couple of years later, AIDS was to dominate the international media as the most deadly killer disease, without a cure.

Cassandra felt so shaken by the turn of events that when she presented herself to the chief's office to ask for permission to go home for the funeral, the grief and remorse visible on her face were very real.

Cassandra was not surprised when she came back to learn that Juliet had filled her place. She was of course glad about it but she dreaded the gloating she would have to endure from her colleague when the team returned.

So with all that going on, it would not be untrue to say that Cassandra had no time for wanderings into strange realms although it would not be wholly true to say she had forgotten all about her meeting with Raymond, or that occasionally she did not indulge in daydreams about him. There was, however, no time to idolise or fantasise about him. She had taken her friend's advice and was allowing herself to interact more with her officemates, particularly George. By the time Mr Wakilo and his group returned from Nairobi, she and George appeared inseparable. But she had made it clear from the beginning that she considered all that romantic stuff a lot of hooey.

George was a good-looking man, extremely sensitive about his unimpressive stature and mixed breeding. So, he had elected to hide behind a camouflage of inconsequential air. He was regarded as a clown by most people and treated dismissively, except by those who knew him well enough. Such a one was Marie with whom they had worked closely together for almost two years. She knew he was very intelligent, very reliable but rather vulnerable and lonely. She wished that he and Cassandra could form a real bond between them. But although Cassandra took him seriously enough, she allowed him no concessions whatsoever.

"Am I going to see you tomorrow?" George asked one Friday evening as the three friends sauntered out of the tall building.

"I don't think . . . " Cassandra started to say but Marie chipped in quickly with, "Oh, I almost forgot, you're both invited to dinner at my place."

"What's the occasion?" George asked.

"Do I need a special reason to get together with two of my best friends?" It was a spur-of-the-moment suggestion and she fervently hoped that Dan had nothing laid on for the weekend.

"I'm sorry, I don't think I can make it, Marie," Cassandra, who saw through her ploy to get her and George together at every opportunity, said. She had a set of page proofs she intended going through during the weekend.

"Nonsense," Marie retorted, "it won't kill you to forget work and relax once in a while."

17

"It's not only office work which keeps me busy: I have my hands full keeping house for my brother," Cassandra said defensively.

"Cassandra's a wonderful cook," Marie explained with mock seriousness to George. "You have to taste her cooking to believe it. See you both tomorrow," she added, clutching her bag tightly as she prepared to dash through the myriad evening traffic to the other side of the road where Dan was patiently waiting for her. "Seven for eight. Cassandra knows the place," she added over her shoulder and dived.

"Seems the decision has been taken out of our hands," George said. "May I drive you home? I have to know where you live if I'm to pick you up tomorrow."

"I could draw you a map," Cassandra offered teasingly. She was not as insensitive as people thought. She knew that George harboured some illusions about her but fully exonerated herself of all blame. Nevertheless she accepted the lift and when they reached Luzzi, invited him in for a cup of tea. Mellinda, who opened the door, goggled at him appreciatively.

"Hello, Mellie. Meet George from the office. My sister, Mellinda. Take a seat and let Mellie entertain you while I scrounge in the kitchen for something to offer you."

"Why don't you let me deal with that, Cassandra, while you make George feel at home?" Mellie offered but Cassandra brushed her offer aside saying, "I'm sure George would rather talk to you. He sees me at the office every day."

"Would you prefer something stronger than tea, George?" Mellinda asked. "Cassandra's tastes in the refreshment department are rather elementary."

George thought about it for a moment and decided that it would not be politic to go against Cassandra's views. "Tea's fine, thanks," he said.

As Cassandra busied herself in the kitchen, Mellinda, in the mistaken view that George and her sister were embarked on the road to matrimony, set about finding out as much as she could about him. By the time Cassandra came back with a loaded tray, she knew all there was to know, even to the number of times George changed his socks a week.

"I like him," she enthused as soon as he was out of the gate. "He's so cute that if I were an artist, I'd want to paint him."

"Good heavens, I believe you've gone and fallen for poor George, Mellie! Wait until I tell him."

"I've done nothing of the sort," Mellie protested. "But you have my full approval to go ahead."

"I'm sorry to disappoint you but George and I are just what I said – office mates and nothing more."

18

"Are you sure? I distinctively got the impression more was in the offing."

"Not with my encouragement, I assure you," Cassandra told her firmly.

"Oh? Did you know his brother is the famous Prof. Sharp of Physiotherapy at Hill Hospital?" Mellie asked, her enthusiasm unequalled.

"Not my field of interest. How did you find out so much in such a short time?"

"I was interested and I asked questions."

"Good for you. We're going out together tomorrow but I wonder if I'm not making a mistake," Cassandra mused aloud. "I don't want to be accused of leading him on."

"Any time you want a stand in, just knock on my door."

"Why don't you take over right away? Give Horace something to worry about, which reminds me, what are you doing at home? I thought you were on night duty?"

"I exchanged with somebody else. I was feeling low and came home to recuperate."

"Don't tell me Horace has been at it again? Honestly, I don't know what you see in that man; he's an animal!"

"Oh, Cassandra," Mellie breathed with the weariness of somebody going over an old argument. "Horace's not even around. He's supposed to be in Masaka."

But what she didn't mention was that he was rumoured to have taken a certain nurse from the hospital where Mellinda worked with him. Incidents like that were not isolated and she wondered why it still hurt to know that he was cheating on her. Cassandra was right, the man was a beast.

Horace Kalanzi was Mellinda's boyfriend of long standing, who belonged to the school of thought with the view that if you can have one girl, you can have them all or as many as you can handle. He was, therefore, occasionally to be seen with a bunch of them in his Mercedes Benz, driving at wild speed to wild parties. Mellinda was getting more and more disillusioned with him but he had a very persuasive tongue and the money he spent lavishly on her aided his cause. She found herself always forgiving him his philandering ways just one more time, until one more time had now got completely out of hand. Cassandra, she knew, despised her for her weakness and did not bother hiding her dislike of Horace. However, for once today, she let the subject go.

* * *

So the days rolled into weeks and weeks into months since that fateful meeting with Raymond Agutamba.

19

Mellinda watched Cassandra, her face puckered into puzzled lines. Cassandra is a sensible girl – no, not sensible exactly. That is not the right word, she thought, and came up with self-possessed, yes, almost to the point of insensibility. So how could she get herself entangled with a person like Raymond Agutamba whose debauchery was a byword? Careful not to alarm her, she asked mildly, "So what has Raymond been up to?"

"Nothing," Cassandra answered, resuming her seat.

"Nothing? Then why all this sudden interest in him?"

Cassandra shrugged. "He just bought me a cup of coffee and brought me home, that's all."

"The very inimitable Raymond Agutamba bought you a cup of coffee and brought you home intact? I find that hard to believe. But of course being you, I can imagine you telling him to get stuffed when he tried his act on you. However, that he has left no mark on you is cause for celebration," Mellie concluded, still looking at her sister with unease.

"Why, what do you have against him?" Cassandra burst out.

"I don't exactly have anything against the man but I've heard stories about his reputation as a heartbreaker. Not his fault of course," she added hastily, wishing to be fair as she did not yet know what Cassandra's feelings for him were. "From what I hear, women simply throw themselves at him."

"Well," Cassandra said with a short laugh, "you can add me to the list."

"You don't mean that you are . . . ?" the other asked with dismay.

"I do, Mellie. I think I . . . well, I don't know what I think really. I'm confused. I've never felt like this before about any man."

"Tell me about it – I mean, about your meeting."

"There's nothing to tell. We first met at that party Gavin took me to at Christmas, and again today. That's all. He didn't even suggest we meet again. But I can't get him out of my mind and I hate feeling helpless like this. I hate the idea that I'm under the power of another human being."

My poor Cassandra, what an innocent you still are, Mellinda thought, moved by pity even as she marvelled at the power of love. It is quite ironical, she thought, remembering her sister's entreaties to her time and again not to allow herself to be ruled by emotions.

"Take it easy, Cassandra," she now said gently. "Falling in love is a process all normal human beings go through. There's nothing strange or shameful about it."

"I'm not ashamed of it. I just don't feel I'm ready for it. I'm still trying to find out what I want from life, how to go about achieving it, who the real me is. I can't afford to stray now."

"Surely this is one way of finding out about yourself," Mellinda pointed

20

out uncertainly. She deplored Cassandra's habit of deviating into dialectic theorism over every argument. "One way of getting to know your emotional self, to identify your needs."

"I don't have much use for emotions which have no logic to their basis," Cassandra retorted in her usual arrogant way.

"You can't apply logic to every facet of life, you know, and especially not to love. Look, let's see if I can help a little." Looking at the ceiling as if seeking inspiration, Mellinda went on saying, "You are a slow developer, my dear, or you'd know all about this love stuff. The thing to do is to keep a cool head as much as possible, actually, vital in your case."

Cassandra raised her eyes inquiringly and her sister went on slowly, "You see, dear, Raymond is married." She noted with satisfaction the sudden alarm as a result of her statement. "I'm giving it to you straight so that you don't get too much hurt when you find out later."

"Married?" Cassandra echoed harshly.

"I'm afraid so," Mellie confirmed. "True, he and his wife are separated but they are not divorced." After a short, uncomfortable silence in which Cassandra sat like a statue, Mellinda went on, offering crumbs, "That must be the reason why he did not suggest you meet again. He did not want to hurt you, which shows he cares, don't you see?" No answer. "Are you all right, Cassandra?"

"Sure, I'm all right," Cassandra said, but she did not look or sound fine to her.

"Good," Mellie remarked with false heartiness. "I'll get us a little something to perk us both up."

She was not surprised a few minutes later to come back to an empty room. Some things are too personal to share even with those nearest to one, she thought. And heartache was one of them. That's life, she thought, sighing as she sat down to a lonely drink while waiting for her brother to come back. The aroma of cooking wafted from the kitchen, making her realise how hungry she was.

* * *

Mellinda was two years older than Cassandra and three years younger than their brother, Gavin. She was a medical intern at the government hospital, having finished her course the year before. Her boyfriend, Horace, was a young man of doubtful reputation from a rich Ganda family. Cassandra thought her sister too good for him, as did Gavin. Neither could understand her infatuation with him. But he was very rich, by contemporary standards, and quite generous with his money. While Cassandra appreciated the role money

21

could play in one's life, she did not think it the right basis for a relationship. It stripped one of dignity, placing the recipient completely in the hands of the giver, she reasoned.

Gavin came in a few minutes later, with his friend and fellow lawyer, Bevis, younger brother to Raymond Agutamba. Now, why couldn't the idiotic girl have fallen for a man like Bevis, Mellie thought, her mind straying back to Cassandra. He looks solid and dependable, she thought, studying their visitor covertly, in addition to being quite a looker with an impeccable reputation. But many people were put off by his stiff and detached manner. When relaxed and at ease, however, as he now is, he can be a very charming person.

"Playing truant, Dr Nshemere-Mutono?" he asked, smiling at her.

"Mellie, I thought you were on duty or something?" Gavin asked. "Where's Cassandra?" he added over his shoulder absentmindedly as he went through some documents on his desk.

"Gone to bed with a headache," Mellie said.

"She works too hard all right, thinks LI would fold up without her extra efforts," her brother continued cynically. "Do try to cure her of it, Mellie, find her a boyfriend or something to distract her."

Mellinda almost burst into hysterical laughter at the farcical suggestion. "Is she short of admirers?" she asked, glancing sideways at Bevis who seemed wholly absorbed in the kinetic images on the TV-screen. Does he know of his brother's philandering, do brothers also have heart-to-heart talks, boast of their conquests, she wondered. "I'll get you both a drink," she said, getting up abruptly.

Bevis followed her slender figure speculatively, wondering why she looked so upset all of a sudden.

"So what outbreaks are you contending with at the hospital presently?" he asked her lightly as he accepted a glass of wine from her a few minutes later.

"Heartaches," she announced dramatically and then stopped to allow her meaning to sink in. "There's a case of a woman who tried to set herself ablaze when she discovered her husband had been cheating on her. She was lucky she got minor burns only. Another hit her husband on the head with a beer bottle, almost cracking his skull open for a similar reason. Yet another, while trying to stop her husband from leaving their compound, sat on the bonnet of his car which did not make the least impression on him. She fell off as the car gained momentum, and is now in hospital nursing multiple fractures and other injuries, with no one to check on the whereabouts of the errant husband."

"I know you're making it up, Mellie, now admit it, you are," Bevis said, laughing delightedly, a spontaneous, deep-throated chortle: a man's laugh.

"I'm not, honestly. Life's so pathetic it makes me want to howl sometimes. When you work in a hospital, you realise that the life the majority of our people know is hunger, misery, disease and death. Full bellies, comfortable beds and other necessities considered basic are, in fact, luxuries only few of us know. My dreams are often haunted by screams of the pain-wracked, the maimed, the dying, all the helpless victims of our society."

"Goodness, Mellie, you're in a fine tickle of humour tonight. Too much work?" Bevis asked, sobering up.

"She's in Casualty this week," Gavin offered, without turning from his desk. "Or else it's that skunk, Horace. Why don't you let me challenge him to a duel one of these days?" he added.

"Horace's mine and I reserve all rights to him, including knocking his teeth down his throat," Mellie emphatically told him.

"Attagirl, that's the spirit," he cheered her while Bevis gave her a keen look.

Chapter Two

"Feeling under the weather this morning?" Wilson Mukasa, an elderly man transferred from Production to replace Juliet, asked. Juliet had been promoted to Assistant Publicity Manager shortly after coming back from Nairobi.

"I think I'm coming down with flu," Cassandra said, blowing her nose loudly to lend credence to her claim. But the sense of ennui and the red rimmed eyes attested to more than a threatening attack of flu. They were a result of a night long restlessness and confusion.

An hour later, George called her for their usual coffee break.

"What's up?" he asked, scrutinising her cheerless face.

"I don't know what's up, but I know what's down: my spirits," Cassandra quipped.

"Want to tell me about it? What can I do?"

"For all your tomfoolery, you're a very perceptive person, George, but I'm sorry I can't tell you about it although there's something you can do. You can take me to your place this evening and get me deliciously drunk. The rest I leave to your fertile imagination."

"Cassandra!" George gaped at her. Then with his characteristic resilience, he was back in gear asking with a naughty smile, "Are you propositioning me, Cassandra?"

"No, St. Innocent," his companion retorted. "I'm only proposing you take me to tea at the Salvation Army Hostel. Honestly, how plain can a girl be without risking sounding like a tart!"

George clamped his mouth shut and studied her gravely, noting the palpable weariness. "Why don't you get it off your chest? You can always rely on Uncle George to provide a shoulder to cry on."

"Isn't that what I've been endeavouring to get through to your thick skull? A shoulder to cry on tonight?"

"Sorry, Cassandra, tempting as your proposal is, I can't oblige tonight. I already have a date with . . . "

"Spare me the details," Cassandra cut him short. "I should have known you were cheating on me all the time, you miserable rogue."

"Yeah, with a seventy-year-old man! My father's in town and has elected to stay at my place rather than at my brother's, which does not augur well for yours truly. Between you and me and these cups," he added, leaning towards her and whispering conspiratorially, "I suspect the time for my initiation into the family black magic has come before the old boy departs for the hereafter. Can we have our get-together tomorrow evening? That is if you think you can survive that long without me? Otherwise I'll have to sneak you in through the back door."

"I think I can just manage until tomorrow."

"It's a date then."

* * *

"Umm, Marie was right," George commented, sinking his strong teeth into a leg of roast chicken. Baked Irish potatoes, rice, vegetables and green salad made up the rest of the menu. "Yes, you're quite something, Cassandra. I don't mind admitting I've found the perfect woman at long last. I envy the man who gets you."

"You know I'm yours for the asking, George. That's what this whole show is about. Anyway," she continued, enjoying his embarrassment, "this is my insurance for the future in case things don't work out. Don't get up, George, let me break one of my own rules and wait on a man, hand and foot."

"Don't bother to wash up, just dump everything in the sink," George told her. "I have a man who comes in daily to clean and cook. The reason he's not in evidence now is because I gave him an off."

"You did the right thing. I wanted this to be my show. Now," she said a few minutes later when they were in the sitting room sipping some wine, "we're all set for the seduction scene."

"What's bothering you, Cassandra?" George, asked refusing to rise to her facetious remark.

"You are, George. Here I am, practically throwing myself at you and not getting the slightest response. It's enough to make a girl want to retire to the convent," she complained but George, as if expecting her to do better than make poor jokes, continued to look at her unimpressed. "Don't you believe me? I'm twenty-four years old and I've never been with a man. So I want to get it over, to discover what it is people rave about. You should be flattered that I've chosen you for the initiation ceremony."

"And I should be a half-wit if I did not smell a rat. Come on, Cassandra, tell old George. Who's the devil who has upset you like this? Give me a name and I'll gladly throttle him for you."

"How do you know there's a devil in it all?"

"It's surely obvious that when a self-possessed, cool-headed girl starts behaving like a crackpot, then you look for a Lothario. You know I hold you in the highest esteem, Cassandra, and that I could never knowingly do anything that would sour your opinion of me. But I'm also human, and while I'm putting on the act of a Father-Confessor, I'm at the same time having to contend with a host of unruly emotions. I'm going to give you exactly five minutes to come clean or I'll throw you out of my house. I mean it, Cassandra, I can't hold on much longer." After that he went to the sideboard to replenish their drinks. When he came back, he sat down silently and stared at her with a martyred look on his grave face.

"The first thing I want you to know, George, is that I'm a fool. I apologise for embarrassing you and for trying to burden you with my troubles. I thank you for your patience and if you don't mind telling me where I can get a taxi, I'll soon be on my way."

"Now wait a minute," George said, hurriedly getting up and pushing her back in her chair. "You still have two minutes, do you want to use them to tell me what's bugging you? Remember, a shared burden, etc."

"Well, George, since you insist, prepare yourself for a shock: I'm in love . . . with a married man, can you beat that?"

"I'm doubled up with hilarity," George said almost angrily. "Who's he?"

"I don't think you know him. A chap I met at a party."

"That's why you should always stick with me. What's his name? I promise not to challenge him without your express orders."

"I shouldn't even think of trying if I were you. He looks like a pro."

"Thanks for the vote of confidence. Am I going to hear his name or am I going to accost every gorilla I meet in town and ask them for their dossier, including a column on 'Girls I have Known'?"

"Oh George, you make me feel better already. I don't see any harm in telling you his name. Your paths'll probably never cross. He's called Agutamba," she delivered heavily.

"Agutamba, Agutamba, why does that name sound familiar?"

"Agutamba, Banura and Co. A firm of lawyers on the main street."

"Magna Mansions, right? I know the firm and I think I've even met the guy, rather formidable looking. I wouldn't stand a chance against that one, I'm ashamed to admit."

"That's not the Agutamba I meant. That's his brother."

"No kidding! What's the other one look like then?"

26

"Not as harmless as his sibling, if you know what I mean."

"Harmless? Harmless? No, I don't know what you mean. Well?" he said as he leaned towards her intimidatingly.

"His name's Raymond." ˉ

"Raymond, huh? Okay, don't stop now. We have all night."

"There's nothing more to tell except that he's married and separated and probably doesn't know I exist, or doesn't care if he does."

"I don't get it, is he blind or something?"

"Something perhaps. We've met but . . . "

"Just like that? He must be something, this Lucifer. So if that's how you feel about him, why don't you give him a tinkle? You're supposed to be a liberated woman."

"I'm not that liberated, I'm afraid. Hard as it may be for you to believe, George, I too suffer from the modesty syndrome of my sex."

"Well, hallelujah, you've finally admitted to being human too! I don't mind confessing I was beginning to despair of it ever happening. I think this calls for another drink. So where do you go from here?"

"Home, after that drink you've promised, if you'll be so good as to get it for me."

"Anything to cheer you up, princess. First excuse me a minute, I have an idea. . . "

He went in the direction of his sleeping quarters and a few minutes later, Cassandra thought she heard the sound of a telephone being lifted from its cradle but did not give it a second thought. When George came back, he asked her, "If this Agutamba character were to show up here, what would you say to him?"

"I'd look into his mocking face and say, 'Fuck you, Raymond Agutamba. Get out of my life and stay out of it'."

"Hey, hey, I should be careful what I say to the fellow if I were you. He might take you literally. But seriously?"

"Why are we indulging in suppositions? You and I know how remote the likelihood of that is. Let's drink and be merry for tomorrow we die."

"I say, none of that dumb talk. Look, how about a little music? I have a number of cassettes and the choice's yours."

"I should really be getting back home now, but if you're dying to show off your collection, anything mellifluous will do."

"Thank you. I hope Dolly Parton appeals to you as much as she does to me," he remarked, putting a compact disc into the player.

They both listened silently as the cooing voice went through 'Real Love', 'When You Think about Love' and the rest. Once Cassandra got up and went

27

to the bathroom where she stayed a suspiciously long time. In her absence, George switched on the kettle and brewed some coffee. When she returned, he presented her with a steaming mug which she took with bad grace saying, "We were getting on very well with the other stuff, what's the coffee for?"

George did not answer but looked at her worriedly.

"Well, aren't you going to tell me to forget the damned fellow, George?" she added aggressively. It was quite clear that the unaccustomed drink was getting to her.

"Will that make you feel better? Okay, forget the fellow. Is that better? Are you beginning to forget him?"

"Forget who? Oh, George, I love you so much but nothing seems to be working," she said with a catch in her voice.

He watched her helplessly, knowing he dare not comfort her for both their sakes. After a few minutes, he cocked his head, listening intently. "I think I hear a car, don't you? I wonder who could be calling at such a time. Hold the fort while I check."

Cassandra could hear nothing. "Either you're psychic or you're trying to get rid of me in a subtle way."

"Just stay put, honey, this could be the moment you've been waiting for – the moment of truth."

"For heaven's sake, George, quit kidding. What moment, what truth?"

"Trust me, will you?" was all George said before he went out chasing after shadows, or so Cassandra thought.

The moment of truth! In spite of herself, she could not help stealing a glance at her face in her pocket mirror. She dabbed at the telltale marks of tears and applied a little salve to her dry lips. Of course George was fooling as usual because there was no way Raymond could know where she was, or what she felt for him, or indeed care if he did ... unless ... unless that tinkle of the phone she thought she had heard ... but no, that would be too preposterous even for George.

"He has come. . . for you," George said, looking at her a little strangely from the doorway.

"Who has come?" But in her heart, she had no doubt as to what he meant and hugged the knowledge to herself, savouring the feeling of anticipation. Things like that happen only in books or dreams, not in real life and yet... "George..." she started to say but he cut her short with, "Come on up: he's waiting for you." He held out his hands and she put hers in them, using him as a lever to get up.

"George," she tried again, this time in a voice that would not be easily silenced. Then more softly, "Has anybody ever told you what a wonderful person you are?"

"No, and don't start now because there's no time. But I'll look forward to hearing it from you some day." He looked into her shining eyes and felt a stab at his heart at the knowledge that they were not shining for him.

"I love you, George."

"Careful or I'll begin to believe in your avowal and hold you to it."

"I mean it, George." She raised herself on tiptoe and touched her lips lightly to his cheek before she picked up her bag and flew out of the door, into the mysterious night outside. George followed her lissom figure with a desolate smile. He felt an emptiness inside him that was too great to comprehend. He knew this was the end of his dream and cursed himself for being such a fool for not taking advantage of a chance of a lifetime. But even as he thought that, he knew he would never have been able to look himself in the face again if he had done that to Cassandra. He revered her too much to abuse her trust.

He moved to the sideboard and this time mixed himself a stiff drink. After a third refill, he felt reckless enough to ring up one of his on-and-off girlfriends and suggest a get-together. Any port in storm, he thought . . .

* * *

Outside, Cassandra approached the parked car hesitantly. She felt a wild urge to run back and seek refuge inside. She knew that what she had embarked on, although conforming to modern behaviour, stripped her of any claim she might have had to maiden modesty. But it was too late to reverse the course of events, even assuming that she wanted to. The man in the car sensed her faltering steps and quickly got out to guide her the rest of the way. Without a word from either of them, he put the car in motion and eased it out of George's compound onto the road. It was not until they were speeding along the main road that he turned to look at her, his eyes opalescent in the gloom of the car.

"Who's George?" he asked without preamble. "Is he your boyfriend?"

"Be serious, Ray," she said, his name easily sliding off her tongue. "He called you, didn't he?"

"Yes, he called me," he concurred and waited for an explanation of George's quixotic behaviour.

"Well, would he have done so if he were?"

"That's the part I don't understand, I'm afraid. Would you please explain? I'm sorry, I've no right to ask or expect explanations of your behaviour."

"I don't mind explaining, Ray." Again her voice caressed his name while her eyes made a study of his silhouette. "George's a workmate and a friend."

As he remained silent, she realised how corny her projection of George must appear to him. She went on, conscious of his scrutiny, "Actually, George has been a kind of a shield, you know, from unwelcome attention. You must be aware of what goes on in big offices like LI where every man imagines that he is entitled to attention from every woman. So, George and I teamed up and well, that's the extent of our relationship."

"Then he's either an angel or a fairy. I know he's not blind," he stated, rejecting the simple explanation.

"A fairy he's not: an angel, probably."

"But wouldn't it have been simpler, more natural to form an alliance for the usual reasons?"

"Perhaps. But I did not feel I was ready for that kind of relationship," she said simply.

"Are you ready now?" he asked, taking his eyes from the road briefly to glance at her.

"Please, Ray."

Once again she was assailed by doubts as she realised the irrevocability of the path she was about to tread. She leaned back in her chair and shut her eyes as she drew in slow, steadying breaths. Already she was relinquishing an important part of herself, the ability to stay in control whatever the situation.

Raymond waited for her to regain her composure, guessing a little at the conflicting emotions she must be contending with. He stopped the car and said, "Look at me, Cassandra." She opened her eyes, glazed with fear. "You must not be afraid of me. I'll not harm you. When I asked whether you were ready to enter into a relationship with me, I wanted to be sure that you knew what you were doing and would not regret it later. I'm not going to hurry you or force you into doing anything you don't want to do, or are not ready for. Do you understand?"

"I did not ask George to call you, Ray. He took it upon himself to find your number in the phone book after bullying me into telling him your name. But when he told me you were out there, waiting for me, I felt like a drowning person who had just been offered a life-jacket. The answer to your question is yes. I think I am ready."

The last words were hardly out of her mouth when she found herself in his arms, without a clear recollection of how she got there. He took her to Panorama Hotel which was located a few kilometres away from the city centre. In addition to being a tourist attraction, it was also a retreat to many weekenders wishing to get away from the hustle and bustle of town life. Cassandra had been there only once with her brother and sisters to celebrate her graduation. What am I about to celebrate now, she mused cynically. My past warped views about men and sex or a fall from innocence otherwise known as growing up? Back there, at George's place, I was sure I wanted this man at any cost, why am I wavering now? I'm a woman, with a woman's needs and desires, I cannot forever remain shrouded in innocence, she argued with herself, seeking to justify her unusual compulsions.

"Let's get out and have a drink, Cassandra," Raymond said, opening the door for her. She shivered a little as the cold wind whipped at her and her companion drew her protectively against his body saying, "I'll now be your shield against wind and any other unwelcome elements."

After they were comfortably seated and had been served, Raymond tried to catch her eye from its wanderings. "There's something you should know, Cassandra." He stopped and waited for her undivided attention. Avoiding his eye, Cassandra lifted her glass, studied its contents intently, and put it down again, untasted. "Listen to me, Cassandra," Raymond pleaded, bending towards her and capturing both her hands in his in order to force her to pay attention. The misery in the twin dark pools almost made him retract his resolution but he plunged on notwithstanding. "I'm married, Cassandra," and like a man on the scaffold, awaited the hangman's axe to fall the next few seconds with agonising breath.

"I know, Ray. Does it matter very much?" she asked quietly, her expressionless face veiling the turmoil inside her.

"Yes, it matters, to me. It means I cannot give you more than friendship."

"I'll be content with only your friendship, Ray."

"Oh, my darling, I do believe you mean what you're saying," he said.

"I do," was her grave reply. "What more can you have to give me that you can't give me now as your friend?"

The poor kid, Raymond thought. What a lot she still has to learn about life. He felt a strong desire to keep her untouched by evil as she was now. "Life, Cassandra, is not simple mathematics where given formulae lead to accurate answers. It's a composite of 'ifs' and 'buts', a puzzle nobody has as yet succeeded in unravelling. Love, I'm afraid, is not the answer to everything as romantic novels tell us. I'm not trying to disillusion you but I'd not be half the man I'm if I hid the truth from you, didn't point out the pitfalls in your path or the options open to you. I know you take life seriously and are determined to make it to the top of your career, am I right?"

"That has been my dream so far, my only dream and the sole goal of my life. It was a simple enough goal, possible too but now . . . Now something seems to have gone wrong with my calculations. I'm not getting the correct answers anymore. But as you said, there're no given formulae to the riddle that is life; all one can do is flounder in the dark."

"Christ, Cassandra, you make me feel such a heel. Let me take you back and no harm done," he said harshly.

"No harm done!" Cassandra cried fiercely. "No harm done? Do you know what you're proposing? Tearing my heart out and sending me back an empty shell. You've just given me a glimpse of paradise, don't turn me away at the gate. I suppose I sound silly to you," she added a little self-consciously, "but I've never felt like this before and I've never been good at expressing my feelings either. You must also remember, before you indulge in feelings of guilt, that I took the initiative for this situation. I know how awkward it is but I also know that I couldn't bear to stay away from you. Not now."

"It's all right, sweetheart, you won't have to," he said soothingly. "It was mere bravado on my part: I could not have done it without a wrench. I just wanted you to know the door is still open in case you want to use it. Personally I've been running ever since I met you. It seems I can't run anymore. What's happening between us is, without any doubt, the most wonderful thing that can happen between man and woman. But in our case, it's not the wisest. You are desirable young woman on the threshold of life. You have all your life before you while mine's ebbing away in the mire of my past mistakes. You deserve better than an old wreck like me. Everybody will tell you that, including myself, although it pains me to do so."

"Don't say that, Ray, please, not even as a joke. What happened to your marriage, I'm sure, was not of your choosing."

"Perhaps not but I equally share the responsibility for its failure." He paused, shrouded in retrospective silence, and then asked abruptly, "Would you like to hear about it?"

"Only if you want to tell me. I understand you have a little boy?"

"Yes, little Steve," he answered, his face lighting up immediately. His ray of sunshine, Cassandra thought.

"He'll be five in June," Raymond offered. Another reflective silence before he continued, "Belinda and I married when we were still too young to know what we were doing. In terms of age, I was of course old enough at twenty-six but I did not realise at the time the seriousness of the step I was taking. Neither did I stop to weigh the consequences, the sacrifices that would be required of me, of us both. I was floating on a cloud."

"What about your wife? How old was she?" Cassandra asked.

"Belinda was only twenty-one, beautiful, spoilt, the belle of the ball. I was flattered that she chose me when every man around coveted her. I was in heaven, but not for long. It soon became apparent we both did not have the basics necessary for a good marriage. We were both selfish and far too demanding. It was not long before the bickering and the quarrels started. We endured the situation for as long as we could and then decided to go our separate ways. You may be wondering why we don't get a divorce but there're complications I can't explain to you, and I think I've bored you long enough with my unsavoury past. Let's talk about something more cheerful. Let's talk about you."

"I'm sorry, Ray," she said softly, her voice full of compassion.

"No need to be. I got no more than I deserved and I believe that every experience, good or bad, has an important lesson to teach." He looked at his watch and looked at her. "How about getting back now?"

"Why? Are you late for a date?" Cassandra asked lightly, trying to dispel the heavy atmosphere that had suddenly descended upon them. Some things left unsaid about his marriage troubled her.

"Any date after you would seem like tasting sand after sugar," he said gallantly, his face breaking into a smile. "Actually I suggested going back now because most of these roads are not safe to travel at night. But we can stop somewhere in town and have something to eat."

"Why don't we go straight to your place, Ray?" she suggested shamelessly.

Raymond studied her face before he said, "I live alone, Cassandra, and I dismissed my houseboy before I came."

"We're both adults, we don't need a chaperone, Ray. I've already eaten myself but I could prepare something light for you. I want to be alone with you, Ray," she added more boldly as he looked at her uncertainly.

"Do you really mean that, Cassandra?" he asked, searching her face. A face he thought was the loveliest he had ever seen.

"I do, Ray." As she answered, her gaze on him was steadfast, although in the vicinity of her heart, it was a different story. But she had to go on with it because she knew that she had never wanted any man as much as she wanted Raymond Agutamba.

"You're so full of surprises, Cassandra, you take my breath away."

"Pray that I remain so. I should hate for you to discover that underneath the veneer of dazzling wit was the usual humdrum female."

"I'm sure you could never be that: I'm willing to stake my life on it. Shall we go?"

* * *

Cassandra's first impression of Raymond's house was that of a shadowy giant, still, watchful, as if poised for flight. This was of course in the insufficient light of a pale moon. Later, when she saw it by daylight, she realised, even with her little architectural knowledge, what a beautiful edifice it was, lovingly wrought by its owner's skill.

He opened the front door with his key and touched the wall switch, bathing the room in brilliant light. Cassandra blinked and adjusted to the brightness, and then allowed her eye to travel the length and breadth of the room admiringly. It was both impressive in its design and upholstery, with emphasis on quality rather than on quantity. She wandered around, touching and caressing the fine furniture and objets d'art. Raymond stood still, watching her while she got acquainted with her surroundings.

"I like this room, Ray. It's so bright and airy, and perfect in every way."

"Thank you, Cassandra, and welcome to my humble dwelling." He moved towards her slowly, almost somnolently, and put his arms about her. Cassandra, who had been expecting this very moment, stiffened fractionally, fearful that her ignorance would render her incapable of answering to his needs adequately. But mother nature soon took over, making heat rise up in her loins and spread to the rest of her body, making it a mass of quivering jelly. She raised her face to his in a supplicant attitude and he bent down and touched his lips to hers lightly before he drew back and said, "Cassandra, Cassandra, what am I going to do with you?"

"You're going to love me, Ray," she whispered against his chest.

"Cassandra, wonderful, lovely Cassandra, where have you been all my life? Why didn't I discover you sooner?"

"I think I've been waiting for you to find me, Ray."

"And have I found you now, Cassandra? Are you real or just an illusion? Do people like you still exist?"

"I'm real enough, Ray. Touch," she said, guiding his hand to her breast so that he could feel the pumping of her heart. "What do you feel, Ray, what do you hear?"

"Oh God," he groaned and then his hands feverishly worked on the buttons of her blouse. He gasped with awe as her twin wonders poured out of their confines excitingly erect and challenging.

"Please, Ray," Cassandra stammered, feeling shy at his gaze, so nakedly full of desire. She burrowed her face in his breast, causing a complete revolution of his nervous system. "Ray?" she murmured. "Will you please take me and love me before I disintegrate?"

He needed no further prompting.

* * *

"Christ Almighty!" Raymond exclaimed, springing up in bed some minutes later. He snatched at his robe and leapt off the bed and sat on the edge, his head in his hands, groaning. "Christ in heaven," he swore again under his breath. Cassandra's eyes flew open, frightened by the outburst. She called out his name timidly as she raised herself up, drawing the bedsheet securely around her body.

"Christ, Cassandra, I didn't know as God's my witness. You should have told me . . . indicated . . ." he floundered and reached for his pack of cigarettes on the bedside table.

"What's wrong, Ray? I don't understand."

"Goddamn it, Cassandra, I'm talking about your . . . You're still a virgin, damn it, aren't you?" He made it sound like an accusation.

"A virgin, I see. Is that so terrible?" she asked, truly bewildered.

"Not terrible, no. Actually it's wonderful to find somebody as pure as you but not . . . what I'm trying to say is that I've no right to touch you, I mean, if you've managed to keep yourself intact this long, it would not be right to deprive you of your virtue through a casual affair," he ended ineptly.

"A casual affair, Ray? Is that all it is to you?"

"I'm sorry, I've put it badly. What I mean is that I can never offer you anything tangible as I've already explained."

"And as I've already explained, Ray," Cassandra enunciated, jumping out of bed and going to sit beside him, "all I want from you is your friendship. It means more to me than anything else in the world. Please love me and let me love you in return. But," she added impishly, "if my virginity's proving to be an obstacle to our relationship, I can easily get rid of it . . . with the help of somebody like George, perhaps."

"Over my dead body," Raymond swore violently.

"Then we've come to what is generally known as an impasse, haven't we?" she queried.

And for no reason he could fathom, she burst into peals of laughter. He watched her warily but soon her infectious high spirits got to him and he too started chuckling as the humour of the situation hit him. But reality soon asserted itself and the two of them forgot everything else except the craving of their bodies for a closer union. They touched, explored and discovered in each other a fulfilment neither had ever dreamed of nor experienced before.

* * *

With Raymond's help and love, Cassandra gradually unfolded and blossomed into a truly beautiful young woman. She felt happy and relaxed and radiated an inner joy that was a delight to behold. She became a totally new being that did not snarl and scratch at the merest provocation and found it easy to identify with her fellow human beings as frail children of nature.

35

Raymond was not only her lover but her friend, big brother, mentor, the receptacle of all her hopes and dreams. She was not only happy but idyllically so. She was content to drift along, for once allowing her heart rather than her head to dictate the way. But that did not mean that she had lost sight of her goal. She still strove to excel and seemed to be filled with a fresh resurgence of energy which allowed for better concentration and improved performance. But all this was secondary to loving Raymond which was fulfilment enough for her.

Gone was the egotism, the egregious ambition. It was a kind of retributive irony but Cassandra did not see it as such. Rather, she considered the advent of Raymond as a timely rescue from degenerating into the rat race. She still entertained ideas and dreams of success and saw it as her sacred duty, as a woman more advantaged than most by virtue of her education, to help the rest out of limbo, by pointing out the avenues before them. But it was with an assurance born out of maturity rather than hysterical fervour that she preached the gospel. It was no longer the all-consuming passion as before. She now freely acknowledged the existence of other forces of nature.

George, now a pensive George with the predilection to play the role of godfather to her, continued to be her faithful companion at work. Marie's hope that the two of them might see the light one day was extinguished the moment she met the matchless Raymond Agutamba.

Cassandra's brother and sister at home accepted the turn of events with the nonchalance of their age and did not presume to advise or admonish her. But there was Bevis, and Bevis clearly disapproved of Cassandra's relationship with his brother. True, he was not a member of the Mutono family but he was as close as made no difference. His attitude towards her underwent a perceptible change, piercing even her seemingly implacable indifference to him.

One Saturday evening, when Cassandra was lounging on the sofa watching 'Super Star' on video and Raymond was busy with his sketches on the worktable, she remembered that the meetings for her brother's wedding were due to start. "Will you be coming to the meetings, Ray?"

"No, Cassandra. I don't know your brother that well and my presence might give rise to speculation."

"And of course you don't want people to know about us, do you?" She longed to be able to be seen with him in public, to show him off to her friends, but he insisted on discretion. "I'm your secret lover, sort of mistress really," she added with a trace of sadness.

There was a pregnant silence between them. Then swearing under his breath, Raymond threw down his pencil and bounded to her side. "I don't think that's fair, Cassandra," he protested, turning her face towards him. "You

36

know I love you very much and that I'd love to proclaim it to the world from rooftops, but you also know that I can't. I don't like this hole-and-corner business any more than you do but the alternative's to give you up. I can't do that, not without wrenching out my entire vitals. I think about it constantly, agonise about it and ..." she put her finger to his lips to stop him from going on.

"I know, Ray. It was stupid of me to have raised the issue at all."

"Are you sure you understand, my sweet?"

"Of course I understand, darling, I'm not a child. Now go back to your work while I accompany my saviour down to Calvary."

"Oh you're watching that again?"

"I'm trying to learn Mary's song, you know, the one which goes ... let me see ... yes, 'Try not to be worried, try not to think of troubles that upset you ... don't you know everything's all right, yes, everything's fine and I want you to sleep well tonight ... close your eyes, close your eyes ... ' then what? I can't get the next line, it's so maddening."

"What a sweet voice! You should exercise it more often."

"Flattery'll get you nowhere. Go back to your work, Ray."

"I can't work anymore," he said, studying her worriedly. She looked calm enough outwardly but her voice sounded brittle and unreal. He lifted the remote control and flicked off the set. "Let's go somewhere bright and chic tonight and have a good time. I am in an expansive mood."

"I'm afraid I can't do justice to your expansive mood; I don't have the right clothes." She glanced ruefully down at her cotton print whose only recommendation was its cool texture in the sultry weather.

"You look alright to me," he said, gazing at her adoringly. "Why do women make such a fuss about clothes?"

"Vanity I guess. Vanity and something else more subtle," she replied, treating his idle remark with more seriousness than it deserved. "Something to hide one's inadequacy in. Call it a mask or an armour but whatever it is, it gives one the necessary courage to face this uncompromising world."

"You know, for someone who claims to be an introvert, you have an amazing insight into human nature. Okay, granted that the sheath or whatever is an essential feature of the outward human appearance for one reason or another, what of yourself? What do you need it for?"

"The right type of attire gives me a sense of confidence and well-being. I want to look right for you, Ray, to do credit to your impeccable appearance."

"Umm," he studied her with mock seriousness. "You always look that to me whatever you have or don't have on," he added, grinning wickedly, which earned him a punch on the chest. "Come with me anyway." He stood up and pulled her after him. Cassandra allowed herself to be led to the bedroom, wondering what surprise he had in store for her. He was fond of surprising her with little gifts, more precious for the care and love with which they were chosen and given. In the bedroom, he threw the wardrobe door open and stood aside to allow her a glimpse inside.

"Would you consider this *de regueur?*" he asked, pointing to a beautiful evening dress of shimmering green to which Cassandra's eyes were glued. "What's your verdict, is it good enough to give you that air of confidence and distinction?" he asked as he pulled it out and offered it to her.

"It's exquisite, Ray, I adore it." She twirled it round, gasping with admiration. Its simple but elegant style particularly appealed to her.

"It's just a dress, angel, reserve the adoration for me. Would you like to try it on?"

"Thank you, Ray darling, but you do spoil me."

"I can't help it, you're so spoilable."

When she had put it on, she stood before him and he whistled his admiration, his connoisseur's eye noting the effect of the tight skirt on the sensuous contours of her supple body. He planted a kiss on the delicate skin of her nape and said, "You look sensational but I know what you need to complete the effect; some accessories to go with the dress."

"No, Ray, honestly. My shoes're just right and my bag is all-occasion," Cassandra protested.

"God forbid I should be so presumptuous. What I actually had in mind was this." He put his hand in his pocket and pulled out a small square box. Cas dra took it with tentative hands and looked it over without opening it. "Yo   overwhelming me, Ray."

      :ase, sweetheart, you've no idea what trouble I went through to get it. The least you can do's look at it."

"Okay, you win as usual." She opened the small casket and gazed spellbound at the pendant of deepest green, with matching earrings, nestling on a bed of cottonwool.

"May I?" He removed the necklace from its container and hung it around her neck while she fixed the earrings.

" ank you so much," she said, revolving in his arms to face him.

'   n glad you like them. I was so afraid they might not be the right type but '   woman in the shop was so persuasive she convinced me."

"ᵢou have perfect taste in everything, always." She gazed meditatively arou d the room. Here she had known some of the happiest moments of her life. Here she had completed the revolutionary change from girlhood into womanhood. The room was beautiful, or perhaps best described as perfect. Tears tickled behind her eyelids and she hastily blinked them away. She had no idea why she should feel weepy instead of happy. She fastened her eyes on the only picture in the room of young Steve at age two, fiercely hugging a teddy-bear with his chubby hands.

Cassandra knew that Raymond loved his son very much, and guessed that he was the reason why he did not divorce his wife. He had hinted as much. But he had never elaborated and she had refrained from asking questions. All she knew was that his wife brought the child over once in a while and on those occasions, she was banished from the premises by tacit understanding. She did not begrudge him the pleasure he got from his son's company but she was getting increasingly curious about his other life as a father, as a husband with his estranged wife. What was the wife herself like? He had described her as very beautiful. Was he still moved by her beauty in spite of their other differences? Was that the real reason why he did not let go completely? He had never clearly stated his position with regard to his feelings for her. What of the lady herself? Did she still love him and was it her intention to claim him back at some later date? And where in all this, do I, Cassandra fit, she asked herself.

Raymond, sensing her withdrawal into herself, touched her tenderly and turned her to face him saying, "Say something, sweetheart."

"I love you, Ray, I love you so much it sometimes hurts. Do you know what I mean?"

"I know what you mean, my sweet, and I feel the same about you. I ... I ... wish things could have been different for us. I would have liked to lay my life at your feet, to belong to you entirely."

"Sh ... hh, don't let us go over all that again. Just kiss me and make me feel whole again." She put her arms around his waist and he bent his head towards hers and the two were lost in one of those kisses which threatened to disrupt their plans for the evening.

"Let's go, angel. We'll keep the best for last."

He took her to Hotel Concord in the heart of the city. Cassandra felt elated. Most of their outings tended to be out of town in discreet places. The place was not crowded yet and they were led to a table on the balcony where it was cool and offered a good view of their surroundings. Cassandra looked about her curiously: it was her first time to be inside the place although she had passed it countless times to and from work.

"What'll you drink?" Raymond asked as a waiter hovered by.

"Sherry as usual, please."

"Try something else for a change. Do you have Pernod?" he asked the waiter.

"We do, sir."

"Bring two." When the waiter had left, Raymond leaned back in his chair and asked, "How are things at LI? How's George?"

"Fine to both questions. As a matter of fact, George's thinking of leaving us to further his studies abroad."

"That's wonderful . . . for him, of course. You're going to miss your patron saint though, aren't you?"

"Most definitely. But you should be pleased; you never believed in his *bona fides*."

"But I believed in you although I admit I'll feel a lot easier in my mind with him thousands of miles away across the ocean. What course does he want to do?"

"Graphic Art. He's an artist, you know, and it's in that capacity he works for LI. But he thinks specialised artists will have greater scope in future than run-of-the mill ones."

"That's true of every field: it's becoming a world of specialists. What about you? Wouldn't you like to go for further studies?"

"It has crossed my mind; I'd stand a better chance of forging ahead." Her mind briefly veered to her job and its limitations for a person with ambitions to reach the pinnacle of success. She turned to Raymond and as her eyes met his, the nigglings of discontent fled and were replaced by a feeling of happiness.

"Cheers!" he said, raising his glass to her.

"Hello, Raymond," a man said, materialising beside their table. "Sorry to intrude on you but I saw you as you came in and thought I'd say hi."

"That's all right, James. Ah, this is Bill Okiror, my associate. Bill, meet Cassandra." Cassandra and the man shook hands but he refused the seat offered, saying, "I want to introduce you to somebody at my table. I promise I won't keep him away too long, Cassandra. I hope you don't mind?"

"Not at all," Cassandra assured him but Raymond himself looked uncertain. "Go on, Ray, I'll be all right."

"If you're sure . . . "

"I am."

She turned her attention to other guests in the place, observing that the vacant tables were filling up pretty fast. The third table from theirs was still empty. But as her eyes were about to move further on, a waiter led another twosome there. The man was plumpish, running to fat although still young. His companion was something else, though. She was tall and slender, with the most vivid brown complexion Cassandra had ever seen. Her voluptuous figure was encased in a lilac outfit, with a shimmering pink blouse inside. Her liquid eyes met Cassandra's in their general sweep of her immediate neighbourhood and lingered on her briefly before they moved on. Cassandra on her part was

40

hypnotised by the other lady's poise and elegance and was still studying her when Raymond returned.

"I'm sorry I took so long, sweetheart, I hope you didn't miss me too much?" Raymond asked anxiously resuming his seat.

"No, I didn't miss you too much," Cassandra replied truthfully, her eyes automatically switching back to the table beyond. The object of her curiosity seemed in turn to be taking an inordinately great interest in Raymond's back. She was gesticulating excitedly to her companion who appeared to be ineffectually trying to calm her down. She shook his hand off rudely and got to her feet.

Fascinated, Cassandra watched her sinuous progress towards their table as one would the slithering closing in of a poisonous snake. Instinctively, she knew who the other woman was and her heart reacted swiftly, pumping extra adrenalin, making her shiver inwardly. Raymond, who was facing the other direction was not aware of the newcomer's presence until she stood before him, drawling out his name insolently. He started and stiffened, his gaze slowly rising to her face.

"Ray darling, what a surprise to find you here. I thought you had retired from social life, become a recluse."

Raymond did not answer, and after darting Cassandra a worried look, he turned to look at the intruder warily. Cassandra shivered again as the tension mounted. She wished Raymond would say something, send the woman packing.

"Aren't you going to introduce me to your latest find, darling?" the lady continued, seating herself down uninvited. She turned to Cassandra and treated her to an impudent gaze. "Not bad," she nodded condescendingly. "Not bad at all although I can understand why you might not be too eager to be seen with her in public: people might call you a cradle-snatcher, mightn't they?"

"I'm twenty-four," Cassandra snapped haughtily, involuntarily coming to Raymond's defence. He still had not uttered a word but he held himself rigidly, the tight knuckles around his glass betraying his feelings. Cassandra felt an almost irresistible urge to throw the contents of her own glass in the insolent face but fought it with the last reserve of her control. It was not her fight; she just happened to be caught in the crossfire.

"Twenty-four, eh? A difference of only ten years. Still," she added in a seemingly confidential voice to Cassandra, "men will be men. You and I know that some old reprobates have been known to marry children young enough to be their grandchildren. Only in your case, the question of marriage doesn't arise of course or hasn't he explained that to you?"

Shocked by the enormity of the other woman's malevolence, Cassandra drew away instinctively as if to avoid a blow. At the same time, Raymond half rose from his chair, his face contorted with rage and hissed, "Belinda!" He infused the word with so much force that even his wife looked taken aback.

"Excuse me," Cassandra said, getting up and stumbling away in the direction of the washrooms. She could not stand anymore.

"Belinda," Raymond repeated, his eyes red with anger. "One of these days you'll outdo even yourself and I warn you I'll not be responsible for the consequences. Now that you've accomplished your mission of destruction, why don't you go back to your lapdog and allow him to lick your wounds."

"Why, you're jealous, Ray, aren't you?" she exclaimed with glee. "You surely can't be jealous of that nincompoop in spite of . . . ,"

"I am not jealous," he interrupted her violently. "The scales fell from my eyes long ago and you can go with the devil as far as I'm concerned. But what I'll not allow you to do is to interfere with my affairs."

"Your affair, present affair, that is, seems to have forgotten her handbag," Belinda remarked, her eyes turning to the article in question. "Poor little thing, no woman goes to the 'Ladies' without her handbag. Besides, she'll need her make up to repair the ravages of tears. Don't you think I'd be doing her a kindness if I took it to her?"

"Don't you dare go near her if you value your life," Raymond warned her fiercely. He beckoned to a waiter and asked for the bill.

"Oh, I hope I haven't spoilt your evening, Ray? Don't waste your time worrying about her, you'll soon tire of her anyway, as you have of others before her. You may search the entire world but you're not going to find what you're looking for until you come to your senses and admit I'm the only woman for you, the only one who understands you and can answer to all your needs."

"I knew you were vain, but I didn't know that you were stupid too! You and I are through, Belinda, finished, understand?" He stood up to indicate he was ready to move if she wasn't. Belinda, like a good general, knew when it was wiser to beat a retreat. There would be other opportunities to renew the attack.

"Give the baby-girl a kiss on the cheek for me. On second thoughts, why don't I bring Steve over tomorrow, would you like that? To make up for lousing up your evening."

"I'll see Steve next Saturday as previously arranged," Raymond replied shortly.

Belinda seemed pleased with the reply and gave a spontaneous laugh which in the past had been one of the characteristics he had liked about her but which now jarred on his nerves.

"So the tramp stays nights, does she?" she snarled, her mood suddenly becoming dangerously brutal. "A straying from the rules, that. Remember, Raymond Agutamba, that you're still a married man. Married to me. Don't you ever forget that even for one minute."

"Why don't you go ahead and sue me for divorce?" her husband challenged.

"And wouldn't you like just that! Well, I have news for you. I'll never divorce you. You're mine, Ray, and I intend to make sure that you remain so for as long as I live. So put the idea right out of your head."

"Listen, Belinda, and listen well; if I wanted a divorce, there would be no problem about getting it, believe me. But I made an arrangement with you which I intend to stick to. We agreed to a trial separation of four years and if I remember correctly, the agreement stipulated no conditions as to our mode of conduct. Only one year of that arrangement has gone by. In the meantime, let Steve be our only reason for contact, is that clear?"

"What's clear to me is that you're bonkers over that trash. But let me also remind you that our so-called agreement did not go through courts of law and it holds as much water as a reed basket. Any time I chose I could come back and live as your wife and there isn't a thing you'd do about it. Think about that carefully before you start laying down the law." Their eyes met and held, mirroring all the old long antagonism and clash of wills. Belinda capitulated first and walked away with an exaggerated swagger.

Raymond remained standing for sometime, not paying attention to the curious glances directed at him. His gaze rested on Cassandra's bag hanging forlornly on her chair and he drew some measure of comfort from it and sat down to wait for her.

* * *

Cassandra bent over the washbasin and let her tears flow freely. Afterwards she blew her nose and doused her face with cold water. She looked up in the face mirror on the wall and a drawn strange face, which she supposed was hers, stared back at her. "Why am I crying?" she asked her reflection. She was not in the habit of taking refuge in tears, preferring to face whatever problem with her head up. But now, well, there were a great many things she was doing she used not to do.

"Not feeling too well, dear?" a girl of about her own age at the other sink asked sympathetically.

Cassandra, who had imagined she had the entire room to herself, looked around, startled.

"Don't look at me as if I were a ghost because I'm not," added the other. "I just came in but I guess you were too preoccupied to notice." She expertly tweezed off a stray eyelash with her thin long fingers. "Want to borrow my kit for repairs?" she asked carelessly after summing up the situation. "You don't want to let him know he has that much power over you. Never let a man know he's the beginning and the end of everything for you. It does not do any harm

43

to keep them guessing a little. They're bad enough without our going out of our way to inflate their egos."

Cassandra opened her mouth to protest the erroneous assumption but thought better of it. She found the other girl's chatter therapeutic. She gave her a watery smile and murmured "Thank you," as she reached for the powder puff and eye pencil.

"My name's Samantha," her new pal told her. "Some of the most delightful friendships I've made have started in washrooms like this."

"I'm Cassandra and I'm delighted to make your acquaintance, Samantha."

"Same here," the other beat her chest. "And you can call me Sam. Where do you work, Cassandra, or are you still at...?" but she never got to finish her question.

"Don't say it, please, don't say school!" Cassandra cried violently. "Oh, I'm sorry," she apologised hastily as Sam looked at her in perplexity. "I'm rather sensitive about my youthful appearance because it has already been a topic of controversy this evening and I can't stand another reference to it," she explained sighing. "I work with Lotus International."

The two exchanged telephone numbers and promised to keep in touch.

* * *

In the car in the park, Cassandra and Raymond sat shrouded in sombre silence. Raymond, his eyes staring out in the gloom, played a tuneless tattoo on the steering wheel. Minutes ticked away until Cassandra could not bear it any longer. She glanced at his face and said, "Ray, I-" but he interrupted her saying harshly, "I'll understand if you decide you want to go back to Luzzi now."

"I don't want to go back to Luzzi, Ray, I came to spend a weekend with you. Also I haven't eaten and I'm starving."

"Cassandra!" he cried with relief, drawing her into the circle of his arm. "I'm sorry about what happened up there. I would have given anything to spare you the dreadful experience."

"Hush, darling, it was not your fault. I understand that your past may sometimes intrude on us like this but after thinking about it, I decided I was not going to allow it to dampen my spirits or we may not have much of a life together. It's a fact that you have a past, we all do. But it's also a fact that no amount of wishing is going to erase it away. One does not fight with facts, one simply accepts them."

"Such profundity, such wisdom," Raymond murmured reverently. "Do you know what you make me feel like, Cassandra, with your worldly wisdom?

44

A juvenile, in spite of my being so much older than you, as my esteemed wife kindly pointed out. What hidden depth do you draw on that makes no recourse to age or experience?"

"What has age got to do with it or wisdom? I'm telling you exactly what I feel in my heart. For your sake, I'm prepared to endure anything, and accept whatever life chooses to hand out to me for the great joy of being with you."

"That's the sweetest and most precious compliment I've ever been paid and it makes me feel ever so humble. But listen to me, sweetheart, I did not come into your life with the purpose of disrupting it. On the contrary, I hoped, in my modest way, to enrich it a little. You're too young to give up the struggle for the best and the best is what you deserve. When I first met you, you were all set to conquer the world and all its ills and injustices single-handed . I was awed and impressed. I don't want you to change from that invincible, resolute girl because that's the essence of the Cassandra I love and adore. Go on being confident and indomitable, my Cassandra, and the sky's the limit. Now that I know I can count on your love at all times, I'll endeavour, as much as possible, to shield you from unnecessary embarrassments such as tonight's."

"Surely you could not have doubted the sincerity of my feelings for you for one minute?" Cassandra said.

"Not to say doubted but I'm never free from the fear of what havoc a scene like the one we've just witnessed could do," he replied.

"It would take more than a few spiteful words to sever what we two have between us, don't you think so?" she asked in earnest.

"It would take a cataclysm on my part, believe me," he declared, drawing her close.

They clung together, reaffirming their love while time itself seemed to stand still, watching, waiting; yes, waiting.

Chapter Three

"We haven't heard from the ladies," the Chairman, presiding over the meeting to prepare for the wedding of Gavin Mutono to Tonia Nabbosa, said, his statement embracing Tonia, the bride-to-be; Mellinda, Cassandra and Alexandria, sisters to the groom, and Josephine, Tonia's friend. They were all squeezed on the sofa set while their male counterparts made do with whatever else was available.

Bevis' gaze swept over each face in turn but seemed to dwell a mite longer on Cassandra's or so her guilty conscience told her. She had been giving the proceedings scanty attention as her thoughts kept wandering to Muyenga, wishing herself there instead of here. She returned his gaze boldly and thought she saw mockery in his. Shying away from it, her eyes slid to his hands. Bevis had long, tapering fingers, whose beauty did not detract from his masculinity. They presently seemed to be a little unsteady and this surprised Cassandra. He was the most self-possessed person she knew. Her gaze flickered back to his face and he gave her a brief smile before he picked up the trail of his scrutiny of other faces.

"Tonia? We're discussing the most important day of your life, don't you have anything to say in support or against the proposals put forward? Or a suggestion of your own to make?" he asked.

"I've complete confidence in you, guys, to do your best to make the day the most memorable in my life," Tonia replied, her eyes seeking out those of her fiancé.

"Hear, hear!" a chorus of cheers greeted this statement. "The onus lies particularly with you, Gavin."

More guffaws from the men which Mellinda interrupted with a suggestion for a break, " . . . to allow us to stretch our legs and recharge our vitality. Some of us are beginning to feel faint from lack of circulation and food."

"A good suggestion, Mellie. Any objections?"

There were none and a twenty-minute break was granted.

After a sandwich break, the meeting resumed. Finally, Cassandra heard, with relief, the Chairman making his concluding speech. "Don't forget we have only one more meeting before the big day. Fresh suggestions will not be entertained then."

"Speak now or forever remain . . . " somebody jocularly said.

"How about dinner, Cassandra? As the two of us have been chosen to oversee the arrangements, we need to work out some strateg,y," Bevis said.

Cassandra hesitated. She was hoping that she and Raymond could get together after all and retrieve whatever was left of the weekend, but Bevis' eyes seemed to say that they could read her thoughts which prompted to her say yes, for the sole purpose of contradicting him.

"Certainly, you're welcome to stay for dinner. Gavin and Tonia are going out, so if you think you can put up with me alone . . . "

"I was actually proposing a quiet dinner for the two of us out somewhere; that's if you're free of course."

Cassandra looked at the phone longingly but knew that Raymond did not expect her until the following day unless she telephoned him and asked him to come for her. She looked up and met with that speculative gaze which once again seemed to be challenging her. "I can always make myself free, I suppose. How much time do I have to get ready?"

"I'm driving Mellie back to the hospital. Supposing I come back for you at eight, will that be all right?"

"I'll be ready."

After everybody had left, she tried to ring Raymond, just to hear his voice but he was not at home. Disappointed, she began to prepare for what promised to be a joyless evening.

* * *

"Let's drink to a better understanding between us in future," Bevis said, raising his glass to her. He was more perceptive than she gave him credit for and must have sensed that he had only part of her attention. She perfunctorily returned his toast and the meal dragged on.

"You seem to be very far away, Cassandra, might one ask where?" he asked after several abortive attempts to engage her in more than a desultory conversation.

"One might be considered impertinent if one did, but actually I was wondering what I'd look like in a month after a five-course meal every day," she improvised.

47

"I'm sorry you're not enjoying your dinner. Can I tempt you with another glass of wine? This particular brand, I'm assured, has a low calorie content."

"Don't be touchy, Bevis, I'm enjoying myself very much but I'm sure I've added inches to my waistline in the last hour or so."

Bevis smiled his slow, lazy smile at her quibble. "I don't think you need to worry about your figure, Cassandra. It will always be the same, give or take a few inches."

"Am I supposed to be flattered by that? One always hopes for improvement of one's appearance."

"Don't change, Cassandra, ever!" he said a little intensely, and then gave a hollow laugh as if embarrassed.

"That's too tall an order for me to fill," Cassandra said lightly, wondering about the man sitting opposite her. "But thanks all the same."

"More wine?"

"Thank you. I trust you find me an apt pupil? Wine has never been my drink until tonight."

"What do you and Ray drink?" Too late, he realised his mistake in mentioning his brother's name. Cassandra's face suddenly closed and her eyes filmed over with antagonism.

"What do you have against my friendship with your brother? It hurts nobody."

The hell it doesn't, Bevis thought grimly. Aloud he said, "I didn't say I disapproved of your friendship with Ray."

"You don't have to say it. It has been apparent in your attitude towards me ever since I met him," she contended hotly.

"You're imagining things, Cassandra. My attitude towards you has not changed and is not likely to change for any reason whatsoever."

Without trying to examine his cryptic remark, Cassandra instantly jumped on the defensive saying, "I never knew you disliked me so much before. It's quite a revelation to me."

"For a smart girl, you do let your imagination run away with you. But my feelings apart, doesn't it bother you that Ray has a wife and a child?"

Oh yes it does, Cassandra wanted to admit but instead said "No" in a voice that brooked no argument. Then after a short pause, in a voice still full of resentment, she added, "If my memory serves me right, the sole purpose of having dinner together tonight was to discuss business and not my errant love life."

"You're quite right," her companion admitted equably. "I apologise. Let's adjourn to the lounge where I can easily jot down some notes. Would you like to continue with wine or change to coffee?" Cassandra looked at him incredulously. Her outburst seemed to have had no effect on him at all. Perversely, she found this outrageous and intolerable. You wait, Mr Cool, she vowed to herself, one day, I'll riddle that armour of yours with so many chinks you won't have the courage to look up. "Now," he continued, pulling out a pen and a notebook, "I'm a little unclear as to what our duty entails. What about you?"

Cassandra continued to regard him motionlessly for a few more minutes before she summoned enough control to match his composure. "I was relying on you to enlighten me but I suppose our role is that of coordinators of the different effort groups. So many people have made pledges of one kind or another, but pledging is one thing and delivering, another."

"I suppose you're right. I have telephone numbers of those who can be so reached and will try to keep them to their promises. When will your people start to arrive?"

"Quite soon, I believe. Accommodation's going to be a bit of a problem. I think Gavin's thinking of putting some in a lodge but that will solve only part of the problem because they'll still need to be fed and generally looked after."

"I have quite a big house and I've told Gavin that it's at his disposal."

"That's very kind of you, Bevis."

"It's the least I can do for a friend," he replied, shrugging. "Let's meet again on Monday. Is that all right with you? Where do you suggest we meet? I'm usually tied up until after six during weekdays."

"That suits me fine as I normally don't get home until after five. We could meet at our place unless you have a brighter idea."

"I don't and your place's fine as long as we don't inconvenience anybody."

"Not likely. Gavin rarely gets home before eight and Mellie's just an on-and-off resident. But what are we expected to have achieved by then?" ·

"Hardly anything. But we might get fresh ideas, or . . . anyway, let's meet and see what develops."

"Okay. You're also invited to stay to dinner if you have no other plans afterwards."

"I'll look forward to it, thanks."

In the car outside her house, Bevis said, "I'm sorry about tonight, Cassandra." Cassandra looked at him surprised. She had imagined she had aroused no stronger feelings in him by her reaction to his ill-advised remarks than disdain. "I hope you've forgiven me. I want us to be friends."

"There's nothing to forgive: I just flew off the handle, that's all."

"Then we are friends?"

"Comrades," she said as she offered him her hand to shake.

He was quiet for some time, lost in thought. Cassandra shifted restlessly and was about to open the door of the car to get out when he forestalled her, saying, "Good. As friends, I may then speak to you frankly?" He took her silence for consent. "I've been worried about you, you know, you and Ray. I don't think you realise the kind of position you've placed yourself in . . . let me finish please before you tell me to mind my own business. The situation, you see, is more complex than it appears on the surface both from a legal and a social point of view. My brother, admittedly, is a good man and well-intentioned, but he's not practical. You may not realise it but you're sitting on a time-bomb."

"Aren't you exaggerating a little, Bevis? I know Ray and his wife are not legally separated, but theirs is not an uncommon situation these days."

"That may be so but there are certain peculiar aspects to this case which you don't seem to appreciate. For example, how would you like to be named as a corespondent in a divorce case?"

"I don't think Ray's wife would go to those lengths. They agreed on separation for a specific period, and until that period's over, nothing untoward is likely to happen," Cassandra told him with unconcealed impatience.

"And after that, what happens to you?" he cried. "No, don't answer," he hurried on angrily. "So they have their gentleman's agreement, okay, do you know what that presupposes, Cassandra? Honourable intentions on both sides. But Belinda knows no shame, nor honour, let me tell you. So far she's having the best of both worlds, a husband to support her and freedom to follow her fancy. But as soon as she finds out about you and realises that you constitute a real threat, then the fat'll go up in the fire. As I said, she can either sue for divorce or pack bag and baggage and head back for Muyenga. It would depend on whichever she considered likely to do most harm to Ray. You're not cut out for that kind of life, Cassandra."

"What kind of life am I cut out for, Bevis, do you know? I don't. Not anymore. Don't imagine I haven't thought about all this: I have, a great deal but well, there it is. But you're wrong on one point. Ray's wife has already met me and dismissed me as insignificant," she added expressionlessly. Bevis sucked in his breath and turned to look at her.

"Don't let Belinda's attitude of 'I couldn't care less' deceive you. She's a consummate actress and she'd rather die than let anybody know her true feelings."

"I realise all that but I don't see why it should concern you. I know how deeply I've put my foot in and I know that sooner or later I'll have to pay the price. I'm not a child, I went into it with my eyes wide open and I'm accountable to nobody but myself for my actions. I know you think I'm a fool, but sometimes a fool's paradise's much more preferable to the real world."

"But why, for heaven's sake? It's all so unnecessary and unlike you," Bevis cried, gripping her shoulders so suddenly that both were startled by the impulsive act. Then as suddenly he released her and apologised for his impetuosity. "Sorry, I went off the rails a little. I'll see you to the door."

As she waited for somebody to answer the doorbell, Cassandra turned and studied Bevis, her curiosity aroused by the few glimpses she had had of the inner man in the course of the evening. In the past she had attributed his actions, especially with regard to her, to the worst intentions. But now she was not sure. He had revealed to her, tonight, a side of him which was not all arrogance and indifference. She warmed to him a little and wished they could become real friends like he was with her brother and sister but knew this to be impossible in the circumstances.

"Goodnight, Cassandra," he said, taking a step backwards when he heard the rattling of the lock inside.

"That's the second time you're bidding me goodnight. Do you want me to go to bed hungry?" she teased him, trying to dispel the tension in the air.

"You'll not go to bed hungry because you've already eaten, and as I recall, a meal you did not very much relish," he reminded her with a little smile.

"I'm sorry I forgot my manners; thank you for a very delightful evening, Bevis."

"I was not fishing for compliments, Cassandra."

"But it is customary, isn't it? I mean to say thank you to your escort after a date."

"We're not doing it according to the rules or . . . " he broke off and took another step backwards.

"Or what?"

"It's not important. Goodnight again. Third time makes it all right."

He turned and walked back to his car, a tall, lonely figure. But why lonely? Cassandra wondered, staring after him. Obviously by choice, she concluded shrugging. That night she dreamt that she was in the witness stand with Bevis as the presiding judge. 'GUILTY, GUILTY,' he kept shouting as he banged on his table furiously. She woke up with a headache and a doubtful conscience the following morning.

* * *

Bevis believed strongly in his ability to influence the course of his life to a great extent. He was also dogmatic and uncompromising about his principles and held that the best judge of his own character was himself. Many people who did not know him well took him at his face value and thought him extremely self-centered and standoffish. But those who did, such as his eldest sister,

Stella, knew the other side of him that he did not reveal to the world often.

Stella was the eldest child of the Agutamba family, now married with a family of her own. She was three years older than Raymond and five years Bevis' senior. But even as a young girl, she had had overdeveloped maternal instincts which had enabled her to take care of her brothers and sisters when their mother died early in their lives. She had loved all four dearly but a special bond had developed between her and Bevis. Their father had doted, and still did, on Raymond who was blessed with a sunny nature. Indeed everybody who came into contact with the radiant child could not help but be charmed by him. As a baby, he had been very delicate and although at age ten, when their mother died, he had looked robust enough, nobody ever forgot that it had been touch and go at one point.

The other two children, both girls, had been by far the most precarious, being much too young to be without a mother. But with the help of an aunt, and later a stepmother, Stella had, with loving care, nurtured them through the critical stages of childhood. They were now grown women; Tracy, the elder of the two, living in Europe in self-exile with her husband and Emily, a qualified veterinary surgeon.

Like a mother, Stella liked to make regular rounds of her 'charges', as she still regarded them, and drew some satisfaction from the knowledge that she had contributed considerably to their development. The girls were happily settled in their chosen careers but the boys' lives left a lot to be desired, she thought.

She had not been happy with Raymond's marriage: she was now not happy with the breakup. She knew Belinda's character was lacking in many of the qualities which made for a good marriage, but she was also honest enough to admit that her brother was far from perfect.

Bevis inserted his key in the lock and opened the door. "You shouldn't have waited up for me, Stella." Stella, curled in the armchair, with a flask of coffee and a cup on the table beside her, let the observation pass as she critically studied her brother's face, noting the lack of animation.

After he had divested himself of the jacket and tie and sat sprawling in the opposite chair, she asked, "How was the dinner with Cassandra?"

"I told you that it was purely business. She and I are supposed to . . . "

"I know, something about her brother's wedding. You told me."

"So why ask if you know?" Bevis retorted, annoyed. He had no doubt that Stella could read him like a book.

"What's Cassandra like?" she demanded, following her own trend of thought.

"What's Cassandra like? An interesting question," Bevis remarked and was thoughtful for a few moments. "I've never considered the question, you know but I think you could say she's different from the ordinary girl of today. Very different."

"How so?"

"Well, she's smart, confident and independent; she's of course young and beautiful, as you might have guessed. For more details, you'll have to ask Ray," he added, breaking off abruptly.

"You said she's your friend, Gavin's sister. You ought to know her well too."

"What's the point in all this questioning?" he asked her, getting annoyed.

"Is there a chance of Ray and Belinda getting together again?" Bevis heard warning bells immediately. Stella's mode of communication might appear artless but he knew there was reason and purpose behind every word uttered.

"Well, why not? When Belinda has had her fill of the free woman world, she'll whistle and Ray'll come running," he said dryly. "You know Belinda."

"Yes, I know Belinda. But I also know your brother whom you don't credit with enough sense to see her for what she really is. But what I'd like to know is where this girl, Cassandra, fits in."

Shrugging with feigned indifference, Bevis said, "Well, she knows he's married. She'll simply have to move on when the time comes."

"Then she's the type who moves from man to man?"

"Certainly not," he retorted violently, and then realising that he had just fallen into her trap. He hurriedly qualified his statement by adding, "As far as I know."

But Stella looked satisfied with his answer. "It's the old story all over again, isn't it?" she cried. "When will you two boys ever grow up and stop rivalling each other? Don't you realise that you're both wonderful people in your different ways?"

Bevis winced as if somebody had pierced him in a wound. One of the things he wanted to forget about his childhood was his envy of his more popular brother. In order to appropriate some of the attention lavished on Raymond, he had often gone out of his way to ape the former's every gesture and action. But that had been a long time ago when he didn't know any better. For Stella to level such a charge at him now was outrageous. "I don't think that's correct, Stella. Ray and I have outgrown childish jealousies and rivalries and are devoted to each other."

"That's very comforting to hear," Stella told him in a dubious voice.

"I know that you're drawing a parallel between Belinda and Cassandra," he continued slowly, "but I assure you there're no grounds for that."

"Except that they're women you have both loved," Stella told him bluntly.

"That's another myth which has persisted over the years with regard to

53

Belinda. Everybody, including yourself, cast me in the role of the rejected lover, an impression that Belinda, for reasons best known to herself, has always fostered. It's true I knew her before Ray did but I was never in love with her. I also knew she was wrong for him, but I could not have warned him without risking my intentions being misunderstood. He had to find out about her the hard way. It's not something I've enjoyed seeing happen, believe me. He's my brother for all our differences and the woman who can separate us is not yet born." He stopped to examine his last statement which sounded false even in his own ears. But why is it necessary for me to take a stand on the issue, he asked himself, feeling his irritation rising. "But you wanted to know about Cassandra, didn't you?" he continued regulating his voice to normal. "Well, I've known her almost as long as I've known her brother. I admire her. I think she's a wonderful girl. She and Belinda have nothing in common. They shouldn't even be discussed in the same breath."

His sister watched him thoughtfully for some time before she said gently, "It's not the end of the story, is it?"

"No, it isn't," he admitted grimly and relapsed into silence. The two were stirred from their meditation by the sound of a single gunshot in the distance. "There's somebody wishing us a goodnight," he remarked, some of his humour restored. "Time for bed."

"I want to talk to you about Dome," Stella said.

"What scrapes has he got himself into this time?" Bevis asked wearily.

Dominic, commonly known as Dome, was their stepbrother who had all the makings of a potential playboy. To him, life was one long circus and work, of any kind, his sworn enemy. He had made rounds of all the schools possible and was at his present one on sufferance. He was now due to sit for his 'A' levels but his chances of passing hung in the balance.

"He has not gotten himself into trouble exactly but his mock results were not reassuring and father does not want him to sit this year. He's not really stupid, you know, but he missed out a lot during his suspension in the first term. Father is banking on your support but Dome, on the other hand, is gambling on your veto."

"And the wretch's right, I'm afraid. I rather think that stopping him from sitting would be a mistake, especially if he himself is not convinced of the necessity. Let him try his luck; he still has three months to recoup the lost time. If he fails, then he'll have learnt a valuable lesson from the experience. He could then transfer to another school and resit. If the situation improves in the city, you can send him to us for Christmas holidays. Geraldine spoils him too much."

Geraldine was their stepmother whom they had never learnt to call mother.

"She's simply terrified of him, isn't it silly? And father's getting rather too soft in his old age. Do you think there's any hope of this madness ever coming to an end?" Stella asked, switching to the civil war in the country. "People are tired of fighting, of living violent, unsettled lives. They want peace, they want rest. They want to plan for their future, they want to have a future. How do you people ever manage to sleep at night? I'm sure I'd become a complete wreck if I had to endure this kind of life for long."

"Oh you get used to it somehow and instead begin to suspect the brooding silence and intermittent lulls. But actually you're quite right to worry. The situation shows signs of degenerating into a full scale war any time now. But end it will, no matter how long it takes. What's needed now is a third party to offset the balance of power between the two warring factions and bring the hostilities to an end."

"Or for one of the two to give in," Stella suggested.

"That's not likely to happen. In Africa we don't believe in giving in. We believe in fighting to the end, even if it be a bitter one. The belief that 'he who runs away lives to fight another day' simply doesn't appeal to us," Bevis told her cynically.

"A pity it doesn't. So many lives and property would be saved. I hope you boys are not involved in anything dangerous?" Stella asked, scanning his face worriedly.

"Don't worry. Personally I believe that it's wiser to be a live coward than a dead hero," Bevis assured her.

"A living rat is better than a dead lion," Stella murmured, quoting a similar saying in their language. "I'm going to bed now, it's rather late."

"Goodnight, Stella. See you in the morning."

Chapter Four

Cassandra surveyed the sea of mourners in the living room of the late Horace Kalanzi's mansion in Buziga with a frown. It was funny that she had never been to that house before, she thought, despite the fact that Horace and Mellinda had practically been engaged.

The room had been divided into two parts so as to separate the female mourners from their male counterparts according to tradition. The women sat on mats spread over the wall-to-wall carpet where they talked in hushed voices and conducted their unrestrained grief.

The men, on their part, with a sprinkling of a few women whose knees had become too stiff from disuse to allow them to sit on the floor, as one woman maliciously put it, sat uneasily in the plush chairs, sipping their drinks and making bad jokes. Occasional outbursts of loud lamentation from the other side almost went unnoticed by them.

"Why, oh why did they have to kill you, my son?" one elderly lady lamented, wringing her hands as she gazed at the still form of Horace, her tears making rivulets on her wrinkled face. "Why did they kill you?" she repeated the million dollar question, "since we are all destined to die some day, why hasten your end, Horace, before your time!" But Horace, ashen and still in his glass-topped coffin, was past caring whether it was now, next year or the year after. For him, the struggle was over, for him it was eternal peace, eternal rest.

Cassandra squeezed her sister's hand comfortingly but Mellinda, stiff and dry-eyed, gave no indication of awareness. All around her people were exchanging titbits of gossip, conjuring up lurid details of Horace's death.

"They say his body was bullet-riddled when it was found, a whole magazine must have been emptied into it," one woman imparted with relish. A shudder went through those clustered around her. "They also said that he was stripped naked when he was found a short distance away from here."

"That cannot be true," a respectable-looking lady, who had been listening to these macabre accounts with disapproval, interrupted with austerity. "The

56

people who found him stated quite clearly that he was slumped over the driving wheel, which made them think at first that he was sleeping off a heavy night of carousal. If he had been naked, they'd have suspected foul-play immediately. It was not until they tried to rouse him that they realised he was dead. Nothing from him was missing except his Rolex watch and the cash he might have had on him. Possibly his cheque book too, which is still missing. But his identification, and other documents were all there in his briefcase."

"I wonder what the motive of his murder could have been," somebody speculated aloud.

"With Horace, it could have been anything, especially business," chipped in one of the Miss-Know-It-Alls. "It's a fact that most of his business deals could not stand up to scrutiny."

"How many scrupulous businessmen do you know?" again the same mature lady came to the rescue of the defenseless Horace. A family friend, a relative? Cassandra wondered. "I don't think it's our business to put motive to crime which, in my opinion, is more complex than business rivalry."

"You must be implying politics?"

"Perhaps," the speaker answered, surveying her immediate neighbourhood furtively. "It was no secret that Horace supported the man in the bush," she went on in a low voice. "If it's true, then the conclusion's obvious, isn't it?"

"That's rubbish," somebody else put in contentiously. "If you want to know my opinion, Horace was killed for no other reason than his womanising. Nobody else except a jealous husband or lover would hate him that much to want him dead. He had an endless string of women and any of these could be indirectly responsible for his death," she averred, her eyes sparking venom in Mellinda's direction. One of Horace's rejects, Cassandra decided, looking at her sister worriedly. But fortunately, Mellinda seemed oblivious of all that was going on around her.

"That's rather a naive and simplistic approach to the matter," the girl sitting next to the last speaker rebuked her sharply. "None of us know the motive . . . I hope," she added, insinuatingly, her glance resting on the uncharitable mourner. "Personally, I don't believe in speaking ill of the dead since none of us qualifies to throw a stone. In any case, of what possible help can our wild speculations be to the dead man now or those he has left behind? Leave the detection to those qualified to do it."

"If you mean the police, then you have more faith in their competence and integrity than most of us do," one woman remarked.

Agreeing with her, another one said, "The police are just puppets of the powers that be and will always be, as long as appointments and promotions are subject to political allegiances. They investigate and make reports for sure

57

but..." here the speaker was interrupted by somebody demanding everybody's attention.

"If I may have your ears, ladies and gentlemen: I have two announcements to make. One, the requiem Mass'll take place at ten o'clock at Christ the King Church. Two, we've managed to secure a couple of buses to take those who wish to travel to Kabuwoko for the funeral. A piece of paper'll be passed around later for those who wish to take advantage of this to put down their names. We're charging a nominal fee of one thousand shillings only per person, return. The buses are scheduled to leave immediately after the service and the venue will be at the church. For those who've never been to Kabuwoko and wish to travel in their own vehicles, I have a rough sketch map here to guide you if you care to look at it afterwards.

"Although I initially set out with no intention of making a speech, I feel compelled to say a few words. We members of the late Horace's family are deeply touched by your turning up like this to share our grief. Most of you, I'm sure, knew Horace personally and knew what a dedicated young man he was to the cause of improving our beloved country, Uganda. But because the forces of evil are sworn to the destruction of all bright and progressive sons of this country, Horace had to die. I must not allow myself to get emotional; the Good Book tells us that vengeance belongs to God and God only. And so in his hands, let's commit Horace's soul. Lastly I wish to welcome Father Ambrose Mukasa who's here to say a few words of comfort. Father ..."

As the priest droned on about mortality and eternal life, blah, blah, Cassandra let her thoughts stray to the last time she had seen Horace alive. It had been at Gavin's wedding, only three days before his death. Horace, one of the ushers then, had looked jovial and full of vitality and all the time, Death had been smacking its lips with anticipation, laughing at the slipperiness and vulnerability of the humans, Cassandra thought, stifling a sob. She was determined to stay calm for her sister's sake. Bevis caught her eye and beckoned her outside.

"How's Mellie?" he asked her quietly, his concern apparent in his grave face.

"I really can't make her out," Cassandra replied. "She seems to be in a stupor. She's not weeping or talking; she shows no signs of animation at all."

"That'll come later. She's still too shocked to show anything now. I want to take you both home now. Do you think you can persuade her to leave?"

"Won't it look rather odd if we leave now? Many people knew of Mellie's relationship with Horace. It might give rise to some unpleasant talk."

58

"I never thought I'd live to see the day when the phlegmatic Cassandra worried about the proprieties of tradition!" The mockery in his voice was like a bee sting and made her wince. "I'm sorry," he apologised quickly. "That was uncalled for."

"Why apologise? I always find it enlightening to know what people think about me. Anyway, I was actually thinking about Mellie, not myself. I wish Gavin were here, I feel out of my depth."

"I think you've been quite admirable in the circumstances; you've managed to keep Mellie together so far."

"I wish I could believe you. I've failed to persuade her not to go to Kabuwoko tomorrow. She's made up her mind to go."

"That's why I think you should go home and get some rest. I'll come with you tomorrow of course."

"Oh, will you? That's a load off my mind. I confess I was not looking forward to confronting those people alone with a zombie-like Mellie. I don't know whether we'll ever repay you for your kindness. All this must be an unwelcome imposition on your time."

"On the contrary. I like helping friends and praise from you is reward enough," he said gallantly and she looked at him as if he had suddenly sprouted horns.

"I'll get Mellie now and you can put your proposal to her. I know she'll listen to you." Mellie agreed when it was pointed out to her that she would not be fit to travel the following morning if she did not have sufficient rest.

* * *

The funeral at Kabuwoko was a nightmare Cassandra thought she would not forget for a long time. A number of people, mostly friends and business associates, had driven from the city to the small trading centre to bid Horace a final farewell. It was shortly before midday when Bevis' Toyota Corolla trudged up the uneven, potholed road to an impressively large and modern brick house of Horace's parents. The spacious compound, the adjacent banana plantation and the house itself were all already overflowing with people.

Cassandra's party of four included her sister, her friend, Samantha, who had been exceptionally supportive, Bevis and herself. They got out of the car and nervously joined the throngs of other people in their general mourning. After they were welcomed by long-faced men and women, they were taken straight to the centre room where the body still lay open for viewing.

The room was crowded with women in traditional *busuti* and *lesu*, their heads turbaned, and their grey, haggard, tear-stained faces making them look

59

like clay images. The men, in their *kanzus,* looked less strained but no less woebegone.

What's the point of life, Cassandra wondered as they stood gazing at the still form of the man, who not so long ago, had been an integral part of their web. What's the point if the climax of it all is to end up looking like a wax-image? Her resolution to remain calm, after all she had not even liked the man, buckled under the turgid, plaintive atmosphere and she felt an urge to join in the frenzied keening. She glanced at her sister and was relieved to see tears coursing down her pain-ravaged face.

"I don't think we're very much welcome here," Samantha whispered after they were seated.

"I think you're becoming paranoid, Sam," Bevis told her. "These people's attitude to us and all the other dudes from the city is natural enough. Horace was murdered in the city by a person or persons unknown. These people don't know most of us and cannot help associating us with the crime. Our turning up here's no proof of our innocence. In fact, we might have come to gloat or spy for our masters. Incidentally, they're treating this as a political killing, so who's to say who's who? See their point? I don't think they're likely to poison us though and a baleful look never killed anybody."

Cassandra agreed with Bevis. They, the strangers from the city, did indeed look out of place in their Sunday best and ridiculous black ties and armbands. Rich ornamental dress, traditionally, is for festive occasions. At funerals, people are expected to don rags as a sign of sorrow.

"I'm going to suggest that as soon as the interment is over," Bevis continued, "we head back to the city. Judging by the heightened activity, I think the service is about to begin. If we give it an hour and a half, or two at the most, we should be leaving this place around five." Cassandra and Samantha agreed. The only signs of life from Mellinda were quiet sniffs in her handkerchief.

The sermon, which was the usual call for repentance and dedication to God, was followed by speeches eulogising the departed, fulsome and lengthy until the gathering clouds above them recalled the organisers to the unremitability of time.

On the way back to Kampala, Cassandra, who sat with the mute Mellinda in the back of the car, had plenty of time to reminisce about the events of the last few days, and to realise how much she had come to depend on Bevis and respect his sober judgement. She at the same time felt guilty at not having given Raymond much thought. But it seemed more natural to turn to Bevis during the crisis since he was, after all, a family friend.

That morning, when they were about to leave for Kabuwoko, Bevis had asked her whether she had informed Raymond about the tragedy. "I couldn't get him but I left a message for him," she had replied.

"I talked to him after I left you last night and put him in the picture. Of course Horace's murder hit the news headlines but he might not have known of the connection to Mellie."

"That was very kind of you," Cassandra remarked awkwardly. She wondered why mention of Raymond by his brother always made her feel wary and suspect hidden meanings in his most innocent remarks. And yet his decency and integrity were unquestionable.

* * *

"We're tired and hungry, Jossi, what do you recommend?" Cassandra appealed to their domestic help after ushering in her two female companions. Bevis had excused himself, saying he needed to check on something. "I'll be back later to help you cope with what might crop up in the latter part of the evening."

"Leave everything to me," Jossi said, feeling in his element.

"I hope you have enough to go round, Jossi?" Cassandra probed anxiously. "Mr Agutamba's coming back and I expect a few other people to drop in although I don't think they'll expect to be fed."

"Everything has been taken care of, Miss Cassandra. Mr Agutamba left me enough money to buy food before you left this morning."

"He did? I didn't know," Cassandra muttered. "Did my brother call while we were away?"

"No, but there were other callers asking for Miss Mellinda. The other gentleman called too wanting to talk to you shortly after you left." At Cassandra's inquiring look, he elaborated, "It's Mr Agutamba's brother."

"Oh, all right, thank you." She hurried to the sitting room, impatient to get to the phone. "You have the bath first," she told Samantha. "I've some urgent calls to make."

"Must I?" moaned Samantha, without moving from her sprawling position on the chair. "I don't mind telling you that if I went to sleep now and never woke up again, you'd never hear me complain. My whole body feels as if it's been through a wringer."

"The road was certainly bad but you can't blame Bevis for holding up his speed. We would have been worse off if the rain had caught us on the way."

"I'm not blaming him at all. In fact if you don't mind my saying so, I think he's a wonder man."

"Aaaaha, so? I used to think 'love at first sight' was a myth but now I know better. You have my blessings."

"You don't mean that of course. I got the impression that he's otherwise occupied."

61

"Possibly. Bevis is a very private person and keeps his affairs to himself. But I couldn't wish him a nicer person. But remember, who dares wins. And a timely warning: Bevis is a very fastidious person and the way to his heart is not through a sweaty, dusty body."

"Say no more. You might go further and tell me the secret of your success, though!"

"Coercion, no less. You love me or else. Honestly, Sam, to hear you talk, one would think I had it all my own way."

"And don't you? Two of the most attractive men in town in love with you, what more do you want, a whole squadron?"

"Two?" Cassandra said, absently going to check on her sister. There hadn't been any sound from the bedroom since they returned. Mellinda was lying down on her bed, her face turned to the wall. Without disturbing her, Cassandra tiptoed out, and finding the sitting room vacant, reached for the phone.

"Miss Cassandra, it's you, isn't it?" Joseph, the man who kept house for Raymond asked and Cassandra confirmed her identity. "I'll call the master, don't go away, he's just sitting outside on the balcony." Although Cassandra spoke passable Runyakaaro, Joseph preferred to conduct his dialogue in Luganda, and very broken Luganda at that.

Luganda, once considered the general medium among Bantu tribes, had now been relegated to a market language in the city, and even that in a very peripheral sense. A good number of the market vendors spoke intelligible English and Swahili. But there were people like Joseph who insisted on speaking it to all and sundry.

One day Cassandra had asked Raymond why he spoke to Joseph in Luganda when their mother tongues were more or less the same.

"I'll answer that with a question of my own," Raymond had said. "Why don't we, that's you and I, communicate in our own language instead of English?"

"I suppose because people of our generation were brought up speaking English, especially those born in the city. It's the only language not susceptible to rub the sensibilities of the different ethnic groups up the wrong way. And let's face it, English's here to stay unless we're prepared to start from zero. I can't see any other language that would be tenable and acceptable to all."

"I agree with you entirely," Raymond rejoined, chuckling. He found Cassandra's tendency to descant on every subject pedantic and amusing. "But I know of a certain group of people who wouldn't, whatever your arguments. But to return to Joseph, in his world, Luganda's the *lingua franca* just as English is in ours. Why don't you try chatting with him in Runyakaaro so that you can compare his fluency in both?"

"No, no. My interest in asking was purely academic. I prefer to leave things as they are. I like his diction, don't you? He's almost lyrical in his speech, and so full of fancy idioms. I like to quote him as a conversational ploy sometimes."

"How exploitative of you. Poor Joseph!"

"Poor nothing. He gets to be talked about, and if that isn't fame, I'd like to know what it is. Think how good for his ego if he knew."

"Yes, if he knew."

Now for some reason, Joseph sounded so excited that his words seemed to be spat directly from his nasal passage. "What's with Joseph, has he won the National Lottery or something?"

"Cassandra!"

"We're back, Ray."

"Oh, Cassandra! How was it?"

"Harrowing."

"I can imagine. How's Mellie?"

"Holding on. Did you get my message?"

"I did, sweetheart, but could not get back to you because I had a business dinner last night. If I'd known earlier ..."

"Never mind, your brother deputised quite adequately for you. He was exceedingly invaluable as a matter of fact."

"Umm, I can imagine," Raymond remarked dryly. "Any chance of seeing you tonight?"

"None, I'm afraid. Mellie can't be left alone and I'm expecting some people to drop in later."

"Perhaps I could come by later too?"

"That would be marvellous, but wouldn't that be rather dangerous driving at night that side of town?"

"The only danger that could turn out to be fatal is my spending another night without seeing you."

"Oh, Ray, I've missed you so much."

"Tell me more of that when we meet. I love you, sweet Cassandra, always remember that."

* * *

True to his word, Bevis was back shortly after dark to help her cope with the unexpectedly large influx of people that evening. "How's Mellie?"

"She's lying down. My immediate worry is what to do with all these people. I don't think I have enough drinks to go round."

"That's easily fixed: I'll nip down and collect a few beers and sodas. But are you sure you're up to keeping another wake?"

"Personally I wouldn't mind but I'm not sure Mellie can stand the strain. I'm sorry to be laying every burden at your door but I just don't know what to do," she lamented, momentarily deprived of her usual air of self-reliance.

"Poor brave little woman," Bevis mocked tenderly. "Why don't you simply regard me as a surrogate brother while Gavin's away?"

"Oh may I really? But I'm practically doing that already. You're a good sort, Bevis," she adulated, making him wince at her grading.

"No, I'm not a good sort, Cassandra," he responded with heavy sarcasm. "I'm essentially selfish and I help people only when it suits me. I'm happy to be able to help now but I never do anything that I don't like doing, no matter what other people think. Always remember that, Cassandra."

Cassandra felt bewildered by his censorious tone and wondered what she had said to ignite his ire. A man of different facets, she thought.

"Ask Jossi to put some empty crates in the car please," he added in his normal voice.

"I'm coming with you," Cassandra said quickly. She had no intention of tting him pay for the drinks; there was a limit to the dependence act. "Just give me a minute to put on my shoes."

"So who is around so far?" Bevis asked on their way to the nearest supermarket.

"I should say the whole metropolis!" Cassandra exclaimed. "Actually they're not less than twenty people inside there. Mostly Gavin's and Mellie's friends. On my side, there's Samantha of course, George, Marie and Dan. I'm also expecting ... I mean Ray said he might come by later."

"Of course." There was a palpably uneasy silence between them before he went on, "Let me make a suggestion if I may; don't extend your hospitality beyond midnight. You could both do with some rest and if I were your doctor, I'd put you both on the absolute rest list and allow you no visitors."

"You too, Bevis, have had no break either."

When they got back from the shop, Cassandra took him straight to Mellinda's room, leaving Samantha to deal with the drinks. "You can safely leave us alone," Bevis said, pulling a chair close to the bed.

"All right, I'll see to the guests," Cassandra said, closing the door behind her and, as usual, marvelling at the ease with which Mellinda and Bevis accepted and treated each other. And yet her own relationship with him was always tinged with overtones of mistrust even long before she met and fell in love with his brother. At one time it did not matter what he thought of her in the least. But recently, she had come to admire some qualities in him and crave for his approval in return.

The front room was humming with voices and drinks were flowing freely.

64

"I think she's ready to receive her visitors now," Bevis said a few minutes later.

"Do you think she's up to it?"

"She has calmed down a little. Perhaps you could give her a little food to restore her strength. Something light, you know. What would you recommend?"

"Some soup and toast perhaps. I'll tell Jossi to prepare it."

"I'll see to that. You go to her, she might want to talk first."

"How're you, Mellie? Are you sure you can face this rabble? I can tell them you're not feeling well and allow only a few in the bedroom," Cassandra said, embracing her sister. The demonstrative gesture took Mellinda by surprise and went a long way to show how much Cassandra had changed since meeting Raymond. Although she had not been exactly cold, she had lacked spontaneity of character, preferring to employ words, usually terse and succinct, as her mode of communication.

"I'm fine, Cassandra dear. I'll change and go and greet these people. It's the least I can do. What do you suggest I put on, what does a widow without a widow's habit put on in the circumstances?"

"A widow, Mellie?" Cassandra asked, not sure whether the other was joking or not. A poor kind of joke, she thought.

"Yes, a widow, Cassandra. I can see by your look that you think I'm hallucinating or beginning to crack up, but I'm not. Horace and I have been secretly married these past three years."

"I don't believe it," Cassandra exclaimed, gasping. "But why, Mellie, why?"

"Why did we get married or why the secrecy?"

"Why did you marry him in the first place?"

"For the usual reasons, I guess. I loved him and he made me happy in the beginning." She was thoughtful for some time before she went on, "Horace was different in those days and he knew how to bend me to his will."

"Why the secrecy then?"

"Well, it seemed romantic at the time – no, the truth is that I couldn't summon up enough courage to face Dad with it."

"But why did you have to do it then? I mean get married. It's not as if you had to. You could have remained friends and married afterwards if you still wanted to."

"I know. And don't think I've not regretted it a thousand times since but at the time, I did not think twice when Horace suggested it. I thought it was great fun."

"Christ, Mellie, marriage's a serious undertaking, not something you do on the spur of the moment."

"I know, oh don't I know it! But three years ago it looked like a bright idea. But don't go jumping to the conclusion that I was conned into it. I wanted it as much as Horace did. We were both too blinded by passion to think straight. I know you can understand that now, if not anything else. Horace was..." her voice dwindled to a broken note.

"Take it easy, Mellie," Cassandra said, proffering her own handkerchief. "You don't have to talk about it if it upsets you."

"But I want to talk about it to you," Mellinda insisted, blowing her nose. "I know you never liked Horace but that's because you didn't understand him. Many people thought him shallow and pompous but he wasn't like that in the least. If he had a fault, it was that he craved to be liked and accepted. That's why he spent his money so extravagantly in order to impress people and buy their friendship. It was an obsession with him. I can't imagine how he resisted murdering you — oh God, Cassandra, he was murdered and here I am joking about murder, ooooh, ooooh!"

"Easy, easy, Mellie, please," Cassandra pleaded ineffectually.

"I'm sorry but I can't help remembering how he used to say that he wished u could like him just a little. He was so scared of you and Gavin that he dared not bribe you with gifts like the rest. I'm not trying to make you feel guilty, Cassandra," Mellie added on observing signs of annoyance on her sister's face. "I'm just trying to show you how vulnerable he was. He said my loving him reassured him and made him feel wholly a man. Oh ... ooh ..."

"I understand and I'm sorry I misjudged him. But recently you were not happy together, were you?" Cassandra asked cautiously.

"No, you're right, we were not very happy. But it was mainly my fault. When we decided on this secret marriage, we also agreed that we'd make it public as soon as my course was over."

"And?"

"Well, truthfully, I was beginning to have second thoughts about the whole idea. Horace seemed so different from the man I had married. He used to be open and confiding but of late he had become secretive and suspicious. He started to flirt outrageously and, although he assured me often enough that these affairs meant nothing to him, I could not help being jealous, I mean I was only human. But shortly before Gavin's wedding, our relationship had begun to improve. We had long discussions, made plans for the future and he was willing to let me choose the right time for coming out in the open. One would think he had a premonition of his death." After making this remark, Mellinda sat very still, striving for control. Jossi arrived just then with a tray of snacks which she promptly declared nauseating.

"Please, Mellie, just a little," Cassandra begged.

"Al...r...rright, life goes on apparently." After a few unenthusiastic attempts to eat, she put the spoon down and asked Cassandra in a small pathetic voice, "How am I going to get along without Horace?"

"Hush, dear," her sister soothed. "I know what I'm going to say may sound presumptuous to you but I'll say it all the same. You'll get over your loss in due course and learn to cope on your own. I also consider it a blessing in disguise that your marriage was still a secret or it might have had some other repercussions. I suggest that we keep it between the two of us, of course assuming that Horace did not confide in anybody else about it."

"He promised me and I know he would not have broken his word to me. Anyway, he was not close to his family and he had no real friends except hangers-on. But one other person already knows, Bevis."

"How did he – yeah, I guess you must have told him."

"Yes, I did in case I needed legal advice."

"But why should you? Nobody would suspect you of killing him – I'm sorry, forget it. Bevis is a good choice anyway, and he'd never blab about anything. Let's get you dressed, the sooner you face these people, the quicker it will be over."

The evening turned out better than expected. People were sympathetic but not overly so. George and Samantha kept up a constant repartee which made everybody feel at ease without the need to keep gloomy countenances. The only cloud, as far as Cassandra was concerned, was Raymond's failure to turn up as promised.

As she bid Bevis goodnight, after everybody else had left, he made her promise to call him in case she needed him for any reason, no matter what time of night or day. "I'll be checking on you tomorrow of course, but promise me that between now and then, you won't hesitate to contact me in case of any emergency."

"Okay, Bevis, although I can't imagine anything happening to necessitate my disturbing you again tonight. I have Samantha with me, so ... The evening wasn't too bad after all, was it? Kind of therapeutic for Mellie, I thought."

"Mellie's a brave girl. All she needs is time and understanding friends. She'll be okay provided we can keep this marriage business under wraps. What about you?"

"Me?" She gave a little hysterical laugh. He knew Raymond's inability to come had clouded her evening in spite of her overbright manner. "I don't think I'll need a sedative to induce sleep although I might need something in the nature of an earthquake to arouse me."

67

"Good. Make sure you're securely locked in for the night. I'm expecting to hear from Gavin either tonight or early tomorrow. He might even ring here. Goodnight."

"Goodnight, Bevis, and thanks very much for everything."

* * *

Two days after Horace's funeral, Cassandra decided to report back on duty. "I'll check on you at lunchtime," she told her sister.

"I don't think that's really necessary," Mellinda told her. "You and Bevis are treating me like a potential suicide but nothing could be further from my mind, I assure you. As a matter of fact, I'm thinking of reporting back on duty."

"That's not a bad idea but don't rush things," Cassandra cautioned. "You're also going to be prepared to face a nasty time, I mean the kind of death Horace died always gives rise to rumours and speculations."

"Don't worry about me, I can handle that. But keeping busy will not give me time to brood."

"You're quite right there. I feel quite relieved."

In the offices of LI, nothing looked changed or different. People were, as usual, hurrying up and down corridors with files and briefcases tightly clutched under their arms. The noise of telephones and typewriters was going at the usual tempo. Life indeed goes on, Cassandra thought. She approached her office hesitantly, trying to shake off the lingering fog of the last few days. But that Horace's death was not a dream was made evident by the first telephone call she received on entering the room.

"Hi, princess! Seen the *Mirror*?" George inquired breezily over the phone.

"You know I don't read that kind of trash, George," Cassandra told him. "Anything else like maybe your doctor has recommended sealing your lips for a couple of months?"

"My brother tried that some years back but I brought in a second opinion who instead recommended the curbing of his libido haaahaaah – sorry, but I am serious though about the news. I'll bring the paper over to you, you'll love it."

She had hardly put the phone down when it rang again. "LI, can I help you?"

"It's Bevis here, have you seen today's issue of the *Mirror*?"

"No, but somebody's bringing me a copy. What's the excitement about?"

"I'll ring again after you've had a chance to read the article," he said.

"I might not be here," she objected, not liking to be kept in suspense. "I have a meeting at ten."

68

"I 'll try to get to you before then. Besides, I'm collecting you for lunch, so we can talk then."

"All right, but all this suspense's very distractive," she complained.

"I'm sorry but I'm in the middle of something. I promise to talk to you later." Click.

"Here, page three, top is what you want," George said, pushing the paper on her desk.

Cassandra looked at the article indicated whose heading, **KALANZI'S WIDOW SCOOPS ALL,** was splashed across in bold type. *"As circumstances surrounding the death of the young business tycoon, Horace Kalanzi, continue to baffle the police, the tireless efforts of the Mirror have succeeded in unearthing information which adds spice to the story,"* Cassandra read. *"This information,"* the article went on, *"relates to the late Kalanzi's last Will and Testament which has come as a great surprise to the bereaved family. More of a shock to them, however, is the revelation that their son had been secretly married and it is to this widow, one Dr.Mellinda Nshemere-Mutono, that the deceased has left the bulk of his estate.*

"A member of his family, who spoke to us on condition of anonymity, stated categorically that the parents of the late Kalanzi had no knowledge of the marriage and repudiate it outright. Asked whether they intended to contest the Will, our informant said that they have every intention of doing so. Look out for our next Friday issue for more illuminating details on the case."

After reading the article, Cassandra pushed the paper away with a sigh and sat lost in thoughtful silence.

"Is it true?" George asked, watching her eagerly.

"The marriage is, but this," she indicated the article, "is as much news to me as it is to you. Mellie did not mention it to me. Logically it makes sense of course. I can't imagine why none of us ever thought of it. We all knew Horace was a rich man."

"He was rich? He stank of the stuff. Do you realise that your sister's worth millions and millions of the best!"

"That may be so but she's going to have to earn it by the time she's through. Knowing the acquisitive nature of our people, she'll be lucky to escape with her skin intact."

"Don't be a wet blanket, Cassandra. Always look on the bright side of the picture, which in this case is that when all the hysteria's over, Mellie can sit back and call the shots, and at her age, whew!"

"Well, rich or not, I call the shots in this office and I say it's time for you to go, so go!" As he was halfway to the door, Cassandra called to him and said awkwardly, "Thanks for the information, George, and thanks for coming over the other night. I never had time to thank you properly."

"Don't mention it. That's what friends are for."

69

Cassandra looked at her watch and put the notes she would need for the meeting, which was due in a few minute's time, together, vaguely wondering why Bevis had not telephoned.

* * *

At the end of the meeting, Mr Ndiwalala, who had succeeded Mr Wakilo (who had gone abroad for a course) as chief editor, asked Cassandra and Collin to stay behind. Both resumed their seats, automatically eyeing each other warily. Neither had use for the other.

"Shan't be long," Mr Ndiwalala said, noticing Cassandra's fidgety manner. It was a few minutes to one and Bevis would be waiting for her outside shortly.

"Ahmm, two things," the chief finally said, pushing his file aside. "I want **The Return of a Hero** on my desk before three this afternoon, I think you're dealing with that, Collin? I also want **Clap of Thunder,** that's yours, Cassandra, isn't?"

"That's mine too," Collin cut him short.

"All right, see to it that they're both here before you go for your lunch then. I'm meeting the author this afternoon and wish to straighten out a few things with him. You can actually join us if you wish, Collin: Mr Ogwat's coming at two thirty."

"I'll check to see if I can manage it, Mr Ndiwalala," Collin said without enthusiasm. From previous experience, he knew that sitting in that kind of meeting meant having every awkward question turned to him to answer.

"Good. The second reason I wanted to see you two together is about the invitation from Uganda Television to do a short profile on LI in their **Guest of the Week** programme. What do you think of the idea?"

"I think it's excellent," Collin replied promptly with his usual assured air. "Especially from the publicity point of view."

"Do you agree, Cassandra?"

"Yes, certainly. Of course much will depend on how we project ourselves on the screen."

"You're both right but let's not get carried away. This is not a publicity campaign."

Collin looked at him pityingly before he said, "I certainly didn't mean to suggest that we go armed with banners but on the other hand, it would be a pity if we didn't take advantage of the opportunity offered. It's not every day that one gets a chance to do a little propagation using a public media free of charge."

"I have no quarrel with that as long as it's kept within limits. Do you have anything to add, Cassandra?"

70

"I just wanted to know how we two come into the picture."

"I should think that was pretty obvious," Mr Ndiwalala replied impatiently. "I want you two to represent LI."

"I see," she remarked, glancing at her colleague who looked immensely gratified. Cassandra had a sudden urge to take the wind out of his sails. Turning to their boss, she asked with a sweet smile, "What about you, Chief? Nobody can portray LI more effectively than you, in my opinion." It was true in the sense that of the three, he had been with the firm the longest.

"Thank you, Cassandra, but I think I'll pass. I have so much to do, I don't see how I can fit it in."

Outside Mr Ndiwalala's room, Collin faced Cassandra and asked with undisguised disgust, "Was all that necessary?"

"All what?"

"All that flattery? You know the man knows as much about publishing as the man on the street." Cassandra agreed with him entirely but was not about to say so.

"An exaggeration surely," she said instead. "Besides, it does no harm to know your colleagues have confidence in you."

"I find that interesting coming from you," Collin remarked with a sneer. "After all the trouble you've gone to to convince everybody that you're self-confident, dynamic, omnipotent!"

"Encouragement and flattery are two different things," Cassandra responded, trying to keep her temper. "We all need the former and only fools bask in the latter. Excuse me," she swiftly let herself inside her office and shut the door.

"Blast Collin!" She drew a deep breath and went out, where Bevis was waiting for her. "I'm sorry I'm late."

Bevis looked at his watch before he said, "Only a few minutes which is not bad for an upcoming young career woman."

"I don't need that, Bevis."

"My turn to apologise. But actually I was talking to Kizito and didn't notice the passing of time." He studied her flushed face and said, "You look as if you've quite recovered from the nightmare of the last few days. You look quite, uh fetching, Cassandra."

"Aren't you the gallant gentleman today!"

"Aren't I always?"

"Sure ... Anyway, what do you make of this business of the will in the papers? Have you talked to Mellie, what does she say about it?"

"Yes, I've talked to Mellie. Apparently Horace had hinted at making his will but she didn't give it a second thought and it completely escaped her mind during the last days of grief."

"Naturally. Poor Mellie. I might have to stay with her the rest of the day. She was making good recovery but I can imagine the horrible effect of this on her."

"I have two pieces of news; first about Mellie: she has, with my encouragement, moved temporarily to her friend, Josephine's place."

"Why was that necessary? Was she being pestered?"

"Not exactly, but until we know the contents of the will, it might be more prudent for her to be incommunicado."

"You mean her life might be in danger?"

"Not so fast, Cassandra. This is merely a precautionary measure. There's nothing for you to worry about. At a place like Luzzi, she's likely to get too much unwelcome attention, that's all."

"You don't have to hide it from me. I know you think that her death might be to some people's advantage, isn't that so?"

"Well, let's say that we can't afford to take chances. It would help a lot if we knew the contents of the will, other than relying on reports from the papers."

"How many kinds of wills are there?" Cassandra wanted to know.

"As many as there are testators who make them. But broadly speaking, most wills are simple documents couched in legal terminology to fit one or other of the prototypes. I sincerely hope that Horace had the sense to make his a simple one. But if the *Mirror* is to be believed, the relatives are all set to contest it. I don't know the strength of the fortune in question but I believe it's vast, by our standards. If that's the case, then Mellie is in for a lot of unpleasantness before probate can be granted."

"Poor girl! Pandora's box couldn't have contained more horrors," Cassandra mused.

"But don't forget that imprisoned in the box was *Hope* too. When all the fuss is over, Mellie'll emerge a young woman of independent means. Wouldn't you say that was worth all the worry and anguish?" he asked with a trace of mockery.

"I don't know. I know that money plays an important role in our lives but I think that its value is sometimes overrated."

"That strikes me as peculiar coming from somebody of your generation!"

"I don't belong to a fold like sheep and my views are my own," Cassandra almost snapped. "And another thing, if you think that's the reason Mellie was attracted to Horace, you're quite wrong."

"I know Mellie enough not to misjudge her so grossly," Bevis told her. "But I thought you disapproved of the relationship yourself?"

"I did. I could not stand Horace and was inclined to be impatient with Mellie. I feel so awful now. Hey, where are we going?"

"Since there's no point in your going to Luzzi, I thought we would eat lunch together, if you don't mind."

"That's kind of you. I suppose I could see Mellie later in the day as I'm not expected back at the office."

"That brings me to the second piece of news I have: Gavin has telephoned confirming their arrival on the five o'clock flight. I thought you might want to come with me to meet them."

"I'd love to, thanks. I'll have to go home first though, to see that everything is ready. Alex must have gone back to college by now too."

When they were seated in the dining room of the Boulevard Hotel, he asked her what she would like to eat.

"You choose please," Cassandra said indifferently, turning her attention to the room and noting with approval the graceful decor. She could understand why a person like Bevis would prefer it to the numerous other restaurants which had mushroomed in the city. It was quiet, cool and restful, with a noticeable absence of the open-air circus which pervaded most of the other eating places.

Bevis, mindful of Cassandra's distaste for rich food, ordered something light for both of them. "What would you like to drink?"

"A soda," she said, and then for some reason, was reminded of Raymond, which brought a small secretive smile to her lips.

"What's amusing?" her companion asked.

"Some inconsequentiality this place brings to mind," she replied, the image of Raymond refusing to leave her. She wondered what he was doing at this time.

What Raymond was doing, at that precise moment, was sitting opposite his wife in a restaurant, and as was their way, arguing heatedly. For some time now, he had been trying to make sense of the symptoms of their son's illness as described by Belinda, without success.

"What does the doctor say?" he asked patiently.

"Do you seriously expect me to take Steve to a doctor alone, meet all the preposterous expenses as if he has no father?" Belinda exclaimed.

"I give you enough allowance to cover all contingencies, including doctors' bills, Belinda. Besides, I don't see how a mother, genuinely concerned about the health of her child, could stop to quibble about payment of the doctors' bills first. You know I'd never shirk my duty where Steve's concerned."

"What do you know about the duty of a parent, Ray?" she flared. "You see him only when you can spare the time from your trollops."

"You set the terms, Belinda, remember?" her husband reminded her. "I went along with them because I was tired of arguments. But I'm quite capable

73

of looking after Steve , without your help, should you find him too much of a burden. He's my son and by right should be with me, under my roof."

"Your son, your son you say? What proof do you have that he's your son?" she challenged him.

"Is his parentage in doubt, Belinda?" Raymond asked on a dangerous note.

"Did I say that?" Belinda prevaricated, looking a little scared. "All I said was that if you had the sentiments of a normal parent, you'd be as worried as I am about him. You'd arrange for us to see a specialist to find out what's wrong with him."

"Enough. Let's go," Raymond said with finality. He got up and beckoned a waiter to bring the bill.

"Where're we going?"

"We're going to pick up Steve and take him to see a doctor. Isn't that what you want?"

"But I can't right now, I'm expected back at the office," Belinda protested.

"They'll understand when you explain to them the urgency. I have to cancel all my afternoon appointments too. After all, our child comes first."

"You think I'm making this up, don't you?" It had actually crossed Raymond's mind but he resisted the temptation to say so.

The doctor, a quite well-known pediatrician in town, did not show undue concern. He was inclined to think the parents, especially the mother, overanxious with little to go on. He ordered some lab tests which would not be ready until Monday and sent them home with some mild painkiller.

"Are you now satisfied that Steve's not in imminent danger of premature demise?" Raymond asked sarcastically of his wife on their way back from the clinic. The object of their discussion, if discussion it could be called, was in the back of the car happily playing with his toy car.

"Were you really impressed with that Dr. Omogodo ... Omogodi, or whatever his name is? I wasn't. But at least he did not dismiss my fears as baseless or he wouldn't have ordered those lab tests."

"But naturally, what did you expect? You were going on and on about these mysterious symptoms, so he had to do something to shut you up. After all, we're paying him, aren't we?"

"So you took us to a quack! I should have known that's what you'd do. Why didn't we go to a hospital where there're specialists in childhood diseases? But we didn't and had to end up with a quack because you begrudge every minute you spend away from your precious business!"

"That was a specialist, Belinda, for heaven's sake. Is there nothing I can do right in your opinion? Look in the back of the car and tell me whether that child needs intensive care," he shouted, unwisely taking his eyes off the road which almost led to a head-on collision with an oncoming vehicle.

"Then why are you reluctant to take him and keep him with you overnight?"

"Is that what all this whole exercise is about? Why didn't you say so in the first place? Are you going away and what has become of your precious Mrs Njuki?"

"I'm not going away and even if I were, it wouldn't be any of your business," Belinda retorted.

"Except only in as far as it concerns the well-being of my child. If you want him to stay at my place overnight, it's fine with me. Any more tricks up your sleeve?"

"You should at least give me credit for being a caring mother, Raymond Agutamba. The only reason I want you to keep him for a few days is so that you can observe him yourself. My fears might, after all, be the result of my over-protectiveness. Staying alone as I do, I'm apt to become prey to all sorts of imaginary horrors," she said pathetically, almost succeeding in making Raymond feel sorry for her. He noted the 'overnight' had turned into 'a few days' but let it go. She was a good mother to his son, of that there was no doubt. So it was possible that her worries were well-founded. Besides, he loved having the little fellow around. It was also high time Cassandra met him anyway.

Steve loved his father with the possessiveness children of broken marriages usually accord absentee parents. They romanticise them and idolise them until they assume images of heroes and angels rolled into one. They are always associated with hugs and kisses and all things that are good and exciting while the caretaker parent, whose role it is to correct and censure, is very often regarded as the unfeeling, uncaring oppressor. And so it was with young Steve. His father was a superman, a demigod whose company he could never get enough of. It was always a tug-of-war at the end of every visit to drag him away. "Why can't I stay with my daddy?" he would innocently ask. "All my friends at school stay with their daddies, why can't I?" Neither parent had a good enough answer although Belinda always made it appear that the blame lay entirely with his father.

"I'll drop you at your office and take him straight home. You can bring his things later."

Belinda sighed with disappointment. She had hoped to have her husband's company a little longer but obviously he couldn't get rid of her fast enough.

* * *

Cassandra got out of her trance and said, "About this evening, what time do we leave for the airport?"

"I would suggest four if that's alright with you," Bevis told her.

"Four is fine."

"That's settled then. I'll drop you at Luzzi after lunch and pick you up at four then."

"You don't really have to drive me to Luzzi, Bevis, I can easily get a taxi."

"It's my pleasure, Cassandra. Remember I never do ..."

"... anything that I don't want to do," she finished for him, dryly.

"Yes, that's right." He gave her a speculative look. Was it possible, he was thinking, that she could be so unaware of what a powerful weapon her beauty was if she chose to use it? Maybe that's what makes her exceptional and singularly attractive; the quality of naivety, he reflected. "As I said, it gives me much pleasure to be of service to you," he added.

"Don't overdo it or I'll suspect ulterior motives."

"Suspect all you want but I bet you'll never even come close to the truth. Shall we go?"

* * *

Tonia's homecoming was not like anything she had imagined. There was no welcoming committee, armed with jocular missiles and a brass band to receive her and her spouse from their curtailed honeymoon. Only Bevis and Cassandra were at the airport to receive them. Not even Mellinda or her own family knew of their unexpected return, so Bevis said as the four sat in their living room discussing the grim circumstances surrounding Horace's death and his secret marriage to Mellinda.

"I knew about the marriage," Gavin said, startling everybody into immediate attention. "That is, he told me just before the wedding mine, not his."

"How could you have known and not told me about it?" Tonia exclaimed accusingly.

"I had other things on my mind," he told her, winking lewdly, but got no blushing response for his pains.

"Indeed how could he have told you when he promised Mellie not to tell anybody until she agreed to it?" Cassandra also asked.

Bevis said nothing but his expression indicated his interest too.

"Well, don't look at me as if I've sprouted horns," Gavin said grumpily. "Anyway, you all know my regard for Horace was not the highest. In fact I don't mind confessing now that I detested the fellow, and deplored his relationship with Mellie, which at the time, I took to be just that: a mere friendship which, hopefully, would one day peter out. The night he told me the exact nature of it, thereby shattering my secret expectations, he also swore me to secrecy. That's why, my dearest girl," this to Tonia, "I could not tell you or anyone else about it. Although the knowledge burnt a hole in my heart, I had given my word to the fellow to be broken only under certain conditions like now prevailing. To explain myself further, the information could only be divulged in the event of something happening to him."

"Good God, are you saying that he expected something to happen to him?" Bevis exclaimed, looking horrified at the thought.

"And did nothing about it!" Tonia cried.

"How extraordinary!" Cassandra added her voice to theirs. "Tell us about it."

"With your permission I will, in my own way," Gavin stated irritably. "At the party at Freddie's, he took me aside and told me about the marriage, breaking a promise, as it were, he had made to Mellie, but added that circumstances warranted it. He went on to say that there should be somebody close to her to look out for her interests in the event of something happening to him. He then proceeded to tell me about his will and that he had made me sole executor of it. The revelation of his marriage to Mellie was of course a great shock, but the additional information was staggering. Do you realise what this makes Mellie? A very rich woman!"

"You men make me sick!" Tonia unexpectedly attacked him. "What about the news that his life might be in danger, it was of no importance I suppose? All you could think about was how rich Mellie would be if he died!" she accused, attracting the surprised attention of all three.

When Gavin was sufficiently recovered, he hastened to defend himself, "Of course I feel terrible about his death but at the time I did not take him seriously. Even you can't deny that he was a bit of an exhibitionist, so how could I have believed him? But since the news of his death, I've been having guilty feelings about it, wondering whether there wasn't anything I could have done to stop the tragedy."

"Poor Horace, all you ever did was criticise and snub him. You never gave him a chance. Did you ever wonder what your sister saw in him, Gavin, did you?" Tonia continued the assault.

"Give me a break, darling, I...." Gavin started to say but it was Cassandra who managed to calm down her sister-in-law. She knew exactly how Tonia was feeling, having experienced similar feelings herself and the need to expunge them.

"All you're saying is true, Tonia dear," she soothed. "None of us treated poor Horace decently enough to get to know him better. But we truly mourn him and have been flagellating ourselves ever since he died. We failed Mellie too because, as you say, we never stopped to ask ourselves whether there mightn't have been something special she saw in him. Our regrets are sincere albeit too late."

"Yes, Tonia," Bevis echoed, "what Cassandra's saying is true and it should be a lesson to us all not to judge people by their appearances. You shouldn't distress yourself unduly, though. Horace's gone from us and no amount of sorrowing can be of the slightest help to him now. But we can make amends by helping Mellie to recover from her loss; Horace, wherever he is, would appreciate that, I'm sure."

Tonia looked from one person to the other embarrassed, and then smiling weakly said, "I'm sorry, guys, I don't know what came over me."

"Hush, darling, what you said is true," her husband said placatingly. "We're all guilty and deserve to hang our heads in shame."

"Can I get you all a drink? Tonia, what would you like?" Cassandra went for refreshments and the other two begged Gavin to go on with the tale.

"There's isn't much left to tell. I should have quizzed him further about his fears but it was in the middle of the night and I was getting married in the morning; I wasn't at my brightest. That's my only excuse. But what I can't work out is why he hung around knowing he was in danger."

"Perhaps he was planning to go and left it too late," Bevis reflected. "Or perhaps he was betrayed to his enemies before he could execute his plans. I suppose we shall never know."

"What enemies did Horace have, I mean, why would anyone want to kill him?" Tonia puzzled.

"How can you put sense or logic to the acts of maniacs?" Gavin exploded. "Look at the hundreds of thousands of people killed in the last decade or so. Has anybody ever come up with a plausible explanation as to why such wholesale massacres were necessary? Is there any way such heinous acts can be justified?"

"These, as you say, are not acts of sane people who reason like normal people," Bevis observed. "But they have reasons for what they do, even if they do not make sense to the logical and more balanced intellect. In the context of our own circumstances, the schizophrenic tendencies of most of our leaders account for a good number of prevalent waves of homicide. Elimination of political opponents is by no means confined to the unfortunate backwater region of our country. It's practised worldwide. The difference's that in most developing countries the methods tend to be crude and obvious."

"What difference does it make what methods are employed as long as they all end in human destruction?" Cassandra retorted hotly. "The act, whether cunningly carried out or not, is beastly and an outrage against humanity."

"Perhaps I didn't make myself clear enough: what I meant was that in civilised societies, elimination of political enemies does not always mean termination of life. There're other different ways of neutralising an enemy without going to the extreme. Unfortunately, the kind of regard for life we see here seems to be in its early stages of inception."

"You have raised a couple of interesting points there but I'm averse to turning this into a general discussion on the different concepts of the sacredness of human life and the rights and freedoms thereof," Gavin remarked. "But putting it in a nutshell, the law of the jungle appears to be still supreme. The state whose main duty is to protect the lives and property of its citizens does not acknowledge the trust or appreciate the enormity of it. Nobody has the right to take another's life except as by law established. If I were asked to rewrite the laws of this country, I 'd limit capital punishment to only three categories of offenders, to wit, murderers, people convicted of robbery with violence and the dirty dogs who sexually abuse the weak, and the young and innocent. But now settling every score by murder has become the order of the day."

"By all this I suppose you mean that Horace was killed for political reasons?" Cassandra asked her brother.

But it was Bevis who answered her saying, "I've been trying to find out what I can about Horace generally, the last couple of days. I particularly wanted to find out his political leanings and I think I'm now in a position to state that the evidence towards that end is overwhelming. He was apparently involved with what's known as 'Internal Rescue Action'. I got this from a reliable source."

Cassandra remembered the titbits of conversation she had overheard at Horace's house after his murder but still found it difficult to believe. "Not the Horace we knew surely. He wasn't capable of that kind of pertinacity," she said.

"A few minutes ago, we all agreed that perhaps we didn't know much about Horace, didn't we?"

"Yeah, you're right. Do you think Mellie knew?"

"I'm inclined to doubt that. He'd have wished to protect her."

"I think that explains some of the exhibitionism you accused him of, Gavin. It must have been all part of the act."

"And a very effective one, I must say," her brother remarked. "He took us all in, didn't he, with his playboy impersonation. A pompous young man with more money than sense, who'd take him seriously enough to inquire into his activities?"

"Apparently somebody did," Cassandra pointed out.

"It does look like that on the surface," Bevis agreed with her. "But I'm more inclined to believe that he was betrayed by somebody close to him or a plant in the organisation. Squabbles among the ranks can't be ruled out either, especially about money. Many fellows in these outfits are motivated by nothing less than the desire to enrich themselves."

"You make them sound so mercenary," Tonia remarked.

"Not as a rule. Some of them are highly principled chaps, willing to stake their lives for what they believe in. But as you know, it's not always easy to separate the wheat from the chaff."

Cassandra cast her eyes at the wall-clock and quickly got up, saying, "I better go and see about dinner."

"Don't bother, Cassandra," her brother said, arresting her movements. "We're eating out tonight."

"You've chosen a fine time to tell me after Jossi has gone to the trouble of preparing a grand meal to welcome his new mistress home," Cassandra grumbled.

"Jossi will have many more opportunities to impress Toni. Tonight, we're taking you out. But first, Bevis' taking me to see Mellie, dear," this to his wife. "This should give you ample time to do your unpacking before we come back for you."

"Oh I think I'm too tired to deal with that today, or go out either," Tonia declared, not at all pleased with her husband's unilateral programme for the evening. "I think we should eat at home tonight. I don't want to start on the wrong footing with the most important man in my new life."

"The most important man, Jossi? Do you hear that, Bevis?"

"Yes, dear, he is," his wife continued. "Until I know which is which end of the kitchen knife."

"May the gods preserve me from the peculiarities of women! Let's go, man, before I'm tempted to make this the shortest marriage ever in history. And don't forget, wife mine of a few days, that divorces are my speciality." With that, he and his friend hurried out of the house, leaving behind a pair of giggly girls.

"Men can be so inconsiderate," Cassandra commented. But silently she applauded her sister-in-law's firm stand against her brother's dictatorial tendencies.

"Wait until you're married," Tonia rejoined darkly.

"So says the veteran of seven days," Cassandra laughed. "Come, I'll help you to unpack while you tell me all about it."

"About unpacking ... I feel so exhausted. The flight from Mombasa was okay but the Fokker from Nairobi was an absolute nightmare."

"Oh I'm sorry. Why didn't you book onto a bigger aircraft?"

"Full up. But what I'm probably suffering from are the effects of delayed

80

shock about this business of Horace. How's Mellie, really?"

"Well, she's being frightfully brave about it ... you'll be able to judge when you see her yourself."

"We were terribly shocked when we got the news, Gavin in particular. I didn't quite understand it at the time and attributed it to his concern for Mellie. Now I know better of course."

"Yes, he must be carrying a load of guilt. The last days have been awful for us too, and on top of that we've had to deal with this unsolicited publicity about the will, especially Mellie."

"But it's nice isn't it, I mean," she went on uncomfortably, "having more than memories for comfort. Of course if anything were to happen to Gavin, I don't think I could bear it." Cassandra diplomatically kept quiet as she wondered why it should be different for her as if only she were capable of deep feelings.

Tonia herself did not dwell on her blunder long, her nature being such that she was not one to sustain a disagreeable thought for long. She was already afloat on another plane of thought, hoping fervently that she and Cassandra were going to become friends since they would be living in close proximity with each other. She knew she preferred the easygoing, sunny-natured Mellinda, but since it was the other one in whose company she would be thrown constantly, she hoped she would be able to crack the formidable shell and reach out to her too.

"Yes," Cassandra said after a short pause, "the importance of money should never be underestimated. For example, I can see my father vacillating between anger at Mellie for her questionable behaviour and gratification that she at least had the sense to marry a rich man. In other words, if one must drown, one should do so in deep water to justify the act. My father, like most men, is very practical where money is concerned."

"And your mother?"

"An incurable romantic, I'm afraid. She would have preferred to see her daughter in white lace, on the arm of a handsome young man. Poor Horace was hardly anybody's idea of a Romeo."

"Except Mellie's."

"Too true. Yeah, you're right. He was her Romeo and perhaps of many other females. Oh, what a lovely *kanga!*" she added, pulling out of the bag she was unpacking a bright piece of cloth and holding it aloft.

"Do you like it?" Tonia asked eagerly and proceeded to show her what she had bought her and the rest. "And this is for Bevis," she added, unfurling a short-sleeved shirt with a bright design.

"Bevis?" Cassandra repeated blankly.

"You don't seem to think much of the idea. What's wrong with it?"

"Goodness, there's nothing wrong with your choice. It's the idea of Bevis in it that I find intriguing. I've known him for many years but I don't remember ever seeing him out of his suit."

"Well, it's high time he did then and we'll see if his body tattooed with tribal markings or is scarred," Tonia retorted. "You know, it's all very well to take life seriously but one must balance it with a little fun now and then. Do you think Bevis ever has time for amusements?"

"I really wouldn't know," Cassandra answered vaguely. She had always taken Bevis for granted ever since she'd known him, a mere presence, as one usually does a brother's male friends whom one is not physically attracted to.

"Have you ever met his girlfriend?" Tonia persisted.

"No, have you?"

"No. But I thought that under the circumstances, you'd be more likely to have met her?"

"You mean double-dating with Ray, that sort of thing? The two are very different, you know. I don't think they even move in the same social circles. Of course I've met him at Ray's place but he has always been alone."

"Gavin's always inquiring about a Lucy ... no, I think it's a Jane, but he does not seem to think much of her chances of success."

"Success in what? Oh, I see what you mean. But you promised to tell me about your stay in Mombasa, Tonia, what did you find to do all day long?"

"That's a funny question to ask a honeymooning couple," Tonia giggled. "But I'll tell you all the same. We ate, slept, danced, not always in that order. We were inclined to follow our whim. There were plenty of bazaars to visit with all sorts of curios and costumes with fantastic designs. Gavin bought me a couple of outfits, they are unbelievable, especially one in a sort of silk material. But unfortunately I can't put them on yet until I have 'unloaded'. I even talked him into buying some very colourful landscape paintings. I'm done with living, or rather sharing bachelor quarters. I want a real home."

"You're quite right, this place's rather bare," Cassandra remarked, looking around the room critically. "What are the people like, are they friendly?"

"Extremely so, but what I liked most about them, is their liveliness, their gaiety. Everybody there and everything is so vibrant. You feel it in the brightness of the climate, the colourful dresses, the richness of the food they eat; everything. There's music in the air, the sea, I swear that even when I slept I never stopped hearing the throbbing of drums."

"Sounds like you were in love, Tonia, with ...,"

"I ..."

"... Mombasa!" Cassandra completed her sentence.

"I got carried away," Tonia confessed before she resumed. "The climate is very hot though this time of year, so most of the time we were out of doors was spent under gaudy umbrella shades, sipping cool drinks and watching the antics of other tourists. Sometimes Gavin would venture into the water. He said he used to be a swimming champion at school, was he?"

"I really couldn't tell. He might have been," Cassandra replied with sisterly loyalty.

"Personally I was not about to risk my life and that of Junior here," Tonia went on, patting her slightly bulging belly, "in that endless expanse of water. The truth, though, is that I've never learnt how to swim because the thought of it terrifies me. Most of my nightmares are dominated by death from drowning. What do you think that signifies, a cowardly or timid nature?"

"I'm afraid I can't help you there; I don't take dreams seriously. Where do you want these?" Cassandra asked, holding forth a new pair of bed-sheets.

"Oh, just anywhere. I still have to decide what goes where. About dreams: I'm personally very superstitious and will never undertake a long journey if I meet a woman first thing in the morning which is why I've never been on one before because the first person I always meet in the morning is myself   in the mirror."

"You've just concluded one, a long journey, I mean," Cassandra said dryly.

"And see how it has ended. But all in all, we were having a good time until the news of Horace's death. What a way to go! I keep seeing him as he was that Saturday, so full of life and gaiety. Why is it that the people one least expects to die are the ones who do? Do you think he really knew?"

"He'd have to have been a real cool one to put up such a show. He might have suspected, but which man's ever free from the shadow of death these days? Horace might have suspected that his life was in danger but I doubt if he realised how close the danger was." The two were silent for some time, remembering the dead man. "I better join Jossi in the kitchen now," Cassandra said, breaking the silence. "That reminds me, I have to show you around, can we do it tomorrow?"

"I know the geography of this place as much as you do, Cassandra," the other protested.

"I mean formally. Sort of hand over, if you see what I mean."

"No, I don't see what you mean," Tonia replied. "I've no intention of taking over anything around here, as you put it. I've no experience in running a home and I'm relying on you to teach me."

"That's very flattering of you and I promise to help wherever I can, Tonia, but from today, you're the mistress, which means that you issue the orders, and make the decisions. I'll just be your helpmate."

"I'd prefer you as a mentor."

"All right then, your advisor whose advice you don't always have to follow," Cassandra said.

"How about a sister, a dear sister?" Tonia suggested, dimpling irresistibly, and Cassandra responded by stepping out of character and embracing her, saying warmly, "I'd prefer that too."

"Oh, I hope we shall be friends, Cassandra, sister-friends."

"We already are that. I think Gavin's lucky to have you. Welcome to the Mutono family."

"Thank you, Cassandra; you're not so bad after all. I confess I was a little bit scared of you in the beginning."

"Silly girl, I'm quite harmless, I assure you," Cassandra said surveying the piles of articles they had unpacked. "Will you be able to carry on on your own if I leave now?"

"Of course I will, thank you." Cassandra gathered up the empty bags and left Tonia humming happily to herself as she went about tidying up with a proprietary air.

Chapter Five

The next day being Saturday, Cassandra planned on spending most of it with Raymond, but instead of collecting her as usual, he telephoned to say that he could not and asked her to take a taxi.

The taxi dropped her outside the gate. After letting herself in, she slowed down to a stroll in order to savour the peaceful atmosphere of the warm afternoon. Halfway, she checked her steps and stood back to gaze at the house whose beauty never ceased to overwhelm her. Today, it looked almost ethereal as it lay grandly against the grassy breast of a large hill, its loveliness accentuated by the opalescent afternoon sun. She thought how easy it could be to be happy in such surroundings, to attain the serenity and spiritual contentment that most people know only in their dreams.

She strayed to a rose garden below the front windows, but just as she bent down to inhale the sweet perfume of the blooms, a bumblebee took exception to her interference and registered its annoyance in loud threatening tones. Cassandra beat a hasty retreat to the front door.

"Cassandra!" No matter how many times she heard her name pronounced in that special husky tone, it always sounded sweeter than any other endearment. "I'm sorry I could not come for you," Raymond said, searching her face anxiously.

"It doesn't matter, Ray, for here I am, in one piece," Cassandra replied, yielding to his embrace. When, still locked in his arms, she opened her eyes, they fell on the most beautiful child she had ever seen. He was about five, with round big brown eyes and a light complexion that was agonisingly too reminiscent of such another striking face.

He was dressed in brown jeans and a blue T-shirt with the caption 'Happy Kid' on its front. But Cassandra thought no kid could have looked further from happy than the one facing her. His mouth was pulled out in an ugly pout and his eyes sparked off intense hatred at the interloper in his father's arms.

Raymond felt her stiffen in his arms and swivelled round.

"Your son?" Cassandra asked evenly.

"Yes, that's Steve." He detached himself and walked towards the kid.

"He's a very beautiful child," Cassandra whispered close behind him.

"Thank you. Come and say hello to Cassandra, Steve," he coaxed, bending down to take the little boy's hand in his, but Steve quickly hid both hands behind his back saying, "Shan't. Don't like her." After this pronouncement, he rushed away, leaving the two adults horror-stricken.

For some time, neither moved nor spoke. Cassandra felt absurdly upset by the child's rejection of her although she reasoned that under the circumstances, it was only natural. She turned and gazed at the man beside her who seemed even more perturbed than her. "Don't look so solemn, Ray, he's just a baby. He doesn't know what he's saying."

"But he has been so expertly coached that he believes it. I'm not angry with Steve but with his mother for burdening him with her own neuroses. I'm sorry, angel, I had no idea things would turn out this way."

"Don't worry about me, darling, he's the one," she added pointing in the direction Steve had taken, "you should worry about. He's young and confused and he needs your reassurance. Please go to him."

"Not yet. He needs time to reflect on his behaviour. He should not be encouraged to think he can always blackmail people into feeling sorry for him by misbehaving."

"Do you think that is wise?" Cassandra had no personal experience with children. The little she knew of them being confined to book knowledge. Her own younger sister and brother were her junior by only a few years.

"I do," Raymond stated grimly. "He can't learn early enough to deal with consequences of his own actions."

"Well, if you think so. Meantime I'll help Joseph in the kitchen to prepare something Steve might like."

"I'm sorry, sweetheart, Joseph's sleeping off the effects of one of his heavy nights. That's why I couldn't come for you, I had nobody to leave Steve with."

"In that case, I'll take over his domain and see what I can do."

"That's a terrific idea. One bite of your delicious cake and Steve'll be your slave forever," Raymond enthused but Cassandra, remembering the venom reflected in the little boy's eyes, was inclined to be skeptical.

"I didn't know he'd be here this weekend," she remarked idly as she busied herself with bowls, spoons and measures. Raymond was perched on the corner of the kitchen table watching her. "The switch please," and the mixer whirled into motion.

"I think I told you he's been sick?" Raymond said, raising his voice above the buzz of the machine. "Well, his mother was getting positively cranky about him, so I decided to keep him here for a couple of days to make my own observations."

"Oh, I hope there's nothing seriously wrong with him?"

"So far I've seen no indication of a virulent disease but we shall know for sure on Monday when the lab tests are out. Belinda thought... never mind. I suppose it's all part of the game."

"Poor Ray, the role of part-time father seems to irk you, doesn't it? I don't pretend to understand the problems of your marriage, but it seems to me there's need for you and your wife to get together and sort out your priorities. Once the two of you know how to balance your needs in the context of your situation," Cassandra offered.

"Top on my priority list is the well-being of my son and I'll not allow anybody or anything to jeopardise that," Raymond stated decisively. Too late he realised how that could be interpreted by Cassandra. "Oh, Cassandra angel, I didn't mean it the way it sounded to you, truly," he pleaded, jumping down and putting his arms around her stiff body. "How can I make you understand the horrors, the bitterness that I must endure because of my past mistakes and weaknesses?"

"You could try explaining, Ray," she said quietly.

"Yes, I suppose I could, my darling, and I will one day soon, when I think you're ready to take it. I owe you that much."

"You owe me nothing, Ray, that you've not repaid a hundred times over. You've been exceptionally frank with me right from the start and I'm grateful for that."

"No, Cassandra, I've not been a hundred percent frank with you. I-"

"Oh, but you have, about the things I consider important to our relationship. The rest doesn't matter. Go to Steve and make peace with him while I finish my cooking," Cassandra suggested.

As he made no move to follow her advice but remained still, studying her worriedly, she pushed him gently towards the door.

"Let me finish what I set out to say." He leaned his back against the closed door and went on, "My greatest fear, the nightmare which stalks me day and night is that one day you're going to walk out on me. I'm a selfish person as you've probably discovered by now. If I were not, I wouldn't have allowed things between us to get this far. But I need you, sweet Cassandra, and I don't want to lose you. Before I met you, I made resolutions which bound me to a certain course of action. This is what I want to explain to you although I'm not sure that at the end of it all, you'll not despise me and wish you'd never met me."

"Despise or hate you? I could never do that, Ray. But I don't think now's the time for explanations. Out there is a little boy waiting for you to tell him you love him very much. Please go and find him and reassure him."

"Okay, angel, but one more thing; you must never doubt my love for you whatever happens. Promise me that, Cassandra."

"I promise, Ray," Cassandra answered, leaning against his chest. 'Whatever happens': the ominous words sent a cold chill along her spine. At that critical moment, the door squeaked open, startling both into guilty immobility. Cassandra glimpsed a reddened eye in a tear-stained face before it was withdrawn, followed by the furious banging of the door and the sound of running feet.

"Jesus!" Raymond swore harshly.

"After him, Ray, quick," Cassandra said urgently. She waited until he was out of the kitchen before she allowed her emotions free rein. "It's ridiculous," she said aloud, "but I'm scared of a mere kid."

"Are you all right?" Raymond asked, coming back some few minutes later.

"I'm fine. How's Steve? I probably should go home if I upset him so much."

"Don't even think of it. He has calmed down and will feel even better after tea, I know."

"Where shall we have it? I'm almost ready." Whenever the two of them were alone, and weather permitting, they loved having their tea on the balcony overlooking the beautiful grounds.

"Let's have it indoors, saves the carrying and fetching."

Thirty minutes later, Raymond's patience with his son was beginning to wear thin. "Eat your cake," he ordered but Steve simply sulked in his chair. His huge eyes were brimming with tears and he refused to touch his tea or the tempting chunk of cake placed before him. His father had tried cajoling, threats, all to no avail. The child obdurately stared at him, making Cassandra feel like a monster.

She got up from her chair abruptly. "I think I'd better go."

"No, wait," Raymond said, springing up too. "Nobody's going anywhere. Are you going to take your tea like a good boy, Steve, or do you want me to make you do it?" he asked, moving towards the little boy's chair threateningly. Just then, the sound of a car pulling up outside stopped him in his tracks. His eyes turned quickly to the window overlooking the drive. "It's Bevis," he said with obvious relief. For a moment he had feared it might be his wife. "I'll let him in," he added, striding away.

Cassandra cringed inside at the thought of Bevis witnessing her mortification. Still standing, she grasped the edges of the table and waited.

"Hello, Cassandra. Seems I'm just in time for the tea-party, eh, Steve?

You still here, how come? Come on, a big hug for your uncle." He lifted the boy out of his chair and hugged him affectionately. Steve responded fiercely, burying his face in the sanctuary of the broad chest, his little body heaving with silent sobs.

"Hey, hold it, soldier, you're drenching me!" Bevis protested mildly as he held him back and contemplated his dejected face. "What is it, little warrior, lost a battle?" He raised his eyes to the other two inquiringly, taking in Cassandra's pinched look and Raymond's grim appearance.

"I'm afraid Steve has not been on his best behaviour today," his brother explained.

"Is that so, young man?" Bevis darted Cassandra another look. "You and I have a bone to pick, Steve, what do you say?"

"Don't like her," the child mumbled. "She stole my daddy." Cassandra flinched and held to the chair even more tightly until her knuckles hurt.

"That's nonsense, Steve," his uncle reprimanded sternly. "Look, your father's here, right? Now, when somebody or something is stolen, you don't see them anymore. They disappear completely. But your daddy's here, and will always be here where you can always find him when you come visiting. He has not disappeared, which means he has not been stolen, do you understand, Steve?" he asked gently and the child nodded reluctantly after a nasty look at Cassandra. It was clear he did not believe a word his uncle said. Whoever had inculcated into him the idea of Cassandra's guilt had done a good job.

"Excuse us, folks," Bevis said, clasping Steve more tightly. "I think Steve and I will go for a short walk. Save some of that wonderful cake for us please."

"Oh, God," Raymond sighed. "Sit down, Cassandra, please. I don't know what to say; Steve doesn't normally behave like this."

"You said he's been ill. Sick children tend to be irritable," Cassandra remarked in the wise-woman tone she usually adopted when confronted with imponderables in their relationship. "Let's get on with our tea."

"Have I ever told you how wonderful you are, Cassandra?" Raymond exclaimed with relief.

"Once or twice but I'm not averse to hearing it again."

They went on with their banter, rather forced on Cassandra's part, until the wanderers' return.

"Here we are, looking forward to our tea," Bevis announced cheerfully. Steve looked wary but calm. "But before we sit down," his uncle went on as he squeezed the little hand clutching his encouragingly, "Steve has something he wishes to say to Cassandra." He shoved the boy in her direction and Cassandra awaited his approach nervously.

"I'm sorry I was naughty, Cassandra, please forgive me. I think you're a nice lady and I...a...a.. am going to...o...o... to like you," he recited stammeringly. Then he stole a backward glance at his uncle, who nodded his approval. Cassandra, feeling as if she was on trial, gathered the stiff little body and hugged it perfunctorily, sending an embarrassed look to her face-saver.

The latecomers then proceeded to demolish the huge helpings of cake with relish and drink their tea with gusto, young Steve conducting the operations from his father's knee.

Cassandra listened distractedly as the two men discussed current events. As soon as tea was over, she announced her intention to leave. Raymond received the news dolefully and Bevis offered to drive her back. "Just give me a few minutes to keep a date with Steve outside." The boy joyfully skipped to his side and linked his hand in his, looking very much like any normal five-year-old.

"Must you go now, Cassandra?" Raymond asked.

"I think it would be best."

"You're still upset?"

"I'm not upset ... well, maybe a little. But I don't hold it against the child. It's only natural he should resent me. But let's not despair, it's not the end of the world."

"It's the end of my day. Let's spend the whole of tomorrow together, okay?"

"Well," Cassandra said cautiously, "you can call me: I'll be in the whole day."

"Steve will not be here tomorrow," Raymond stated firmly. "I'll see to it," he said as he held her in a close embrace until the sound of returning footsteps on the cobalt outside wrenched them guiltily apart. "I'll call you," he whispered, pushing her into a chair before he went to the door to answer the excited summons of his son.

"Daddy, Daddy, guess what? I saw kites, Uncle Bevy showed them to me, and so many birds saying, squeak-squeak, in the tree. Come, Daddy, you can see them too – hurry! And Daddy, I want to stay here with you and Uncle Bevy for always and always, may I please? If I'm very good, Daddy, please?"

"Hey, slow down, buddy," his father said laughing, as he bent down to scoop him up in his arms. "Now, one thing at a time..."

Cassandra thought she had never seen Raymond so happy and carefree. I have no place here, she thought wistfully. These two are sufficient unto each other. With the child here, I'd always feel like an interloper, while his absence would forever condemn me.

As her eyes veered away from the two, she caught Bevis watching her with a pitying smile. "Ready?" he asked her quietly.

Cassandra got to her feet. "I'm off, Ray."

"Okay, Cassandra, I'll give you a call. Say goodbye to Cassandra and Uncle Bevy, Steve," Steve waved vigorously to Bevis, his hand wavering perceptibly as he turned to Cassandra.

* * *

"Don't fret about Steve, Cassandra, he'll come to like you in time," Bevis offered solicitously as they turned out of the drive.

"I'm not fretting about anything in the least," Cassandra snapped. "But isn't this where you say 'I told you so?' "

"Perhaps, but I'm not going to."

"How most considerate of you!" she mocked. She did not know why she was goading him into a quarrel but she needed a punch-ball and he happened to be there.

"Let's not quarrel about it, okay?" Bevis said roughly, the closest Cassandra had ever seen him get to losing his temper.

"Sorry," she said grudgingly and the two lapsed into silence. Some minutes later she noticed that they were not going in the direction of Luzzi. "Where're you taking me?" she demanded.

"I thought that, unless you've strong objections to my company, you might care to have dinner with me? You're not expected home yet, are you?"

"I come and go as I like. I'm not a school girl any more," she added, glancing at him suspiciously. Surely he must know I spend most weekends with his brother, she thought. "But there's no need for you to saddle yourself with me. I don't want to interfere with your plans for the evening," she added ungraciously.

"As it happens, I've no other engagement for the evening. I want to stop at my place to change into something more suitable." Cassandra glanced at him and thought how much more relaxed he looked in casual wear.

"Something wrong?" he asked, sensing her scrutiny.

"No, nothing. I was just thinking that this is the first time I've seen you dressed like this."

"Really? I can hardly credit that. What's your verdict?"

"You look more human."

"Ouch! I can feel pain too."

"I'm sorry, I didn't mean to offend."

"You didn't. The suit's very much the stock-in-trade of the professional class. Sort of window-dressing but a feat worthy of martyrdom in our kind of climate, I can assure you."

"Whatever happened to the *Kaunda* suit?"

"It's still very much in vogue but the finish of most of our local products leaves a lot to be desired. I sometimes think that the need to save the odd shilling here and there at the expense of quality and precision is mostly responsible for the inability of our local markets to compete with foreign products even on their home ground. Thus you find that a man of discernment wishing to wear a *Kaunda* suit will have to order it from Britain, which country will have imported it from South Africa."

Cassandra laughed enjoying his nimble humour. "Not from Zambia?"

"Not from Zambia since we don't have direct trade relations. Besides, they probably order theirs from South Africa too, men of discriminating taste, that is. No pun intended there, by the way."

"What a cynic you are, Bevis."

"A realist, Cassandra, not a cynic. Do you mind coming in for a while?" he asked, drawing up before a hideous brick building.

Cassandra stepped out of the car glancing around curiously. It was strange that in spite of their long association through her brother, she had never been to Bevis' house. What a contrast between Raymond's and this, she thought, giving the place another quick, puzzled look.

Bevis' finger had hardly touched the bell when the door was flung open by a middle-aged, amply proportioned woman in the garb of a housekeeper.

"Mr B," she exclaimed beaming, "I didn't expect you back so soon."

"Well, I'm back, May, but only to change. I won't be needing dinner. This is Miss Mutono. My housekeeper, May, Cassandra."

"How do you do, May?" Cassandra greeted, offering her hand. She was answered by a wide welcoming smile and an open appraisal.

"Is she your lawyer friend's sister?" May asked.

"She is. How clever of you to guess," Bevis answered, mocking her a little. It was apparent to Cassandra that the two enjoyed a more cordial relationship than that of master-servant.

"I can see the resemblance," the housekeeper declared, squinting at the visitor short-sightedly. Cassandra thought she was stretching her imagination a trifle. Nobody had ever remarked on any resemblance between her and Gavin although she supposed that some family traits existed.

"You could be right, May," Bevis remarked, gravely treating Cassandra to a microscopic study. "Yes, I think you're right, May," he repeated before he firmly steered her inside the house, which gesture May took as a dismissal and left.

"I hope you don't mind May's familiarity," Bevis said as he showed Cassandra to a seat. "She's been with me for a long time and treats me as a son. It follows then that she takes a great deal of interest in every girl I bring home in the hope that that particular one might turn out to be the bait that will ensare me to the altar."

"I see. Do you provide her with a great many of them?"

"I beg your pardon? Oh, you mean girls? Hardly. Here, have a drink, I shan't be long." He handed her a glass of sherry. "There's some music here too," he added, inserting a cassette in the player, "to while away the time." He pressed the button and the room was suddenly plunged into a melodious symphony by Steve Wonder crooning "I just called to say I love you" in his haunting voice.

Her drink in hand, Cassandra got up and wandered around the inelegant room. She could not see Bevis' imprint anywhere. The mediocre furnishings secured in drab and discordant colours plus the unattractive building she had glimpsed outside, all conspired to dismantle the picture she had formed of him as a refined and fastidious man. Of course, she admitted to herself, her judgement contained an element of prejudice arising from the temptation to use Raymond's tastes and preferences as a standard measure.

She gave the room another puzzled glance. The whitewashed walls boasted of no decorations except two paintings of ordinary scenic landscapes such as those usually displayed on shop verandas. She moved to the more vivid one, attracted by the artist's liberal use of colour. It depicted a flock of tropical birds in flight. Cassandra looked at it long and reflectively, envying the birds their airiness of body and freedom of spirit.

"What do you make of it?" Bevis asked, coming to stand beside her.

"I confess to complete ignorance of works of art," Cassandra said, "although this one seems simple enough to understand."

"Yes, it's simplicity itself, but what a marvellous cacophony of colours!" He lingered over the painting a few minutes more before he said, "Let me relieve you of your glass. I think we should be going now. I'll just inform May."

He disappeared in what Cassandra assumed to be the kitchen wing. She turned and picked up her bag and started for the door but never made it there. Suddenly the world seemed to erupt beneath her feet as the sound of machine gun and other heavy artillery split the air. She clutched her bag tightly and stood frozen to the spot. This kind of pastime was becoming a frequent occurrence lately but it was not the kind of thing one got used to. Every time volleys of shots were unleashed on the unsuspecting citizenry, they threw them into frenzies of panic, especially as there were never any plausible explanations afterwards.

When her senses were together once again, she sprinted in the direction she had seen Bevis take and met him at the kitchen entrance hurrying back inside.

"Are you all right?" he asked, taking her hand and guiding her back.

"I'm fine," she gasped.

"May," he turned to address the rotund figure staggering towards them, "tell Juma to lock the gate immediately and all of you should stay indoors until we know what all this is about, is that clear?"

Bevis then led Cassandra inside and made her sit down before he went to the door to make sure that his orders were being complied with. He then locked it, closed the windows and drew the curtains. May could be heard doing the same thing in other rooms.

"So much for our evening out," he remarked, coming to sit beside her.

"Not my lucky day, is it?" Cassandra commented ruefully.

"The battle scene seems to be Mbuya Military Barracks," Bevis remarked listening intently to the thundering noise.

"Are you sure? It sounds so deafeningly close," Cassandra stuttered, her teeth beginning to chatter. Normally she did not scare easily and despised people, women in particular, who turned to jelly at the slightest sign of danger. But lately her constitution seemed to be undergoing a profound change, turning her into a shadow of her old self.

"I think that's because we're on a corresponding hill and are receiving the impact direct," Bevis explained. He got up and poured them both a drink saying, "We might as well try to steady our nerves while we wait. It might be a long wait at that."

Cassandra picked up her glass with shaking hands and took a few cautious sips before she felt calmness return. "What do you think is the cause this time?" The previous pandemonium had been attributed to rebel activities although it was common knowledge that a small disagreement between brigade commanders could easily set off the fireworks as well.

"It's hard to say," Bevis replied. "The crossfire could either mean warring factions within the same barracks or an invasion from some other place. But don't look so frightened, Cassandra, we're as safe here as anywhere else."

"I'm sorry I'm putting on a poor show."

"Don't be silly. The noise itself alone is enough to send anybody into a funk. I...," the telephone shrilled suddenly, startling them both. Bevis went to answer it.

He talked for some minutes before he returned to his seat saying, "That was a friend of mine, John Zilaba. He tells me the conflict is between Makindye and Mbuya, which doesn't surprise me. Obviously Makindye is the besieging force."

"I hope it won't spread to the rest of the barracks."

"Yeah. That could lead to carnage galore but I imagine the high command is still capable of containing the situation before it develops into a free-for-all contest."

The next caller was Raymond who had also heard about the shoot-out. After speaking with his brother briefly, who explained the circumstances of Cassandra's presence at his house, he asked to talk to her. "What cursed luck, darling! Are you all right?"

Cassandra assured him that she was. "But the noise here's terrifying. Do you mean it's all quiet there?"

"Not even the squeak of a mouse can be heard. Are you sure you're okay?"

"Perfectly. How's Steve?"

"In bed asleep. I don't think you can make it home tonight but I'm sure Bevis'll make you comfortable."

"I'm sure he will," Cassandra said, turning to glance at her host, but he had discreetly left the room. "I better hang up now, Ray, I have to strain to hear you. Call me tomorrow please. I'll be in the whole day. Do you wish to speak to Bevis again?"

"Al..rr..right," Raymond replied, reluctant to let her go. "I hope you can make it home early. I'll ring you then. Take care of yourself."

"You too. Good night. I'll call Bevis now ..." she had hardly got the words out when a thundering blast seemed to shake the very foundations of the house. She stopped dead, her hand rigid around the instrument.

"Come and sit down," Bevis, who had materialised suddenly beside her, said, prying the receiver from her hands. Raymond's frantic voice could be heard demanding to be told what had happened. "Talk to you later," Bevis said to him briefly and put down the phone. He led Cassandra back to her seat, keeping his arm comfortingly ar und her until the tremors had passed and they were enveloped in a temporary balmy silence. But not for long: a spurt of gunfire followed, which seemed to go on indefinitely. Then a relative lull, after which an intermittent spate of shots ensued, signifying the waning enthusiasm of the warring parties, and hopefully, heralding the ceasefire.

Bevis switched on the radio for the nine o'clock news in the hope that mention of the disturbance would be made but in vain. The newscaster's voice, with a marked accent, droned on about innocuous days' old news: the President was reported to have received a delegation from North Korea; the Minister of Home Affairs had praised the high standard of discipline of the police force at a passing-out parade at the Police Training School, Naguru; the government of West Germany had signed a trade agreement with the Uganda Government; an outbreak of rinderpest was reported in the western part of the country, and so on and so forth. Bevis snapped off the set, swearing, "Rinderpest outbreak for heaven's sake! Where do these people live, on the moon?" He paced the room a couple of times, his tall silhouette throwing comical shapes on the walls in the dim candlelight.

The room was lit by a single candle. This was a normal precautionary measure during times of insurgence, a relic of the turbulent seventies.

At about nine-thirty, things seemed to calm down somewhat and eventually the racket subsided completely.

"I think we might survive yet," Bevis said, getting up to replenish their drinks. "The worst seems over."

"I guess so. Is there any way of ascertaining the situation?" Cassandra asked.

"I don't think so. I know one or two chaps in the army but I hardly think this is the time to disturb them. We'll just have to sit tight and wait a little while longer, I'm afraid." He lit a cigarette, watching her contemplatively. "If ʊu were thinking of going home now, I'd have to discourage it. We don't ᴋnow how long this lull's likely to last. Even if it means a complete halt to the fusillade, it'd still be foolhardy venturing out and risking running into bands of wandering desperadoes or unexpected roadblocks."

Cassandra, who had actually been thinking along those lines, denied it promptly. "It would be madness trying to traverse the town now. But I'd like to ring home and let them know I'm safe."

"I'll get the line for you."

Cassandra spoke to her sister, Alex, who was spending the weekend at Luzzi, and put her in the picture.

"Golly, rather you than me. Lucky I decided to spend the night here; it must be real bedlam at the institute."

"Well, that's it in a nutshell. I understand the newlyweds have gone roller-skating, why didn't you tag along?"

"I think I'm getting a little too old for the coattails, don't you? Besides, how could I enjoy myself when Horace has just been buried, oumph?"

"Okay, you've made your point, no need to get upset," Cassandra checked her impatiently, thinking that Alex had not been all that fond of Horace. But of course she had adored the presents he showered on her and the rides in his Mercedes Benz which raised her social status with her peers. Gosh, I'm turning into a cynic, Cassandra thought, stealing a glance at Bevis as if he could read her thoughts.

"Anyway, I hope to be home tomorrow as early as I can make it. Stick around and I'll fill you in on the rest of the details."

"You mean you're spending the night at...?

"Of course. Would you rather I spent it in the barracks entertaining the soldiers?" Cassandra retorted tartly. "Goodnight, Alex."

"She doesn't think it proper for you to spend the night here with me?" Bevis asked with a wry smile.

Cassandra shrugged indifferently. "I don't see that it's any of her business really as long as you don't mind."

"How could I mind when you're here at my invitation, Cassandra?"

"I'm not sure I'm not turning out to be a nuisance. You can't have anticipated all this when you kindly invited me out to dinner."

"You know that I ..."

"... never do anything that I don't want to do," Cassandra interjected triumphantly, a little of her sang-froid restored.

"Yes, that too but I was actually going to say that I love having you here."

"Well, thank you, but why are we being so polite and proper like strangers?"

"I don't know the answer to that. We can perhaps attribute it to the strangeness of the evening. Would you like some more light? I think we're now back to normal, if you discount a few prowlers seeking to take advantage of the situation."

Just then May marched in, and without so much as a by-your-leave, switched on the table lamp on the desk and then marched out again with the candle. A few minutes later, she reappeared, this time ready to talk.

"I think the Good Lord has seen it fit to spare us this time, Mr B," she sighed, her benign glance embracing Cassandra as well.

"I think he has, May."

"I declare I've never seen the like of it before, not since the 79 Kampala battle with them *sabasabas*. What do you think is happening now, Mr B? The boys are saying that it could be you-know-who, do you think it's true?"

"It's possible, May. Anything's possible," Bevis, suspecting he could easily be quoted as an authority on the subject, answered cautiously.

"It's a shame, Miss Cassandra, for this to happen on your first visit here."

"We do have our excitements too where I live, May, although this sounded far more serious than anything so far experienced. These things do have a way of escalating, don't they?"

"Well, there's nothing anybody can do but wait. Haven't we always waited? I say to myself again and again that when it's time for one to go, one goes; when it isn't, one doesn't go," she imparted portentously. "How many people survived the holocaust of the early eighties only to die later of nothing more than a snakebite?"

"Thank you for cheering us up, May, but while Cassandra might have survived the kick-up yonder, she's likely to die of starvation unless something is done about it quickly. What do you think?"

"Oh, I'm sorry, Mr. B, I should have realised you'd not be eating out after all. But what with the sounds of the guns still ringing in my ears, I declare I'm not myself."

"That's understandable, May. We're all a little shaken up. About supper..."

"Leave everything to me, Mr B, I know just what you both need."

"Why does she call you 'Mr B'?" Cassandra asked after May had majestically stomped away.

"A compromise between familiarity and respect, I suspect. She's competent in spite of her loquacity: I leave everything to her." His eyes seemed to be challenging her to comment. He suspected that she was mentally comparing his brother's place to the one she presently found herself in, to the detriment of the latter. He hoped that was all she was comparing.

"And apparently she does very well," Cassandra remarked neutrally, her eyes automatically giving the austerely clean room a sweeping glance.

"The place," Bevis explained, "does not belong to me. I undertook to caretake it for a friend three years ago. Now it seems I can't get rid of it until ne owner returns from his self-exile. I took it on as it was: the only piece of furniture which belongs to me in this room is that writing table."

Cassandra almost gave an audible sigh of relief. She hated to be wrong about people. "But wouldn't you find yourself displaced if your friend were to return suddenly?"

"I doubt he'd do that. In any case, my own house should be ready long before that happened. Actually, it's ready and only a few finishing touches are remaining. Hasn't Ray ever taken you along to see it? He's very proud of the work and calls it his masterpiece. It really is a beautiful house even if it's I who says so. You ought to see it."

"Perhaps I will one day," Cassandra remarked, wondering why Ray had never mentioned it to her. He told her about most of his other projects.

"Perhaps you will, one day," Bevis repeated softly.

Their simple meal over, Bevis asked if Cassandra was ready for bed.

"I suppose I might as well. I don't think we're likely to get any more news tonight."

"Wait a minute," he said, fiddling with the radio until he located the BBC Africa Service for the eleven o'clock news, but Uganda was not even mentioned, which in a way was reassuring. "Anything serious would have merited airtime."

"May I show the visitor to her room?" May asked after clearing up.

"I'm reserving that honour for myself, May, thank you." After she left, Bevis got up briskly, saying, "A date to remember, wouldn't you say? I'll show you to your room."

The room readied for her was small, impersonal, the walls a stark white and the floor bare, except for two Turkish rugs spread alongside the two single beds on either side of the room. A visitors' room, Cassandra concluded.

Bevis switched on the bedside light and snapped off the wall switch. "It's not much but I hope you'll be comfortable here."

"I'm sure I will, thank you," Cassandra replied, her eyes on the bed ready to receive her. A night gown of flimsy material was spread out on top. Her distaste for the garment of some strange woman must have been apparent for her host, after giving her a thoughtful look, said, "My sister's, I believe," pointing to the offensive object. "I don't know whether you've met Emily?"

"I've met the eminent doctor," Cassandra answered dryly.

"I can see it was not love at first sight," Bevis, smiling wryly, remarked. "She can be a little brusque with strangers at times, especially female strangers she regards as security risks to her brother!"

"You don't say brothers?" Cassandra asked and looked at him curiously. For a minute, she thought she had caught an unguarded look in his expression but it was gone before she could read it properly. A hurt?

"No, not brothers. So far, no female has ever posed a risk to my impregnability." The words 'so far' were loaded with nuances but Cassandra was not sure of what. "I see your face radiating with eloquence," he continued, "is it because of something I've said?"

"Yes, in a way," she replied, thinking that the sum-up of Emily's attitude to Raymond explained what had been puzzling her since their meeting. But now everything fell nicely into place, explaining the outright rejection of her by the other girl.

"Anyway, I'm sorry about that," Bevis said as he waved towards the bed, "but we had to make the gesture. What you do or don't do with it later is entirely up to you."

"I'm sorry if I appear ungrateful but..."

"That's all right, Cassandra. I believe in frankness too. Good night."

"Good night, Bevis."

* * *

It took Cassandra a long time to fall sleep after she had settled down for the night. The night was shrouded in sinister silence that lent it a more perilous air than the rumpus of a few hours before. An indeterminate moon made a halfhearted attempt to penetrate the darkness. Cassandra forced herself to relax as she ran through the day's events, seeking to review them objectively. Young Steve's reaction to her was what anybody would expect from a child of such a marriage although the intensity of the emotion in one so young was a little unnerving. Anyway, time would show whether he would ever come to accept her or not.

Her thoughts then strayed to her sister, poor Mellie. How would I feel if I were to lose Ray, she wondered. The very idea seemed too horrible to contemplate, so she hurriedly tried to reroute her thoughts into a more pleasant channel. Only none immediately presented itself. She plumped down her pillow, turned on her side and shut her eyes. As she finally drifted into an uneasy sleep, a hazy image of Bevis, handsome, detached and eternally mysterious loomed over her, blocking out all other images.

It seemed to her that she had hardly closed her eyes in sleep when she was awakened by a loud shattering noise outside. She sat bolt upright in bed, not sure whether she had indeed heard anything or had dreamt it. The door to her room opened and a shadowy figure walked in.

"Are you all right?" Bevis asked.

"I'm fine now. I was awakened by a terribly loud noise. Did you hear it too or did I imagine it?"

"You didn't imagine it. There was an explosion a few minutes ago. Will you be able to go back to sleep or shall I get you something to drink?"

"No, nothing to drink, thank you. Perhaps you could sit down for a few minutes and just talk to me," she added, feeling very nervous all of a sudden.

He obeyed and perched precariously on the edge of the bed. He took her hand in his and felt it tremble. "What's the matter, Cassandra, are you cold?" He tried to peer into her face but she pulled her hand away saying breathlessly, "I'm sorry, I'm behaving like an idiot. Please go back to your room, there's nothing to be afraid of, is there?" How absurd I must sound, she thought, annoyed with herself.

"I don't mind sitting with you a little. Just try to relax. No harm's likely to come to you."

"I know. I'm just being silly really. Don't worry about me, I feel fine now."

"Okay." He left without another word and was back almost immediately with a glass of water and some white tiny pill he pressed on her. "Take it; it'll help you to relax and it has no aftereffects."

"All right. I hope it does the trick," she said, swallowing.

"It will if you give it a chance. Good night. I'm next door in case you need me."

After Bevis had left, Cassandra fell asleep almost immediately. She dreamt that she was in Raymond's arms and felt so warm and secure that she did not wake up again until it was broad daylight. She lay back a little while longer trying to adjust mentally to the strange surroundings she found herself in. Her dream had been so vivid that she was now having difficulty accepting it as only that, a dream. The fog in her mind was, however, soon dispelled by the entrance of May with a loaded breakfast tray.

"Good morning, Miss. Something to put in that empty stomach of yours."

"Good morning, May," Cassandra answered, pulling the sheet up to her neck. She had dispensed with the stranger's night gown and did not think May was the type of person to approve of people sleeping in the nude. "But you didn't have to go to all that trouble of bringing me breakfast in bed," she added. "I was about to get up."

"Trouble's my business," stated the indomitable lady firmly, yanking the curtains apart and throwing the windows open. "A lovely day we're having after the goings-on of last night. I declare I never slept a wink."

But her positively glowing appearance belied her claim. "Neither did Mr. B, judging by his drawn face," May continued, giving Cassandra a sly look.

"I slept soundly myself and woke up only once when that big blast went off," Cassandra said truthfully.

"I heard that too. What's the world coming to, I ask you? Pop-pop-pop, day and night; nobody's safe from those flying bullets. But you wait and see," she added darkly, "those wielding those weapons will have them pointed at themselves one day. As the Good Book says, those who live by the sword shall die by the sword. Where's Amin and his henchmen now?"

"Not dead as they deserve, not all of them anyway," Cassandra factually told her.

"They're not here, are they? Now you're no doubt wanting to get down to business. The master, before he left for his tennis playing, charged me to feed you on a good and hearty breakfast. So you sit up and eat," she ordered, clasping her arms across her ample bust and showing every intention of staying put until Cassandra had swallowed the last morsel.

"All right, May, but I'd like to have a wash first."

"You wash. I'll just pop the eggs in the oven to keep them warm." She went and Cassandra retrieved her clothes and dashed to the bathroom for her morning ablutions.

* * *

Towards morning, Bevis had been awakened from his sleep by the noise of barking dogs, clamorous and insistent from his next but one neighbour who kept a couple of brutes. He tried to stretch his hand and reach for his watch on the bedside table but encountered some unexpected resistance. His hand appeared to be pinned down by some weight of a warm, cuddly object. Dash it, where am I, he cursed, his heart leaping to his mouth. He turned cautiously

101

to look at the person lying beside him and almost went into an apoplexy attack at the discovery. "Cassandra!" he exhaled slowly.

But how in the name of sanity did I come to be here, he wondered silently. I know I went back to my room after giving her the sleeping pill, and in fact lay awake thinking about her, my mind conjuring up all sorts of impossible situations. But they were confined to the imaginary and nothing in the world would have induced me to translate them into action. And yet, here I am, waking up in a bed I have no business to be in and without any idea of how I got there! But of one thing he was sure. He did not go there of his own volition or he would have remembered. The whole thing didn't make sense to him but for the sake of his sanity, he felt he had to unravel the mystery.

He glanced again at his sleeping companion and felt panicky at the thought of her waking up before he stole away. How would he face her, what would he say to her? It was urgent for him to get away, but when he tried to pull his hand away, the slight movement disturbed the sleeping girl who stirred slightly and snuggled even closer. But by gradual manoeuvres, he was eventually able to extricate himself without waking her.

In his room, he reached for a pack of cigarettes with trembling hands. He rarely smoked except when under great mental stress as he was now. The fact that he could not remember a thing about how he strayed to his visitor's room was extremely frustrating. He cringed at the thought that he might have behaved in a manner that could be construed as depraved and cowardly by his guest. If only he could recall just one little detail. But the more pressure he exerted the more blank his memory screen became. Instead, scenes unrelated to his present predicament interfered with his concentration; scenes from his early childhood, the most vivid of which related to the death of his mother.

His mother had died when he was about eight and it was said that he had been very attached to her although he himself could hardly recall that. According to his family, her death had affected him more than the other children, resulting in some psychological problems for him like wandering about at night. He would be discovered in strange places without the faintest idea of how he got there. On being asked the reason for his wanderings at night, he would, it was claimed, always say he was looking for his mother. The image of a sad little boy suddenly flashed before him and he experienced a momentary intense feeling of loneliness.

Years later, he had learnt that what he had been suffering from was a form of emotional disturbance called somnambulism or sleepwalking, as it is more commonly known. But it had been many years ago; he had adjusted to his loss and outgrown his disability. Was it possible there could be a relapse after all these years? And yet there could be no other explanation for his strange behaviour.

He shrank from the thought of what must have been Cassandra's reaction to the invasion of her privacy or worse. She could not have known or guessed at his mental state. To an ordinary person who knows nothing about the illness, a sleepwalker appears normal in every way although, to all intents and purposes, he is deaf and blind as he records nothing of what he sees or hears. Cassandra could, therefore, have attributed his actions to the worst intentions imaginable. The fact that he had woken up peacefully at her side was of little comfort.

What repercussions his nocturnal wanderings would have on their relationship needed no straining of the imagination to see. She was his brother's girlfriend and as such, taboo to him as long as that state of affairs existed. While he might think him a cad, he dared not imagine what Raymond would call him. To attempt an explanation would be futile, as he could see neither believing him. What was he to do, he wondered.

By daylight, he had worked himself into such a state that he could not face Cassandra. He also felt he needed medical advice on his state of health. He therefore decided to leave the house before she woke up, after writing her a note of apology.

* * *

"So Mr B...I mean Bevis...Mr Agutamba has gone to play tennis?" Cassandra asked as she toyed with her breakfast, with May standing over her, her indefatigable voice providing background entertainment in competition with the Sunday morning programme on the radio. She was puzzled by his behaviour and a little piqued, she admitted.

"Yes," May answered. "It's like his religion, if you see what I mean. He never misses a game on Sunday if he can help it, although after the goings-on of last night and you being here and all, I confess I didn't expect him to go haring off as if all the devils in hell were after him. Not even did he take his usual morning cup of coffee. But men will be men. I should know, having been married to one for twenty solid years, although Mr B doesn't behave so queerly like most of them do – oh my!" she broke off to exclaim with such vigour that Cassandra started alarmed.

"What is it, May?"

"It's that letter he gave me and I clear forgot about. What will I forget next, my name no doubt. 'May,' he said, 'when the visitor gets up, be sure to give her this letter. Don't forget,' he urged. He knows how forgetful I am, you see. And now here I am talking while the letter waits to be read!" She dipped her hand inside her spacious apron pocket and pulled out a sealed envelope which she handed to Cassandra and waited.

Cassandra studied the envelope thoughtfully, wondering why Bevis should write to her when he could have talked to her directly or entrusted a verbal message with May.

"Aren't you going to read it?" May asked, unable to contain her curiosity.

"Later," Cassandra answered absently. She was toying with the idea of ringing up Raymond to ask him to collect her from here, but at the recollection of her experience of the previous day, she quickly discarded it. How inconsiderate of Bevis to leave her stranded when he knew she wanted to get back to Luzzi as soon as possible! But the taxi rank was probably not far and the morning looked calm enough in spite of the night of violence.

She was still pondering Bevis' uncharacteristic behaviour when the letter beside her cup caught her attention and pricked her curiosity. She picked it up and ripped the envelope open.

"Cassandra," she read, *"I don't think that you'll want to see me again after last night. I've therefore taken myself off with due dispatch to avoid embarrassing you further. To say that I'm sorry is to understate it but I say it all the same.*

Always BA.

PS: I'll send the car back around nine. You're free to use it as you please. I shan't need it for a while."

Cassandra felt bewildered after reading the letter. She had no clue as to what Bevis was referring to. Why shouldn't she want to see him again and what was he apologising for? She read the letter again, this time slowly but still drew a blank. She went over the events of the night before in an effort to discover the reason behind Bevis' self-reproach. He had behaved like a perfect gentleman throughout, polite and solicitous of her comfort, even to the extent of insuring that she slept soundly by giving her a sleeping pill. Sleeping pill! Was that the clue to his apparent dilemma? Was he afraid that she might have suspected ulterior motives behind his actions? But why should he think so unless he had guilty feelings about it, and why would he feel guilty about it unless the heinous thought did actually cross his mind? But no, not Bevis.

Apart from the fact that he did not like her very much, he would never resort to such dishonourable measures, or would he? He was a man, after all, and there were few men who could rise above their baser nature, she knew. But wouldn't she have had a suspicion of some sort, sleeping pill or no sleeping pill? But there was his admission to the crime veiled in innuendoes and self-reproaches, what more evidence did she want?

She felt a deep sense of disappointment that Bevis, for whom she had recently developed a grudging respect, was no better than any other male rogue who pounced upon defenceless women under the cover of darkness. But what she could not understand was why, having gone to the trouble to conceal his evil intentions, he should think it necessary to come in the open now when he could have kept mum and she would have been none the wiser? Unless at some point he had reason to think she was consentient with whatever was going on. But that was preposterous of course, unthinkable! But as her anger threatened to get the better of her, she remembered her vivid dream about Raymond and wondered, with increasing discomfort, if there was a connection with what had actually taken place, or supposed to have taken place. She hurried to the window for a breath of fresh air where May joined her a few minutes later.

"Who're those?" she asked mechanically, watching two sturdy youths outside the servants' quarters.

"The tall one's Juma, the shamba-boy and the younger one, that one looking this way's Byensi, my son," May revealed reverently. It was apparent Byensi was the apple of her eye.

"Does he also work here? He looks a bit too young to be out of school," Cassandra remarked.

"He doesn't work here, not in a manner of speaking, that is. He only helps out now and then, cutting the grass, washing the car and doing other small jobs for Mr B when he's not learning to repair machines. Mr B said he's a natural born mechanic and found him this job in a factory. He can now repair anything from a flat iron to a car engine. He has got the room next to mine and the least he can do to show his appreciation for Mr. B's kindness is to help around whenever he can."

"You must be proud of him?"

"Oh, he's a fine boy. I have two other children who're girls and already married. Excuse me," she added, hurrying to answer the ringing phone. "That was one of Mr B's friends wanting to talk to him but I... Oh, there's Mr B himself back sooner than I expected." She hurried to open the door as Cassandra tensed up. A minute later, however, May was back to say that it was somebody else driving Mr B's car who had come for her.

**

It was true that Bevis played tennis most Sunday mornings with his friend, Dr Mugodi. But from his sombre appearance when he appeared at the latter's door that morning, it was quite clear that it was not the thought of the invigorating exercise that was uppermost on his mind.

On being ushered in by a dishevelled, red-rimmed James Mugodi, he

105

apologised saying, "I'm sorry to drag you out of bed so early on your only day of rest."

"Who's talking of rest?" the doctor protested good-naturedly as he removed his spectacles and rubbed his tired eyes vigorously. "There's no rest for sinners in this world or didn't you know? I've been up betimes trying to catch up on my reading. I can't imagine why I ever took up medicine when I could have got as much satisfaction ministering to the souls of the flock."

"But think of the pleasures of the flesh you would have otherwise missed," his friend kidded.

"There *are* fleshes and fleshes and it's a fact that there are those the sight of which I could very well do without. Besides, I wasn't thinking of being cloistered in a monastery. Your ordinary church minister, with a little training in counselling, has a wider female clientele than your Kampala street consultant. But come in please. I hear it was a night of fun and games at your end? I can't say you look the worse for it; only a slight haggardness around your eyes which could be Old Man Age beckoning. I've of late noticed an alarming increasing resemblance between my pate and the Kalahari desert," he added, patting his receding hairline solicitously. Bevis' hand automatically ran through his luxuriant hair too as he acknowledged his friend's wry humour with a smile.

"Have you discovered what all the hullabaloo was about?"

"Not yet, but my guess's that it was triggered off by the usual power struggle in the army hierarchy. We should be used to these constant melodramas but one can't help being apprehensive that one day the sparks will set off a conflagration that will go beyond the borders of mere bickerings."

"I don't think 'mere bickerings' is the right way to describe the avaricious wrangling which characterises the top dogs in the country. It's a matter of time now, judging by the frequency and magnitude of these clashes, before the roof carves in. Most people are betting on sooner rather than later. The surprise is that it's taken so long, given the kind of political turmoil prevailing."

"The situation's becoming more fluid with every passing day and in its bid to ward off the inevitable, the administration is tripping itself left, right and centre. But even so, it's not easy to topple an established government with a national army. Not until the common man himself decides that it's time for a change. Look at Mozambique, Angola, Chad, Sudan, Ethiopia and the rest of them. Some of these guerrillas have been in the bush fighting close to a decade. For fairly quick action, massive popular support is essential."

"I suppose you're right. You legal chaps seem to have your fingers glued to the political pulse all the time."

"It's the nature of our work," Bevis replied as his eye wandered about the shabby but masculinely comfortable room. It was hard to believe that the

106

same room had once glittered and sparkled under the expert management of James' ex-wife, Helen. How had he, in the space of under two years, managed to erase all the traces of his brief stormy marriage? Was this an indication of the struggle within to forget or a seal to the end of an old chapter? Two years could be as vivid as yesterday or a mere speck on the memory. He turned to scrutinise his host and found the other's eyes watching him speculatively.

"So my friend, it's not yet time for our game, nor do you look as if you can't wait to get started...?" Bevis' preoccupied air had not escaped him.

"Let's go to your study, James, I have a problem."

"Don't we all?" the doctor exclaimed while covertly submitting his visitor to a more professional examination. "Problems are part and parcel of life, intrinsically woven into the fabric of our existence. Come," he added, leading to a side room he used as a study, "and get it off your chest."

"Now," he said when they were both seated on either side of the desk, "what seems to be the trouble? Do you wish to consult me in my professional capacity or as a friend?"

Bevis thought it over and said, "Both, I guess."

"How can I help you? Are you worried about your health, Bevis?"

"Broadly speaking, yes," Bevis admitted and ruminated awhile, trying to find the best way of putting it. "Do you consider somnambulism a serious mental disorder and what causes it?"

If his friend was surprised at the question, he did not show it. Maintaining his professional composure, he remarked, "Two questions. Well, I'm just a physician as you know, not a psychoanalyst, but from the little I know on the subject, I 'd not call somnambulism a serious disorder, that's in the sense that it's crippling in any way, or cannot be cured, once the root-cause has been established. It's more commonly to be found in children with unstable backgrounds who have been deprived of a normal childhood. In other words, somnambulism has its roots in anxiety neurosis, abnormal or inexplicable fears and worries. I think I've covered both your questions, Bevis."

"Yes, thank you, James. Actually I knew all that, more or less, but I needed to talk it over with somebody. Is it recurrent, to your knowledge, I mean after an intermission of more than twenty years, is it possible for a person to suffer from similar attacks? Damn it, I've not sleepwalked since I was a kid, until last night."

"What happened last night?"

"I wish I knew. I just know it happened."

"Okay, let me put it this way. Were you particularly under some kind of stress, I mean apart from worrying about what was going on in the barracks?"

"Well, it's a long story," Bevis started hesitantly.

"We have all day, so shoot."

So Bevis told him of Cassandra's unexpected presence at his place, omitting such details as he did not consider relevant to the case. But he did not try to minimise the depth of his feelings for her or the effect of her unpropitious proximity. "I was determined to be the perfect gentleman and had every confidence of carrying it off. After all, I'm not new at the game," he added, laughing mirthlessly.

"So I take it this girl does not know how you feel about her? What exactly is her attitude towards you, do you know?"

"Quite amicable, at least of late," Bevis said slowly. "We've known each other for a long time and I've often had the horrible feeling that she regards me as a brother, or as close as makes no difference."

"Surely not or you wouldn't be here to tell the story."

"What story? That's the whole point of my being here because I can't remember a damned thing about what happened or did not happen," Bevis groaned.

"Let me see if I can make myself clear: if she was indifferent to you as you claim, don't you think she'd have bawled you out of your hypnotic state and back to your senses? You must realise she couldn't have known you were not responsible for what you were doing unless she had prior knowledge of your condition. Did she?"

"Of course not. I myself had completely forgotten all about it. Only members of my family know about it unless — no, that would not be in keeping with his character. Anyway, that brings me to the other point I was about to make in regard to our relationship. Some months ago, something happened which had a tremendous effect on both of us but let me come to that later."

"So let's assume that up to last night, she was unaware of your feelings for her..."

"There's no evidence to show that even last night she interpreted my actions correctly. She could have attributed them to my caddish nature."

"Let's just assume it for the sake of argument."

"So, all right, let's assume. I've sometimes been tempted to make a clean breast of it but it wouldn't have worked."

"Why not? What's the obstacle?"

"As I said earlier on, the introduction of a new element in our relationship changed it completely." He stopped and sighed heavily before going on. "This girl, Cassandra, is Ray's girlfriend."

"Raymond? Yes, I can see that would constitute an impasse from your point of view," James said. He looked at his friend sympathetically. "But I thought Raymond was married, in fact I distinctly remember attending his wedding, was it seven or eight years ago?" Not that matrimony, holy or

- otherwise, ever deterred anybody from an extramarital game anyway, he thought wryly.

"He and his wife are separated."

"Then he plans to marry Cassandra?" The situation's even more hopeless than I thought, James mused.

"I doubt that," Bevis stated flatly, and his friend wondered whether his certainty was based on factual evidence or unwillingness to accept the unacceptable.

"He hasn't shown any signs towards that end so far. Belinda, his wife is bad news all round and would do everything to stop that happening, including using their only child to give her greater bargaining power: Ray's inordinately attached to his son. No, I don't think he'd divorce Belinda to marry Cassandra," Bevis added slowly, reflectively.

"I thank God there were no offspring to my short marriage," James stated, "but I'm diverting. Let's see what we've got: we know how things stand between you and Cassandra, which I suspect's the cause of the buildup of emotional pressure behind your relapse. Briefly then, your long repressed coveting of your brother's woman came to the fore when she was served to you on a gold plate, so to speak. You would have hardly been human if you had not felt any temptation. But being the gentleman you are, you opted for further repression. Do I read you correctly so far?"

"More or less."

"Well, then, you let this pressure build up to such a level that it had to be released somehow. That's when your subconscious decided to step in and take control. In medical terms, this is known as an interaction of the body and the mind. It's generally accepted by all branches of medicine that thought processes and emotional reactions alter the functions of the body tissues, but you don't want to hear all that baloney. What I'm trying to prove to you is that there's no cause for alarm. The condition's not chronic or retrogressive. Once the pressure is released, the constraints extirpated, I don't doubt that was done in your case, however inadvertently, the cause will be eradicated. But as I mentioned at the beginning, this is not my field. If you wish, I can put you in touch with somebody more qualified to allay your fears."

"No, my friend, I have every confidence in you. What I needed most was a willing ear to make sense of my jumbled fears. You've done more than that."

"Fine. Let's finish off then. We've established cause and effect; it now remains to find a permanent remedy. Since you don't seem predisposed to join in the race for the fair Cassandra, the only practical solution I can offer by way of suggestion is that you find a substitute. I know this sounds rather inept, I mean you don't need me to tell you that, you must have considered the option already. What I'm trying to do is give credence to your perhaps half-formed thoughts and ideas. You and Jane had something good going, I thought? I don't imagine it would be too much of a hardship trying to love her."

"Jane's all right but ..."

"She's not Cassandra?" James cut him short with a twinge of irony.

"Let's say she's not the right girl for me. I wish I believed in kismet. Then I would sit back and wait for it to be fulfilled and if Jane was it, then there would be no more to be said. But you know me, James, I don't kindly take to defeat and I hate compromise even as a last resort. Don't get me wrong," he hastily added when he saw something like surprise on the other's face. "This is not meant to slight Jane in any way. She's a fine girl and with the right kind of man, she can make a wonderful wife. But she's not for me: I'd make her miserable for the rest of her life."

"What you actually mean is that she's not your type? I wonder. Sometimes a little pragmatism helps in responding to the challenges of this world, you know. Idealism went out at the turn of the century. So either go after Cassandra with all you're worth or—but I think I've stuck out my neck as far as I dare. Now you have my permission to tell me off like 'physician, heal thyself first' et cetera."

"The only thing I want to say is that I appreciate your help very much. With your permission, which you've already granted, I wish not to be uncomplimentary but personal and offer a piece of advice too. It's been about two years since you and Helen split up, what are your future marital plans? Contrary to all these aphorisms drummed into our ears daily, women are not all the same. It's high time you put your unfortunate experience behind you and picked up your shield again. A doctor, like a church minister, needs a wife to protect him from all those predatory female clients."

"Every man needs a female companion on a permanent basis, including you, Bevis. Actually," the doctor went on more soberly, "I've been giving the matter a lot of thought lately but I'm still plagued by memories of my experience with Helen.

"Rightly or wrongly, I believe that failure for a man to hold the love of a woman is a reflection on his manhood. I'm looking for somebody capable of repairing my punctured ego, if I may use that euphemistic phrase. Meantime, I've not exactly taken to the mountains. I'm still capable of appreciating women, I enjoy their company and even admire a few. But I can take them or leave them. In truth, we're very much alike; we're both looking for Miss Perfect."

"While the Miss Perfects might be looking for the Mr Perfects whose images we don't measure up to?" Bevis put in.

"Right. And so the search goes on *ad infinitum* while we depreciate in

110

value with every passing year," James added, smiling a little as he cradled his potbelly.

Bevis' eye wandered to the wall clock: the time was quarter to nine. "I promised to send Cassandra transport at about this time. Do you mind if I trespass on your kindness further and borrow your driver, James?"

"Not at all. I'll track him down for you. It's his day off but I'm sure he's still around. Meantime, come and make yourself at home in the dining room. Judging by the clutter, áll should be in readiness. After that, a brisk game of tennis for an hour or so is indicated. Doctor's orders."

"Thank you, doctor. I'll do as you suggest. Here're my keys. Tell Muyinde to get his instructions from Cassandra as to her destination," Bevis impassively added. His friend eyed him keenly for a moment, started to say something but changed his mind and left him frowning.

Chapter Six

As soon as Cassandra entered her office that Monday morning, she knew it was going to be one of those days. The pile of files on her desk immediately brought on a colic attack, and on checking her desk diary, she saw marked down two appointments with exacting authors which she had completely forgotten about.

About nine thirty, when she was beginning to make inroads into the heap before her, the intercom summoned her to Ndiwalala's office for an unscheduled editorial meeting – all typical of a Monday morning. But this was the one day she craved peace and solitude.

"Well, ladies and gentlemen, that's about all for today unless you have something else to add," Mr Ndiwalala said an hour later. Nobody seemed inclined to prolong the meeting. "Good. The meeting is adjourned. Incidentally, I want you to handle Mr Ekoch when he comes at eleven, Cassandra. When are you meeting with Model Printers, Collin?"

"This morning at eleven. After that I'm expected at AAFDOL for the meeting scheduled for two o'clock this afternoon."

"Looks like you have your hands full for today." Turning to Cassandra, "Don't forget to impress upon Mr Ekoch the importance of this joint venture with IMS, but, and this is the crux of the matter, leave him in no doubt about the impossibility of paying part of his royalties abroad. Apart from the intricacies involved, it would be contravening exchange control regulations. Do you think you can handle it?"

The audacity of the man! Does he think I'm an idiot? Cassandra fumed silently. Aloud she said sarcastically, "All I have to do is remember the salient points you've just outlined, sir."

Mr Ndiwalala eyed her sharply, not sure whether she was serious or making fun of him. "I don't have to remind you," he went on stiffly, "that though this

112

particular author's thorny, he produces best-sellers and is, therefore, our bread and butter."

"I promise to handle him with kid gloves, Mr Ndiwalala," Cassandra declared solemnly, inviting another dubious glance from her boss.

* * *

Of Heroes and Bandits. The words swam before Cassandra's eyes crazily for some time but her disciplined mind eventually overcame her riotous emotions, making it possible for her to concentrate on her work. By the time Mr Ekoch came, she was ready for him and able to bring him into line with their viewpoint.

"Oh, how I hate Mondays!" Marie sighed, dropping in the chair just vacated by Mr Ekoch.

"If you have a story to tell, tell it and scoot," Cassandra said belligerently. "Sorry, Marie. I'm just longing to take it out on somebody and you conveniently presented yourself."

"Just had a dose of the chief's company, I presume?"

"You presume right."

"An editorial or a pow-wow between the two of you lovebirds?"

"Don't push it, Marie," Cassandra warned. "I can easily get off with 'while of unsound mind', you know. I've just had Ekoch too."

"And you're having me now, poor you. Actually I stopped by to ask whether a decision on *Politics of the Gun* has been made. The file is not in the registry and I'm meeting Kareeba this afternoon."

"Wait a minute, I seem to recall seeing it on Wilson's desk..." After a short search... "Yes, here it is. Let me mark it to you first ... why do you want it?"

"I want to know whether his manuscript has made it to this year's publishing list. The author is coming to discuss the cover illustration with me."

"But surely that's a bit premature even if we were going to publish his work?"

"Well, you know prospective authors, they are like expecting mothers – all a twitter at the word go. So how was your weekend? How's Mellie? Dan and I almost dropped in yesterday but weren't sure whether you'd be around."

"I was in actually, most of the day anyway. I ... get it for me please," referring to the ringing phone.

"LI, can I help you?" Marie automatically intoned the standard jingle and listened, her mouth opening into a wide, wolfish grin. "I'm afraid I'm not the one, but if you hang on a tick, I'll put your angel on ... for you." She extended the receiver to Cassandra.

"Thank you. And now you can take the file and disappear."

"Sure, angel, have fun," Marie said, picking up the file and going out of the room.

"Have I got the right person this time?" Raymond asked, his voice quivering with laughter.

"If it's me, Cassandra, you want."

"Have I ever wanted anybody else since I met you?" he declared, sobering up immediately.

"Aaaahaah," Cassandra grunted noncommittally.

"How effusive you sound this morning, darling! Absolutely titillating."

Cassandra thought she detected a trace of mockery in his voice and hastened to explain, "I'm sorry, Ray, I'm a bit fussed this morning."

"I understand. Mondays are like that. That's why I thought the sound of your voice'd act as an antidote to the grayness of mine."

"You flatterer! But it's heavenly to hear your voice too, Ray."

"Would I be presuming too much if I suggested lunch?"

"That sounds lovely but I thought you had an appointment with Steve's doctor?"

"In the afternoon. I must see you, Cassandra, before then."

"You sound desperate, what is it, Ray?"

"If you don't know the answer to that, then perhaps I better collect you right now and start enlightening you."

"Oh, Ray! One o'clock?"

"One's fine. Till then, sweetheart."

After she had replaced the phone, Cassandra allowed herself the luxury of a few minutes' retrospection on the events of the last couple of days, in particular the night before with Raymond, which exercise made further concentration on her work next to impossible.

She had spent a good deal of that Sunday morning pondering Bevis' cryptic note, which she still carried in her bag. Although her instincts had pushed for an outright denial of the implications it contained, the more she examined the matter the less confident she became of her ability to consign the whole affair to the rubbish heap. She even came to accept, albeit reluctantly, that she must have unconsciously created the impression that she was in accord with Bevis' actions, prompting the remorse in him afterwards. But even so, why did he feel he was wholly to blame? It did not make sense.

Fortunately for her, at home everybody was preoccupied with her sister's affairs to notice her sombre mood. "I intend to apply for letters of administration immediately," Gavin told his audience. "Horace made a perfectly tenable will. So I don't expect any major problems. The other party would be foolhardy to lodge a claim."

114

"Did Horace make any provisions for his parents in the will?"

"He did and quite generous ones too. He bequeathed to them his up-country property and a hefty financial settlement. I don't think they have cause for complaint. The problem, I suspect, stems from some disgruntled relatives who wrongly believe that they've been diddled out of their rightful inheritance."

"According to our African customs...,"

"African customs be blowed!" Gavin cut in inelegantly.

"Do you think..."

Here Cassandra stopped paying attention and turned her mind to the evening ahead which she was half-dreading, half-looking forward to.

* * *

"What's the matter, Cassandra?" Raymond asked as soon as he took one look at her closed face.

"What do you mean? What makes you think there's something wrong with me?"

"Hey, I'm sorry, I asked a simple question. I've known you long enough to know when you're not yourself." He gave her another speculative look before he went on, "Look, if you're still brooding about yesterday, I want to talk about that."

"I don't want to talk about yesterday," she almost snapped.

"Then I'm right," he said quietly. "But we cannot avoid the subject of my son forever. So let's talk about it openly now. First of all, I want you to know that I did not mean to put you on some kind of trial, believe me."

"I believe you but listen, Ray..."

"No, you listen to me," he silenced her with unusual vehemence. "Come and sit beside me here," he invited in a gentler voice and made room for her on the settee. "I want to talk with you, not at you across a sea of carpet. Good, now let me go ahead with what I started to say. I love you very much, Cassandra. I guess you know that?" She nodded, wondering where this was leading to. It was not what she had been expecting, so guilt-ridden was she that she could not help jumping on the defensive. "I spent the whole night worrying about you, about us," Raymond went on. "And regretting what happened yesterday."

"There's no need to blame yourself, Ray. You could not have foreseen Steve's reaction to me."

"True enough. Anyway, I think it's high time I put you in the picture about how things stand with me. I know that you must have often wondered why I don't divorce Belinda."

"That's entirely your business, Ray," Cassandra put in quickly. Perversely, now that the moment she had longed for was at hand, she felt reluctant to face

115

it and wished for its indefinite postponement. "I don't want to come between you and your son."

"You won't come between me and Steve, Cassandra. Sure, Steve's important to me, but so are you. Yesterday was an eye-opener for me; it made me realise how unfair I've been to you, expecting you to take me at my face value. Your future could be very affected by what is happening between us now, or so I flatter myself thinking it could. So I propose to put all my cards on the table and let you make your choice."

"I made my choice six months ago, Ray, remember? It was not an easy choice for me but I've never regretted it. If I felt unhappy or dissatisfied with our relationship, I'd not hesitate to end it." She stopped and examined her statement for any falsehoods but found none of any weight. It was true that she had sometimes longed for a straightforward relationship with a promise of some permanence in it but she did not let it spoil her pleasure in the present until she came face to face with reality mirrored in the accusing eyes of a little boy. Then her confidence ebbed and a lot of uncertainties set in. But now, with his eyes watching her eagerly, she felt that this was not the time for sombreness. "Tonight," she continued softly, "I don't want to have to deal with weighty issues and make wise decisions, Ray. I want to feel silly and wanton; I want you to wave your magic wand and carry me into dreamland where I can lose myself completely. I have missed you, darling, haven't you missed me?"

"I've missed you too, immeasurably. It's been a long time. Come closer, angel, we have a lot of ground to cover." But even after taking her in his arms, he remained still, as his earlier impression of something not being quite right persisted.

"Ray?" she stirred restlessly.

"Still with you, sweetheart," he responded and shook himself out of his uneasiness. "I have an idea, let's dine out and relax a bit."

"Why do I get the feeling that you don't want to be alone with me tonight?" Cassandra queried him, half-teasingly.

"Do you want to bet on that?"

"I'm not a betting woman but you can go ahead and prove me wrong."

Sometime later, as she stood gazing out of the window at the darkening sky, and hoping that it would not rain, her thoughts once again leapt to the previous evening with Bevis. She remembered, with amazing clarity, everything that had passed between them, however insignificant; everything except the unrecorded incident which had been monopolising her thoughts most of the day and continued to intrude on her persistently.

She turned to look at the sleeping man, wondering whether she had succeeded in allaying his suspicions, but could read nothing on his tranquil face, so uncannily like his brother's in sleep. *

Wincing, she turned back to the window and pressed her face against the cold steel bars. It was going to rain after all; the evening was unusually hot and humid for September. She carefully unfastened one of the windows and pushed it slowly back to let in a bit of fresh air but it squeaked a bit, disturbing the sleeping man behind her. "Are you all right?" he asked groggily.

Cassandra let the curtain fall and without answering, turned and walked back to the bed where she perched herself on the edge, watching him.

"What's wrong?" Raymond asked again, groping for her hand.

"Nothing. I want to go back early but I didn't want to disturb you."

"What's the time? Why do you want to go back so early?"

"Two reasons. One, I'm expected back and two, I don't like you driving late at night."

"Still haunted by last night's events?"

"Last night's events?" she echoed with instinctive alarm, but almost immediately realised that he was referring to the military disturbances while she was allowing feelings of guilt to override her mind. Guilty? Certainly not! She was more sinned against than anything else, so why carry on as if she had connived with Bevis? "Oh you mean the confrontation at Mbuya?"

"Yes. There wasn't any other, was there?" He looked at her speculatively for some time before he said, "I still think we should have a serious talk about yesterday. I want you to know my reasons for opting for a certain course of action. The..."

"We've already agreed that tonight..." Cassandra started to say but he cut her short with, "That was before I realised how deeply you had taken this business of Steve to heart."

"You have it wrong, Ray. If I look preoccupied, it's because I have other matters on my mind. Matters that have nothing to do with you and me."

"What are these matters, Cassandra, against which our relationship seems so trifling?" he asked, propping himself against the headrest the better to observe her.

"Don't sound so harsh, Ray. It's not like you." The two stared at each other, with Raymond showing no signs of relenting, until Cassandra was forced to go on. "The problems I'm talking about are not more important than our personal concerns but they are more pressing."

"Such as...?"

"Such as the death of my sister's husband," she said. A little more gently she added, "I know Mellie has been putting on a brave show but I don't think she's all that cool inside, and this stupid will is not helping matters."

"Good God, Cassandra," Raymond exclaimed, highly amused, "trust you to talk disparagingly of a fortune everybody else finds impressive." He studied her indignant face, thinking how incongruous within the context of the modern girl she was. She claimed to be ambitious and desirous of reaching the top, but the top of what if not of the influential rich set?

"I suppose you think I'm naive or fake?" Cassandra charged, correctly guessing at his thoughts. "I don't despise wealth *per se* but I think the way people fight over property like dogs fighting over a bone is disgraceful. If you want to live a comfortable life, why don't you go out and work instead of waiting for somebody to die so that you can scramble for his possessions?" she retorted censoriously, sounding very much like her old self: impatient and unsympathetic of human failings, Raymond thought, heaving a sigh of relief.

"These are difficult times, Cassandra, and lucrative employment for the majority of people is very hard to come by," he explained tolerantly. "Our shilling, as you know, is not worth the paper it's printed on. So dead men's fortunes are easy pickings now and have been from time immemorial. It's unfortunate that up to now nobody has seen it fit to reconcile the customary practices and the civil laws governing inheritance. The inherent discrepancies still allow for the exploitation and improper grabbing of property, very often leaving the immediate family almost destitute."

"What does the law say exactly? I mean, how's the property supposed to be shared out? How much is the wife entitled to?" Cassandra asked with interest.

"If I remember correctly," Raymond said cautiously, "the wife's entitled to 15%... hey, wait, I didn't make the law!" He broke off to protest at her accusing look.

"What happens to the rest of the 85%?" she demanded.

"Let me see ... 75% goes to the children of the deceased and the remaining to the rest of the dependents. That's of course when somebody dies intestate."

"But that's unfair to the wife who might have contributed equally to the acquiring of the property!" Cassandra cried indignantly.

"I agree but that's the law. Most of these laws were made a long time ago and are foreign-originated."

"Don't!"

"Don't what?

"Don't give me that nonsensical excuse! This habit of blaming all our mistakes and shortcomings on imperialists should stop. I mean we've been independent for twenty two years for heaven's sake, why can't we redress these so-called blunders of theirs to suit our own requirements?"

"I doubt whether you'd be happier with African-orientated laws," Raymond remarked dryly. "Don't forget that according to African traditions, a woman's no better than a chattel, bought and paid for. The customary laws we have don't favour the woman because they are more ancient than the imported laws, having been made to suit the society as it was then."

"I know," Cassandra snapped, "by men."

"Well, why don't women of your type get together and agitate for the changes you think would serve your present-day needs better?"

"We shall, don't worry."

"I'm not worried. As far as we men are concerned, things could stay as they are for all we care. In fact, we shall fight you tooth and nail to preserve the status quo. I say, how did we get into this stuff of women's rights and what not?"

"Horace's will, the late Horace, that is," she added with a catch in her voice.

"Hey, easy, angel! It takes time to accept tragedies of this nature," Raymond soothed.

"I didn't even like him," Cassandra wailed.

"I know. Go easy on the guilt complex, okay? You probably weren't the only one. I didn't know him very well but from what I've heard, he seemed an insufferable whatnot."

"How can you say that?" Cassandra rounded on him, making a complete about-turn.

"I'm sorry," Raymond said, his unease about her nervous state resurfacing. "So Gavin's the executor of the will," he said, switching the subject. "Quite interesting. If Mellie's the only beneficiary, I don't see any major problem in having the will probated. That's a layman's view of course."

"Gavin's of the same opinion actually and thinks the relatives are using intimidating techniques to make Mellie relinquish her claim on the estate. He doesn't think they'll go as far as taking legal action. We shall know soon enough anyway."

"Are you still set on going back?"

"I must. People keep dropping in and it would be unkind to let Tonia cope with all that on her own."

"I'm sorry to be so insensitive but I hate to share you even with your own family." And I don't, Cassandra thought, giving him an unreadable look.

* * *

At Luzzi, Cassandra found her mother waiting for her, a huffy expression on her face. "Mama, how nice to see you back so soon!" she exclaimed, rushing to embrace an older, plumper version of herself.

119

"Not soon enough from what I hear," Mrs Mutono replied dryly.

"And what do you hear, Mama? You know how dreadfully things get exaggerated on the bush telegraph." She kicked off her shoes and sat beside her. "Where's everybody?" she asked the hovering Tonia.

"The party broke up soon after you left. Alex has gone back to college of course and Gavin..." Here she stopped and seemed to swallow something like a lump in her throat which Cassandra recognised as anger at being deserted by her husband, during what, in all fairness, should still be their honeymoon. "Gavin," Tonia went on, "has gone to meet with his associate over this business of the will. And Mellie, believe it or not, has gone back to the hospital to work. She said she needed some distraction. I was afraid you might also decide to spend the night with-eh... Marie," she added ineptly, looking fearfully at the old woman. But Mrs Mutono was paying little attention to their conversation as she looked around, bewildered.

"This doesn't look like a house in mourning to me," she observed.

"Well, what did you expect to find? A log fire in the compound and wailing women inside the house?" Cassandra asked dryly.

"I wish you wouldn't adopt that tone with me, Cassandra," her mother complained. "I at least expected to find Mellie and Gavin here. Certain decencies must be upheld even in your ultra-modern society."

"I stand corrected, Mama, but we can't mourn Horace forever," Cassandra articulated slowly as if to a half-witted child. Tonia deemed it prudent to withdraw at this juncture. "Who told you about what happened, Mama?'

"The bush telegraph, as you call it, since none of you thought it important enough to come with firsthand information," her mother told her reprovingly.

"Gavin came back the day before yesterday. So whom did you expect to go gallivanting around the countryside, Mellie or myself? It's only a few days since Horace was buried, you know."

"I understand. How's Mellie taking it?"

"Bearing up. How's Daddy, Lionel and Aunt Sophie?"

"Lionel's busy preparing for his finals but your father's back's playing up a bit. That's why he couldn't come to look into this dreadful affair himself."

"There's nothing to look into, Mama. Gavin has everything under control."

"I'm talking about the appalling death of this so-called husband of Mellie but you refer to it as if it were an outbreak of some sort. Is there a reason for this?"

"Not exactly," Cassandra said hesitantly, wondering whether to tell her mother about the will and all the hullabaloo it was causing. "There's a little bickering about the will Horace left. Why don't we go to the bedroom where I can tell you all I know? You look a little tired, have you eaten?"

"Tonia gave me some food but I was too tired and worried to eat. Let's go to the bedroom."

"A minute: let me tell Tonia you're retiring." In the dining room, the table was already laid for supper. "Goodness, Tonia, you haven't eaten?"

"No, I just served mother." She used the appellation awkwardly and Cassandra smiled in sympathy. "Poor Tonia, what a frightful welcome into the Mutono family!"

"I'm quite adaptable really, I'll cope. Do you think she'd like a cup of tea or something before she goes to bed?"

"Mama does not subscribe to the 'something' but a cup of tea might help to ease her into sleep. I'm not up to keeping awake until the small hours talking. Don't disturb yourself, though, Jossi knows how she likes it."

"I'll make it: it's high time I learnt too," Tonia remarked with unnecessary intensity, Cassandra thought.

* * *

"So how much of this affair have you been told, Mama?" Cassandra asked her mother soon after joining her in what was generally known as the 'girls' room'.

"For the sake of expedience, we'll assume I know nothing. So start from the beginning and tell me everything. Was Mellie actually married to this gangster?"

"Horace, a gangster, whatever gave you that impression, Mama? You saw him at Gavin's wedding, did he look like a gangster to you?"

"Do they wear badges? Besides, I saw hundreds of young men. How was I supposed to know which one was Horace?" Mrs Mutono retorted.

"Well, you can take it from me that Horace was not a gangster and don't let Mellie hear you call him that."

"I'm sure I'm not all that callous."

"I'm just cautioning you. Horace was an ordinary young man who happened to be luckier than most in that he was rich. And also unlucky enough to fall victim of evil forces."

"Get on with the tale, Cassandra," her mother urged her impatiently.

"Okay, listen then and I'll tell you what I can." And so she told her mother, as succinctly as possible, about the marriage of her eldest daughter, of the untimely death of the-son-in-law she never knew, and of the legacy which would make Mellie quite rich when all the fuss was over.

"What kind of business did this man do?" Mutono, whose fixation about Horace as a man of dubious reputation was not easily dispelled, asked.

"I'm not quite sure," Cassandra confessed, regretting having taken so little

121

interest in Horace's affairs. "I know he owned a number of properties, both commercial and residential. I think he was also involved in import-export trade. But a gangster, Mama, would Mellie have married him?"

"Oh do stop harping on that, child, it was just a slip of the tongue," Mrs Mutono remarked wearily. "But if he was so honourable, why this shilly-shallying about their marriage?"

"That's a question only Mellie can answer. I'm sure she and Horace had their reasons. What Mellie needs right now, though, is comforting, and not upbraiding, Mama," Cassandra warned.

"I'm sure I know my duty, Cassandra, I don't need guidelines from you on how to handle my daughter. I'll do whatever I think necessary for her own good. Talking of duty," she added after a short awkward silence, "I think I'd be failing you if I didn't mention that there are rumours circulating about you too."

"What rumours, Mama? I assure you you don't have to worry about me. I can take care of myself," Cassandra said loftily, dismissing the subject.

"Just like that? Well, I have news for you Miss High and Mighty: I can't help worrying about you; it's been like that ever since you were born." She was quiet after the outburst, struggling to control her anger. She found Cassandra's arrogant manner infuriating. But at the same time, she felt apprehensive because she knew that denying reality does not make one less vulnerable. "Oh Cassandra, why?" she cried, abandoning her authoritative, dignified approach. "I had hoped for better things for you."

"What things and why me in particular?" Cassandra asked warily.

"Well, for one, I thought you had better sense than to get entangled with a married man," her mother answered bluntly.

"Obviously your informant omitted to mention that this married man is also separated from his wife."

"Is he going to marry you then?"

"Is marriage the only thing going for women, Mama? Why aren't you happy with Mellie then?"

"That's entirely a different matter. It's the underhand way they went about it we object to. But for you, a married man, what's the point? Who'll want to marry you after that?"

"Would it surprise you to learn that I don't plan to get married? Marriage's not everything, you know. You have a couple of unmarried sisters yourself who look just fine to me, happier than some of the married women I know, as a matter of fact."

"You really think so? I could tell you a tale or two about your 'happy' unmarried aunts."

122

"But there are many married women who never stop wishing they were single again," Cassandra persisted. "Haven't you, for instance, ever regretted giving up your job to become a full-time housewife?"

"Why should I? I have everything a woman could ever want."

"A husband, a home, children, the ultimate fulfilment for every woman," Cassandra enumerated with a sneer. "You know, Mama, you live in the Dark Ages. Today, women have more going for them than the subservient role designed for them by men. Marriage is no longer the only goal. I'm not saying that marriage has no purpose to serve, it has. It's still an honourable institution but it has ceased to be a must for every woman. Single women are no longer looked upon by society with pity, at best, and as misfits, at worst. Quite a number of them are, in fact, happy, and living meaningful lives."

"I can't dispute that: we're all made differently and have different needs. But I still maintain that if this man truly loved you and you loved him, you'd both wish to marry and spend the rest of your lives together. That's the test of true love."

"We're talking about marriage, not love, Mama. I don't have to marry him in order to live with him, you know," Cassandra retorted, shocking not only her mother but also herself. She had never considered the idea at all before. The words slipped out in defiance intended to shock her mother into silence.

"Ah, the truth at last! Now you listen to me, Cassandra. I've no intentions of telling you how to live your life: you're old enough to decide that for yourself. You also have the right to decide whether you throw it away or not. But as your parent, I should be failing in my duty if I didn't try to correct you where I thought you were going astray or advise you. I'd hate to see you hurt, Cassandra, especially when it's not necessary. You've so much potential for happiness and fulfilment. All you have to do is reach out in the right direction," her mother pleaded emotionally, for in this second daughter of hers, she had hoped to realise her own unfulfilled dreams and desires.

Silently, Cassandra got up and went to stand by the window, her back towards her mother. There was silence in the room for some time. Mrs Mutono's eye was trained on the neat, erect figure, wondering whether she had not gone a little too far in belabouring the truth. She experienced the familiar emptiness in the pit of her stomach and chafed at her impotence to save her daughter the pains and sufferings she knew lay in store for her. She ached to take her in her arms, hold her, and comfort her, but of course Cassandra was no longer a little girl. The only way she could help her was to try and talk and talk, in the hope that a little of what she said would filter through. Looking at the stiff back

123

now, she could not help wondering what was going through that arrogant head of hers.

What Cassandra was feeling was a mixture of emotions, anger not excepting. She felt annoyed with people presuming to know what was best for her as if she was an imbecile. What she was doing was for herself and not for anybody else and only she would bear the consequences. Anyway, her mother was wrong in thinking Raymond was merely using her as a source of amusement. If he were, he would not have been so frank with her right from the beginning, knowing that by doing so, he risked losing her. She had always known their parting was inevitable and accepted it, initially with stoicism and lately not without pain. But there was nothing in that to prove anything to his discredit.

Her mother seemed to guess at some of the thoughts passing through her mind when she said, "I wish I knew this young man of yours." She waited for a reaction but when none came, she went on, "I've no doubt he's an admirable young man, but he's also a married man, Cassandra. If you were foolish enough to do what you said, you'd live to regret it. It may appear tragically romantic at first, two young people desperately in love, discovering each other too late but that state of affairs rarely lasts. What will happen then when the magic's gone? I'll tell you; pain, regret, heartache, even recriminations. Is it worth it all, your good name and your future? Think about it, Cassandra."

Cassandra turned abruptly and faced her, her cool face hiding her feelings, and said in a hard brittle voice, "Don't generalise, Mama. People have different attitudes to different situations, and what might appear like a tragedy to you might be heaven to me."

"I don't doubt that in the least, Cassandra. All I want for you is to be happy in whatever you choose to do," her mother replied, feeling her way more cautiously. She could, as a mother, be blunt and forthright; it was her privilege. But she did not want to prejudice her cause by appearing to be meddlesome, the typical 'mother knows best', anathema to all growing children. "But," she continued after rearranging her thoughts, "I want you also to know that your hurts and your pains are my hurts and pains too. That's what parental love's all about; indeed that's what real love's about."

"Thank you, Mama," Cassandra said with a deep sigh. "I'm sorry we don't see eye to eye on these matters, but as I've already said, you have no reason to worry about me. I'm still the same egoistic child whose eccentricities caused you such despair. I'm not about to change for anybody, or do anything, especially if it compromises my future."

"Cassandra...," Mrs Mutono, still not satisfied by Cassandra's offhand manner started to say but her daughter silenced her with, "No more talk tonight. You're tired, I'm tired, why don't we shelve everything for another time? I'll

124

see if that cup of tea's ready and bring it to you. Then I'll see if I can locate Mellie and tell her you're here."

"What about Gavin?"

"Gavin can keep. You don't have to wait up for him, you'll have a chance to talk to him in the morning."

"I hope you understand, Cassandra, why I've had to be a little harsh in my approach. My intention was not to hurt you but to stop you from getting hurt," Mrs Mutono pleaded, arresting Cassandra's progress to the door.

"You've already explained that, Mama," Cassandra replied, almost curtly. Then, seeing the hurt expression in her mother's eyes she relented and went back and sat beside her on the bed saying, "I know you care about what happens to me and want the best for me. But I'm not a child anymore, and I don't want you to worry about me unduly. Trust me, Mama," she added placatingly, "I wont let you down, I promise." But the last words came out shakily and Cassandra felt tears run down her cheeks unbidden. Her mother responded tenderly and encouraged her to expurgate herself of whatever grieved her soul with floods of tears so long held in check. Cassandra cried so rarely, even as a child, that to see her eyes wet was almost a welcome experience to her mother.

After a few minutes, the bout ceased as suddenly as it had started. "I guess you know now I don't live in a fool's paradise," Cassandra drawled with a wan smile.

"I now know that you're grown up and I don't need to worry about you." Her mother patted her on the back with affection. "All will be well, daughter, if you keep your head."

When Cassandra came back a few minutes later with the tea, her mother was fast asleep, her face calm and relaxed.

* * *

Cassandra was aroused from her reverie by a loud thump on her door which heralded the entry of their office messenger, Jimmy.

She looked at Collin's memorandum about the Writers/Publishers Workshop due in a month's time for which she and Collin had been selected to represent LI. In addition to representatives from other publishing firms, literary societies, booksellers and other interested organisations in the country, participants were expected to come from East and Central Africa. Various papers would be presented and discussed, and LI had been asked to write on **The Future of the Publishing Industry in Developing Countries**. The topic was vast and challenging and from the lengthy loose minute on the file, it was apparent Collin meant to give it fair treatment.

125

There was an appreciable number of women participants, especially writers, and Cassandra got to know a few quite well, in particular a lady from Kitwe, Zambia, whose book entitled **Born under the Wrong Star** received moderate acclaim. They talked long and exhaustively on the status of women in an African society, their problems and limitations in a 'man's world'. "It still is, you know, in spite of human rights guarantees by the UN Charter," Olive Kalyafe averred.

"Don't I know it," Cassandra cried with feeling. Olive was much older than her but she had fresh and exciting views on a range of subjects although her hobbyhorse seemed to be the social injustices suffered by women the world over. "What remedial measures do you recommend?"

"The issue has many aspects. Firstly, there's the lack of awareness which must be tackled. Women must be sensitised about their rights, especially women in rural areas. Secondly, and maybe by far the most effective tool, is education. More women must have access to education. The numbers of female school-going children is still far below that of the boys. Personally I won't even consider numbers because we lag too far behind. I'd advocate for free primary education for girls to enable us to cover the gap. I don't know the situation here, but in Zambia women account for 51% of the 73% illiteracy rate."

"I imagine the situation is not much better here," Cassandra replied. "Tell me about your views on improving the women's lot. Do they have anything to do with your becoming a writer?"

"In a way ..."

"Yes?" Cassandra encouraged her eagerly.

"Oh, there's nothing remarkable about my life; it's the usual unsuccessful marriage, also childless, in my case. Then the emptiness, the nothingness... followed by the desperate need to find direction again, to fill the void. When I recovered from the tragedy of my marriage, I seriously thought about making a career out of writing. Yes, you could say that it's my tragic experiment with marriage which changed my entire perspective and enabled me to look at the fate of women globally rather than as an isolated experience of one single woman in Kitwe, Zambia. But what I wrote in the beginning could hardly rate as literature. I was still too full of anger and my first flirts with the pen came out as ravings of an unbalanced mind. But it helped to purge my mind of bitterness and self-pity. It was important that I relate my experience to other women's and refrain from personalising the issue. As a matter of fact, this is my first publication. I'm just a late starter."

"But a very promising one, in my opinion."

"I guess I'm lucky and it's to Heinemann that I owe it all. You could say it discovered me after I had been turned down by all the local publishers. I have a file full of rejections weighing almost a kilo."

"Surely not! But wait a minute. I thought you told me your trip was sponsored by the Zambian Literary Society?"

"And so it was. Don't you know success begets success, Cassandra? Now that I've been acclaimed as a successful writer, all those who had not wanted to have anything to do with me can now afford to welcome me warmly into the fold."

"Don't sound so bitter, my dear, make use of the belated support to pile success unto success. I imagine you already have something else brewing, give a clue?"

"I better not until it takes shape, Cassandra, but I promise to give your firm first option when I'm ready."

"I guess that's good enough."

Two days later the workshop closed and it was back to the daily office routine for Cassandra. She, however, looked forward to the resumption of Raymond's companionship, although remembering the turbulence which had characterised the period following his son's illness, she decided she would be more circumspect this time.

Her mind briefly strayed to those two months, especially the day she first realised how much Raymond's child meant to him: much more than she herself did.

"Why 'pavilion'?" Cassandra remembered asking on that Thursday which she had marked as the turning point in their relationship.

After collecting her from the office, something unusual in itself, Raymond had driven straight to some hideout in the back streets with the inappropriate name of 'The Pavilion'.

It was a small, neat, double-storeyed building which structurally or otherwise bore no resemblance to a pavilion.

"Why 'pavilion'?" Raymond asked, his face breaking into a smile. "Quite catchy, isn't it? Conjures up images of wide open spaces, and cool long drinks under attractive shades."

"But that's a misrepresentation surely?" Cassandra argued.

"Perhaps, perhaps not, who cares? All the owner wants are patrons and you must admit they come in droves." Following the direction of his eye, Cassandra had to agree with him.

All the booths, which were made of bamboo with an intricate pattern, were full. They drank their tea in silence for some time and then Cassandra asked, "How's Steve?"

"Steve," he repeated with a heavy sigh.

"He's not well?" she inquired gently.

"To look at him, you wouldn't even know he was sick," he said frowning.

"He's sick then? What's he suffering from, what did the doctor say, Ray?" Cassandra cried, quite alarmed. She had never seen him like that before.

"The doctor called it leukopenia. He's ordered some more tests but he seems to think the first ones were conclusive."

"Is leuk – whatever you call it, the same as leukemia?"

"Apparently not. But it's also an infection of the blood which results from deficiency of white cells in the bloodstream."

"Is it very serious?"

"It's serious enough, even fatal if not treated early. The doctor seems to think an operation's indicated to remove the spleen which is the major agent in abetting the disorder."

"Oh, I'm sorry, Ray!" Cassandra cried, sharing in his pain and anxiety.

"Thank you. You know," he added reflectively after a short pause, "I've been doing a lot of thinking lately about a lot of things, especially my role as a ther. I don't deserve that honourable title."

"Don't be too hard on yourself, Ray. It's not your fault Steve's ill. People, young and old, fall sick all the time. It's part of our natural heritage."

"Even so, I can't help feeling guilty about it. There must have been times when Steve wanted me, cried out for me and I was not there to comfort him or drive away his childish fears."

God, I don't understand all this, Cassandra thought. "I don't think you've been negligent or remiss in any way. No father could be more indulgent or caring. I saw you together only once but I thought you were quite marvellous with him."

"Oh, Cassandra, you don't understand at all. I could afford to be all those things because it was only part-time, don't you see? The rest of the time I was free of responsibilities and able to follow my inclinations," he cried fiercely but Cassandra had a feeling he was repeating a litany of accusations levelled at him by his wife. "Now, do you see why I feel such a fraud?"

"Take it easy, darling. I do see what you mean, indeed I do," she assured him soothingly. "But you can now devote as much time as you wish to nursing him back to health, can't you? Surely your wife would not object to that."

"Oh yes, I intend to," he declared with relief. "In fact," he went on more cautiously, "that's what I wanted to talk to you about. We've decided, that is, I think in order for me to be fully involved in the nursing of Steve during the crisis, it's necessary for him and his mother to move back to my house. It'll make everything easier all round," he ended, avoiding her eye.

Cassandra was quiet for some time, digesting the meaning of his message.

128

"I see," she said quietly at last. "In actual fact you're saying it's all over between us, aren't you?"

"No, Cassandra, I'm not. This is only a temporary arrangement, until Steve's out of danger. But while the two are at Muyenga, it won't..."

"I understand perfectly, Ray," Cassandra interrupted. "You don't have to spell it out."

She marvelled at her ability to stay calm in the face of what amounted to being unceremoniously ditched. Well, it did not come as a surprise to her that faced with the choice between her and his son, he should choose the latter. It was quite commendable really, what any man worth the name would do. But it hurt all the same.

"Would it be possible to collect my stuff now?" She kept a few necessities at his place which she could easily bundle into her handbag. The sooner the break the better.

"You make me feel cold-blooded, Cassandra," he protested. "This need not affect our relationship. We'll keep in touch and meet whenever possible."

Cassandra raised her eyes and scrutinised his face to see whether he really believed what he was saying. She knew once his wife moved back into his house and his life, it would take a miracle to dislodge her. She had already sown the seed of guilt into his conscience, to nurture it to fruition would be child's play for a woman of her capabilities.

"Cassandra...," Raymond started to say, his voice pleading, but she stopped him with a 'please don't' look. She did not think she could take more insults to her intelligence or that her wounded heart could endure more blows. "Alright, let's go."

Just before they reached Luzzi, he stopped the car and once again tried pleading with her, saying, "Please try to understand, Cassandra, that I could not have acted otherwise even at the risk of being misunderstood by you."

"I've already said that I understand, Ray, what more do you want me to say?"

"Do you really? Look, bear with me a little longer and I'll explain my position. Steve's all I have in this world; he's my only child. If anything were to happen to him ...Lord!" he groaned and stopped as if to go on demanded more courage than he possessed. After some moments of silence, he resumed, "I 've let him down once, I don't want to let him down again, especially when he's sick. Perhaps you think I'm pampering my oversized ego, and perhaps I am, I don't know. But there comes a time in a man's life when he needs to prove his worth as a man. I feel I've been given another chance to prove that I'm capable of being a worthy parent. To fail that test now would take something vital out of my life. You're a principled person, Cassandra, you wouldn't think

129

much of me if I turned my back on my responsibilities, would you?"

"There's no need to justify yourself to me, Ray," Cassandra remarked, managing to keep her feelings of desolation from showing, "as long as you're satisfied that you're doing what's right. We'll probably meet some day if the world doesn't end tonight."

"Don't sound so cynical, Cassandra, it's not like you. I'll keep in touch if I may, may I?"

"Do what your conscience tells you," Cassandra said curtly and got out of the car.

Chapter Seven

During the following days, Cassandra found herself yearning more and more for a place of her own where she could hide from the prying eyes of her family.

"I want your advice on how to get a place of my own," she asked Marie one day.

"Why the hurry to be on your own when the rate of insecurity's on the increase. Fighting with your sister-in-law already?" Marie asked, her flippant tone belying the concern she felt at the desperation visible in Cassandra's manner.

"No. My relations with Tonia are excellent and I want to keep them that way. But I've been considering the idea for some time now and lately I've come to realise that it's not only desirable but imperative too," Cassandra explained dispassionately.

"Oh, I see, big girl now needs privacy, et cetera. Okay, okay, I have a dirty mind," Marie interrupted herself to say at a chilly look from Cassandra. "You're serious, and so am I. Now, let's see....you want a place that's central enough, easily accessible and with our type of roads, the two requirements don't necessarily go together. But to go on, you want running water, electricity, relative security my dear, you're asking for the moon!"

"I realise it's not going to be easy but..." Cassandra shrugged.

"I have a better idea," Marie interrupted her excitedly. "Why don't you move in with me now so that when I vacate, you can take over the house? It belongs to the company as you know and your moving in now would give you an edge over other applicants."

"It sounds perfect. Have you set the date?"

"Tentatively, yes. But don't worry, I'm rarely in."

"That's not what I meant, Marie."

"I know. I'm just teasing. How's Prince Charming?" Marie asked, switching the subject.

"He's all right, I guess," Cassandra answered guardedly. "I don't get to see him very often these days. His son's sick."

"That's too bad. He's an only child, isn't he?"

"Yes," Cassandra answered, getting up. "I better get back to my office." Marie reserved her comment, divining problems of the heart.

Four days later, when Cassandra emerged from the tall building, she was surprised to see Raymond's car parked outside. She hesitated, not knowing whether to go on or flee. She had heard nothing from him since that day when he had so expediently disposed of her. A hot rush of anger at the memory made her head boil and she checked her steps a few paces away from the car and almost glared at him.

Raymond, whose eyes had been fixed on her since she appeared, guessed at the reason for her hesitancy. He uncoiled himself from the car and came to meet her. "I thought I'd give you a ride home."

"Really? How kind of you!" Cassandra drawled without making any attempt to enter the car. But the nearness and the lethal dark-brown eyes played havoc with her mental controls.

"Please?" he begged with a smile. The warning drums fell silent and Cassandra glided in.

"How's Steve?" she asked as soon as the car started moving.

"No change. He'll be operated on Monday."

"Is he admitted yet?"

"Yes. Can we pass through Muyenga, Cassandra? I need to talk to you."

Cassandra looked at him sharply. A sarcastic rejoinder as to whether his wife had given him permission was trembling on her lips when he forestalled her saying that Belinda was not staying with him. "It was never her intention to move back, just a ruse to keep me on a tight leash," he ended bitterly.

Cassandra tried to harden her heart but the pain and wretchedness mirrored in his face unnerved her. "I don't have to rush home," she said carefully.

At the front door, they were met by a screaming telephone inside the house. Raymond picked it up with shaking hands and Belinda's voice screeched at him, "Where have you been? I telephoned the office and was told you'd left early but you were not at home either. Where have you been?"

"Has something happened to Steve, Belinda?" he asked with panic when he managed to cut through her tirade.

"What more do you want to happen to him, hasn't enough happened already?" his wife retorted querulously.

"Then may I ask why you're hounding me like this? I wasn't aware I

132

needed your permission for every step I take. I told you this afternoon I'd be calling later in the evening, didn't I?"

"Oh forgive me, most High and Mighty One," Belinda parodied with irony. "I'm just a distracted mother whose only child lies on the brink of death and don't know what I'm doing most of the time. But of course I don't expect a superior being like you to understand vulgar emotions like parental love, fear and concern over a loved one. No, I don't."

"Are you finished?" Raymond asked through clenched jaws.

"No, I'm not, you bastard! I..." But Raymond slammed down the phone, giving her no chance to deliver more vitriols. ·

For some time, there was silence in the room as he stood quite still, his eyes glassy like a sleepwalker's, Cassandra thought. "Do you think these are the hands of a potential murderer?" he asked heavily, opening his clenched fists.

Cassandra, now as still as he, watched him quietly, her heart filled with anger and hatred for the other woman. She wondered why her type always resorted to insults and vulgarity to assuage their wounded egos. Although she had heard only Raymond's part of the conversation, she could easily guess that his wife, grieved by something, had let loose her wrath. She sincerely hoped she was not the cause.

"God," Raymond swore, bunching his hands into fists again. "I...I..." he brought them down on the table, making the telephone jump noisily.

"Hush, darling," Cassandra said, going to him and unclasping his hands. "Come and sit down and I'll make you something to calm you down." She led him to a chair and after handing him a glass of brandy, left him alone to regain his composure.

In the kitchen, Joseph grinned his welcome. "You've been away too long, Miss Cassandra," by which she understood she had been missed.

"Indeed I have, Joseph. What treat do you have for us tonight?" she asked, bending to peep in the oven where two tender chickens lay sizzling in fat. "Umm, smells good, looks good too."

"Your favourite, miss, ordered by the master himself," Joseph imparted importantly.

"The master, eh?" Cassandra remarked, wondering how Raymond could have been sure she would come. Either he had a poor opinion of her powers of resistance or an exaggerated faith in his own magnetism. Anyway, whichever, he was right and here she was as if nothing had happened between them. "What time does the master usually visit the hospital, Joseph?"

"After dinner, although at times I believe he passes there before coming home... Ah, you know about the little one being sick?"

"Yes, I know," Cassandra answered crisply, and firmly closed the kitchen door behind her.

At the entrance to the sitting room, she paused and quietly watched Raymond. He was sitting quite still, the fixed expression in his eyes well beyond her scope of comprehension. Some intuition made him turn and look in her direction but it seemed it took him some time to bring her into focus. Immediately he did, he got up and came to meet her, saying, "What can I say, Cassandra?"

"There's no need to say anything, Ray. How do you feel?" she asked, searching his face.

"Like a damned fool. Sorry about that. How about a drink?"

"I dare not, Ray. Mother'd take one sniff at me and consign me to purgatory. She's convinced that drink is the ruination of the young generation. She has discovered religion in her middle age." Abruptly Cassandra stopped when she realised she was jabbering.

"Are you okay?" Raymond asked.

"Sure," she said tightly, her anger at his taking her for granted returning. She glanced outside at the fast fading light and then pointedly checked her watch.

"I suppose you wouldn't consider spending the night?" Raymond asked, his eyes pleading. "I know I have no right to make demands on you but it would comfort me very much if you spent just tonight with me. Tomorrow is Saturday. Please?"

Cassandra looked away from him and gazed at her hands as she weighed the situation. All her instincts warned her against rekindling the flame between them but in spite of the resentment and sense of betrayal she felt, she knew she was still under his spell.

Her eyes turned to his face, looking for signs of knavery, of deceit but instead saw only the misery and despair, and the need to unburden himself.

"I'm afraid to spend the night alone," he confessed. Cassandra felt her chest contracting and knew she could not turn her back on him, whatever it cost her.

"I'll ring home and tell them not to expect me." As she got up to go to the telephone, he caught her hand saying, "Have I ever told you what an angel you are?"

"A few hundred times, could be more," she joked, her spirits lifting. "But if you still feel the need to drive the point home, I suggest you engrave it in gold and reserve it for my tombstone when I die." She was about to turn to go to the telephone when he jumped up, throwing off her hand as he cried hoarsely, "Don't talk about dying, not even in jest." He then moved away from her, his steps jerking and his breath coming in short gasps as if he had just run a marathon. Too surprised to say anything, Cassandra watched him mutely. At last she went to where he was standing with his face in his hands and said, "Ray? What is it? Please tell me," she added, urging gently.

"I'm sorry, I'm behaving like a prime candidate for the madhouse," he replied with a half-smile, seeming to come to grips with whatever was bothering him. Then abruptly, "Tell me, Cassandra, what do you know about dreams?"

"Well," Cassandra replied hesitantly, searching for a clue to his fitful manner, "nothing beyond the dictionary definition which says dreams are sequences of scenes and feelings occurring in the mind during sleep. On the other hand, Freud's interpretation is that dreams are unconscious impulses which pass from the unconscious to the conscious mind where they are revealed as dreams. Why do you ask?"

"I have this recurring dream night after night," he answered quietly. "The scene never varies in the slightest: I'm standing on the porch next to that variegated creeper, looking down a deep chasm. It's not wide, a meter or so, but inside it looks so dark and fathomless and very sinister." He stopped and swallowed, reliving the fear of his dream.

"Yes? What happens next?" Cassandra prompted.

"Across this rift is my son's stiff and shrivelled body lying in a coffin on the grass. And surrounding it a band of men, hammers in their hands, ready to drive in the last nail. Steve," he went on hoarsely, "raises his pathetic frail hand, calling to me to save him from death but I'm too terrified to jump over the narrow trench although I know that his life depends on my reaching him in time.

As I stand there, petrified with fear, the people around start jeering at me, hurling insults at me and calling me a selfish, despicable coward. They move in one body towards me, their voices raised high. At the same time the undertakers swing their hammers high, galvanizing me into instant action. I shut my eyes and plunge forward. Of course I fall in the pit and wake up terrified just before I hit the bottom. Although I know it's just a dream, I can't stop seeing Steve's huge frightened eyes accusing me." He stopped and shivered.

"Poor Ray, you must stop blaming yourself for Steve's illness or you'll get a nervous breakdown," Cassandra said, choosing her words carefully. She knew she was on slippery ground here. "Don't you see the nightmare and everything else are products of your own distorted mind, a projection of your own fears and imaginary guilt?"

"No, it's not like that," he muttered.

"Then what is it? Personally, I think that it is and unless you stop torturing yourself, you're not going to be of much help to a sick child. Children are

135

very sensitive to atmosphere and Steve'll absorb your fears and anxieties. Do you think that will help him? He needs you strong and confident, Ray, to infuse in him the will to fight for his life," Cassandra earnestly exhorted him. She was surprised at her own ability to cope and knew that with anybody else, she would not have had the patience or inclination. She based her rating of a man on moral and physical strength, among other qualities, and the greater the ability to withstand the rigours and exactitudes of life the greater the entitlement to esteem, in her opinion.

But although she didn't know it, and would have repudiated it if suggested, her ideas of a real man, and of Raymond in particular, verged on the romantic. What did she know of a man pursued by a nameless, inexplicable and inescapable fear of losing an only beloved child? What did she know of a guilt-ridden mind which welcomed mental flagellation as the only let up on feelings of self-doubt and self-contempt? But she was still young and still had a lot to learn about real life and real people. In a couple of years, perhaps even less, when nature had put on her the stamp of experience, something of a wiser, more mature woman would emerge.

Raymond had responded by shaking off his despondency and eagerly grasping at her words as if they were from the Book of Wisdom. "Perhaps there's something in what you're saying," he conceded. "I confess I've been rather introspective lately and I know that in a crisis like this, it can serve no purpose but to bog me down deeper into the mire of misery. I think you're my talisman, Cassandra, and I feel already cheered for having you here."

Later as she lay awake, she tried once more to bring order to her own confused mind. There were still many things she did not understand about Raymond, which probably accounted for her continued ambivalent feelings towards him and lack of connection between her actions and convictions. But she recognised the need to get better organised mentally, and to review their relationship in the light of his present state of mind. It was obvious to her that his preoccupation with his son's illness was having a harmful effect on him. He probably needed her, or thought he needed her in his most vulnerable moments. But did she want to expose herself to emotional upheavals and uncertainties again? She knew she still loved him very much, of that there was no doubt. The short period of their separation, which had been a living hell to her, clearly testified to that. But also remembered were the pains of rejection, the utter sinking into the dumps.

She shifted slightly and instantly his eyes flew open. "Can't you sleep?" he asked woozily.

"I can but I haven't tried yet."

"Why? It's past midnight," he added, wriggling around to have the electric clock on his dresser in view. "What're you thinking about?"

"That you brought me here for a talk and we haven't started yet."

"It's in the middle of the night, Cassandra, for heaven's sake," he started to bluster but she cut him short saying, "I love midnight talks."

He was silent for a while, trying to gauge, in the uncertain light, how serious she was. From her unnatural stillness, he concluded that she meant to have her talk. He reached for her hand and felt it tense in his. "Okay," he said finally, "where do we start? First," he continued, "I have a confession to make: I 've missed you so much these last days I thought I'd go out of my mind, and I probably would have if I had not been too preoccupied with Steve's health."

"But why didn't you try to contact me, Ray? I too was concerned about Steve and would have appreciated some information." She was not complaining but stating a fact.

"I know, angel, but after I bungled our last meeting, I was not sure of my welcome. Today though, with one thing after another, I felt that I had to see you at all costs. I have a difficult time ahead of me but I thought that a little spell in your company, however brief, would give me the necessary courage to go on."

"I don't know what to say, Ray," Cassandra whispered, overcome.

"Just say you love me, sweetheart, and give me your trust and understanding. I'm not always as articulate as I would wish to be, and that evening of last Thursday I seem to have been particularly jabbery. What I had meant to ask you, and wish to ask you now is your patience to bear with me during this trying time."

As Cassandra did not reply immediately, seeking the right words to convey her feelings, Raymond's control seemed to snap, unleashing a flood of emotions as he cried, "My son lies on the brink of death, Cassandra, my only son and hope for the future. Do you think it's selfish of me to indulge in a little self-pity and crave for a sign from you that you care a little!"

"It's not that, Ray," Cassandra assured him. "My love, you know, you have. Now I pledge my trust in you and my cooperation, my understanding too."

"Thank you, my dearest. I know you're a wonderful girl and that I can depend on you. But it's not going to be easy for either of us. We may not be able to meet or communicate as often as we'd like. But remember that wherever I am, and whatever I'm doing, you'll always be foremost in my thoughts."

"And you in mine, Ray. I'm glad we had our talk after all, for all my fears and doubts are now at rest."

"Fears? Doubts? Oh, my beloved, were it possible for me to love you as I would!"

"Hush, darling, we must be thankful for the blessings we have. What we don't have is nothing compared to what we have."

"My little sage, is there nothing you don't have an answer to?"

137

"Yes, one: why are we sitting on top of the bed, shivering in the cold when we could be snug inside?"

"May I answer that in my own way?" he replied, lowering her gently down.

When he dropped her home the next morning, he promised to keep in touch but it was to be more than a week before she heard from him again. Her sister, though, kept her abreast of Steve's progress. It appeared that he had been making satisfactory recovery after the operation only to have a relapse later, dashing his parents' hopes. Feeling concerned for Raymond, Cassandra tried to call him, first at his residence where there was nobody to pick up the phone. Next she tried his office and spoke to his partner, Mr Okiror.

Two days later Raymond returned her call and sounded in good spirits, putting an end to her fears. "Steve's off the danger list," he informed her, "and all things being equal, we should be out of this place in a week or so."

"Oh, I'm so glad."

"He'll continue being on treatment for sometime of course but he appears to have pulled through. Incidentally, your sister paid us a visit."

"Mellie did?" Cassandra asked.

"You sound surprised? I know I don't rank high in her esteem but she told me she's interested in childhood diseases."

"That's the field she wants to specialise in, yes. I've been trying to get in touch with you, Ray."

"I know, angel, and I'm sorry I couldn't have called earlier."

"I understand, Ray. Our workshop's opening on Monday, I think I told you about it. I'll be away from the office for two weeks. What's the best way of communicating?"

"Let me see, why don't I ring you at home in the evenings?"

"All right," Cassandra said, trying not to allow her disappointment to show. She had been hoping for something more definite than that.

"How's the kid?" Tonia asked when she had finished speaking.

"On the mend. I understand Mellie paid them a call."

"She took a big chance on the wife recognising her, didn't she?" Tonia remarked, sitting up expectantly.

Cassandra shrugged. "She's a doctor and Ray's wife can't very well stop her from carrying out her duties."

"How do you feel about all this Cassandra?" Tonia ventured.

"About all what?" the latter asked fiercely.

"I mean," Tonia fumbled, "he and his wife being in close contact daily."

"She's his wife, isn't she?" Cassandra retorted cuttingly.

"Are they back together?" Tonia plunged on regardless.

"Not as far as I know." The other's crisp reply implied the end of the conversation but 'in for a penny, in for a pound' was the way Tonia saw it and asked even more boldly, "Then why aren't you at Muyenga holding his hand?"

"Obviously because I'm here listening to your drivel," Cassandra snapped, finally managing to douse her sister-in-law's ebullience. Tonia felt saddened by the lack of intimacy between them, but she had long accepted the fact that Cassandra was not the type to share her troubles and joys even with those closest to her. In spite of this, however, she embarked on a ceaseless campaign to get her to unbend a little.

"I should feel snubbed, I suppose," she observed after a short silence, "but I don't. We're both of an age, have a lot in common. I don't see why we can't get on well."

"Don't we get on well?" Cassandra asked dangerously.

"You know what I mean. We live in the same house, eat at the same table, but we could as well be passengers on a train for all we know about each other."

"I know all about you," Cassandra put in quickly with a smile.

"I know; I'm an open book," Tonia remarked wryly and waited.

"Actually I'm thinking of moving out," Cassandra said, after a thoughtful silence. She raised her eyes and met Tonia's shocked ones. "I think it's time," she added.

"Oh, but you can't, Cassandra," Tonia cried, impulsively rushing to the other girls's side and taking her hands in hers imploringly. "I mean you and Mellie going away at the same time. People will think I've driven you out of your brother's house."

"Now listen, Tonia," Cassandra said, " it's natural that I should want to move out now, and that you and Gavin should want to be alone. But if I stayed on, that would indeed strike people as strange. Gavin's a family man now, or will be soon," she added, stealing a glance at the perceptible bulge in Tonia's middle. "He has you now and does not need his sisters to keep house for him."

"Where're you going to live?"

"I'm thinking of moving in with Marie. Then after her marriage, I can take over the house. It's rented by LI."

"It's more than a thought then? But I need you, Cassandra, I mean how am I going to cope without you, especially when my time draws near?" Tonia wailed.

"For heaven's sake, Toni, I'm not going to the moon, only a few kilometres away," Cassandra exclaimed in near exasperation. "I've not even told anybody else about it."

"Really?"

"Yes, really," she mimicked but not unkindly.

"Gavin will never hear of it," Tonia stated with more optimism than factuality.

"Let him try to stop me. He's not my keeper, you know."

Cassandra belonged to the new feminine breed which liked nothing better than crossing swords with machomales. She grinned evilly at Tonia, knowing how easily scared the latter was of her husband's bursts of temper. After that, the two lapsed into silence until Tonia's sharp ears picked up the click-clack of a high heel on the gravel outside. "That must be Mellie," she chimed, brightening up. "She'll tell us all about her visit to the sick child."

Cassandra was also hungry for more morsels of information concerning Raymond although her pride recoiled at showing her curiosity.

Throughout Tonia's barrage of questions, Cassandra remained cool and distant but as soon the latter left the room, she asked quickly, "Will Steve ever be well again, Mellie?"

"To tell you the truth, I don't know. I made it my business to look up his case but there's still a great deal I don't know about the disease. Take for instance this near-fatal relapse, which, in my opinion, was most inconsistent. However, he seems to be showing significant improvement now but don't expect miracles, Cassandra. That kid is going to be an invalid for a long time. It's not going to be easy for you and Ray. You must be prepared to use all the patience at your command to maintain a rational stance."

But contrary to Mellie's pessimistic prognosis, Steve was well enough to be discharged inside of a month and Cassandra and Ray resumed their somewhat precarious relationship.

* * *

"Come in," Cassandra called in response to the peremptory knock on her office door and Collin marched in with a sheath of papers in his hands.

"I thought you might want to glance over these notes before I have them typed and submitted," he said in what for him passed as a genial tone but was in fact just short of imperious. Cassandra subjected him to a moment's silence as she struggled to gather her wandering senses together. "Is something wrong with me? You're staring," he said irritably.

"No, of course not." She transferred her gaze to the said notes which he still clutched in his hands and asked, "What are they about?"

"May I sit down?" Cassandra gestured to the chair opposite. "You know of course that we're supposed to submit a report on the workshop we both attended? Well, I've made a rough draft and I'd appreciate it if you could spare a few minutes to go through it and let me have it by lunch time tomorrow.

With your suggestions and recommendations of course."

"It's fairly long but I'll do my best."

"Of course it would have been better if we could have incorporated our ideas right at the start. But when I came looking for you yesterday, I was told you had reported sick," he said accusingly. "It's not that I'm trying to monopolise the proceedings, I've enough to do as it is. But I thought that with reports of this nature, it's better to deal with them while ideas are still fresh in the mind. Besides, Ndiwalala's sure to call for it before the next production meeting."

"I appreciate all that, Collin, and I have the highest regard for your conscientiousness. I don't really think it matters who prepares the report as long as it is prepared," she careened on provocatively and thought she saw him wince. "Besides, you've had more experience at this sort of thing and are by far better at it than I. You can also see that the two weeks away from the office have somewhat set me back," she indicated the heaps of files on her desk awaiting her attention. "I understand Wilson has had his leave extended?"

"Yes, I know. I endorsed it. His health is not what I'd call robust," he added pompously. "At his age, he should have retired long ago. Well," he added standing up, "I hope you won't forget to let me have these," he tapped the notes on the desk, "by noon tomorrow."

"I said I would," Cassandra replied shortly.

After he had left, she mused on what kind of report he would give her this year. It should be an equitable one, she reasoned, since she no longer posed a threat to him on the promotion ladder. But why not though, she quizzed herself and felt a little saddened by her honest self-analysis. She had used to revel in the challenge and excitement of the contest and the constant call on her vitality.

There was another knock on the door. She wanted to say "Go away" but instead she invited the caller in.

"Mr Kiiza sent me here to ask if you've any work I can take off your hands," Hamis Kamugye, a junior editor, said.

Cassandra gazed at him speechlessly, regretting her uncharitable thoughts about Collin of a few minutes ago.

"What about your own work?"

"We're having a rest period in our section now. It happens every end of year."

" "Do you know how to research these work reports?"

"No, but I'm pretty quick at learning if you show me," Hamis answered with an assuredness that was, for Cassandra, reminiscent of her early days with the firm.

"Good, here's what you do..." she opened a file and proceeded to show him.

Maybe I need a lesson in psychology, she mused after Hamis left with a load of files, which allowed her to breathe a little. But she did not feel any more kindly towards Collin.

* * *

Cassandra normally enjoyed good health which she boosted with light exercise. But that month of November saw her constantly dogged with ill-health that was baffling in the extreme. She caught more colds than she had had to date and felt general fatigue which she could not relate to any specific complaint.

"My goodness, Cassandra, you look the perfect ad for the caption, 'Only a Few Days Left to Live'. Whatever's wrong with you?" Marie asked bluntly.

"Nothing."

"Honestly, you look awful, have you seen a doctor?"

"I'm not ill, Marie, just out of sorts," Cassandra protested.

"Just see him all the same and he'll put you right or people will soon start saying you're suffering from this dreadful disease they call 'slim'."

"Maybe I will. I hear Mr Wakilo's due back in a month's time. Is it true?" she asked in an effort to steer the conversation away from the touchy subject of her health.

"Yes, so I gather. But not as the Chief. He's being elevated to the rank of Director now that Mbone's retiring at long last. How're you getting on on your side? Is it still daggers drawn with Collin?"

"Not exactly. We haven't exchanged shots in a long time. I think he now sees me in a different light."

"You have changed a little – but for the better, believe me."

"And on that note, I'll make my retreat to my office. Everybody else seems to be on leave except me," Cassandra added mournfully as she got up.

"Maybe if you saw a doctor, he might recommend a few days' sick leave," her friend suggested tactfully.

"I don't need a doctor, Marie," Cassandra almost screeched. Then more composedly she quipped, "You forget there's one in the house, our house."

"And so there is. What does she say?"

"Stop nagging, Marie," Cassandra cried and left.

* * *

After a whole month of earnest prayers to God, Cassandra's fears soon crystallised into a real nightmare. That she had nobody else but herself to blame, she did not doubt at all. She was not only guilty of negligence but stupidity as well, a crime she found difficult to forgive herself. Having accepted

142

full responsibility for her predicament, what remained now was to decide on how to deal with it. She did not know, could not guess at Raymond's reaction to the situation, preoccupied as he still was with his son's ill-health. Nor did she want to make him feel in any way compromised. So she tried to bear the burden alone although she lacked neither friends nor sympathisers. But confidences did not come easily to someone of her nature.

Her sister watched her uneasily as she seemed to lose her vitality daily. When she could not bear to keep silent any longer, she decided to tackle her.

One hot Saturday afternoon, she invited her outside for a chat and without preamble asked, "Are you all right, Cassandra?"

"What do you mean?"

"I mean you don't look well to me."

"Why does everybody keep harping on my health?" Cassandra retorted defensively. "Surely I should be the first one to know if I were ill."

"Perhaps you know and you don't want to admit it," her sister shot back. "Why're you losing weight if you're not ill?"

"Oh, for heaven's sake, stop putting me through the third degree, Mellie. I'm not fitted with a stabiliser against weight loss, nobody is."

"Don't be flippant, Cassandra, you know what I mean," Mellie sternly admonished. "I may be only two years older than you but I've not always lived in a cocoon like you. I have much more experience of the world."

"So? Come to the point or leave me alone, okay?" the other belligerently said.

"Look, I'm on your side, Cassandra, I want to help you," Mellie said soothingly. "I'm your sister as well as a doctor. I remember what a comfort you were to me after Horace's death. Won't you let me repay a little of that gratitude by confiding in me?" She waited a little before asking, "Is it Ray?"

"No, it's not Ray," Cassandra replied reluctantly. "I really don't know what's wrong with me, at least I'm not sure."

"But you think ...you suspect you might be pregnant?"

"I think I am. There's no other explanation and I should know the signs."

"You did not take my advice then?"

"That stuff you gave me made me sick all the time."

"Why didn't you come back to me? You know there are other methods. All right, it's too late for that, anyway." Mellinda was still for a moment, her high forehead knitted in deep thought. "I'll take you to a friend of mine on Monday who can help you. He has a clinic in town."

"You don't have to escort me there like a child," Cassandra returned ungraciously. "Just give me his name and address and I'll find him."

"Oh Cassandra!" Mellinda felt like weeping with frustration but she knew that her sister was not herself. She had had to adjust to so many emotional changes and accommodate a number of new attitudes in such a short time that it was inevitable she should feel a little strange and alienated. In time there would be a return to normalcy, after she had fully come to terms with her situation. In her heart right now, she was probably crying her guts out, asking God, 'Why me?'.

So ignoring the snub, Mellie went on, "Okay, I'll telephone right now – what time shall I tell him to expect you?"

Cassandra quickly refreshed her memory...a sub-ed at ten in Collin's office, Production at two... "I can pass there first thing in the morning."

"Let's say eight-thirty then, and Cassandra, have you thought carefully about all this?"

"What do you think? Of course I have," was the curt reply.

A week later, Mellinda broached the subject again. Cassandra had duly presented herself to the recommended doctor who had examined her and confirmed her condition.

"The results are positive, Cassandra, ten weeks at a guess."

"I see," Cassandra replied expressionlessly. "I never had any doubts really."

"I understand you're not married?" the doctor went on cautiously. Of course he already knew all that, having been fully briefed by his colleague but he was groping for an opening. He had never in his life met a girl who made him feel so ill at ease and superfluous. In contrast to her sister's effervescent nature, this one was cool almost to the point of rudeness. He thought about the man responsible for her condition and felt a little sorry for him. He knew that he himself lacked the daredevil courage which inspired some men to storm impregnable citadels in order to prove their manhood. This chap, whoever it is, must be one of those, he reflected, although looking at the stunning beauty, any man could be excused for being rash.

"No, I'm not married," Cassandra was replying coldly as much as to say 'It's none of your business'.

"So what plans do you have. Would you like me to umm, arrange..for...er...er...you to terminate the pregnancy?" God, she made him feel like a peddler trying to pass off worn-out goods as new! He passed a clammy hand across his perspiring brow and braved a look.

"You mean help me to abort? No, I intend to keep the baby," and with her tone managed to convey that he, and not she, was the object of pity.

"But surely I understood from your sister that..."

"This is my problem, doctor, not my sister's," she articulated. "All I came for was your professional confirmation of what I already suspected. The rest is up to me. How much do I owe you?"

"Okay, Cassandra, the decision's yours of course," the doctor said as he wrote out a prescription for her. "You may pay at the counter as you go out."

So intimidated was he that he dared not tell her her sister had undertaken to meet all the financial expenses. "But in case you should need me, say you change your mind ..." he ventured but got no further.

"I shan't change my mind, doctor. Thank you and goodbye." She got up and left him gaping.

Mellinda, who had been given a full account of the visit, now said, "Have you thought about your situation carefully, Cassandra?"

"What's there to think about? I'm expecting a baby, and contrary to other people's concepts of what needs be done in such a situation, I intend to keep it, full stop." A little less snappily she added, "I know my decision may appear somewhat impractical to you but I'm not about to change it."

"Okay, okay, have it your own way. Have you told Ray about it?"

"No."

"Why not? Don't you think he has a right to know? Besides, this could precipitate the desired change between you two."

"By desired change I suppose you mean marriage? Well, I'm sorry to disappoint you but I don't want to marry him, not on those terms, anyway. I'm quite capable of taking care of my child single-handed," she declared defiantly.

"I have no doubt you are, my dear," her sister commented placatingly, "but even in this so-called permissive society of ours, a certain amount of stigma is bound to attach to a child born under such circumstances. Nor is it smooth sailing for the single mother either. A child needs both parents in order to grow up healthy both in body and mind. You can't play both roles and you've no right to deny the child its heritage."

"I don't have much choice, do I?"

"Oh yes, you have, Cassandra, two choices, in fact. You can either discuss it with Ray or, if the worst comes to the worst, have the ..."

"No," Cassandra exploded. "I'm not going to play God. I don't have the right to decide who lives and who doesn't. That is His prerogative and His alone."

"That sounds funny coming from you, the rationalist. Okay," she went on hastily, "let's approach it from a different angle; have you thought what this is going to do to your career? It's bound to affect it adversely."

"I don't see why it should. There are many female single parents who have illustrious careers. I don't see why I should have fears about mine. I've not lost sight of my goals in life. This is only a minor setback."

"You call having a baby a minor setback?" Mellinda cried incredulously.

"What would you call it, a catastrophe? This is 1984 for heaven's sake, not 1900," Cassandra retaliated impudently.

"Fine," Mellinda said, sighing audibly and just managing to resist a strong urge to slap her sister across her arrogant face. Instead she transferred her wrath to a mosquito on her arm which she squashed with satisfying savageness.

"Would a little consideration for the people who care about you like your father and mother be considered old-fashioned?" She added with heavy sarcasm. "Have you thought what this is going to do to them on top of my recent debacle?"

Cassandra was quiet for some moments, raising Mellinda's hopes that she had reached her at last, but in vain. All Cassandra said was, "I wish I could spare them but I have my own life to live."

"I have no more arguments left," Mellinda said with an 'I wash my hands of you' sort of gesture. "May I ask one last question though, of a more personal nature and will you promise to answer it truthfully?"

"Go ahead."

"What stops you and Raymond from getting married, and I'm not thinking of now? I'm wondering why you've never considered the idea before. To me nothing could be more natural for two people who love each other as you claim, unless..."

"Unless what?" Cassandra asked threateningly.

"Unless what people say about him's true; that he's just a philanderer and a degenerate," Mellinda answered recklessly.

Cassandra did not immediately flare up as her sister expected. Not because she agreed with her distorted and slanderous character image but because there was no way she could convince the already prejudiced Mellinda otherwise. Raymond was one of those men whose looks and manner condemn them outright. Every look they give a female seems like an invitation, every smile a caress. They are called natural charmers who sometimes find themselves paying heavily for it like when a misguided woman imagines herself deceived and turns vindictive and begins mudslinging.

Recently though, Cassandra had started to wonder whether she herself had not read more than she was meant to in those beguiling smiles, those mesmeric eyes and those solemn avowals. How deep were his feelings, how durable, she had been asking herself lately. But loyally she rose to her lover's defence saying, "Ray's not a philanderer, Mellie. In the first place, he has always been honest with me and never led me to expect more than he could give. I know he'd marry me tomorrow if circumstances allowed, but he has problems and I don't want to use my pregnancy as a weapon. In any case, marriage has never been a factor in our relationship and it's not going to be now. Nor have my views changed much on the subject. I still regard it as a form of slavery. I don't honestly think I'm the marrying kind. I'm too independent to make the conventional good wife. No, marriage is not for me now or ever."

"So marriage is not for you," Mellie repeated unbelievingly, "then why, oh, why didn't you guard against such an eventuality?"

"I told you ..." Cassandra started to say but her sister cut her short irritably, "I know, I know. Forget I asked the question. Let's talk of practical matters: what are your plans exactly?"

"I haven't made any yet. I shall continue to work for as long as I am able of course."

"I didn't mean that. When are you going to tell Ray, for instance?"

"In due course. There's no hurry, is there?"

"And Gavin, the people at home?"

"You think I should make a public announcement or put a notice in the papers?" Cassandra retorted.

"Look, why are you making this more difficult than it is already?" Mellinda patiently tried to reason. "Try not to jump down my throat every time I ask a question or make a perfectly reasonable suggestion, Cassandra. Gavin's not only your brother but he's in a way responsible for you because you live under his roof. Do you think it fair on him to learn about your condition from his drinking cronies or other outside sources?"

"How do you suggest I go about it?" the beleaguered sister asked sullenly.

"Let me handle it for you, okay? But it would be more diplomatic if you took Tonia into your confidence. She could be useful in checking Gavin's wrath."

"Wrath? Wrath against who?" Cassandra immediately cried contentiously. "How did Tonia come by that ungainly mound? The way you talk, you'd think I've set a precedent!"

"You know, Cassandra, I sometimes despair of you, truly I do, with your lofty views and unrealistic attitudes. But even you must know there are different rules for men and different rules for women. You may not like it but it doesn't change the facts an iota. We live in a man-dominated society," Mellinda told her. "Besides, they were planning to marry," she added pointedly, "which makes all the difference. Anyway, morals are not the issue here. You're old enough to decide your own future. What I'm talking about is showing a little regard for the feelings of people who care about you like Mum and Dad. Look," she added impulsively, "I'm going home for Christmas, why don't you come along too? The country air'd do you a lot of good and it'd give you a chance to let Mum know how things are with you."

Cassandra, her eyes narrowed, seemed to mull over the idea, raising Mellinda's hopes once again but eventually, with a shake of her head, the former said it was impossible. "I can't afford the time away from the office and I'd be grateful if you did not say anything about me to anybody."

"I won't if that's the way you want it but I think it would be kinder to let them learn the news from you or a member of the family rather than from gloating neighbours."

"Listen to who's talking!" Cassandra taunted but her sister, with utmost patience, explained that it was because of that very mistake she herself had made that she was trying to make Cassandra see the folly of her course.

"I'm genuinely worried about you, Cassandra, and I hate to leave you in this situation." Mellinda had applied to and been accepted by a medical school in London to specialise in pediatrics. She had taken two years' leave of absence from the hospital and planned on leaving early the following year.

"Couldn't you get your firm to recommend you for a course abroad? I'd be more than willing to pay for it." And she certainly could afford to; Horace's will had successfully passed probate after the contending parties had wisely decided not to proceed with their claims. Mellinda was now a young woman of means.

"Thanks, Mellie, but it's not possible."

"Why, Ray?"

"Partly. But there are other considerations too." Like you want to show the world how tough you are, and how tenaciously you cling to your stupid principles, Mellinda thought, her heart filling with pity and tenderness for this intractable sister of hers. She was so infantile in many ways, in spite of her air of superiority.

"But you can't stay here. I mean you'd be uncomfortable after I'm gone."

"I know that. In fact I've tentatively arranged to move in with Marie so that when she gets married, I can take over the house."

"When's that, I mean the marriage?"

"After Easter."

"Whom will you stay with after she moves out? It's a pretty rough neighbourhood."

"I'll have Alex."

"Alex's all set to go abroad after her exam but maybe she can be persuaded to postpone the trip until September. It'll give me time too to plant my feet before I can look around for a suitable college for her."

"No, don't do that. A disappointed Alex would be worse than a no Alex. I'll manage somehow. How long has Tonia got to go?"

"I don't know exactly but less than two months I'd say. Why?"

Cassandra shrugged. How amazing, she was thinking, that the pregnancy which was hardly evident at the wedding should have expanded to such incredible proportions in only three months. It's a matter of time now before people's glances start riveting on me. She winced at the thought.

"Are you all right, Cassandra?" Mellinda asked, watching the play of emotions on her face worriedly.

"It is this heat," Tonia answered for her as she waddled towards them, bearing a tray of refreshments. "I don't know why you two elected to bake yourselves like this," she complained. "Personally I'd be happy living an amphibian life."

"So who asked you out if you don't like the heat?" Mellinda chafed good-naturedly.

"Where my husbands are, there will I go to serve them," Tonia declared and proceeded to do so.

"I knew there was something about you that attracted my brother," Mellinda went on teasingly, "for we Mutonos love to be waited on hand and foot."

"Yes, I know. My beloved master did mention your forebears once dabbled in slave-trade," Tonia rejoined, looking about her pleasurably. The heat was letting up a little and a welcome breeze was rustling the treetops, making her feel good.

Cassandra, never at her best in small talk, especially with people of her own sex, listened to them with a growing sense of isolation. She gulped down her drink and excused herself.

Chapter Eight

"One would think Horace's death would have been forgotten by now and his soul allowed to rest in peace," Gavin muttered as he read the day's issue of *The New Dawn*. Tonia, who was reclining on a chaise lounge grunted sleepily. "Listen to this," her husband added reading aloud, "'The Minister of Agriculture blah, blah ... called on Mzee Kalanzi of Kabuwoko. It will be remembered that Mzee Kalanzi lost his beloved and only son four months ago at the hands of unknown gunmen. The Minister, who is on his cotton promotion tour of the area, took the opportunity to pay his and the government's condolences' – rather late in the day, wouldn't you say?" he broke off to expostulate to which Tonia groaned concurrence. "It goes on to say that the government categorically condemns the wave of indiscriminate killings which is sweeping through the country, especially the urban areas."

"So what's being done to arrest the situation...ouch!"

"What is it, darling?" Gavin dropped the paper and rushed to her side.

"It's gone. Just a small ache in the back, rather sharp! I've been having them since last night, probably due to indigestion."

"A small ache, my God! Don't you have the sense to know better? Small aches have a habit of growing into big aches, you know. Let's get the doctor immediately."

"Stop fussing, Gavin, I still have two weeks to go."

"Who says? I say we call the doctor now and seek his professional advice. What do we have to lose? You get ready while I put through the call."

"Surely you're not suggesting that I—?"

"Don't argue, darling. Better to look foolish now than sorry later." Eight hours later, Tonia was delivered of a four-and-a-half kilogramme baby girl who displayed every sign of being high-spirited.

"She's so cute, Tonia," Cassandra said the next day, watching her niece in fascination. Did we all start out looking like this, she wondered and was startled by her unexpected deep interest. To her, babies had always been messy and

150

tiresome creatures she generally regarded with indifference. But, mindful of her own condition, she had of late started to take a keen interest in the mystery of creation, absorbing as much information on the subject as she could lay her hands on.

"Yes, she is, isn't she?" the new mother crowed proudly. "God, I can't believe I've brought a new life into the world!" The baby gave a piercing scream at which Cassandra smiling, said, "There's proof that you actually did. Can I get her out?"

"Yes, do please. I wonder why she's crying now."

"Perhaps she's hungry," suggested Cassandra, cradling the jelly-like form.

"I'm not allowed to feed her yet."

"Good God, she'll starve to death."

"Not she. She gulps that glucose stuff as if it's from the spring of life. I'm almost scared to put her to the breast."

"She's fallen asleep again," Cassandra whispered. "I'll put her back and then you can rest too. That's why I'm here."

"I'm too excited to sleep," Tonia declared but within no time, her eyelids slid over her eyeballs and she was out like a candle. Cassandra moved her chair to the window where she sat watching the hive of activity in the hospital grounds below and reviewing her own life to date, with an overwhelming sense of dissatisfaction. So engrossed was she with her own thoughts that she did not hear the gentle tap on the door, nor see the visitor enter until he was standing before Tonia's bed, gazing down at her.

"She's asleep," she said irrelevantly.

"Yes, she is," he echoed gravely. He had a bundle of magazines in his hands which he carefully placed on top of the locker beside the bed. Then unhurriedly, he moved to the babycot and bent to peep.

"I can hardly see a person here, can you? Only a pink blob with a hint of mouth and nose. I suppose the eyes are there too but I can't see them."

Cassandra breathed a sigh of relief at his innocuous remarks. She had dreaded their first meeting since that incident almost four months back, but apparently she needn't have worried. He had probably long relegated it to the 'matters of no importance' compartment with his usual air of competence. Well, that was okay, fine with her, no? Then why the sense of outrage?

"Don't let Tonia hear you say that," she rejoined lightly, trying to match his nonchalance. "She thinks hers the most beautiful baby ever born."

"I suppose every mother feels that way about her offspring. I have it on indisputable record that my own mother could hardly take her eyes off me for wonderment," he joked, smiling a little. He replaced the mosquito netting over the cot, and with slow, deliberate steps walked towards her. "So how have you been, Cassandra?" he asked, leaning against the window sill, and subjecting her to a searching gaze.

'So how have you been', the words rang inside her like the voice of Nemesis. She felt an overpowering desire to laugh or flee from the room but controlled it. Instead she raised her eyes to his, trying to discover whether sincerity or mockery lay behind the words, but his face was as inscrutable as ever. "Cassandra?" he repeated but in a gentler voice, making a shamble of her earlier deductions. She rose to her feet abruptly, not sure what she intended to do and suddenly the world went into a spin and she reeled into his arms.

"I'm sorry," she whispered weakly as she tried to steady herself.

"You're not well, Cassandra!" he cried with alarm

"I'm fine, Bevis, it's just the heat. Please let go of me." ·

"Cassandra!" he said again, tightening his grip, and he felt her tremble in his arms. He searched her face again before he carefully lowered her into her chair. "Are you sure you're all right?" He scanned her wan face before taking in the rest of her body, noting the heightened voluptuousness. "Have you been sick?" he persisted.

"Stop putting me through the grill, Bevis, I told you I'm all right," she retorted irritably.

"I'm sorry, I don't mean to pry but...." He stopped as a preposterous idea struck him. But why preposterous? Because of Raymond's disability unless ...unless...oh, no, but surely that would be even more absurd. His eyes inspected her body once again, noting how more provocatively outthrust her bust was, and how rounded her slender form. His gaze went back to her face, studying it, searching for more clues to substantiate his suspicions. Cassandra, who had regained some measure of composure, returned his gaze defiantly, daring him to trip himself further by his comments. She instinctively knew that he had guessed about her and was about to let off steam.

"Have you told Ray?" he asked harshly, his eyes shedding their drowsy look behind which he normally took refuge.

"No," she answered briefly.

"Why not?" he asked and waited for her answer with bated breath. He watched her keenly in order not to miss the slightest nuance in her manner.

"It's none of your business, is it?" Cassandra retorted, making him flinch. He fumbled for his cigarettes and resumed his position by the window, seemingly lost in thought. Cassandra breathed with relief at his curtailed interest in her affairs, her gaze moving from his immobile face to follow the writhing of cigarette smoke out of the window.

The silence in the room deepened and palpitated until, raising his eyes to her face, he asked again, "Why haven't you told Ray?"

152

"I said... all right, if you really must know, it's because I was waiting for the right moment."

"There will never be a right moment for Ray for this kind of information," Bevis said sharply. "Don't I beg you..." he started to add but was interrupted by the entry of a nurse who dimpled at him, acknowledged Cassandra with a cold glance, peered at both her patients, and after fussing around a bit, went out, leaving behind a vibrant silence.

"You were about to dictate my future conduct with regard to your brother," Cassandra reminded her companion acidly.

"Not dictate, Cassandra, just advise you. I was about to ask you to hold off your disclosures for a little while longer, please, for Ray's sake."

"For Ray's sake, why?"

"I'm sorry I can't explain now. Will you trust me?"

"I don't see why I should when it's obvious you don't trust me. You've been trying to separate us for a long time and I know you'd be glad to see our relationship dissolve into nothingness. You now fear this new element might confound your machinations, isn't it?"

"I don't think I could convince you that my concern is not only for the good of my brother but of yours as well. Anyhow, all I ask is that you give me the benefit of the doubt until I'm in a position to explain myself fully."

"And if I should refuse? What will you do?"

"Cassandra," he cried, his eyes pleading with her, but she set her lips obstinately. After a short uncomfortable silence, he said abruptly, "I must go now. Will you tell Tonia I called?"

"She'll be disappointed not to have seen you," Cassandra said mechanically.

"I'll call again." She nodded and turned her eyes back to the window until she heard the squeak of the door behind him.

* * *

Bevis hurried from the tall building like somebody in whose wake all the hounds of hell had been let loose. He looked neither left nor right but made straight for his car in the car park in which he slumped down heavily, his body breaking out in a cold sweat.

Fate? Coincidence? But he believed in neither! Only people deficient in a sense of direction and commitment evoke fate as the author of their fortunes. His personal belief was that with enough determination and the right kind of motivation, man could, to a large extent, influence his own destiny. It was with this in mind that he had set out, at his slow, measured pace, to woo Cassandra,

153

the pace dictated more by his obsessive fear of failure than a sense of caution. He had believed that victory would eventually be his because Cassandra was too vital to his happiness, the axis around which the fabric of his dreams hung together.

But because he had hesitated and temporised, he was now faced with the worst dilemma of his life from which he could see no escape. And yet he could not sit back calmly and wait to see what would happen. He had two options: to tell Cassandra and risk dire consequences or tell his brother and reap no less retribution. What a snare, what a tangled web, he thought with despair as he lay back against the seat, urging his dulled wits to work the oracle but to no avail. Instead, recollections of past events jostled for attention in his mind, in particular the incident of the night he first came upon Cassandra and Raymond together.

He eased his tie as a familiar pain at the memory stabbed him in the chest, interrupting the breathing process. When he had sufficiently recovered his normal heartbeat, he allowed himself to relive the scene although he knew the experience offered neither succour nor balm to his suffering spirit. But to deny it would result into more intense restlessness.

He had of course heard rumours about Raymond's latest 'enchantress' but they had left him unstirred. His brother's affairs were a byword since his separation from his wife and stopped short of being scandalous. Most of the time Bevis did not even get to meet some of these doxies, so ephemeral were they. It was therefore with great shock, when one day he chanced upon Cassandra and his brother at the Elite. Cassandra, his Cassandra, his very own preserve, was the Cynthia of the moment for Raymond's amorous escapades; it was utterly unthinkable, completely unacceptable.

Although the Elite was hardly his idea of a spot for relaxation and amusement, being too noisy and boisterous, Bevis knew Jane adored such places and feeling in good humour that evening, he had deferred to her choice.

He opened the swing door, took one step inside, his eyes automatically sweeping across the multitudinous heads as one normally does on entering such a place, and then froze. At a table towards the rear, with his back to the entrance, sat Raymond and opposite him unmistakably Cassandra, her face flushed and glowing. Fortunately for him, she was too engrossed with her companion to notice her surroundings or she would have spotted him immediately. Bevis stood rooted to the spot, incapable of any action except to stare at the pair.

"Let's take the table over there," Jane, blissfully unaware of the reason for the tableau, suggested, indicating a vacant table on the other side of the room. She had not seen Raymond; Cassandra she would not have recognised.

"We're getting out of here," Bevis said, making an abrupt about-turn, his jaw crunching on the words savagely. "We're leaving now," he added, swinging her round by the elbow.

"But why?" Jane, bewildered, asked as she trotted after him in her high heels. His answer was a mad rev of the engine as he swung out of the car park and catapulted onto the road.

"Wow, are we practising for the suicide race?" his companion exclaimed, her arms flailing in the air to keep her balance. She swallowed angrily and turned accusing eyes his way. "What's got into you, Bevis?" No answer. "I thought you liked the Elite. I mean, I didn't force you to go there, you chose it yourself." Still no response. The speeding street lights only afforded her a dim side-view of his face but she sensed a fierce tension in him, raw and riotous. She felt pricks of fear. It was so unlike him to act like that and she couldn't think of what could have happened in such a short time to account for the change.

After they had been driving for some time in complete silence, Bevis removed his hand from the wheel and passed it through his hair with weariness. "I'm sorry, Jane," he apologised without looking at her and then resumed his brooding silence. 'Sorry, Jane', Jane mimicked silently, smouldering with justifiable rage. 'Sorry, Jane' and that settles it! But a glance at his granitic profile changed her mind about giving vent to her indignation.

They ended up in an obscure little place, whose mediocrity was reflected in its indiscriminate clientele. Jane looked around the hideous little hall full of noise and smelling of body sweat and cheap perfume, perplexed. She knew Bevis to be meticulous almost to the point of fanaticism, how most peculiar of him then to choose such a place for his evening entertainment! What was behind the abrupt switch from the Elite to this Copula Bar-Restaurant? She sifted through impressions, rearranged snatches of conversation in an effort to solve the puzzle.

Bevis, his face more impassive than ever, sipped his drink slowly and silently, seemingly unaware of Jane's inner turbulence. After a few minutes of heroic silence on her part, in which self-induced coughs, heavy sighs and nervous fidgetings had drawn no response from her companion, Jane sank back into her chair resignedly. Bevis raised his eyes to hers, studied her absently, and then pulling himself together gave her an apologetic smile, which barely touched the corners of his mouth, but nonetheless a smile with the capacity to melt an iceberg, and said, "I'm sorry, Jane, but there was somebody there I did not care to meet."

"I gathered that much. Who was she?"

"Not a she," he refuted quickly, too quickly, stiffening a little. "Somebody you don't know."

"Obviously." And at that profound observation, a deep silence descended upon the two. She devoted the rest of the evening to space-gazing until some drunk directly opposite mistook her unblinking stare for overt overtures and leered at her disgustingly. Indignantly, she turned stormy eyes at her companion who forestalled her expostulations saying, "Let's go." He beckoned a waiter and paid the bill, leaving behind almost untouched drinks.

Halfway back to town, he said apologetically again, "I'm sorry for lousing up your evening. You'd have had more fun curled up in your settee, listening to music." Jane was a pop music addict.

"Alone?" she asked.

Bevis shrugged and concentrated on his driving. He turned into the siding leading to her block of flats, drove past the gate and stopped the car in the cul-de-sac ahead. Jane waited tensed up.

"I'm not good company tonight, Jane," he said quietly. "We'll get together another time." Silence fell between them and Jane allowed it to stretch into minutes before she asked in a controlled, almost fatalistic voice, "It was a girl who upset you back there, wasn't it?"

"Jane dear, there's a part of me you don't know anything about and are better off knowing nothing about," he said prevaricatingly and tried to take her in his arms but she pushed him away.

"Oh yes, tell me exactly where I stand and don't mince words – oh, I'm sorry, Bevis," she apologised, choking on her sobs. Her moods were mercurial and evanescent, Bevis thought, taking the small, pointed face in his hands and studying the normally lustrous, intelligent eyes, now clouded with tears and dejection. God, at times like this, I feel like a heel, he thought as his mind came under a heavy barrage of 'ifs'.

"Dear Jane," he murmured huskily, rubbing his cheek against her velvet one. She clung to him, begging him to take her back home with him.

"I don't want to spend the night in that lousy apartment."

"Listen, Jane, I'm really whacked tonight, but I promise we shall get together again soon and I'll make it up to you."

"But I want to be with you tonight," Jane shrilled, abandoning herself to the indignity of begging. She knew he hated it when she became maudlin and weepy. She wished she didn't love him so much, it would be so easy to be calm and detached. If only she had a little insight into his mind, knew just what it was he sought most in a woman. She felt an unreasonable and burning jealousy against the other woman, whoever it was, who had upset him, and longed to shower him with abundant love and make him forget her, at least for tonight. But she knew she stood no chance and his next words confirmed this.

"Now, Jane, you know that I'd also like to be with you tonight but I can't. Let me ring you tomorrow and maybe we can arrange something, okay?" Jane

156

was a wonderful girl and he regretted the necessity to be so brutal to her but he needed to be absolutely alone tonight. It was beyond his capacity to hold one girl in his arms while every part of him craved for another.

"I'm sorry I don't want to put pressure on you but I don't want much, just your company for tonight, that is all."

"Don't sound so humble, Jane," he chided, his voice rough with emotion. "Any man'd be lucky to have you."

"But I don't want any man. I want you, Bevis, don't you understand?" she exclaimed, on the brink of another downpour.

"Jane, baby," Bevis said in a weary voice, "we've been through all that before. I'm very fond of you but I don't think I'm the right guy for you. I don't want to mislead you into thinking that someday ..."

"The hell you don't!" Jane exploded, jerking herself free. "Who's talking of a lifetime? I'm talking of tonight, not tomorrow, not next week or next year but tonight; just one fucking night. But you Mr Clean Conscience must spell it all out for me so that I don't get the wrong idea! Do you know what I think about people like you who hide behind your so-called consciences to justify your cruelty and insensitivity to others? Inhuman, miserable wretches. One little detail you seem to have overlooked, Mr Clean Conscience is that you've been using me. Taking everything I got to give and giving me nothing in return. Well, this is all finished now. You go to her, whoever she is, and we'll see if she can give you half as much as I've given you or love you as well. Don't say more," as Bevis opened his mouth to reason with her. "And don't call me." She opened the door, shaking with rage and banged it behind her viciously. She ran the short distance to the gate without glancing behind.

Bevis watched the diminishing diminutive figure absently. He waited until he saw a light come on in one of the flats on the second floor before he turned the ignition key and allowed the car to glide gently down the slope. Of course he and Jane would be together soon, depending on how long it was usually how short, it took her to swallow her pride and contact him, her opening sentence invariably a resentful, "I thought you'd ring me?" to which he would blithely answer, "But, Jane baby, you said you never wanted to hear from me again, remember?" He could always hold out longer than she but he was not proud of being the worshipped rather than the worshipper. And he knew he deserved every word of her contempt. But his heart beat as fast and as warmly as hers, only it beat for another. How simple it would all be if she were that other!

Perhaps as a gesture of contrition, he should be the first to call her this time as soon as he got back to his house and suggest they spend Sunday together. But a flashback to the scene in the Elite and he knew this could not be. The following afternoon found him speeding towards his brother's house to verify

157

what he already knew in his heart to be the irrefutable truth.

He mopped his brow, recalling his wandering thoughts to the present. The situation was desperate, even explosive, and called for bold measures, the form of which made him shudder with apprehension. His loyalty to his brother and his sense of honour demanded a coming out in the open about the whole misadventure but his survival instinct counselled caution in the hope that a miracle might occur to render it unnecessary. But he was no believer in miracles, and judging by Cassandra's mood, his time was running out.

He thought about his brother's wrath as he drove out of the hospital grounds and wished there was a way of sparing Cassandra the outcome.

Chapter Nine

"I want to name her after you and Bevis and I want both of you to be the godparents. Alex will be the third," Tonia bubbled, her mind full of delicious thoughts of her baby and the bright future.

Cassandra, who was scanning an article in *Single Parents* magazine, reluctantly closed it and lifted her eyes to her sister-in-law, giving her full attention. "What, who?"

"You and Bevis. Baby's to be named after you both and you're to be her godparents," Tonia repeated, a smile lighting up her face. "But 'Bevis is such a boorish name. I mean what can you do with a name like that, how can you feminise it? With yours, there's no problem. She can be simply 'Cassandra', 'Cassy' and so on. But 'Bevis'? If she were a boy ..." She knitted her brows in deep thought. "What does the initial 'L' stand for?"

"Lance, I think."

"So I could call her 'Lancia' or ... what?" she mused, inviting Cassandra to share her perplexity, her most pressing problem the choice of names, the latter thought enviously.

"Why don't you name her Bovina, Lancia or Blanche for both?" she suggested a little roughly. "What's in a name, anyway? I mean," she added more gently, "they all sound quite fine to me, rather unique, actually. What about a surname?"

"Oh, didn't I tell you? Gavin gave her 'Namara'."

"A good name. Do I read meaning into it?"

"Yes, there is. You know what fuss you people of Kaaro make about the gender of the offspring. So when I asked Gavin whether he was disappointed about our firstborn being a girl, he assured me that he was satisfied with a girl and called her Namara."

"Quite an answer, that. Incidentally, first baby girls are considered a

159

blessing to a marriage. I suspect originally it was intended to console the unhappy couple and eventually turned into a superstition. But don't all African societies accord more importance to the birth of a boy than that of a girl, yours included, Tonia?"

"I suppose so but we're more subtle about our preferences. Are you going out tonight?"

"Would you like me to? Am I getting on your nerves?"

"You're deliberately trying to misunderstand me, Cassandra," Tonia grumbled.

"I'm sorry, Tonia, and no, I'm not going out. Actually I thought I'd stay and lend a hand. You're not strong enough to be up and about yet and the new maid, Suzi, still needs some breaking in."

"I appreciate the sacrifice, Cassandra, but I can manage I think. I'll have to soon anyway, when you go."

"Tonight, I'm staying in," Cassandra stated firmly. She had been trying to get in touch with Raymond but in vain, by which she concluded that he was still preoccupied with Steve's health. But he could at least acknowledge her calls even if he couldn't spare the time to see her. Anyway, he had warned her to expect this kind of thing as long as the kid's health was still a cause for concern.

A car hooted at the gate and after a few minutes it drove in. Jossi, looking important and mysterious, marched to the front door to let in whoever it was, Gavin most probably. Cassandra, in the act of getting up to check on the recalcitrant Suzi and refresh her memory about her duties, stopped dead in her tracks at the appearance of their caller. Raymond, looking impossibly handsome, loomed hesitantly in the doorway. Her heart did a suicidal somersault as his brilliant eyes met hers and held them briefly before he turned to Tonia, who was urging him to come in, and said charmingly, "I'm sorry I'm calling at a most inappropriate hour, but I was in the neighbourhood and could not resist the temptation to pass by and offer felicitations on the arrival of your new baby girl, Mrs Mutono."

"Call me Tonia, please, won't you? And how most delightful of you, Ray ... may I call you Ray?" Tonia, ably rising to the occasion, gushed. "Won't you sit down please?"

"Only for a few minutes. I know how demanding a new, and a first baby, for that matter, can be. I don't want to disorganise you."

"Oh, she's a good baby actually, hardly cries. Cassandra and I have just named her Lancia, after Bevis, you know, who's to be her godfather," she prattled happily. "Only I can't think of another name." Cassandra gave her a surprised look which drew a wink.

160

"Perhaps you might consider a coalescence of the names of the other two godparents," Raymond suggested gravely.

"How very clever of you. Why didn't we think of that, Cassandra? Let me see, Cassandra and Alex are the other two," she confided. "How would you go about it, Ray?"

"I'll leave that to your ingenious powers. I don't want to spoil your fun." He smiled his most captivating smile, almost knocking the breath out of her and then turned to Cassandra, who up to this moment had not said a word.

"Can I get you a drink, Ray?" she asked, a little flustered by his intense gaze. She knew Tonia was watching and recording their every gesture. He pretended to think it over, his eyes never leaving hers as if seeking her guidance.

"Okay," he said eventually. "Just a little one, please." Cassandra got up and left as Tonia was asking about Steve's state of health.

When she came back with the drinks, there was no Tonia.

"The baby," Raymond mouthed. "I really shouldn't stay long, I don't want to be in the way. Gavin not home yet?"

"He should be along any time now. Oh, Ray, you shouldn't play tricks like that. My heart almost stopped beating at the unexpected sight of you!" she rebuked with mock sternness.

"I know and I apologise. I should have telephoned first but I did it on an impulse. I suppose I can't persuade you to come out with me?" he asked hopefully. There was no reason why not, Cassandra thought. Tonia herself had been urging her to and she knew Gavin would not be long in coming. Meantime, Tonia had Suzi and Jossi on hand.

"I'll tell Tonia," she said, getting up, but that lady herself was already back in the room, proudly bearing forward her offspring for Raymond's inspection and admiration. Cassandra stood spellbound as she watched the big man receive the tiny swathed bundle with the utmost care and drool over it appreciatively, to the mother's gratification. With a catch in her throat, Cassandra moved away, determined that tonight was to be the night for the long overdue news of her own condition.

But as usual, they were no sooner together alone than she forgot about it. His presence always had the effect of making it impossible for her to remain cool and sober. Luxuriating in the intense joy of their reunion, she decided that the news could wait a little longer, relegating the worries of tomorrow to tomorrow. Tonight she wanted nothing weighty on her recaptured bliss.

"Do you think it's healthy to want somebody the way I want you?" she asked sometime later that night. "It somehow smacks of decadence to me." The question might have sounded idle to Raymond but he knew Cassandra rarely indulged in pointless chatter and the puckered lines on her pretty face confirmed his guess.

161

"Don't be ashamed to confess your love, Cassandra, for love's life and life's love. Better put, 'she who has never loved has never lived' unquote. Love's one of the basic human needs, the essence of our very existence. I believe in love and I believe in the purity of our love in spite of the anomalous circumstances in which it abounds. If I'm wrong, then my whole concept of life is wrong, as must be the whole doctrine of humanity.

"Before I met you," he continued, "I didn't know the full meaning of life. I went through the motions of living, sure, but I had no idea how one's existence could be enriched just by giving oneself to another. Loving you has taught me a lot of things, in particular the joy of living. This, and much more does your love mean to me, my angel. Without it, I'd go back to my sham existence, lacking the motivation to keep me going."

"You know I feel the same about you, Ray, and these last few days without word from you have been hell. I know life has been trying for you but I hope that the worst about Steve is over." Glowing with happiness she relaxed, her doubts and fears, as usual, swept aside by Raymond's convincing line of argument. They wished each other pleasant dreams and drifted into a blissful sleep.

It was an hour later, eleven-thirty by the wall clock, when the telephone shrieked, jerking Cassandra awake. "Telephone," she said, shaking Raymond gently.

"What?" he bolted upright, his eyes wide with alarm. He lurched out of bed and grabbed the ringing phone gasping, "Belinda? What is it?" He listened, his hand automatically pressing the switch for the table lamp. "Calm down, Belinda, I'll be right over." His face taut, he replaced the receiver and hurriedly started to dress.

"What is it, Ray?" Cassandra asked, handing him the various dress items. "Your shoes, jacket, watch, anything else?"

He looked around distractedly, extracting his briefcase from its stand and saying, "I don't think so. That was Belinda," he added, "Steve's having a bad turn. I have to go and see what we can do."

"I'm sorry," she said quietly, trying to make herself unobtrusive. She was recalling her mother's warning, ".... he already has a family from which you'll always feel excluded." But she confidently thought that the knowledge of her coming baby, their baby, would provide that special link now missing to make their harmony complete.

At the door, he stopped and looked back at her as if he had just become aware of her and the unsatisfactory position he was leaving her in. "Will you be alright?"

"Don't worry about me, Ray. Take care."

162

"Lock the door after me. I'll let myself out of the gate and lock it from the outside. Kapasi, the *shamba* boy, has the duplicate key in case I'm not back early enough. I love you, angel," he touched her briefly, absently, his eyes far away and unreadable. Cassandra shuddered, experiencing a sudden attack of *deja vu*. She locked the door and dragged her feet back to the cold, empty room.

That was just the beginning of the successive nightcalls. They became so much part of their evenings that Cassandra started to hold her breath until she heard the ominous ring. Sometimes Ray answered the summons, coming back moody and reserved, and sometimes he just talked soothingly, making his wife promises of more vigilance on his part. Cassandra was confused and could not help wondering whether these interruptions were a nightly routine or only coincided with her visits but could not ask Raymond without risking being misunderstood.

Under such circumstances, the propitious time to reveal her own condition became more and more elusive. The atmosphere was always tense as she and Raymond strained to act normally and convince themselves that everything was as it should be. But nothing was ever the same after the night of the first call. Raymond was solicitous rather than tender, reawakening Cassandra's fears and doubts with greater intensity than before. For a long time she had known the kind of relationship she had let herself into. But she had not wanted to face reality. Now reality had caught up with her. So why didn't she call it quits and go? But she simply couldn't contemplate a life without Raymond, especially now, when her condition made her more vulnerable and in need of his reassurance. She also still hoped that the knowledge of their coming baby, once in his possession, would effect the desired change in him, and bridge the gap that was daily growing wider between them.

One relatively tranquil day when Raymond seemed in a more receptive mood, Cassandra decided to disclose her condition. She had rehearsed the scene several times before, with her working up to the subject gently. But now under his keen eye, and uncertain of how long their time together would last uninterrupted, she found herself blurting it out.

"What did you say?" Raymond asked, alert but as yet registering no emotion.

"I said that I think I'm pregnant, Ray," Cassandra repeated in a voice that shook a little.

"I thought you said that," came the harsh grunt. He was still and silent for a few minutes. "Are you sure?" he asked at last.

"Would I joke about a thing like that?" Cassandra cried. "I saw a doctor and he confirmed my condition."

"Impossible!" he uttered the one word forcefully and it rose and hovered between them, before it landed in her lap with a shattering impact.

She turned it over as if unsure of its meaning before she said with acerbity, "I beg your pardon?"

"I said it's impossible and I meant it. When was this, when did you see the doctor?" Cassandra drew herself up sharply at the inquisitorial tone. Whatever was prompting him to ask the unnecessary questions seemed not to allow for her feelings at all.

"I saw the doctor two months ago. I should have told you then but the opportunity somehow never arose until today."

"Why're you telling me now?" His voice was controlled but the atmosphere was beginning to vibrate with strong emotions; the wrong kind, from Cassandra's point of view.

"Why? I thought you'd want to know. After the doctor, the proud father's normally the next one to know," she answered with thinly veiled sarcasm.

"Then you're on the wrong track, baby. Whoever the proud father of your child is, I'm not he." His words were terse and declamatory and stung as they were meant to.

"What do you mean, Ray, what are you saying?" Cassandra cried stunned as she jumped up. "You don't mean what you're saying, you can't."

"Yes, I meant what I said. For the sake of clarity," he added coldly, "I'll repeat: I'm not responsible for your condition, Cassandra."

"Are you suggesting that I've been going with other men behind your back?" she exclaimed angrily, perspiration breaking out on her brow. She could understand his not wanting to shoulder the responsibility but to suggest that she, Cassandra, was capable of playing around like a common slut was insulting and unforgivable and she could not let it go unchallenged.

"The facts seem to suggest so," was the brutal reply.

"Oh yeah? What facts? I'll tell you what the facts *are*, Ray. The facts are that you're so afraid of responsibility that you'll go to any lengths to deny it. What you've always been scared of is making a commitment, isn't it? You've weaved around yourself a shroud of invisible obstacles and insoluble problems but you've never come out in the open about them. You've never even bothered to find out what my views are on the subject," she went on, unheeding of his strange stillness. "Well, you've been worrying needlessly because you've never been in danger of being entrapped by me. I can and will take care of my baby without any help from anybody. My only reason for telling you was because I thought you'd want to know. It seems I was grossly mistaken."

By the time she came to the end of her tirade, Raymond's expression had changed from chilliness to puzzlement. His response was slow in coming, as he weighed her words first. But when it did, it was firm and unfaltering: "Damn it, Cassandra, you know me better than to suppose I'd shy away from responsibilities I believed to be mine. This one, however, happens not to be one of them. More explicitly, it's physically impossible for me to be. That's all I'm prepared to say on the matter.".

"But I'm not prepared to accept it," swiftly, angrily Cassandra retorted, her eyes flashing. "What makes it impossible for you to be? I never saw you take measures to that end. Of course the woman's always expected to take care of such unimportant details, isn't it, since she's the one who'd end up holding the baby, literally," she ended bitterly.

"Look, Cassandra," Raymond interjected, "you and I seem to be talking at cross purposes. A while ago you accused me of pleading nonexistent excuses for my procrastination but you couldn't be more mistaken. I've loved you in a way I've never loved any other woman and nothing would have given me greater joy than forging a permanent relationship with you. I told you this often enough and I meant it. I also attempted to tell you, on several occasions, why this could not be but you always warded me off, remember? What I tried to tell you then and what I want to tell you now is that I can't have children. The only mistake I made was in not forcing you to listen to me then. In all conscience, I could not ask you to marry me, thereby depriving you of what every woman craves, the feel of a baby in her arms." Then in a voice shaking with anguish, he cried, "The problem exists, Cassandra: I'm sterile."

"Sterile, you! I don't believe it!" Cassandra stared at him with incredulity. Then an unwelcome recollection of a certain warning seemed to squeeze all life from her. "But you have Steve..." she whispered, wishing the ground could open and swallow her up. The realisation of his unwelcome confession hit her squarely in the face.

As if from a very long way, she heard Raymond say after a deep sigh, "Yes, I have Steve." He stood up to pace the floor and Cassandra followed his figure with unseeing eyes. Then with a suddenness that made her shrink away with fear, he was in front of her, towering over her, his eyes burning with an unfamiliar emotion.

"I have Steve," he repeated, "but that was before I developed the condition which resulted in my sterility."

"I still don't believe it," she said dully, fatuously, averting her face from the relentless scrutiny. "You never told me."

"I've told you now. In any case, would it have made any difference? Obviously there's somebody else."

"There's nobody else," she answered, but even to her own ears, the denial sounded hollow. The image of Bevis suddenly obscured her vision, mocking her and daring her to claim divine visitation. Unable to hide her confusion, she slid off her chair and went to stand by the window overlooking the front of the house. "There's nobody else," she repeated, her back turned. Raymond did not reply and for some time the two were enveloped in heavy silence as each struggled to dispel the nightmare and make sense of the senseless.

Cassandra, her eyes fixed sightlessly on the view outside, felt a cauldron of emotions churn away her defences. I must get away from here fast, she told herself, before I disgrace myself. Her eyes were beginning to sting with unshed tears but she held them back and swallowed painfully. I must not cry, she exhorted herself, exhaling asthmatically. But in spite of herself, rivulets of tears started to run down her cheeks unbidden. She rubbed at them angrily with her hand and forced herself to be steady by taking deep breaths before she turned to face Raymond again.

Raymond had resumed his seat, filling the silence with thoughts which ran on a crazily undulating plane, casting Cassandra as an angel one minute and a villainess the next. But out of all these convolutions, one dominant thought stood out, chilling his blood and filling him with nausea: the thought of Cassandra in the arms of another man, the thought of the betrayal of his trust and faith in her. He had elevated her in his mind, putting her on a pedestal, all her own, how could he ever believe in any other human being again? How could he face another day, another tomorrow without her?

What did it all mean, that Cassandra had been making a fool of him? He looked back to the time since he met her, examining her words, her expressions, those endearing gestures imprinted on his memory and deep down knew the very idea to be next to impossible. There had to be another explanation ... supposing that .... dare he hope...? Doctors had been known to err before in their diagnoses, his would not be the first case in medical history ... but after so many years of trying, consulting with the best specialists in the field, how could it possibly happen? What a joy if it were, what a dream come true!

He got up quickly as Cassandra turned away from the window, eager and excited to share his conclusions with her. "Come, let's sit down and see if we can't make sense of this mystery. We could both be approaching the problem from wrong angles," he suggested in a gentle voice.

"There's nothing to talk about, Ray."

"I see." After a long pause he asked, "Who, Cassandra?"

"Who doesn't matter," she replied and watched the transformation from the Raymond she knew to a stranger, take place.

"No? My God, Cassandra, I trusted you, believed in you as I've never believed in anybody else, don't I even rate an explanation as to why? Who was it, Cassandra? Damn you, I must know, don't you understand?" He moved towards her with slow, menacing steps but Cassandra did not even flinch. Her eyes loved him and pitied him but he was too blinded with anger to see beyond the surface. "Who was it?" he repeated. "Surely I have a right to know after all we've been to each other."

"And who are you to talk of rights, Ray, to demand explanations of my actions? Don't you think that I too had a right to know about you, to make my choices and decisions? What difference does it make now anyway? When I walk out of this house today, I'll just be a memory to you, and hopefully, not for long. Our relationship was destined to end anyhow and now is as good a time as any. I'm sorry it had to be this way but all things considered, it should make it easier on your conscience."

"I don't think you're being fair to me: you're all set to paint me a rogue and you the wronged party because you don't want to answer my question. Fine, I can't force you. I don't want to deprive you and your lover of the fun of a good laugh at my expense. My God, Cassandra, don't you feel even a little remorse for the sucker you've been stringing along? "he cried bitterly.

"It's a little late for recriminations, Ray. Let's do the sensible thing and part without further ado."

"As simple as that? It was nice meeting you, wish you the best? I wish I had your fortitude, your philosophical outlook. But I'm very human, Cassandra, weak and vulnerable and inside me is an ache that is beyond my capacity to bear." The last words were whispered in a voice that had suddenly grown hoarse with emotion. Cassandra felt her body begin to shake as if from a fever attack. "What do you want me to say?" she whispered through chattering teeth, hiding her face in her hands. "That I'm sorry? I'm sorry a hundred times, a thousand. I never for one minute wished for this to happen. It was all a horrible mistake." Then the fibre between self-control and the need to abandon herself to the expression of despair she was feeling snapped and she broke down, wheezing and heaving. She rushed out of the room, opening the first door she came to in the passage which happened to be the visitors' washroom. She locked the door behind and slid down on the marble floor as the pipes in her head burst open, unleashing floods of tears until the last drop had been squeezed out. Ten minutes, twenty, she seemed to have lost count of time, but sometime later, she heard the ring of a telephone, hopefully to summon him to his sick son's bedside. If it were so, it would give her the chance for a quiet exit. She kept her fingers crossed until she heard the sound of a car engine start outside. A couple of minutes later, she let herself out and bade goodbye to the place where she had known both happiness and sorrow.

* * *

"Water's the main problem here as you know," Marie said by way of briefing the new occupant of 17 Mpafu Road a few days later. "It trickles in between six and eight in the morning, so it's up to you to see that the plastic water containers are always filled. Massy can attend to that of course but she needs to be reminded all the time. The trouble with employing relatives is that you can never have a proper émployer-employee relationship. They always assume they're doing you a favour."

"Why employ them in the first place?" Cassandra asked, looking around the badly kept place. Well, she was not a relative and she would see to it that all that changed.

"Security, that's why. I feel safer with my own kith and kin. But they're not part of the lease. You can send them packing any time you want."

"I don't have 'kith and kin' myself since Alex's locked up on the other side of the war zone. Besides, I like Massy and I think she'll get to like me in time," Cassandra said. "Anyway, when you leave, I intend to ask Samantha to move in with me. It's the only promise Gavin managed to extract from me, that I would not be staying in the house alone. I know the two of you don't hit it off," she added, "but I need somebody here. She's not all that bad really once you get to know her. All that brashness is just her way of saying boo to the world."

"If you say so," Marie said, shrugging. She had no interest whatsoever in exploring Samantha's psyche. "And now, are you going to tell me what has happened to precipitate all this?"

"All what? My moving here? Surely I thought I explained all that and you..."

"I don't mean that," Marie cut her short and waited. She had a feeling that Cassandra was in some kind of trouble and it pained her that she did not trust her enough to confide in her. "I don't really want to force confidences, Cassandra," she said stiffly as Cassandra's face immediately assumed a closed expression.

"You're right," Cassandra burst out finally, "something has happened ... between Ray and me. But I'm not ready to talk about it yet. I'm not as brave as I'd like people to think, Marie. Sometimes I believe I don't have any guts at all," she concluded weepily.

"I think you're wonderfully brave, Cassandra, and I know you'll emerge from whatever's afflicting you whole. But remember that you can always count on me for whatever help I can render."

"Thank you, Marie for being so understanding," Cassandra whispered, and gave a gusty sigh.

"Don't tempt me to renege on my promise and beat the truth out of you ... but okay, okay," she added soothingly, "I'll stick by what I said. But talk to somebody, talk to Mellie. You'll feel better after unburdening yourself."

"When I said I can't talk about it, I meant exactly that, Marie, or you'd have been my first choice."

"But you can at least tell me whether you and Ray have broken up, can't you?"

"We have, yes."

"But you can't tell me the reason why?"

"I'm sorry, Marie, I can't."

"And you still intend to have the baby?"

After a short pause in which she checked an indiscretion trembling on her lips, she simply said, "He's all I have." What would he look like, his father? Who was his father? She closed her eyes tightly as if to shut out some unpleasant image. Marie watched her, her heart swelling with pity for her, but checked an impulse to demonstrate her feelings. Instead she said practically, "The sooner you get Samantha to stay the better. I'll stay with you until Dan returns from the East. After that, you can move into my room and leave the smaller one to your friend."

Just then, the phone rang. "It's Mellie, Cassandra," Marie called to the retreating
figure. "I'll go have a pow-pow with my kinswoman."

Mellie, with the privileged position of a sister, was more direct and insistent in her queries but met with no more candour than Marie before her.

"All right, I'll see if I can't get more information elsewhere," she threatened.

"Don't call Ray, Mellie," Cassandra warned with panic.

"I'm not going to call Ray: I'm going to call Bevis."

"Bevis knows nothing," which was true in a way.

"We'll see. Let's talk about something else; have you started ante-natal clinics? I told Dr Mwangusa to expect you."

Bevis was more evasive if anything, claiming he was rushing to court at the time of Mellinda's call, and skirting around the issue when pinned down to specifics. "Is there nobody who can tell me what's going on over there?" Mellinda cried with frustration.

"Have you asked Cassandra herself?" Bevis asked fatuously.

"What do you think? She would not tell me anything; that's why I turned to you," she said with a hint of disappointment.

"I'm sorry, Mellie, but ... look, let me ring you sometime when I'm more settled, okay?"

"No, it's not okay but I suppose I can't force you if you don't want to say anything," Mellinda replied gloomily.

"I don't have anything concrete to tell you, Mellie, or I would. As soon as

I have anything ..." he promised, tugging at his tie with his free hand. He was aware how unconvincing he sounded.

"It's that stupid pregnancy, I know," Mellinda postulated. "If she'd followed my advice and got rid of it, all this to-do would not be there."

"Mellie!" the man on the other end of the line exclaimed faintly. It really is hot, he thought breaking out into a sweat. He glanced outside through the window and was surprised to see big drops of rain pelting the rooftops.

"I'm sorry if I've shocked your moral sensibilities, Bevis," Mellinda continued, sounding anything but sorry. "But we live in a material world and must consider all options open to us before making irrevocable decisions, don't you think?"

"Ahaah," he grunted noncommittally. He cleared his throat, desperate for something sensible and soothing to say, but Mellinda had not finished. "I know your brother is not a bad man but his relationship with Cassandra was ill-conceived and doomed right from the beginning. The mistake they both made, in my opinion, was to allow it to run the whole span, if you see what I mean."

"Yeah, well, I understand your concern and share it to some extent and I promise to go and see Cassandra ... should have done so ages ago anyway," he added under his breath.

"That's a relief. I knew I could count on you," Mellinda remarked effusively. "All she needs is somebody sensible and reliable like you to guide her. She's so immature for all her sophisticated airs and arrogance."

"You know there's nothing I wouldn't do for Cassandra, for any of you, don't you? Anything that was within my power, that is," he added huskily. "I'll give it a shot anyway and let you know how things stand."

"I suppose I'll have to be satisfied with that and I'm very grateful to you, Bevis."

Bevis carefully replaced the receiver and passed a handkerchief over his glistening brow. Retribution had caught up with him and he could not put off the confrontation any longer. But once again he had not reckoned with fate. Almost immediately after his talk with Mellinda and resolve to face up to things, calamity struck the Agutamba family and he was once again forced to leave the Cassandra issue pending.

Chapter Ten

Belinda sat by the phone waiting impatiently for the doctor to return her call. She constantly got up to wander agitatedly around or tiptoe to the bedroom to check on her sick son. She felt alone and very frightened and a rush of searing anger at her husband who seemed to have lost interest in his son's welfare. That fool of a doctor had assured them that Steve was out of danger when they took him for a check-up two weeks after his discharge from hospital. His blood count was stable, he had said, and his response to the new drug satisfactory. Belinda admitted that Steve had looked cured and healthy and after a few days had allowed him to resume his schooling, relaxing her vigilance over him. But that did not mean that he did not need his father's care; even healthy children do, she thought.

If only she had stayed with him the whole day instead of going off to a wedding reception in the afternoon after a morning at the beauty salon. But he had looked all right and she had left him in the care of Mrs Njuki, her housekeeper, whose concern for the child was almost as great as hers.

"Oh thank God you're back," a distraught Mrs Njuki cried, meeting her at the entrance when she returned at seven in the evening. "I was almost going out of my mind with worry."

"What has happened? Is Steve worse?" Belinda asked, kicking off her high-heeled shoes and rushing inside the flat without waiting for an answer. Mrs Njuki bent down and picked up the discarded shoes. "What happened?" Belinda asked again in a hushed voice, her hand on Steve's high forehead.

"A few minutes after you left, I went to check on him and found him hot and delirious. He was calling for you and for his father but I didn't know how to get you."

"You didn't try to give him anything at all like aspirin, did you?"

171

"I know better than to do that, Mrs Agutamba," the housekeeper replied, offended. She loved Steve like her own son and Mrs Agutamba had no reason to doubt her.

"I'll call his father. We must get him to his doctor immediately," Belinda said, turning to go but at the sound of her voice, Steve's eyes fluttered open and he croaked out weakly, "Don't leave me alone, Mummy."

"I won't, baby, I won't, darling," his mother assured him soothingly. A big lump jumped in her throat, playing haywire with her vocal chords. Tears stung the back of her eyelids but she blinked them away, adjuring herself to remain calm. Mrs Njuki placed a chair behind her and she sank into it gratefully, the tiny hot hand in hers.

After a few minutes, the child's eyes closed and he dropped off into a fitful doze. The temperature was still worryingly high, the delirium subjecting his weak body to spasmodic twitches. She got up quietly and tiptoed out of the room to try to raise her husband on the phone. She got Joseph instead, who informed her that his master was not at home. "He left a few minutes ago."

"Was he alone, and did he say where he was going?" she demanded.

Joseph, resenting her peremptory manner, took his time in answering. "He was alone," he said shortly.

"You lying, old fool, you think I don't know what's going on there? You tell him that his son is very sick the minute he comes back," she banged down the receiver, shaking with anger and frustration. Mrs Njuki watched her pityingly, thinking how it was like her to fly into a temper at a time when she needed to keep all her wits about her.

"Perhaps you could talk to the doctor yourself, Mrs Agutamba," she suggested tactfully.

"Yes, yes, I better do that." Belinda reached for the phone again but a female voice informed her that the doctor was not back yet. "Is he still at the clinic do you think?" With Mrs Njuki holding Steve, I could drive there, she was thinking.

"I don't know," the indifferent party at the other end of the line said. What a moron, Belinda thought. She left a message for the doctor to call her as soon as he got in but without much hope that it would be delivered with the urgency it required. "No luck," she told the other woman, her lower lip quivering like that of a child about to burst into tears. She flopped into a chair and asked for a glass of cold water. Her head was pounding, heralding a severe attack of migraine. Everything seems to be conspiring against me, she thought self-pityingly. If Steve was suffering from an ordinary ailment, she could have rushed him to the nearest clinic or medical centre, but with his recent

172

complicated condition, it was imperative that his doctor be informed of any adverse change in him.

Oh God, she wailed silently, please don't let my child die. Why me and why my child? Haven't I suffered enough for both? Please dear God, don't let anything happen to him, I pray you. She devoted the next few minutes to a fervent prayer in which she promised to do anything if her son was spared. It was a prayer borne out of desperation and uttered in earnest; a prayer she had been uttering ever since Steve fell critically sick.

Belinda was not a religious person, and other than making her feel better that she had committed the fate of her beloved son into the hands of the Almighty God, half of what she was saying was mere rhetoric. In all her life, she had never consciously thought about her religion. To her, like to many people of her generation and upbringing, religion was simply a way of life, like the observance of many other customs and traditions handed down from generation to generation. With the advent of Christianity and other imported faiths, a new order had emerged, superseding some of the old tribal customs and beliefs or coexisting side by side in the absence of fundamental conflicts.

So Belinda, born of Christian parents, was baptised and confirmed in the faith as a matter of course, and when it was time for her to get married, she was united to Raymond Agutamba in holy matrimony. From time to time, when convenient or absolutely necessary, she took part in the rituals of her church but without the sincerity or devotion of the true believer. But whenever she was in trouble, it then became necessary for her to invoke the powers of the omnipotent Being to come to her aid. God then became real, his help indispensable and his mercies boundless.

She reluctantly aroused herself from a self-induced trance and went to the bedroom. As she neared the sickbed, it struck her that Steve was unnaturally still. Was he...? Her breath caught in her throat and then came out in short painful gasps as she covered the short distance in bounds. She stretched a timid hand to touch him, and thank God, he was warm and breathing. Her heart dropped back in its cradle and she sighed with relief. Even his fever, of its own, seemed to have broken. But she still had to get hold of the doctor. She checked her wristwatch. It was close to eight, surely he must be home by now. After one lingering look at her sick child, she went back to the sitting-room to try the doctor's number once more but was again met with an impasse: the doctor was not home yet, and no, the answering party had no idea where he could be.

"Still not home?" Mrs Njuki asked, placing a teatray on the table next to her mistress.

"No. I'll try Raymond again although I don't have much hope of his being home either or he would have gotten in touch." But in her heart, she feared that he might have misconstrued her earlier call as yet another ruse to pull him away from the arms of his lover. In her desperate bids to get him back from her rival, she had been known to resort to such measures.

"Mr Agutamba has not yet returned," Joseph answered in an infuriatingly cool voice which left Belinda wondering whether he was telling the truth or acting on orders.

What about Bevis? she thought in desperation. Only in extreme circumstances would she consider appealing to him. Long ago, she had conceived a burning hatred for the man, a hatred borne out of rejection and humiliation.

* * *

She had first met Bevis at a camp for Guides and Scouts after her A-levels and been attracted to him instantly. Bevis, who was at that time a second year law student at the University, as she learnt later, was unlike any man she had known. His extraordinary looks aside, he displayed an unusual lack of interest in the female sex and an incredible air of cynicism for one of his age. In spite of that, Belinda found herself strongly drawn to him but her overtures were received with disdainful patience like the pranks of a naughty child.

It was through her relentless pursuit of him that she had met the more tractable Raymond and fell in love with him. But in spite of the triumphal conclusion to her campaign, her resentment against Bevis had not subsided and she had made a vow to herself that she would get him one day and bring him down to his knees before her. However, now was not the time to dredge up old grudges. She needed his help and knew it would not be denied where Steve was concerned.

"I'm very sorry to disturb you, Bevis," she started nervously as soon as he answered, "but I need to locate Ray urgently. Might you know where he is? He hasn't been at home the whole afternoon."

"I definitely don't know where he is, Belinda, and I categorically refuse to be dragged into your brawls," Bevis said uncooperatively.

"I'm not trying to drag you into anything and I wouldn't have bothered you if it were not for Steve."

"What about Steve?" he asked sharply.

"He has had a relapse, Bevis, and I can't get hold of his doctor. If I could get Ray to go and look for him ... but he's never at home, doesn't even bother to find out how his son is doing, damn him and his women!" she expostulated and broke down weeping.

174

"Take it easy, Belinda," Bevis soothed gently. "We shall find the doctor and we shall find Ray ... now, let me see... I'll try to get hold of Omoding first, I know a few places where these medics hang out. By then Ray should be home; I'll contact him for you, okay? Try to keep calm; we'll be with you soon."

"Oh, thank you, Bevis," she said relieved. "I'm sorry if I've spoilt your Saturday night."

"Don't be silly. Steve's health is a priority and my concern too."

After replacing the receiver, he turned a worried face to his guest and said, "There goes bust our evening plans. I'm sorry." But he actually felt relieved not to have to pretend to emotions he did not feel. Mellinda's call was still haunting him but he had not yet marshalled enough guts to face Cassandra. On top of that, his partner was seriously ill and he was having to take most of his urgent cases in addition to his, which meant a good part of his time was spent in court without enough time to attend to paperwork or personal matters.

"Who's Steve?" Jane asked. She was naturally disappointed but tried not to let it show. Bevis had been so moody and elusive lately that to have him whisked away the minute he showed signs of equanimity was a blow she did not deserve. But accepting it with bad grace would not work for but against her.

"Steve is my brother's kid I told you about who's been seriously ill recently, remember? Apparently he's having a bad turn and I must go and see if I can locate his doctor. Would you like me to drop you at your place on my way to town or would you rather stay here?"

"I'd rather wait for you here."

"It might be a long wait, Jane," he warned.

"It doesn't matter. I'll be here when you return if May doesn't poison me before then. She's definitely off me these days."

"She's just worried about her son's disappearance." May's son, Byensi, had gone to work one morning about two weeks back and had not returned. Bevis suspected he had gone to join the bush war: so many idealistic young people were running away to join the rebels in the bush in the struggle against what they called a tyrannical regime. Many of them had never seen another regime of course but if they survived, they would have something to compare with.

But May, on the other hand, was convinced that her son was dead and Bevis let her think so for her own safety.

* * *

175

Dr Omoding checked the patient carefully, and after a thoughtful silence confessed himself baffled. "I cant understand it, did you check his temperature properly? It reads almost normal now. You say he seemed alright this morning?"

"He had a restless night but the temperature was not high. But it had risen to 105 this afternoon and an hour later had dropped considerably."

"Let me have a look at those drugs I gave you." Belinda passed them on to him and he studied them silently, a frown draping his face. "Agranulocytosis again," he murmured to himself.

"What's that? Another complication?" Belinda, who had caught only the tailend of the long word, cried out in alarm.

"No, nothing like that. Just a reaction to the medication," he soothed. He caught Bevis' eye studying him somberly and gestured in the direction of the other room.

"Perk up, Belinda, the doctor'll do all he can. Stay with Steve while I try to make sense of this, okay?" Belinda nodded, her eyes misting over. Steve was awake and moaning weakly.

"Mummy? Don't leave me alone," came the pitiful voice from the small bed.

"No, I won't, darling. I promise I won't leave you alone," his mother soothed, her chest heaving with emotion.

"And will you take me to see Daddy tomorrow?" the laboured words whistled like wind through dry leaves.

"And I'll take you to see Daddy tomorrow."

"And will we stay with him for ever and ever?"

"Yes, my precious, we'll stay with him for ever and ever."

"Will Cassandra stay with us too?" His mother caught her breath in her throat, startled.

Forcing herself to utter the hateful name she went on, "No, baby, Cassandra'll not stay with us."

"Tell Uncle Be...be...eevy that Cassandra is a ni... ni..i..ce lady."

"Uncle Bevy?"

"Tell Uncle Be...eevy..." he started to repeat fretfully but the effort proved too much for him and his voice trailed away.

"All right, darling, I'll tell him what you say," Belinda assured him and tucked him in. "Now lie back and rest and when you wake up, Daddy and uncle Bevy'll be here."

"To take me home?"

"To take you home." Oh, pray God, not home, Belinda sobbed confusedly. She shut her eyes and sent a shuddering earnest entreaty heavenward, asking for her son to be spared. "He's all I have, Lord, he's my life!"

* * *

"Okay, doctor, give it to me straight. It's serious, isn't it?" Bevis asked, as soon as they were out of earshot.

"I'm afraid it's not good. It's not good at all. I've no doubt that it's agranulocytosis which, if you remember, was responsible for his first relapse after the operation. I can't understand why he keeps rejecting these drugs. Most patients find this one quite tolerable. There's only one left we haven't tried so far but unfortunately we don't have it in our depleted medical stores."

"Perhaps some private hospital or clinic ..." Bevis started to say hopefully but the doctor shook his head. "We don't have that much time to shop around. We can order it from Nairobi if they have it. I'll get in touch with a doctor I know at the Aga Khan immediately and make inquiries. Time is our enemy, I'm afraid. It might be even better to pack off the patient for treatment there unless one of you can be ready to travel, say tomorrow, to pick it up?"

"Of course Raymond would be ready at the word go, and so would I. Just write the prescription and give us the details."

"That's excellent. Without the booster he's been getting from the medication, that child is going to be a prey to a host of infections. I'll go and make that call immediately and let you know. I'll leave the patient here for the time being. No sense in having him admitted until we know the next step. Give me your telephone number, I have Raymond's already."

"Here's mine," Bevis said, scribbling on a piece of paper. "But I'll most likely be here with Raymond or at his place." The doctor picked up his bag preparing to depart. "Don't you have some instructions for Belinda before you go?"

"Oh yes, indeed, if only to boost her morale, poor lady."

* * *

Raymond was dreaming that he was attending a noisy party with drumming and feet-thumping when his sleep was suddenly disturbed. At first he thought it was a continuation of the tormenting dream in which somebody had decided to improve on the proceedings by jumping on his head, causing a conflagration of countless stars. But then a voice like his brother's penetrated the cobwebs in his head. He started awake and muttered disagreeably, "Hell!"

"More hell awaits you if you don't get up right now." Bevis accompanied his words with a shove. Another wrenching shake was applied to his shoulder as he evinced no desire to be ordered around by remaining still. "Man, it's hardly ten o'clock and you smell like a brewery. What do you do, bathe in the stuff?"

"I resent your attitude, Bevis, I resent it very much," Raymond said with as much dignity as his throbbing head and recumbent position could allow. "What're you prattling about anyway? I wish to be left in peace." He burrowed deeper under the covers and gave a simulated snore.

"Peace? You talk of peace? If you want peace, then you ought to treat others with a little more consideration."

"I'll not discuss my private affairs with you, Bevis."

"I don't know what you're referring to but I'm here because your child is critically ill and Belinda's going out of her mind with despair. You should be by her side right now, comforting her. Does it sound like I'm prattling to you?" Bevis asked coldly.

"Steve!" Raymond cried, shooting upright, but almost immediately cowered back as sharp needles went in and out of his head. "But he's not ill," he moaned with minimum body movement this time. "The doctor assured us the worst was over." He searched his brother's face pleadingly but found nothing there to dispel his fears.

"Oh God," he whispered, cradling his face in his hands.

"Look, old chap, try to get yourself together," Bevis admonished but not unkindly. "I suggest you take a quick shower before I drive you over." But Raymond made no move except to pull his hand slowly away from his haggard face.

"The doctor said he was out of danger," he repeated in a monotone.

"That was two weeks ago: he says otherwise now. So hurry. Steve needs you, Belinda needs you and the doctor wishes to talk to you. I'll make a brief telephone call from the other room while you get ready."

Bevis went to the phone and found himself dialling Gavin's number and asking for Cassandra. The phone was answered by Tonia. "Don't bother Gavin, I'll talk to him another time. How's my namesake?"

"Sound asleep. We've seen so little of you lately," she chided gently. "Don't forget the baptism is on the eleventh."

"No, I won't. Can I speak to Cassandra if she's still awake?" He did not know exactly what he wanted to say to her, probably just to hear her chilly voice.

"Didn't you know?" Tonia was saying, "Cassandra moved out almost three weeks ago."

"Oh, really? I didn't know. Where's she staying now?"

"With her friend, Marie. I expect to see her tomorrow. What should I tell her?"

"It's not important, Tonia. Give my regards to Gavin and good night." After that he telephoned his house and briefed Jane on the situation.

* * *

"The medicine's available but Dr Shah thinks it would not be a good idea to send it all the way here. He suggested, and I agreed with him, that we dispatch the patient immediately. He has undertaken to make the preliminary arrangements so that there's no unnecessary delay. As I've already told Bevis here that time is of the essence. I'm not trying to scare you but we need to move fast. I'll go and get my referral papers ready while you two talk it over."

"There's nothing to talk over, doctor, you go ahead with the arrangements," Bevis said. Raymond simply sat there with a dazed expression, appearing surprised whenever directly addressed or required to comment.

"It's very important though that no matter how high his temperature is, you don't give him any medicine. Use compresses if necessary and keep me informed of any change, however slight. I better go and get my papers in order now. Fortunately I have the file with me at home."

"I hope your passport is up-to-date, Ray, you're travelling to Nairobi tomorrow," Bevis said firmly.

"Sure, sure," replied the other absently, after which the two joined Belinda at the sick child's bed and tried to persuade her to rest.

"Ray and I will take turns at watching over Steve," Bevis assured her.

She accepted a cup of hot milk from the solicitous housekeeper and took the two tablets the doctor had given her for her migraine. She and her husband had barely exchanged a word, and to Bevis' relief had confined her criticism to reproachful glares.

Bevis was just dozing off in the chair with the shaded lamp slightly behind him when an anguished howl jerked him awake. He shook off the lethargy, cursing himself for succumbing to exhaustion when he was supposed to be watching over Steve. He got up and went to stand beside his brother, peering into the small bed. "He's dead, Steve's dead!" Raymond moaned shakily. "My son's dead, Bevis."

"Are you sure?" Bevis asked, even though he knew that the question was unnecessary because he could see that at a glance. The child lay unnaturally still, his eyes staring vacantly. He touched the small body, still warm but without a single flutter of life anywhere.

"Oh God, no," he groaned into his hands. "Kind, and merciful Father, this is not true; it cannot be! An innocent child, a lovely and only beloved child, why?" He felt a heaviness descend upon him until he felt as if he was strangling.

He had known Steve from the day he was born and had loved him like his own son. Precocious and wilful he might have been but precious and lovable too without a doubt, he lamented inwardly, conscious of his brother's sob-

179

racked body beside him. He pressed the palms of his hands over the slight face, bringing down the final curtain.

Belinda, slightly disturbed in her induced sleep, stirred a little and muttered incoherently. Both men stiffened, their own grief momentarily forgotten and turned to look at her apprehensively. She gave a shuddering sigh, turned over to the other side and went right back to sleep.

"The doctor," Bevis muttered, fumbling for the slip of paper in his pocket which had his number.

"Of what use is he now?" Raymond burst out bitterly. "He must have known Steve was going to die and did nothing to help him. My son, my only hope for the future gone from me forever," he quivered. Bevis looked on helplessly before tiptoeing out of the room.

"It's most unfortunate, most unfortunate indeed," the doctor intoned in a deep pompous voice on being apprised of the tragedy. Irritated but controlled, Bevis asked with a hint of reproach, "Aren't there arrangements that must be made?"

"I'm sorry, please forgive me but I've not taken it in properly," the doctor apologised. "I'll make arrangements for the transfer of the body to the hospital and then I'll come over. How're the poor parents?"

"Raymond of course is shattered but Belinda doesn't know yet: she's still asleep." He dreaded being the one to break the dreadful news to her and had hoped the doctor could do it, using his professional mannerism to cushion the blow. But was there any way one could lessen the impact of such a tragedy? Perhaps it might be better if he himself undertook the painful task rather than a relative stranger. He sighed heavily and listened to the doctor clucking on, "Oh dear, oh dear, what a prospect, what an awful prospect to awaken to!" He was quiet for a short time, no doubt conjuring up the terrifying occasion before he finally said, "I'll be over shortly."

As Bevis was replacing the receiver, he became aware of the housekeeper hovering uncertainly close by. "How's Steve, sir?" she asked in hushed tones.

"Steve...Steve..." Bevis tried to speak, to tell her, but the words got caught in his throat, making him stutter. He stared at her with a glazed expression. She couldn't know of course, how could she, he thought. Mrs Njuki suddenly felt a chill run through her body and shivered.

"But, sir, it can't be, how can it? He was alive this evening. He was sick but not dying. I've seen him worse and he recovered," she rambled on, her voice rising. "He's asleep, he must be."

"Pull yourself together please," Bevis ordered, pushing her into a chair. The last thing he wanted to deal with was a hysterical woman. "You and I have to pull ourselves together to see to things because there's nobody else," he urged with outward calm. "Belinda's asleep and doesn't know yet but you can imagine how stricken she will be when she wakes up. Raymond of course is too devastated to do anything."

"Yes, sir," the kindly lady replied, trying in vain to stop herself from shaking. "I'm sorry."

"Good. Go now and get dressed and come back here." She shuffled away, bent almost double, her bunched fist stuffed in her mouth to choke back the sobs.

Left alone, Bevis thought that he should ring up Emily, other relatives and friends who could be reached by phone. He would then arrange to put an announcement on the air. But first he tiptoed back to the room to check on the occupants there, but stopped right at the door. Inside, Raymond had removed the body of his dead son and sat with it clutched tightly to his breast, while tears ran down his ravaged face.

Bevis' own heart swelled with terrible pain at the pathetic sight until he thought he'd burst. He took an unsteady step backward and turning, lurched drunkenly to the sitting room where he slumped into a chair, gasping.

"Oh God," he whispered under his breath, and felt a terrible urge to abandon himself to grief too. A few minutes passed before he pulled himself together. A show of grief was a luxury he could not afford at the moment. There were matters to attend to and he the only one in a position to do it.

'Look, Uncle Bevy what my Dad bought me... Here Uncle, I know how to read... Uncle Bevy...' God, never to hear the piping voice again, see the sweet face!

He felt himself faltering again and wondered how his brother must be feeling. Belinda too would surely go out of her mind when she came to know. Whatever her other faults, she had loved Steve dearly and been a good mother to him. What comfort could he offer such people, what hope? He needed Emily beside him; the burden was too much for him to carry alone.

He looked at his watch and realised it was almost daybreak. There were a hundred and one things to do – good God, where would they bury him? The problem had completely escaped his mind. The ongoing civil war had divided the country into two zones with the guerrillas controlling most of the southwest and the government the rest. The communications between the two warring parties had long been reduced to the sound of gunfire only. Poor Steve, poor innocent mite, deprived of even the right to rest alongside his ancestors! What a world! Sighing deeply, he reached for the phone to make his list of calls.

Chapter Eleven

"What did the MD have to say about it?" Marie asked her friend in a gentle voice. They were sitting in Marie's office, she at her worktable, looking across at Cassandra who sat looking awkward with the frontal weight she carried.

She averted her face sideways to hide the angry tears gathering in her eyes before she replied, "He said that I should not regard this as a reflection on my ability, but I'd like to know what it is."

Marie made sympathetic noises. She understood exactly how Cassandra was feeling. She felt indignant at the injustice meted out to her friend in the recent changes in the editorial section in which Collin had been promoted to the position of Chief Editor after Mr Ndiwalala absconded into self-exile. Indeed everybody had expected Cassandra to step up to the post of Senior Editor. But to their surprise, a completely new person from outside had been brought in and appointed to take over from Collin.

Marie had suspected that Cassandra might not have been promoted simply because she had spurned Mr Wakilo's sexual advances. There could be no other explanation for the committee to disregard Cassandra's abilities even if she were relatively new on the job. But knowing how the other would react to such a suggestion, Marie decided to underplay the personal angle by attacking the problem from another, saying, "You must realise that as a woman, the odds were against you right from the beginning." Gender issues were up Cassandra's alley. "What I mean to say," she went on hurriedly, after colliding with a black look, "is that in such a contest, a man always starts out with advantages over a woman. The interviewers are almost always men and it stands to reason that they'd favour their own kind. Sheer male chauvinism, if you like," she added, forestalling the retort trembling on Cassandra's lips. "Secondly, in your case, not only were your sex and aptitude for the job being considered but your state of health too."

"What's wrong with my health?" Cassandra snapped.

"Nothing from your point of view. But you're pregnant and naturally a woman in such a condition is considered to be the least suited for a job which's quite demanding in terms of time and devotion. Not if there is a choice, anyway."

"What do you mean?" Cassandra demanded, outraged. " I put in more time than most people around here. You sound as if you're on their side!"

"I'm on your side, Cassandra," Marie soothed, climbing down from her high stool and coming to join her at the low table. "But," she added solemnly, "I'm realistic enough to have an objective view."

"It is easy to rationalise a grievance when you're not personally involved, isn't it?" Cassandra remarked scathingly.

"That's not fair and it's not like you to sound so petty," the other mildly objected. "As your friend, I want you to succeed as much as you yourself do and as a woman, I regard any injustice done to you, because of your sex, a general issue. But I'd seriously advise you not to allow this setback to affect your excellent performance. It won't take them long to realise their mistake."

"I don't think I have to go out of my way to prove anything," Cassandra said stiffly. "Anybody who thinks I'm not doing a good enough job is free to say so."

But in spite of her protestations, she continued to work as hard as before and readily extended her cooperation to the new head of her section, making things easier all around.

At this stage in her life, it was more than devotion to duty which made it necessary for Cassandra to keep as busy as possible all the time. She feared that idleness could easily lead to an invasion of self-pity and melancholy and endeavoured to fill the emptiness which surrounded her with sinister persistence with the old familiar routine of activity. But it was not always possible to keep her mind absolutely free from retrospecting on the past events. Nights were the worst when she lay alone and sleepless in her bed. Flashes of past joys and sorrows, still vivid enough to disturb, intruded on her, arousing a deep and urgent need to fill the aching void left by Raymond.

But it was not as if she lacked company from men. She received her share of the usual passes as any other young lady of her attributes. But in her condition, she could not feel but irritated at such attention, especially from Bevis.

After Bevis had learnt of his brother's break-up with Cassandra, his feeling of concern for her overcame his initial trepidation and he decided to face her with the truth.

"Sleep walking, ha!" Cassandra remarked nastily. "I've heard of a great many excuses but yours stretches the imagination."

"It's true, Cassandra," Bevis pleaded. "Why would I lie to you or seek to malign myself."

"Because you banked on my not believing you. Nobody would believe anything as far-fetched as that," Cassandra replied witheringly. "Actually the laugh's on me," she added; laughing unpleasantly. "You see, I thought of you as a pretty harmless person, incapable, or more accurately, disinclined to sullying your reputation by stooping to trickery to achieve your ends. But then it had become such an obsession with you to separate me from Ray that you were prepared to try anything to achieve it, am I not right?" .

"As a matter of fact there's some truth in what you say, Cassandra," Bevis admitted without flinching and Cassandra gazed at him, stunned. She had expected a hot denial, or at worst one of his self-virtuous claims like 'I was thinking about you' but not this blatant confession. Before she could recover, he went on, "I wanted your relationship with Ray to end because I knew there was no future for you in it. I knew my brother and the complex problems of his marriage. But more importantly, I wanted you for my own. I love you, Cassandra, I have loved you for a long time. But believe me, I would not employ such dishonourable means to compromise you into accepting me. What I told you is the simple truth. If you don't believe me, you can ask any member of my family. They'll confirm what I've told you."

"No, thank you. The less I have to do with the lot of you, the happier I'll be. I wouldn't believe anything coming from any of you, anyway. That's one valuable lesson I've learnt from my experience."

"Oh, Cassandra, I've never lied to you, have I? Why can't you believe me? You're the last person I'd deliberately wish to harm. I love you so much, I want to marry you!" Bevis pleaded, almost on bended knees, but pleaded in vain.

"In my scheme of things," Cassandra retorted with arrogance, "there's no place for a husband, let alone one encumbered with the name Agutamba."

"What about the baby you're carrying, is there no place for a father for him in what you call your 'scheme of things'?" Bevis asked sharply. "That child is part of me, whether you like it or not, and I'll not allow you to exclude me from his life completely."

"And what will you do about it, sue me for violating your parental rights?" Cassandra sneered. "Let me tell you something, Mr Lawyer, before you start threatening me with legal action. I alone can tell the father of this baby I'm carrying," and here she touched her protruding middle to emphasise her point.

"Surely you're not thinking – you can't be planning to pass the baby off as Ray's, or can you?" Bevis stared at her dumbfounded.

"Look, how can I possibly make it any clearer that what I do is none of your business? By your own admission, whatever took place was a misadventure and a most regrettable one at that, if true. Mind you, I'm not saying I believe you. But, if for the sake of argument we were to assume that I do, I see no reason why you should feel concerned about it at all because the very circumstances under which this came to pass absolves you of any responsibility."

"You still love him, don't you?" Bevis, whose mind was running on a slightly different track, stated almost with disdain. Cassandra did not answer but regarded him with hostile eyes. "Well," he went on, trying to sound unconcerned, "although my intentions are suspect to you all the way, I wish to give you a piece of advice. Forget Ray, Cassandra, he's not the same man you knew. The death of Steve has affected him greatly and unless you're expecting a miracle, you have a big disappointment in store for you."

* * *

This was no exaggeration on Bevis' part. Raymond was a morose, cheerless person who hugged his grief jealously to himself as if it was the only precious link with his departed beloved son.

"He'll go completely bonkers if he goes on like this," Bevis remarked to Emily one Sunday afternoon. The two sat in the gloomy sitting room while waiting for their brother to shake off his inertia and join them. They had got into the habit of checking on him together or severally like a recalcitrant child.

"All he does is drink and grieve," Emily lamented. "Isn't there something you can do, Bevis?"

"What can I do? He's a grown man and he's not sick, not in the real sense," Bevis replied dryly and added, "All I can do's try to reason with him although today I intend to go further and use threats." Grimly he recalled the visit Raymond's partner, Bill Okiror, had unexpectedly paid him at his office and frankly expressed his grave worries about Raymond's continued absence from office. "I know he's had a terrible knock, poor chap, and he has all my sympathy, but life must go on, you know. Work has accumulated steadily these past weeks and I'm at my wits' end to know what to do. I've tried talking to him, trying to rekindle his interest with update briefs but he keeps saying he's not ready to take up the reins again."

"I know. He says the same thing to me," Bevis commented. He spoke heavily, he was not sure what more he could do. His brother seemed to be relishing his state of deep melancholy and met every attempt to help him overcome it or rationalise it with strong rebuffs. "You don't know how I feel, nobody does," he retorted bitterly one day. "My son lies buried in a cold grave and you dare tell me to forget it and carry on as if nothing has happened!"

"Nobody's asking you to forget Steve, Ray," Bevis had tried to say soothingly. "I too loved him as if he were my own son and miss him very much but..."

"You'll marry and have children of your own," Raymond snapped, adding piteously, "and I never shall."

"You too can start anew, Ray. You're still young enough," Emily had chipped in and made the further blunder of suggesting that he and his wife could reconcile since they had suffered a mutual loss. "Belinda is changed, Ray. She's very remorseful about all that happened between you in the past and is ready to try again if you'll let her."

"Don't talk rubbish, Emily," Raymond had silenced her violently.

Arousing himself from his train of thought, Bevis sighed with the weight of responsibility and asked Okiror, "What do you want me to do?"

"Tell him I can't cope with all the work on my own and I'm considering subcontracting. I don't think he'd like that. Nor would I but we cannot afford to dither any longer. We have deadlines to meet and contracts to honour. Law suits would be quite suicidal in our present financial state. You might even add that we're even beginning to lose clients."

"I don't care what method you use to jerk him out of his stupor," Emily concurred and then started to weep quietly, while her brother looked on helplessly. But a few minutes later, the appearance of Joseph requesting an audience with her in the kitchen dried up her flow with surprising suddenness.

"What is it?" she snapped, looking about the cold kitchen critically. The two had never hit it off. Emily abhorred Joseph's fondness for the bottle and distrusted his shifty manner. Joseph, on the other hand, who was constantly harassed whenever she was around, defied her as much as he dared.

"There's nothing to cook for lunch," he mumbled, looking at his feet, embarrassed. He hated betraying his master's lapses but he knew the 'madame' expected a meal and what would he prepare it with, stones?

"No food? What do you mean 'no food'?" Emily exclaimed, flinging cupboard doors open. "Why's there no food in the house, what have you done with the money? I'm not a stranger here, you know, and I know my brother lets you buy all the provisions for the house. So you tell me why there's no food, not even a bean," she ended with disgust. "What're you waiting for? Go and buy food now, if you haven't drunk all the money."

"I'm not a thief," Joseph retorted indignantly, "and I'll not stay here to be insulted," he added, taking off his apron and flinging it on the table. He then headed for the back door and disappeared.

"Hey, where do you think you're going?" Emily demanded, angrily trotting after him. "Who gave you permission to be off?"

"I'm going and that's that," Joseph flung at her over his shoulder and hurried to his sleeping quarters. He was longing for a drink and welcomed the spat with Emily as a good excuse to cut loose. He had been hemmed in too much lately, not daring to leave his master alone in his state.

Emily's strident voice echoed through the house attracting Bevis' attention. "What's the matter?" he asked, joining her in the backyard.

"That stupid old fool says he's not going to work today."

"He probably deserves a day off," Bevis said, sizing up the situation. He suspected an altercation in which Emily probably hurled insults at the poor man.

"But there's nothing in the house to eat, how can that be when I know how foolishly lavish Ray always is with money? He must first explain why he's not bought any supplies." Just as I feared, thought Bevis, regarding his sister thoughtfully. Emily had the knack of putting underlings' backs up which made her unwelcome in most of her relatives' kitchens.

"Don't interfere too much in Ray's domestic arrangements for heaven's sake. This would be a bad time to lose Joseph," he warned her. "Let's go back. We'll think of something for lunch."

"I thought I heard voices," a dishevelled figure bending over an empty fridge remarked. "There's not a stick in the damned place," he muttered, banging the door shut.

"What about the freezer?" Emily suggested helpfully, darting to the said machine but this was not only empty, it had been defrosted and cleaned. "Your faithful retainer has apparently hogged down the lot."

"Probably wasn't much to begin with," Raymond muttered unconcernedly. He led the procession back to the sitting-room and dropped into a chair, his head in his hand. "Where's Joseph? He could get you folks something," he added vaguely.

"He's taken the day off," Bevis put in quickly to forestall Emily's diatribe. "Why don't you let me take you both out to lunch?"

Raymond raised his head, a dubious look painted on his suffering face. "I feel like hell."

"And no wonder; always happens once the laws of moderation are ignored. Emily here is dying to mother you," Bevis added dryly, earning himself a scowl from that irascible young lady. "Would you Emily?" Emily flounced out of the room. "When do you reckon you last had a meal, Ray, and I mean a real meal, not *muchomo* or whatever?"

"I'm not much into food these days."

"What about Joseph, has he given up on life too? You need him you know. If you're not more careful, you're going to lose him."

"Oh for heaven's sake, none of your 'I know better than you' nonsense please. You run your household and I'll run mine," Ray retorted, unrepentantly.

"Take this, Ray, and you'll feel like a new man in no time," Emily said, coming back with a glass of clear liquid for her brother.

187

"My old self's fine, thanks. What's this anyway?" he added suspiciously, holding the glass aloft, with an unsteady hand.

"I'm not trying to poison you, if that's what you think," Emily joked humourlessly.

"Dear sister, nobody would blame you if you were; certainly not I," he added to himself. "Down the hatch then." He took the contents in one gulp and then shook himself like a wet dog. "I'm a good boy, I am," he intoned in a childish voice, and then went suddenly rigid, his mouth slack and his red-rimmed eyes staring as if he had seen a ghost. His two visitors, equally stupefied by the unfortunate slip, stared at him open-mouthed. The words were an exact reproduction of Steve's piping voice after a heroic act like taking bitter medicine.

For some time, nobody uttered a word or moved. The silence was so total it echoed in their ears. Then suddenly, Raymond's grip tightened on the glass and with a curse he hurled it at the opposite wall, missing hitting his brother by a fraction. He gave a bellow like a tormented animal and, burying his head in his hands, started to heave with sobs. The other two watched him tense and anxious, too overcome themselves to help him. Then Emily sprang to her feet to go to him but Bevis held her back saying, "Leave him alone, Emmy, he needs it," meaning the crying. But Emily wrenched herself free and rushed to the side of her brother, murmuring to him soothingly.

"This is too much," Raymond cried out. He got up violently and stomped away, leaving behind a bewildered Emily.

"You still have a lot to learn about men, Emily," Bevis said without sympathy, "Why don't you do something practical like stocking the depleted food store? Here's some money." He counted out a handful of thousands and put it in her willing hands. "Take my car." Emily looked uncertainly in the direction Raymond had taken. "Go on," Bevis urged. "I promise you by the time you come back, Ray'll be in his Sunday best, ready to take the city by storm. I hope you won't mind our deserting you but it's time for a man-to-man talk and I know you've been itching to take broom and brush to this place," he added, gently teasing her.

"I told you Joseph is no good," Emily responded forcefully, her usual dour spirits immediately restored. "Look at the grime and clutter. I swear I don't know what he does the whole day." Bevis also let his eye wander about the once splendid room, now covered with dust and giving off a general air of disuse.

What would Cassandra think of Ray's deterioration, he wondered inwardly, and allowed himself to dwell on the complex relationship between the two. Since the death of Steve, Cassandra's name had not, to his knowledge, crossed Raymond's lips. Did it mean he had put her out of his mind completely, or was he still too upset by what he considered her betrayal to bring himself to talk about her? Cassandra was not the type of woman a man forgot easily.

Pursing his lips grimly, he sought out his brother in his sanctuary to ram into him a few home truths. The threat to his business, which he had started single-handed, brought him out of his stupor, arousing instant concern. "Why did James go moaning to you, why couldn't he come to me?" he thundered.

"Guess he didn't want to worry you and..." Bevis got no further. He was rudely interrupted with, "Didn't want to worry me! Whose business is it, anyway?"

"Yours of course. Look, Ray," Bevis, pretending to be alarmed by the violent response, hurriedly interjected to extricate himself, "I was just reporting what Okiror told me. You can sort out your problems together when you meet, which I hope will be soon."

"You can bet on that. I'll be in the office before sunup tomorrow to check things over. God knows what's been happening in my absence."

It was the longest and most animated speech Raymond had made in a while and it made his brother sigh with relief. He could now cross him off his priority list and turn to other matters.

* * *

The civil war which had been showing signs of slackening suddenly gained momentum. The rebels overran the whole of the Western Region and closed in on the centre.

As usual, rumours, real and imaginary, were rife in the city, throwing the entire populace into a chaotic existence. Insecurity and lawlessness became the order of the day as armed thugs turned on the citizens, plundering and murdering indiscriminately. Once again people sought refuge behind locked doors. The two girls at Mpafu had, out of sheer bravado, refused to move out of their house. But every night brought its own terrors and every new dawn was awaited with suspended breath.

"I did not know it was going to be this scary," Samantha said after one particularly terrifying night. "Last night was like the day of Armageddon, wasn't it?"

"It was certainly bad," Cassandra agreed, examining her drawn face in the mirror.

"You look like hell," Samantha commented helpfully.

"I feel like hell," the other agreed.

"When do you start your leave anyway? You look like a drum major."

"Thanks a lot, but I could do without some of your inspiring comments today ," Cassandra said with sarcasm. She still had about three weeks to go and had no intention of spending them hiding behind curtains and peeping through keyholes every time a leaf fell on the roof of the house. Samantha had been relieved of working evening shifts which was a bit of a relief but no definite comfort to Cassandra. Her friend might be warmhearted and willing to help but she was flighty and might not be able to cope very well in an emergency.

"I suppose I could move to Luzzi for the period," Cassandra one day said, thinking aloud.

"You want to go to your brother's place?"

"For the duration, yes. Do you mind?"

"Mind? Are you kidding? I've been having nightmares in case you started labour in the night, I can tell you! I was going to suggest the move myself if you hadn't brought it up yourself." Actually that was stretching the truth a little. The idea had come from Bevis who had been using Samantha as his contact to know how Cassandra was faring.

"You see, the death of his son has traumatised my brother so much it might take him a long time to be himself again. But in the meantime, I don't want Cassandra to feel abandoned, especially in her condition. Keep me informed of her welfare, Sam, and if you think there's anything I can do, anything at all, please let me know."

"Substitute lover or dummy?" Samantha mocked him with her usual bluntness. Bevis smiled wryly in spite of himself. He had believed himself to be the embodiment of subtlety.

"Don't the two mean the same thing?" he asked laconically.

"Not in my vocabulary, they don't. But you can rely on me to keep your secret."

"Thank you. And please keep this conversation from Cassandra."

"Of course. But as a matter of interest, why have you suddenly become an outcast?"

"We collided on something," Bevis said vaguely.

"Yeah, I can imagine. She's extremely touchy these days, quite understandable of course."

"You're a good friend, Sam, try to keep her from moping."

"Cassandra is too sensible to waste time feeling sorry for herself, and I bet one day she'll discover the real you."

"Ah, one day," Bevis repeated under his breath.

* **

190

At Luzzi, Cassàndra discovered that she couldn't very well avoid Bevis. Nor could she display open animosity towards him without arousing speculation. So she decided on a middle.By the time her baby was born, the atmosphere between them had thawed considerably to make it possible to fit him back in his old place as a family friend.

Bevis was, at this time, feeling more and more restless. He was a man who was used to knowing exactly where he was going every inch of the way and hated the limbo state he found himself in. After their child was born, he thought Cassandra would change her attitude towards him, but he was still making no headway with her and yet he found it impossible to put her out of his mind and make other plans. It was in this mood of uncertainty that Jane had left him.

"How could you let a girl like Jane slip out of your fingers, man?" his friend, James, had remonstrated with him.

"She did not just slip out, I let her go."

"That's what I mean. She was tired of being on the shelf and why, because of the immortal Cassandra? If ever that girl was out of your reach, she's more so now that she is expecting your brother's child. I can't imagine why you waited that long to make a move? You should have made her love you."

"Caveman style? I'd be out of my mettle," Bevis said, amused.

"Then how about pleading? What's the use of being a good lawyer when you can't plead your own case? What do you plan to do now? Vegetate until the princess wakes up?"

"You've got your metaphor mixed up, mate."

"That's not important. Why don't you ask Jane to come back? You surely look at a loose end without her."

"Yes, she had her uses, poor kid, but it wouldn't be fair to her. She really wanted to do this course. She wants to make something of herself and I won't be the one to stand in her way."

"Perhaps she's trying to prove something," James said after searching his friend's face for signs of remorse in vain. "Your rejection of her must have given her an inferiority complex that she's trying to overcome by redirecting her energies into more practical channels. I have no doubt a sign from you would reverse the course."

James's insight into Jane's psychology seemed to be more accurate than Bevis'. Although Jane had gone about securing a scholarship with grim determination, the main reason behind it was to jolt Bevis into making up his mind about her. When he let her go without a struggle, she knew she had gambled and lost. But even after she had left to go abroad, it was still on the table that a sign from him indicating his need of her could bring her galloping back.

But although Bevis missed her badly, he knew that he could not, in all conscience, do that. The only meaningful commitment he could ever make to a woman would be to none other than Cassandra. She was in his blood. Only she could give meaning to his life. It did not matter very much that she still kept him at arm's length. Just being in her company and being allowed to see his son once in a while was a comfort of sorts. The little fellow was growing to be every inch an Agutamba and he couldn't help being proud of him.

* * *

One day when Stella was visiting, Bevis could not resist the temptation to boast about him.

"You never told me there was a kid," Stella accused him, jumping to the natural conclusion that Benjie was Raymond's child.

"I suppose because the subject never came up," Bevis replied, his blood running cold. It was a state of affairs he was going to have to learn to live with until Cassandra came to her senses and decided otherwise.

"The subject never came up, what do you mean?" Stella exclaimed, greatly excited. "How can you calmly say that when we've been racking our brains trying to find a solution to Ray's problem? Don't you see this is the perfect answer? This child could in time come to fill the vacuum left by Steve's death."

"Benjie has nothing to do with Ray's problems and I'll not have him used as a tool. He's just a baby, Stella, Cassandra's baby."

"I realise that and I'm not suggesting anything wicked like separating him from his mother. All I'm saying is that Ray should be encouraged to take an interest in the kid. Since Steve's death, his zest for life has been on the wane. If this kid should capture his interest, he'll have something to encourage him to go on from day to day, to fill him with hopes of tomorrow. Your brother has had more than his fair share of suffering, Bevis. I'm surprised you did not think about this yourself."

"Strange as it may seem to you, Stella, I do have a life of my own to live," Bevis replied sarcastically. But no sooner were the words out of his mouth than he regretted allowing the bitterness inside him to show. Stella would not hesitate to use it to rake up old feuds.

"How can you say that?" she charged with disapproval. "We've always stood together as a family and I'm sure if circumstances were reversed, Ray'd do no less for you."

"Would he?" he challenged dryly.

"We're made differently, Bevis," Stella said, avoiding a direct answer.

192

"You're the stronger one, the pillar of the family. We all depend on you in times of crisis because you're sensible, dependable and openhearted. You should be flattered that you're thought so highly of."

"I am," he replied shrilly and fell silent, trying to check his resentment. What's the matter with me, he asked himself. His nerves were on edge and he felt very vulnerable and alone. But it ran against his grain to unveil his feelings and the myth of superman was what his ailing ego presently needed. He sighed deeply, willing calmness to return to him before he said, "I did what I could, Stella. Emily and I did not spare ourselves. I wish you could have seen Ray after Steve's death. He was completely devastated."

"I'm sorry if I sounded critical but I'm worried about Ray. Do you think Cassandra'd object to his taking some interest in – what did you call him – Benjie? It might help him to stop mourning Steve."

"That's a question only Cassandra can answer."

"I guess you're right," Stella readily agreed but her brother was not deceived by her apparent acquiescence. She would pursue the matter later to her satisfaction, he was sure.

* * *

"It's not a mistake, Ray, Benjie's the very image of Steve," Bevis might have heard her say to Raymond a few days later. "That child is our own flesh and blood I tell you, you cannot afford to lose him."

"You don't know what you're talking about, Stella," Raymond muttered gloomily. He thought that if it were not so painful, he would burst out laughing at the very absurdity of it.

"Go and see the child, Ray, before you make up your mind about it," Stella entreated. "A chance like this does not come one's way often. If this child does not stir up your heart, then you can let the whole idea drop. Trust me, Ray dear, when have I ever lied to you or let you down?" she cajoled.

A reason to live, a chance to be happy again! He had mourned Steven for two long years. Raymond brooded over the possibility long and deeply but it was not that futile hope which one day compelled him to visit Cassandra. It was the morbid curiosity and a touch of masochism to see her again with another man's child. But not even his sister's colourful account of the incredible resemblance Cassandra's child bore to his never-to-be-forgotten sweet Steve had prepared him for the phenomenon before his eyes.

He had parked his car quietly outside the gate, preferring to walk in so that if his courage failed him, he could as quietly disappear. A little inside the gate, he stopped and stared stupefied at the incredible sight before him.

193

Cassandra and a little boy, who was the very image of his dead son at about age two, were playing on the lawn. Am I awake or dreaming, he asked himself as memories of Steve's childhood flooded him, making him feel weak with anguish and longing. He shut his eyes and leaned weakly against the gatepost feeling the strength slowly ebb from his body. Am I going to faint, he wondered for one panicky minute.

The happy babblings and squeals of laughter went on interminably, it seemed to him; now loud and clear, the next minute faint and indistinct. He opened his eyes slowly and was surprised to find the scene fifty metres or so away unchanged. Cassandra, her back towards him, her tight jeans hugging her young pliant body, had a ball in her hands with which she was teasing the infant. The latter suddenly lost interest in the game on sighting the visitor. "Uncle!" he screeched with glee and broke into a haphazard trot in Raymond's direction. Cassandra turned sharply and drew in her breath audibly on seeing who it was. The two stared silently at each other for some time. Surprisingly it was Raymond who recovered first and rushed towards the tumbling child to ¨revent it from colliding with the obtuse trunk of a huge tree.

Cassandra seemed rooted to the spot. For her, the stupor was total and complete. There were times, when in her unguarded moments, she had imagined such a scene, but never with such vividness, such an impact. It was like a dream from which she could not shake herself awake.

Raymond, with Benjjie's arms wrapped tightly around him, gazed at her over the child's head with eyes full of condemnation. "My God, you could have told me, Cassandra," he whispered harshly.

"I was under no obligation to tell you anything," Cassandra, finding her voice at last, retorted defensively. It was natural that she should jump to the wrong conclusion. He took another look at Benjie and burying his head against the little body said, "You don't have to now. What a fool I've been, what a damned fool!" Cassandra gasped and almost shouted a disclaimer.

"Uncle, Mummy!" Benjjie rebuked sharply, impatient with his mother's marked lack of enthusiasm. He was basking in the closeness of 'Uncle', enjoying every minute of being the centre of attention.

"Here, Benjie, come to Mummy," Cassandra coaxed, drawing close and stretching out her arms, but clearly Benjie had taken a shine to the stranger, or could it be a question of mistaken identity, Cassandra thought, alarmed. "Come on," she ordered , and roughly pulled the child away from Raymond's arms.

"You could have told me, indicated," he repeated, his eyes glued to her face. "What a difference it would have made!" he added, murmuring to himself. Cassandra's heart turned over at the sound of his voice and the proximity of his body which brought back all the old sensations, destroying her carefully planned defences. Without a word, she turned from him and walked quickly to the house, hoping he would not follow her.

"Can we talk, Cassandra?" he asked, hard on her heels.

"There's nothing to talk about," she said shortly, deliberately making her voice sound hard and uncompromising. She continued with her swift short strides to the house without stopping or turning. Midway, she realised she was running away from him, and running away from problems was not her style. She stopped and turned to face him.

"We have plenty to talk about," Raymond said, moving towards her, slowly. "I promise I won't keep you long." Stop looking in his eyes, Cassandra admonished herself, knowing how lethal those eyes could be. But her good senses, which should have dictated her next move, seemed to have taken a holiday, leaving only her emotional self to grapple with the situation.

But it did not take her long to realize that she was not the attraction at Mpafu, the magnetism which drew Raymond there again and again. She was saddened by the knowledge but not inordinately so. She at least had a chance to see him and be with him.

Raymond himself became a new man. The discovery that he was a father again gave him a new lease of life and restored his sense of direction. Life became meaningful once more and each day became an adventure. He no longer needed the comfort of a bottle before he fell asleep because it no longer mattered how long he stayed awake. His mind was always full of ideas, plans and dreams for his son. He was determined not to repeat the mistakes he had made with Steve. Benjie's needs, not his own, would come first.

* * *

One Saturday afternoon, Raymond came to Mpafu, as usual, loaded with parcels of toys and whatnot for Benjie. Cassandra welcomed him with the wry remark of, "Have you been robbing the Tiny Tots?" His extravagance made her uneasy, but since spoiling Benjie seemed to give him such great pleasure, she did not have the heart to forbid it although she had no qualms about checking Bevis. Bevis, who was very observant, was not fooled by the sudden affluence in the toy department even without Benjie's innocent remarks. This made him feel angry and more resentful towards his brother than ever before.

"Where shall I put these?" Raymond asked, his eyes eagerly scanning the room. Cassandra indicated the table in the corner. "Benjie?" he inquired, literally quivering with excitement.

"He's asleep."

"Let's wake him up," he suggested, his eyes dancing with mischief like a little boy's. "I can't wait to see his face when he sees what I've brought him."

But Cassandra vetoed the idea. "He needs his sleep; he was rather restless last night."

A cloud of fear immediately overcast Raymond's countenance. "Is he sick?" Cassandra's heart went out to him as she realised what nightmares any childish complaint must stir up in him. "He was just restless due to this relentless heat, but he's not sick," she reassured him.

"Are you sure?" he quizzed, still looking afraid.

"Of course I'm sure, Ray. Why would I lie to you?" She longed to throw her arms around him and comfort him but there was something distant in his manner which did not encourage the kind of intimacy they had once shared . "I'll go and prepare some tea," she said abruptly and left him chiding herself for her weakness. This time he will not call the shots; I will, she decided.

"I hear a car outside," Massy, who was ironing on the other side of the small kitchen said, as she listened intently, her nose beaded with sweat.

"It's probably Sam," Cassandra answered absently. She was brooding over her unsatisfactory relationship with Raymond. Had she been too optimistic to expect him to reciprocate her need for a closer bond such as the one they had once had? Where had all the beauty and wonder gone, the warmth and wealth of feelings, the magic? She could not have imagined it all; it had been there.

She had deliberately let him think Benjie was his son in order to remove the main obstacle to their picking up where they had left off and he had eagerly embraced the idea. She did not know how he had reconciled his sterility with fatherhood. He probably believed his earlier theory that doctors were not always accurate in their diagnoses, and he could be right for all she knew, she thought, endeavouring to absolve herself from the guilt of connivance. Bevis would think her cold-blooded if he knew what was going on behind his back. But it was not his business really; that had been settled between them long ago.

"Sam is working the evening shift," Massy reminded her, breaking her train of thought. "Shall I go and see who it is?"

"By all means." Cassandra said dryly, as usual marvelling at Massy's excessive curiosity.

She now came back heaving and whizzing like an overloaded old truck going uphill.

"It's Bevis," she announced. She called everybody by their first name, a liberty she considered raised her above the ordinary domestic help.

"You either reduce your weight or adopt the snail technique of slow motion," Cassandra said unkindly. She had not as yet digested the impact of her pronouncement.

196

"I said Bevis has come," Massy repeated loudly, ignoring the reference to her obesity, and then avidly waited for Cassandra's reaction.

"In that case, we need another cup," Cassandra said calmly before she reached for it and put it on the tray, added hot water to the teapot and opened the biscuit tin to make sure it contained enough; her actions slow and measured. She lifted the tray and left the kitchen.

Bevis, finding the door open, casually walked in like somebody familiar with the place, his brother thought sourly. "Are you following me?" he asked disagreeably.

Bevis leisurely selected a chair, and after he was seated comfortably, deigned to answer him, in his slow, passive voice, "I did not even know you were here until I saw your car outside." He looked around the room searchingly, his gaze dwelling thoughtfully on the packages on the table.

He nodded to himself perceptibly, as if he had found the key to the puzzle which had been eluding him.

"Looking for something?" Raymond demanded with narrowed eyes, determined to be provocative.

"For somebody, actually. Where's Cassandra?" As if on cue, Cassandra appeared bearing a loaded tray. Raymond jumped up and made a show of gallantry. "Where do you want it?"

"On the dining table, please." Cassandra hurried before him to make some space for it. "Hello Bevis, a cup of tea?" she asked calmly as she busied herself with crockery. Bevis accepted one and sipped it slowly and thoughtfully as he listened to what sounded like a staged conversation between the other two in the room. 'The woman who can separate us is not yet born,': the memory of his words to his sister mocked him as his resentment at the ease with which Raymond had walked back and reclaimed Cassandra mounted.

During a chancy lull in the conversation, he interposed to say he had come to deliver a message from Mellinda. This was not strictly true. His visit had been prompted by the unease he had been feeling since Samantha's portentous hints of surprises a few days previously. He did not know exactly what he hoped to accomplish but he needed to know exactly what was afoot and what his brother had in mind with regard to Cassandra and the baby. "Mellie said she's been trying to contact you without success."

"I know, I got her message. They've clamped restrictions on our phones. No more long-distance calls. Did she tell you what she is so worked up about?"

"Now that you mention it, she sounded quite excited, but no, she did not confide in me."

"Are you sure? You two used to be as thick as thieves and I can't imagine her keeping any secret from you," Cassandra remarked.

"I give you my word. She said that she wanted you to be the first to know."

"To know what?"

"Search me."

"Wouldn't it be simpler to find a phone and ring up your sister rather than playing blind man's buff?" Raymond interrupted irritably what appeared to him like a flirtatious show.

Looking crestfallen, Bevis exclaimed with mock surprise, "Why didn't we think of that, Cassandra?"

"I suppose because we're both clog-heads," Cassandra answered, with dancing eyes, and for no reason at all that Raymond could see, she and Bevis burst into merry laughter, Bevis' low deep chuckle drawing needles through his already irate mind.

"You can ring from my place now, Cassandra, if you want," he rejoined in an unnecessarily loud voice. Cassandra sobered up immediately and looked at him coolly. Had he made the suggestion unprompted, she would have jumped at it. She had been longing to visit all those old familiar spots again, the reservoirs of so many happy memories but he had never, until now, invited her to his house, forcing her to conclude that Muyenga, being too full of memories of Steve, was out of bounds to her and her son. Unable to resist the temptation to deflate his ego a little, she rejected his offer saying, "I don't think it's all that important. I'll ring from Luzzi tomorrow. What do you think Bevis, will you drive me there?"

"Be glad to. And now I must be on my way." He got up heavily, and just when he was about to turn, Benjie, still half asleep, and looking adorably babyish, made his entrance. At the sight of the two men, he stopped, confused, and rubbed at his eyes.

"Come and say hello to Uncle, Benjie darling," Cassandra urged him, going to stand by his side. She did not take his hand, as if leaving the choice of which uncle to greet to him. Benjie took a few tentative steps forward and then stopped, raising his face to his mother's in an appeal for guidance. Raymond smiled encouragingly but Bevis, looking shocked, shot an angry look at Cassandra, which gesture went unheeded. Cassandra was so intent on provoking a reaction from her son that nothing else mattered. Benjie, sucking his thumb sulkily, stood still, refusing to cooperate.

"What's this, an identification parade?" Bevis burst out angrily, unable to restrain himself. Cassandra raised her eyes and for some minutes their cold gazes locked while Raymond looked on amused. "Whatever you're contemplating doing, Cassandra, don't you dare use Benjie or by God..." leaving the threat hanging in the air, he turned on his heels and banged his way out of the house. Raymond turned to Cassandra with a smile on his face, ready to

198

share the joke, but surprised an attentive air on her face, as if she was listening to the fading sound of Bevis' car.

"Don't let old Bevis' outbursts upset you, Cassandra," he said quietly, his sleek beautlful hands playing with Benjie's tight curls. Benjie's dilemma had been resolved for him by the departure of the superfluous uncle. "He's jealous of course," Raymond continued in a confiding manner, a smug smile suffusing his face. "He always has been of my easy conquests."

At these words, Cassandra went rigid. She turned her face slowly to look at him, her eyes dark with anger. "Will you leave too, at once?" she asked tightly.

"Come on, angel, we have a date, remember? First with this young man here," he added, standing up and stretching to his full six feet. He took Benjie's hand and moved confidently towards the table with the parcels but was checked by Cassandra's voice saying sharply, "I meant what I said, Ray. I want you out of my house now. You'll have to look for your easy conquests elsewhere from now on."

"Now look here, Cassandra, I didn't mean what I said, I swear," he pleaded meltingly. "It was just ..." But Cassandra did not wait to hear the rest. She snatched away Benjie's hand and dragged him after her, leaving Raymond standing alone in the centre of the room, looking very surprised.

In her bedroom, Cassandra made straight for the window overlooking the front and a few minutes later, saw him sauntering towards the parked car. Before he got in, he turned and leaned his back against the car, his eyes locating the bedroom window as if he knew exactly that she would be there, waiting for him to appear.

The evening sun caught him sideways, accentuating his good looks. Cassandra waited for the dizzying feeling but nothing happened. Instead she felt hollow and empty as if all her insides had been scooped out. The words 'easy conquest' continued to ring in her ears, making her blood revolt at the humiliating insult. She wished she could hit back at him by telling him he was not Benjie's real father, would he still think himself the ultimate lover? However, a glance at her son's bewildered face made her swallow her anger, promising herself that the time for revenge would come one day. But she could not forgive herself for being so stupid as to think she could turn the clock back. However, she congratulated herself on having been saved more untold miseries by the timely slip of the tongue. From now on, she would be on her guard and eventually, when he was least expecting it, unload him like an excess piece of luggage. That he would be back she was sure. His conceit knew no bounds.

Chapter Twelve

Thankfully the atmosphere at the office was more boisterous. They were preparing for the Frankfurt Book Fair, an annual event which brought publishers, authors, booksellers and all those interested in the book industry together. It was due to take place on the 18th October and the Director's announcement at the last meeting that LI would be participating in the event had caused a stir.

"As you know, we have not been able to take part in this very important event before owing to financial constraints," he had told the meeting. "But now, thanks to the restored peace and security, and the importance our government attaches to our kind of work, we have managed to make fairly good returns and can afford to attend the 38th Frankfurt Book Fair this year. As this directly concerns the Editorial, Sales and Publicity departments, a committee of four people will be appointed in the course of this meeting to look into the necessary arrangements." Cassandra, who was acting Chief Editor during Collin's absence, was selected to chair the committee.

"I think you'll head the team to Frankfurt," Marie remarked later.

"I don't know but I sure would love to go. Do you realise I've never been further than Nairobi?"

"Not for lack of opportunity, I'm sure," her friend commented dryly.

"Don't rub it in, Marie," Cassandra said quietly. She had never told anybody at all, her close friends included, about the exact nature of the breakup with Raymond. Consequently, people like Marie thought the worst of Raymond and every time she saw Cassandra's joyless face, she sent a silent curse to the one responsible for it. "Anyway, there is time for everything," Cassandra added lightly. "Time to travel and time not to travel."

"I rather think it's being able to make the right decision at the right time and stick to it," Marie amended, determined to leave her in no doubt about her distrust of Raymond from the beginning. She was also alluding to the fact that after all she had gone through, Cassandra could still allow Raymond back in her life. She had come upon them rather unexpectedly although so far no flames of fire irradiated Cassandra's face.

"Don't stop there. Tell me what a fool I am and how fools learn from their mistakes," Cassandra whipped angrily. She was doing her best to bury the past but it seemed as if people were determined not to let her do so.

"Only fools who know they're fools ... oh I'm sorry, Cassandra, I don't mean to be so bitchy but you know what this," she indicated her advanced state of pregnancy, "does to me. The person I should be taking it out on is Dan who's responsible for my state."

"It takes two to tangle."

"Cassandra, you're so epigrammatic!"

"Don't be vulgar, Marie," Cassandra scolded but her humour was restored. "What were we talking about before you diverted my attention?

"About your trip to Frankfurt."

"My prospective trip you mean?"

"Oh, you'll go. Take it from me."

"How can you be so sure? Do you know something I don't? Anyway, I hope you're right. If I go, I intend to pass via London on my way back. I'm particularly anxious to look into this engagement of Mellie and George. She sounded genuinely happy on the phone!" she added in a voice full of wonder.

"There's such a thing as genuine happiness, you know, Cassandra," Marie told her gently. "And George is capable of making any woman happy."

"Not any woman; the right kind of woman," Cassandra corrected her, forestalling any further reminiscences on the subject of George. " I wish there was a way of knowing whether I'm going."

"You have got a bad case of the wanderlust there but I hope it's temporary. Anyway, the top management is sitting this Friday; so it won't be long before you know. The reason I know you're being considered as the team leader is because Collin, and not you, has been invited to the meeting."

"That's because I'm only acting as Chief Editor, and I'll bet you a month's pay Collin made it known before taking leave that he'd be readily available if needed."

"Yeah, conscientious beyond the call of duty, that's Collin. But in case you do go and need somebody to take care of Benjie, you can always count on me."

"That's very sweet of you, Marie, but even though Benjie is an angel by general standards, I wouldn't dream of wishing him on you in your present condition."

"Don't be silly. What's one more?"

After it was confirmed that she was going abroad for two weeks, Cassandra asked her sister-in-law to take charge of Benjie. He and her niece, Namara were of an age and Tonia was genuinely fond of him.

"I could have looked after Benjie," Samantha protested unconvincingly.

"I know you could but I didn't want to mess up your working schedule," Cassandra said mollifyingly. Massy was there of course and was more than competent to do the job but somebody more dependable to make decisions in an emergency was needed, and Samantha was not that person.

There was also the fear that Raymond might take advantage of her absence to spirit her son away.

Their relationship had not broken up as expected after that dreadful Saturday. After thinking about it afterwards, Cassandra decided that for her son's sake, she would work towards a gradual, rather than an abrupt, break. She no longer had any illusions about him but she could not help admitting he was genuinely fond of Benjie and good for him. Her own feelings were not important.

Raymond was not very concerned with Cassandra's show of indifference. He knew he had hurt her pride but he suspected that she still found him irresistible and would be ready to eat out of his hand any time he wished it. But he would keep that as a last card. What presently concerned him was getting to know his son better. As long as she went along with that, everything was fine with him. He did not feel ready for a long-term commitment and perhaps never would. What he needed now were light affairs unencumbered with guilt or responsibility. So unwittingly he and Cassandra found a happy medium for their relationship.

Cassandra spent a hectic one week in London shopping and partying, but George and Mellinda looked so blissfully happy together that they made her feel discontented and restless. The sight of the two talking together, laughing and loving awakened in her a tide of longing for something she once had but knew she could never recapture. Besides, she was already missing her son and although, at her sister's insistence, she had talked to Tonia who assured her all was well, she could not help feeling that her place was back home, taking care of him.

Chapter Thirteen

"Benjie's not here?" Cassandra exclaimed on a hysterical note. "Where's he?" she demanded , running from room to room as if to confirm with her own eyes what she had just been told, her high heels echoing hollowly through the quiet house.

She had insisted on going straight to Luzzi from the airport, eager to be reunited with her child at the earliest time possible only to have her hopes rudely dashed.

"Where's he? What have you done with my child ,Tonia?" she screamed full of premonitions.

"Sit down, Cassandra, please. Tonia has something to tell you," Bevis urged her, his own voice harsh and none too steady. She had been surprised and disconcerted when instead of her brother, he had appeared with Tonia at Entebbe airport to collect her. They had not seen each other for about three months now and remembering the nature of their last meeting, she could not help but feel awkward with him. "Gavin told me you were expected today and I offered to meet you as he couldn't," he had answered her unvoiced query. He seemed to be smouldering with suppressed anger inside, which did nothing to add to her comfort.

"What do you mean?" she now demanded in a tremulous voice, turning to him. She felt panic rising swiftly in her chest as her eyes flickered from one face to the other, searching for clues; imploring for mercy. "Has something happened to Benjie?" she whispered.

"Nothing has happened to him, Cassandra, at least, nothing bad," Tonia said. She glanced at Bevis, her large dewy eyes imploring him to bail her out of her peril. But Bevis remained quite still, looking broodingly into space. "Ray took him for a short visit yesterday," Tonia went on, looking defiant. On

203

a less certain note she added," and...and... did not bring him back as promised, that's all."

"That's all?" Cassandra burst out, the relief of knowing her baby was safe, making her voice sound high and impassioned. "And pray, who gave him permission to take Benjie from here? If it was you, then all I can say is that it was presumptuous of you. If I'd known you were going to hand him over to whoever came along, I'd never have left him in your care."

"That's quite unfair, Cassandra. Ray is not just anybody: he's Benjie's father," Tonia argued in her defence.

"And where's he now, do you know?" Cassandra screamed and rushed to the phone. There was no answer at the other end of the line to her frantic call. After a couple of minutes, she banged down the receiver and stood glaring, her chest heaving with anger and apprehension.

"Cassandra?" Bevis said gently, coming to her side. He took her by the hand and led her to a chair.

"Oh Bevis, will you ever forgive me?" she cried, looking at him appealingly, the unshed tears making her eyes glisten like a pair of diamonds.

"Hush, my dear," he murmured softly. "We're in this together, and together we shall find Benjie and resolve the whole problem once and for all. But first of all, you must calm down. You know Ray loves Benjie and would never dream of hurting him, okay?"

"I know, but I also know he'd do anything to take him away from me. He has hinted at it often enough."

"That he'll not do, I promise you. I'm sorry I've mishandled the whole situation from the beginning but I'm going to make sure what has happened now will never happen again," he assured her in a firm voice. He had made up his mind to confront his brother with the truth. He suspected that after recovering from the blow, Raymond would lose his proprietary interest in the kid.

"No, I'm the one to blame," Tonia jumped in. Although she was not quite following the trend the dialogue was taking, she hated to be left out of the picture. "I shouldn't have assumed things but I really believed he'd bring him back as promised. After all, he'd always honoured his word before."

Before Cassandra could react to this further evidence of betrayal of her trust, Bevis swiftly interposed, saying, "This is what I think we should do." He outlined his plan of action and got up briskly.

"I'm coming with you," Cassandra announced, jumping to her feet.

"I think it would be better if you let me handle this alone, Cassandra," he pleaded.

"I must come," she said with determination and the two set off together.

At Muyenga, they found neither Raymond, nor Benjie. Nor could they get any useful information from Joseph except to confirm Cassandra's fears that Raymond did indeed intend to abduct her child.

"He left early in the morning with the kid," Joseph said, staring owlishly at her all the time, his sluggish mind wrestling with unexpected riddles. The two left him and set off to look for Raymond in all possible places but drew a blank everywhere. It was as if man and child had vanished into thin air. Suddenly an idea struck Bevis. "I must find a phone," he announced, bringing the car to an abrupt stop near a small restaurant on the main street. Without further explanations, he left Cassandra in the car, frantic with anxiety.

His sister did not sound too thrilled to hear his voice, which was a promising sign.

"Why are you looking for Ray?" she asked suspiciously.

"Just tell me if you've seen him at all today. If you haven't, say so and stop wasting my time," Bevis snapped.

"Ho-ho, drop the big-brother act if you want my cooperation, although I can't imagine why?"

"No?"

"No. So?" she added aggravatingly.

"Go to hell," Bevis fumed and banged down the receiver. He would have to go to Entebbe and check for himself, although if Emily's attitude was anything to go by, Raymond was definitely at her place with Benjie.

"I'm taking you to Kalungu," he told Cassandra briskly. "May'll look after you while I'm gone."

"Where're you going? I'd prefer to come with you."

"No, Cassandra, you definitely cannot this time," he said firmly. "I'll explain everything later when I come back. Will you trust me?"

"I suppose so. I don't have a choice," Cassandra replied grudgingly. He was grateful that she did not put up any resistance. Poor girl, she is all in with jet lag and the anxiety about Benjie, he thought, his anger surging to the surface again. But he was human enough to feel a little vindicated by the turn of events.

At Kalungu, where he had been living for about a year now, he stopped the car under the extended front porch over the drive and helped Cassandra out. "Miss Mutono's not feeling too well, May, so I'm putting her in your care," he told his bemused housekeeper.

"You're not going out again in this raging storm, Mr B, are you?" May asked him with disapproval. The sky, which had been getting darker and darker by the minute, had finally decided to let go of its oppressive load, flooding the entire place within minutes as only a tropical shower can.

"I have to, May," Bevis said briefly before letting himself out again.

About an hour later, the telephone pealed stridently, startling Cassandra out of her stupor. She lunged for it, beating the lumbering May by a fraction of a second.

"Is that Mr Agutamba's house?" a strange voice asked formally and Cassandra answered in the affirmative. "Can I speak to him?"

"Mr Agutamba is not in," Cassandra replied. "May I know who's calling?"

"My name'll not mean anything to you or even to Mr Agutamba himself but I'm calling on a matter of the utmost urgency. Perhaps you can tell me where I can reach him."

"I'm sorry but I'm not sure where he is right now. But if you care to leave a message, I'll see that he gets it promptly. I'm his wife," she added glibly.

"Oh, I'm sorry, Mrs Agutamba, so stupid of me not to realise you'd be the one to answer the phone."

"That's all right. What's the message?" she prompted, holding her breath.

"It concerns his brother," the voice doled out.

"His brother?" Cassandra breathed, groping for a chair.

"His brother Raymond Agutamba of Encyclopaedic Architects Ltd. You know him? "the voice, faltering over the particulars as if reading them off a card, asked.

"Of course I know Ray. What about him?" Cassandra asked in a cracked voice. "Has anything happened to him? Please tell me, " she begged, almost hysterically. May, attracted by her distressed voice, hurried to her side.

"What is it?" she kept interrupting in a breathless voice until Cassandra hissed at her to keep quiet.

"Don't be too alarmed, Mrs Agutamba, but your brother-in-law was involved in a car accident," the voice informed her. Cassandra gasped audibly and was silent. "This happened on Entebbe Road about an hour ago," the caller went on, trying to give her time to absorb the shock.

"Is he...is he... he..." she struggled to articulate her fears but felt too faint to go on.

"He's not dead but he's badly injured," the man added and stopped abruptly as if he was recalling the horrific scene. "I'm calling from Hill Hospital where most of the victims were rushed."

"Oh, thank God he's alive," Cassandra sighed with relief. "What're his chances?"

"I couldn't tell you that, I'm afraid: I'm not a doctor. But I know he was taken straight to the theatre and is still there now. The authorities should be in a position to put you in the picture soon if you contact them."

"Of course. There's one more thing I'd like to ask you Mr ...I'm sorry, I don't know your name."

"I'm called Kato and I'd like to add that I was one of the good Samaritans who offered to ferry some of the victims of the accident to hospital, in my case, your brother-in-law. You wanted to ask me something?"

"Yes," Cassandra said, feeling her throat go suddenly dry. "Do you know whether Raymond was alone in the car or had somebody else with him?"

"I believe he was alone although I can't be certain ... no, I'm sure he was alone. Was he expected to be travelling with somebody else?"

"Yes," Cassandra gulped. "a little boy, about three years old. Are you sure there was no such person? He could have been trapped inside."

"Don't distress yourself, Mrs Agutamba, I'm positive there wasn't anybody else or he would have been discovered and rescued. I'm definite there was no little boy or child of any kind involved in the accident. Your brother-in-law's car was a complete wreck but it was thoroughly inspected. It was a head-on collision with an overloaded speeding *matatu*. There were no fatalities. Most of the victims from the *matatu* sustained injuries of various degrees."

"Oh, I'm so relieved to hear that, I mean that he was alone. Thank you so much, Mr Kato, for your kindness and for sparing the time to inform us."

"I could not have done less. Raymond expressly asked me to let his brother know and actually gave me the name and phone number. He was in great pain of course but lucid enough to know what was happening around him." At these words, hope flowed again into Cassandra.

"Bee ... my husband'll want to thank you personally. Can you tell me where we can reach you?"

He gave her his home and office addresses. "Unfortunately I don't have a telephone," he apologised.

"We shall get to you somehow," Cassandra assured him and bid him good-bye.

"Benjie's safe," she exclaimed, falling into May's open arms. "My baby was not in the car, May, he's safe," she bubbled, too overcome with relief to care about anything else.

"Please explain what has happened," May demanded, and Cassandra did, her short-lived joy turning into concern for Raymond.

"He's not dead, May, but badly hurt," she said between sobs. "So we must keep our fingers crossed and pray that he survives the operation ... oh, I wish I knew where Bevis has gone. I don't know what to do ... what shall I do, May?" she appealed to the older woman, but before the latter could open her mouth, she ran to the phone, saying, "I ought to inform Emily, do you know her number, May?"

May opened a drawer and indicated the telephone book. Without any thought as to how she was going to break the news, she dialled Emily's number, and got an instant response suggesting an anxious Emily sitting by the phone. "I suppose you're ringing about your son?" the belligerent voice charged as soon as Cassandra identified herself without giving her a chance to state her business.

"What do you know about my son? What have you done with him?" Once again Cassandra was gripped with panic, wiping out all other thoughts from her mind.

"Your son has a father and that father has every right to enjoy his company without you and Bevis hounding him like a criminal," the irascible voice retorted.

"That's none of your business, Emily," Cassandra snapped back. "If you and Ray think..." she broke off with a gasp as mention of the name reminded her of the reason for her call.

"What about me and Ray? What more can you·say that Bevis has not already said, calling me an accessory as if we're in the dock. Is it a crime for Ray to want to get to know his son? Why is Bevis so het up? Benjie's not his son," Emily grumbled. Under normal circumstances, Cassandra would have had volumes to say about that but she was anxious to get to the purpose of her call and cut in rather sharply.

"I did not ring to talk about Benjie, Emily," she said and then felt her voice tremble rather ominously. "I have some bad news concerning Ray. He has met with an accident," she managed to say and was almost tempted to put the receiver down and have done with it.

"Ray involved in an accident?" Emily whispered harshly. "It's not true, it cannot be!" she shouted vehemently, making the telephone wires vibrate with emotion. Then she broke down and sobbed unrestrainedly. "But he's just left me, he was all right ... is he.. . ?" Like herself, she naturally assumed the worst conclusion.

"He's not dead, Emily," Cassandra hastened to reassure her, "but he's badly hurt." In a tremulous voice, she told her the name of the hospital and rang off.

A few minutes after the call to Emily, in which time Cassandra tried unsuccessfully, to control herself, Bevis returned. She hurriedly scrambled to her feet as she rubbed at her tear-stained face and went out to meet him.

Bevis came in carrying Benjie whose arms were tightly wrapped around his neck. Cassandra halted a few paces away, overwhelmed by a feeling of tenderness. It was not the first time she had seen the picture of the man and child together but it was the first time she felt so moved by it. It looked so right, and beautiful. How blind I've been, she thought to herself as she stood savouring the moment and wishing she could hold it forever. But she gulped in a lungful of air and advanced towards the two.

"Is he all right?" she asked, stretching out her aching arms, but Bevis

208

tightened his hold on the child saying, "He's fine, Cassandra, just tired," and hurried past her inside.

"Mummy?" Benjie murmured sleepily and went straight back to his slumber.

"We'll put him to bed straight away," Bevis said over his shoulder to the trailing Cassandra and then ordered his housekeeper, who was hovering nearby, to prepare a bed quickly. The procession ascended the stairs to the sleeping quarters, with May in the lead and Cassandra bringing up the rear.

"Why didn't you ring to let me know he was all right?" she demanded, annoyed at being ignored.

"Not now, Cassandra, please. I'll explain later," Bevis, sounding more remote than ever, gestured with his head impatiently.

"I was worried," Cassandra persisted. "He could have been in the car with Ray..." Once again she broke off in mid-sentence, horror-stricken. How could she be so self-centered as to allow her own personal worries to overshadow the tragedy that had befallen Raymond? Bevis probably knew nothing about it and it was her duty to have told him the moment he arrived. She raised fearful eyes to his, but although her lips opened and closed like that of a dying fish, no words came out. Tears rushed down her face unbidden as she mumbled, "I'm sorry, Bevis." He did not react immediately but waited until May had relieved him of the child and put him to bed. Then he turned to her, his face twitching with pain, and said, "I'm sorry too, Cassandra." He opened his arms to her and she ran into them like a small child in need of comforting. The grimness and desolation in his voice told her that he already knew.

"I'll get you both some tea to warm those chilled insides of yours," May said, falling back on the only panacea she knew for shock. "The little one'll be fine, Miss Cassandra, don't worry about him." Her loud voice broke the spell, recalling the other two to the need for haste and action.

"Let's go down and talk," Bevis suggested. Simultaneously they both turned and looked at the peacefully sleeping child tenderly before they left the room. Bevis felt so elated to see Benjie under his roof although he wished it could have happened under happier circumstances. Cassandra divined some of his feelings but for once did not bridle at his possessive air.

Back in the sitting room, he asked her how she had heard about the accident.

"Somebody called Kato telephoned and told me," she said in a sepulchral voice. "He was on the scene shortly after and offered to take Ray to hospital."

"Did he say which one?"

"Yes, Hill Hospital. I ... ought to have told you immediately; I'm sorry."

"I already knew," Bevis said briefly, regarding her quietly. May arrived with two mugs of hot tea which neither wanted but forced themselves to take. "I saw the wreckage on my way back," Bevis added a moment later in a dull voice. "There was still a crowd of spectators and the traffic police at the scene. I managed to establish that there had been no fatalities although I could not get a coherent picture of the extent of injuries." He looked at her inquiringly but she shook her head. "Mr. Kato could not or would not elaborate. He referred me to the medical authorities."

"That's significant in itself. Let's go and find out," he said and stood up quickly. Cassandra followed suit but more slowly and shakily. The prospect of seeing Raymond mangled and spattered with blood terrified her and made her feel ill.

"If you'd rather not go ..." The agonised look on her face had not escaped Bevis which he had interpreted in his own way.

"I want to come, I must come," Cassandra stammered, getting hold of herself.

The storm outside had abated into a steady drizzle but it was still bitterly cold and desolate with the debris of the floods in evidence everywhere. "What a day!" Bevis muttered gloomily, glancing outside at the grey sky. He told her of his hunch which had led him to Entebbe. "I must have passed Ray as I was going, I can't imagine how I missed him. But visibility was almost zero at the time and my mind was fully occupied."

Cassandra was reminded of her own altercation with Emily and without going into details, told him about her call. "I had just told her about the accident when you came."

"I expect she'll be on her way now. Poor Emily, I was pretty rough with her." After that they lapsed into silence, each with their own thoughts. But as he switched off the engine in the hospital car park, Bevis said with a heavy sigh, "We can at least be thankful Benjie was not in the car with Ray."

"That was my first thought when I heard the news. Poor Ray, he does not deserve this on top of all he has gone through already," she said in an almost impersonal voice.

"No, he doesn't," Bevis said, carefully controlling his voice. "And we don't even know what 'this' entails yet. But let's hope and pray that he lives," he added earnestly, and Cassandra silently echoed his invocation.

* * *

Raymond survived the accident but just barely. He was in intensive care for two weeks after coming out of the operating theatre with pneumonia and other complications due to exposure to the cold and haemorrhaging. Finally his condition stabilised but his right leg, which had been broken, had had to be put in a plaster-cast and his back in braces to hold his injured spine.

He was in so much pain the first few weeks in spite of the opiates pumped into him daily. Cassandra could not bear to watch him. "He's likely to spend a long time in the hospital and probably walk with a crutch or limp afterwards," she recounted to Samantha one day. "I can't bear to see him like that. Why do such things happen?"

"I don't know," Samantha confessed, feeling compassion for the unfortunate Raymond. Turning to her friend, she said sternly, "Apropos the subject of Ray, I have been intending to have a little chat with you about it. Don't you think," she added cautiously, "that you're taking his condition a little too much to heart? I don't want to sound heartless or cynical, and in fact I do sincerely sympathise with him, but these things do happen, you know. You're wearing yourself down, rushing from office to hospital every day. Your child hardly ever sees you now. You leave him asleep in the morning and find him asleep at night. Soon he'll forget you and begin to call Massy his mother. I've no doubt your office work's faring no better. So look out, mate, you're not cut out for the role of 'victim'."

" I don't know what you mean by that," Cassandra said stiffly.

"What do I mean? Well, to put it bluntly, you should not be dancing attendance on a man who turned his back on you when you needed him most. Where are the other flocks of women who were ready to eat out of his hand when he was all right? They have scuttled away like mice from a sinking ship because they have the good sense to know what's what. You know what I used to envy most about you, Cassandra? Your independence of mind and sense of personal worth. Don't lose that quality now; don't allow yourself to become a hostage of your own conscience. It's not worth it and you might regret it later."

"Are you finished?" Cassandra asked coldly.

"Yes, you can now tell me to mind my own business as usual."

"What I do and why I do it is none of your business, Sam."

"I know but I was born a busybody as you know. It's my second nature. Since I've already poked my fat nose into it, I might as well get everything off my chest before I make my oath of silence. What about his wife? How does she take all this?"

* * *

What about Belinda indeed? Since the death of their son, Raymond and his wife had become more estranged than ever before although neither had made

211

the move to legalise their separation. But now, at the time of her husband's accident, Belinda had been considering doing so. She had just struck it lucky with one of the *nouveaux riches* army officers and did not have time for her suffering husband. Her whole attitude towards him was one of acrimony as if his accident had been intentionally designed to wreck her matrimonial plans. She knew this would present a golden chance to Raymond to inflict some revenge on her for her past misdeeds but she made it quite clear that she could pull a trick or two if necessary to achieve what she wanted. "I could sue you for divorce and you wouldn't have a leg to stand on, metaphorically speaking of course," she threatened with ghoulish humour. "I have all the evidence I need, remember."

Raymond suspected she was alluding to Cassandra. "You're talking through your hat, as usual. How many years since you deserted me?"

"I did not..." Belinda started to say and stopped.

"You're quite right," her husband said, reading her thoughts. "It's your word against mine. Under the circumstances, this would not be the most opportune time for your coup. No, Belinda, I'll keep you for as long as it suits me."

"Nothing you can say or do would persuade me to return to you," Belinda told him. "I'll not be tied to a cripple. Never!"

"Cripple or no cripple, you're my wife 'until death do us part', to use your own words," he taunted, relishing the irony of it.

"Don't tempt me, Raymond Agutamba," Belinda warned him. Then she recklessly added, "You'd be no loss to anybody except perhaps your pie-eyed slut. Even she would not wait for the grass to grow on your grave before she sought comfort in other arms." He was opening his mouth to blast her when she proceeded in a conversational tone. "Have you ever asked yourself what the nature of her relationship with your brother is? I have and I made my own conclusions. She's young and pretty, if you like that type, and needs more than a studio portrait to keep her warm."

"What do you mean by that preposterous allegation?" Raymond fumed.

"He asks what I mean," Belinda said as if addressing an audience. "I'm not making allegations, darling, but allusions. I'm sorry, I shouldn't be adding to your torments but I thought you should be warned."

"Get out," Raymond screamed, struggling to raise himself up. But the effort proved too much and he fell back on his bed with a groan, his body breaking out in a sweat. Hot tears of pain and frustration ran down his sunken cheeks. This was the ultimate humiliation, he thought, hating his wife with every part of his being.

·Belinda, nauseated by the spectacle, thought what a caricature of the man he used to be before all this!

"Get out now and don't come back, ever," he quivered, his voice coming out hardly above a whisper.

"Now, don't excite yourself, Ray;" Belinda scolded. "Nobody is perfect, as you yourself have proved again and again before. Let the poor thing have her fling while she still can. It's not going to be easy nursing you back to health; I should know. As for Bevis, he still bears you a grudge for what you did to him eleven years ago. But let me not spoil your fun. I'm sure you're dying to make your own observations."

"I said get out!" Raymond repeated between clenched teeth. He had now regained a little of his calm but still looked close to an apoplectic attack.

As if she had not heard a word he had said, Belinda continued in an equable voice: "It's really pathetic the way you're always gloating about the miracle child   yes, I've made it my business to check it out," this in answer to his shocked look. "Miracles don't happen any more, you know. Sterility's not reversed by change of partners or you would have fathered more than a dozen by now. Anyway, what evidence do you have that this prodigy is really yours? After all, you're not the only one with the Agutamba looks," she added, carelessly delivering the last blow to his very manhood.

In spite of waves of pain shooting through his body, he summoned up enough strength to punch the emergency bell and maintain the pressure until a nurse on duty came running into the room.

"What is it?" she asked breathlessly. Belinda, who had moved to the window, ignored her. The nurse bent over Raymond for a closer look, observing signs of intense distress. She wondered whether he was going to have a heart attack; the rolling eyes and laboured breathing were all symptomatic of the disease. Before she could compose herself to act, he hissed, "Get out!"

"Who?" she asked, perplexed, and drew back a step, scared.

"Get her out, staff, now please," Raymond pleaded more articulately, pointing a trembling finger at his wife.

"Certainly, if she's upsetting you," the nurse replied officiously, and turning, fixed hard eyes on Belinda whom she secretly disliked. Belinda was that type of woman who flaunted her beauty and other feminine attributes, causing envy and jealousy in those of her own sex less favoured. Thus most of the female medical staff, whose maternal instincts Raymond appealed to, were unanimous in their condemnation of her as a hard-hearted she-devil. Their male counterparts, on the other hand, were only aware of her extraordinary sex appeal and perfection of form.

The nurse advanced menacingly towards her with the intention of carrying out her patient's request. "Will you please leave the patient to rest, Mrs Agutamba?" she requested in a cold voice.

Belinda looked the tiny starched figure up and down and smiled contemptuously. "My husband, I admit, was once a ladies' man, but even you, with your limitations, nurse, could do better than a crippled invalid with minimal chances of full recovery," she thrust viciously, before arrogantly stalking out of the room, leaving behind one stricken nurse and one mad patient.

* * *

After the brawl with his wife, Raymond became sombre with frequent bouts of dark moods which prompted his doctors to regard him as a potential suicide. He was churlish with everybody, particularly Cassandra, and yet clung to her with the tenacity of a drowning man to a lifeboat. He would sometimes make impossible demands and when they could not be met, become irritable and vicious.

One day he demanded to see Benjie. Cassandra told him that it was impossible, "You know children're not allowed in the wards," she explained but he screamed at her.

"I don't give a damn about hospital regulations. I want to see my son!"

Cassandra had got into the habit of running to Bevis for advice about anything she could not handle on her own but this was the one topic on which she could not expect him to give judicious counsel. He had never brought up the question of her passing Benjie off as Raymond's son. She had long repented of her folly but knew this was not the time to put the record straight. Raymond's condition was very precarious, according to his doctor who advocated sympathy and gentleness as part of the psychotherapy to help him regain his strength.

A logical and intolerant person by nature, Cassandra had at first found her patience tried to the limit. But by and by, she had learnt to cope and became quite adept at handling his moods. However, of late, she was finding the demands he was making on her time and patience too heavy to sustain.

"I'm worried about you," looking at her drawn face, the ever-observant and solicitous Bevis said to her one day. "You're driving yourself too hard trying to do three jobs at the same time. You'll soon break down if you don't watch out."

"You make me sound like an old car," Cassandra said. "But what three jobs do you mean?" she asked, stifling a yawn. She had sat up late the previous night with a pile of accumulated work all marked 'urgent'. Dividing her time between office and hospital meant she was always behind schedule, a thing she had never allowed to happen before. So after a sleepless night trying to catch up and a hectic day at the office, she felt all in and was not looking forward to the hour or so in the sickroom.

"Yes, three jobs," Bevis repeated with emphasis, looking directly at her. "Mother, full time office worker and voluntary nurse. I've probably got the order mixed up, but basically that's what I mean."

"You're exaggerating a little I think, Bevis. I don't exactly act as Ray's nurse, you know. I just try to help keep up his spirits. It's the least I can do."

"That's very commendable ..." was there a trace of sarcasm? "but unnecessary really. Why do you do it?"

"Do what?" Cassandra asked wearily. When the car stopped before a traffic light, she slid further into her seat as if for a nap.

"Wait on Ray hand and foot. He's got the best medical care this country can offer and he certainly doesn't lack attention with every female in the place treating him like royalty."

Cassandra looked at him sharply and without thinking remarked, "You sound jealous of him!"

"Don't be ridiculous ..." he started to expostulate and then stopped, his eyes flashing defiantly. "So what if I am? He has something I don't have, something I long to have," he added.

"I can't imagine what," Cassandra's voice was larded with indifference, whether feigned or real, Bevis could not tell.

"Quit playing games, Cassandra, you know very well what I mean."

"Oh, Bevis, please, don't let us go over all that again. All I want now is to be left alone," Cassandra implored truculently.

"You mean 'left alone' by me? I apologise for inflicting my unwanted attentions on you but I cannot apologise for the way I feel about you because that's beyond my power. Likewise, I don't feel guilty about my resentment against Ray, my God, he treats you as if he owns you, body and soul!"

"Nobody owns me," Cassandra stated crisply. "In any case, what I do is none of your business."

"And suppose I want to make it my business? I'm tired of sitting back while Ray monopolises the show."

"How can you be so unfeeling, Bevis!" Cassandra exclaimed, inflamed by his perverseness. "Your brother lies helpless on his sick bed while you have everything life can offer, and yet you tell me that you envy him! What can you possibly find to envy about a comfortless situation like his?"

"You're evading the issue, Cassandra, which is that he has you, your love and loyalty, which, in my opinion, is more than he deserves. Marry me Cassandra, please!" he continued in the same breath, catching her off balance.

"Marry you?" she echoed, blinking at him like someone just awakened from a deep sleep. "What do you mean 'marry you'?"

215

"It's possible in your literary world, those words could be called cryptic but I'm a simple man and I speak a simple language," he said without a touch of humour. "When I said 'marry me', I meant just that. Be my wife, live with me for the rest of our lives; have I made myself any clearer?"

"Don't be an idiot, Bevis, you know very well what I mean. It's not as if this was the first time you've asked me!"

"No, it's not," he agreed soberly.

"Well, circumstances have not changed, I'm sorry."

"They have but I think you're just afraid to face up to that fact." He expertly swung the car into a side lane and drove on until he found enough space in which he could reverse before rejoining the main road heading into the opposite direction. All this was done with a purposeful air and vigour which Cassandra found rather intriguing. She watched him silently before she demanded, "What are you doing?"

"You'll soon see," was the enlightening answer.

"Tell me now or stop the car and let me out."

"I'm kidnapping you, satisfied? If you want to get out of this car before I'm ready to let you, you'll have to jump."

Cassandra studied his aggressive face thoughtfully and concluded that he meant it. "Well," she said, nestling down in her seat, "I've never been kidnapped before. I didn't know it could be so thrilling," she mocked.

"I'm sorry for the histrionics but I have to talk to you now, Cassandra," he apologized in his normal voice.

"Don't spoil it please; I like you looking villainous and dangerous."

"Don't make fun of me," said Bevis.

"I'm not making fun of you," she told him, smiling a secretive smile, and suddenly she did not feel tired anymore. Every nerve in her body was alert and tingling and she was very much aware of the man sitting beside her, and not as the usual familiar presence but as somebody capable of disturbing her emotionally.

She sat quite still, almost afraid to breathe lest she lost this new and exciting feeling before she had time to examine it. Her companion, on his part, his jaw still jutting out and his face grim, appeared determined to extract from her, by fair or foul means, the answer he wanted. But in spite of this new awareness of her feelings, she could not see herself abandoning Raymond until his dependence on her moral and emotional support had diminished. Would Bevis understand this? She doubted it. She expected his demand to come in the form of an ultimatum: 'It's now or never.' She could not blame him; he had been patient long enough.

She raised her eyes slowly, intending to observe unobserved but instead collided with his glance, intense and fathomless. She turned away quickly, but not quickly enough for him not to notice the subtle change in her.

"What's the matter, Cassandra?" he asked softly.

"Nothing," she lied. He regarded her a moment longer, until he was forced to turn his attention to the road.

Thirty minutes later, in his charming sitting room, Bevis was still in the dark about Cassandra's feelings for him.

"I'm waiting for an answer to my question, Cassandra," he reminded her.

Cassandra felt herself at a crossroads and incapable of making a snap decision. "I have nothing to say to you, Bevis. You shouldn't have brought me here."

"Nothing to say to me, why, Cassandra? How long are you going to play the martyr?"

"I don't know what you mean."

"I think you do. When you refuse to admit your feelings, to allow yourself a chance to make a life of your own, which is not tailored to fit in with Ray's wishes and demands, that to me is no more and no less than self-martyrdom. Why do you feel you have to go through all that?"

"What do you know about my feelings or the reason why I do what I do?" she shot back angrily.

"That's the point. I don't know and would like to," he answered with mocking humility. More gravely he added, "A while back, you looked happy, almost eager to be with me as I with you. Then all of a sudden you went cold. Why?"

"Please take me back to town." She got up abruptly, sending her bag flying to the floor. "I'd like to go back now," she added, scooping it up and heading for the exit. But Bevis had longer strides and got there before her, barring her progress.

"You're afraid Cassandra," he said slowly, seeming to relish every word. "You're afraid of me."

"I'm not," Cassandra asserted heatedly.

"I think you are and I know the reason why."

"Your imagination is running away with you, Bevis."

"No, it's not. I now know you love me, don't you Cassandra?" he challenged. "Let me hear you deny it if you dare."

Cassandra stared at him as if seeing him for the first time. The coldly logical, abnormally conscientious Bevis, she knew. 'We have a child and that child needs a father. It follows that if you marry me, I will be that child's father' was the reason he had previously given for their union. But the impetuous, impassioned Bevis was completely new to her. She felt completely disarmed and shaken.

"What do you want from me, Bevis?" she asked, spreading her hands in a helpless gesture.

"Not much to begin with, just a simple statement of facts. Do you love me, Cassandra? Just say yes or no."

"You know I do, Bevis," Cassandra whispered, and then looked up startled by her own admission. "But I cannot make you any promises or commitments, Bevis," she cried, turning her head away hastily. But Bevis caught her by the shoulders and forced her to look at him.

"I think I can persuade you to change your mind if you give me a chance, will you?"

"How can I? I don't want to hurt Ray, Bevis. You know that."

"No, I don't know it," he exploded, springing up with such suddenness that she drew back startled. "What about me, Cassandra, what about my feelings, don't they matter?" he demanded, his eyes burning a hole in her face. "What I understand is that you still love Ray. As for me, I don't exist as far as you're concerned, isn't it?"

"That's not true. I'm only concerned about Ray because he's sick. He has suffered enough shocks. Think what it'd do to him to learn that I had deserted him for you, his own brother. It might undermine the progress he's making and damage him irrevocably. Do you want that on your conscience, Bevis?"

"Does what I want matter really? Be honest with me, Cassandra. All these excuses and evasions are nothing but a smokescreen. You could at least have the courtesy of telling me the truth."

"You can be extremely stupid, Bevis, you know. If I didn't love you, why would I... ?"

"Hold it there," Bevis shouted, stretching his hand as if to physically shut her mouth.

"No, you stop interrupting me," Cassandra retorted firmly. "You're so obsessed with what you think I feel for Ray that you cannot think straight. I've tried to tell you on several occasions that I feel I owe it to Ray to stand by him because I'm indirectly responsible for his present situation. Call it a need to expiate my conscience if you like, but that's the long and the short of it. I can't help it if you don't understand me but that's the way I am."

"Which is why I love you. What can I say? I feel such an idiot," Bevis said, sighing deeply and looking at her imploringly.

"You could start by saying you understand."

"I do now, yes, I do. How could I not when you've just answered my question? But as you know, I'm a dull sort of bloke, without a grain of

218

imagination. I believe in what I see and ... oh, I need your reassurance, Cassandra. I need it badly," he added on a broken note.

Cassandra felt exhilarated but hid her feelings from him. Instead she said mockingly, "For a person without imagination, you have a way with words." More seriously she added slowly, "Once Ray is well ... what am I saying? I guess I'm trying to ask you to be a little more patient with me until I feel at ease with myself. I know it sounds selfish bu..."

"I think I understand a little and I promise to play it according to your rules as long as I know you love me. Let me hear you say it again, dearest heart," he begged, taking her in his arms.

"I love you, Bevis," she whispered against his chest and then added, "but it's not fair!"

"What's not fair, my love?"

"The accident happening to Ray at such a time, you know. Why him of all people?" she asked rhetorically and felt his arms slackening their hold about her. "What's wrong, Bevis?"

He looked at her remotely and wondered whether he would ever stop resenting her relationship with his brother. He moved away from her and sat leaning back in the chair, his arms cushioning his head, his eyes studying the ceiling. Cassandra's eyes searched his face, puzzled. "What is it?" she asked again. "What have I done now?" She tentatively touched his face, tracing the fine jaw-line. Bevis shut his eyes, feeling his anger melt away at her tender touch.

"I'm sorry, Cassandra," he apologised, opening his eyes. "I'm handling this clumsily. You can't know how I have longed for this day, craved to hear you say those precious words, 'I love you', to me. But what do I do when the moment comes, carry on like one demented! What a fool you must think me!"

"As a matter of fact I do but don't be too hard on yourself, darling. Leave that to me. Actually I think it's natural that you should suspect my dealings with Ray. After all, I did love him once," she added with her usual candour, making him wince a little. "I too have doubts: I have doubts whether anything will ever go right for me again." She looked at him and he recognised in her a mutual need for reassurance, which made him feel more tender and protective towards her.

"Everything 'll be all right, sweet one," he promised her. "I love you so much that I'll do anything in my power to ensure your happiness."

"I know that, darling, perhaps I've always known ... subconsciously. I wish we did not have to wait. But you'll bear with me, won't you?"

"For as long as you think it necessary, dearest heart."

"And try not to doubt me?"

219

"There's no love without trust, Cassandra," he told her solemnly. "We shall try not to doubt each other." He smiled at her slowly, hypnotically, but still made no move to take her back in his arms. "I love you, Cassandra, I love you very much. I've never said this to any other woman. You're the first one and will be the last."

"I feel honoured. But may I suggest that what either of us did before today should be regarded as history?" She looked at him with a trace of anxiety but he was in no hurry to put his seal to the pact. He sat still watching her.

"Come here, Cassandra," he said at last, and held out his arms to her. Cassandra swiftly rushed into them.

"I try to be honest not only with myself but with other people too, whenever possible," he said, looking into her eyes. "If I told you that I'll forget the last three years, I'd be lying to you. What I can promise you is that whenever I recall the past, I'll try to remember that a good deal of what happened was due to my complacency and conceit. Will you accept that?"

"Yes, I suppose I will. I admire your sense of integrity very much, Bevis, but you must promise too there'll be no more reading between the lines."

"Stop harping on that please. I have so much to say to you and so little time in which to say it. May is supposed to be off but I wouldn't bet on her curiosity not overcoming her to come snooping." The words were hardly out of his mouth when the sound of an opening door in the region of the kitchen was heard. With dramatic stealthiness, Bevis moved away from Cassandra and sat apart, his hands primly folded in his lap.

"When I heard voices, I suspected that you must be needing me, Mr B," May said without batting an eye as she fastened the strings of her apron in readiness to take up her duties. "Of course I'm delighted to see you, Miss Cassandra, and I hope that the little one is in good health?" Cassandra returned her greeting. "That's good. I should be going and putting my time to better use like making tea instead of standing here chattering."

"No, May, really, I mean, no tea," Bevis stopped her as she turned purposefully away. "We don't have time for tea. We're going to the hospital and we're late already as it is."

"How long does a kettle take to boil?" May asked, huffed.

"I'd love that cup of tea, May," Cassandra said and added to Bevis, "we can always get in by the side gate, you know."

"We can?"

"Sure, with a little loose change in your pocket." May lumbered away, pleased.

"I don't want to go to the hospital, Bevis, not today," Cassandra added, surprising him. "I'm prepared to do anything within reason to make Ray happy but I feel today should be exclùsively ours. Does that make me very selfish?"

"It makes you contradictory, my dear one, but then that's part of your charm. A while ago, I could have sworn Ray's well-being took top priority."

"Listen, darling, you're never going to be sure of me until you accept the fact that we three have our lives so closely bound together that whatever one does is bound to affect the other two. Ray is your brother to whom, I suspect, you were very close until I came on the scene. He was also my lover, however repugnant to you that may be. I have always believed in facing facts rather than pretending they don't exist. I've already explained to you why we have to go on as if nothing exists between us, but I promise that this masquerade'll only last for as long as Ray is considered delicate. After that, you'll be my first consideration."

"That could take forever," Bevis argued pessimistically.

"I don't think so although I'd like to believe that by 'forever' you mean that every minute we're apart will feel too long, do you?"

"Indeed I do." Then in a bid to recapture the illusion that he was still in control of the situation, he said, "I'm taking you out. You have one hour to run home and get ready." Looking sideways at her he added, "I wonder if we could take Benjie too?"

"Definitely not," Cassandra said. "Perhaps another time." She smiled at him to soften the blow and he smiled back, accepting the subordinate role in the upbringing of his son. But all that would change soon, he promised himself.

"Another time then," he murmured graciously and tilted her face back to look into her incredible eyes. His senses deserted him, one by one, leaving only the great hunger he felt for her.

"How long have we known each other, Cassandra?" he asked and then chuckled as at a secret joke.

"What's funny?" Cassandra asked.

"I was remembering the first time we met." Cassandra and Mellinda had come to visit Gavin who was his roommate on campus. As Gavin was not around, it fell upon him to entertain the two girls. Mellinda, whom he was already acquainted with, was warm and uncomplicated. But Cassandra, whose existence had hitherto been only hearsay, was another story. "What a hateful hussy you were!"

"Surely you're exaggerating?" Cassandra remarked, unoffended.

"I am not. You were the 'snooty one' in my mind from then on."

"I was only fourteen," Cassandra protested. "But it may interest you to know that I hated you on sight too. You were so conceited you expected every girl to swoon at the sight of you!"

"Now, how would a girl of fourteen know that?" he asked with feigned shock. "I confess I went to great lengths to impress you - Gavin's idea actually, who was set on coupling Mellie and me. She was so sweet."

"I will pretend I didn't hear that," Cassandra said severely.

"You heard it all right and I was about to add that but it was you who captured my attention. I was thoroughly annoyed that you did not seem to think much of me. I could not get you out of my mind after that and that annoyed me even more. When I met you years later, I knew why. I craved your approval so much, I still do. Do I measure up to your dream man?"

"You're more than that, Bevis, you're everything I shall ever want in a man. This may sound corny but I wasn't exactly indifferent to you. Looking back, I can now see why we were always up in arms against each other. What I hated most was your condescending attitude towards me."

"I was just sending out the wrong signals in my blundering way. I used to think I could control my destiny, shape my life according to my needs and desires. But not anymore. From now on, I'll take nothing for granted. So be warned."

"I don't know what you want from me, Bevis," Cassandra remarked with a provocative smile. "I have given you all I have to give."

Bevis groaned and tightened his arms about her. "My God, you are beautiful, Cassandra, have I ever told you that?"

"No, but better late than never. I wonder how many women you've said that to, though."

"A couple perhaps but never from the bottom of my heart. When I look into your eyes, a whole new world unfolds before me. A world full of joy and excitement; a world full of promise. Oh, Cassandra, how I wish I could make you mine now, this very minute!" He buried his face between her breasts and sighed heavily.

"Look at me, Bevis," Cassandra commanded, lifting up his head and pushing it away from her body.

"I can't. I'm not that strong."

"Nobody's asking you to be strong: just honest. What do you feel about me right now?"

"You don't want to know. You'd be shocked."

"Try me." Bevis accepted the challenge and took her back in his arms. They kissed slowly, probingly, infusing the act with mystery and tenderness that went beyond the ordinary. Cassandra did not stop to question the legitimacy of her actions. She felt happy and relaxed as she gave herself up to the enjoyment of a pure and luxuriant taste of true love. It's like being born again, she thought dreamily. The past no longer existed for her, only the present and the promise of a wonderful future ahead.

Chapter Fourteen

When Cassandra next went to the hospital, Raymond received her with cold detachment instead of the fury and tantrums she had expected for abandoning him for a couple of days. Feeling a little uneasy, she tried to draw him out by recounting some amusing tit-bits but he was not in a receptive mood.

"Come and sit here, close to me," he invited, patting a place on the bed.

"Oh, but your leg," Cassandra exclaimed, her eyes flying to his plastered leg hooked to a pully above the bed.

"Don't worry about the old leg. It's almost as good as new though rather superfluous," he said flatly. Then turning to her and seeing the fear in her eyes, he added with a forced smile," Don't mind my gibbering. I indulge in it a lot these days."

"Are you all right, Ray?" Cassandra asked with genuine concern. She was wondering whether he was about to go down with fever, to which he had become prone immediately after the accident.

"Don't look so scared, Cassandra, I'm not about to give up, not before I've done what I want to do, anyway," he added grimly.

Truly alarmed, Cassandra looked at him with wide eyes. There was something fatalistic about his subdued mood.

"What do you mean?" she asked, moisturing her dry lips. "Your leg is mending fast, and the doctor told me the cast on your back will come off soon."

"All that is irrelevant to what I want to say to you."

Cassandra had chosen the mid-afternoon for her visit with care. She and Bevis had agreed to avoid coming at the same time.

Cassandra perched precariously on the edge of the bed and gave Raymond her full attention.

"What I have to say is only for your ears," he announced dramatically. Then for some time he seemed lost in thought, his eyes gazing into space.

"What do you have on your mind, Ray?" Cassandra prompted.

Instead of replying, Raymond stretched his hand for an envelope on the table near his bed. "Read this, Cassandra, and tell me what you think."

"What's this, Ray?" Cassandra asked, fingering the envelope hesitantly.

"Read it and find out," Raymond told her impatiently. She obeyed and pulled out some official-looking document. Mystified, she glanced over it quickly but as certain phrases caught her attention, she went over it again more carefully.

"You're divorcing your wife?" she asked quietly, her eyes still glued to the 'decree nisi' ending an eleven-year marriage between one 'Raymond Rutagi Agutamba and Constance Belinda Kyomuhendo'.

"Correction: she has petitioned for the divorce to which I have no objection," he told her passively. "Isn't it great, Cassandra?" he looked at her keenly.

"Great," Cassandra intoned flatly.

"Yes, we can now make our own plans to get married. As soon as I've signed that, I'll be a free man, ready to make an honest woman of you. That's what you want, isn't it?"

It was not a question but a statement. The presumptuousness of it aroused Cassandra's anger but she held it in check.

"Isn't it exciting?" Raymond went on but his face did not show a trace of animation.

"It's exciting but rather sudden," Cassandra remarked. "I need time to take it in properly."

"You've been thinking about it ever since we met, sweetheart," he reminded her, rather insensitively. "I want to legitimise Benjie's birth immediately."

"Oh, if that's the reason you want to marry me ..." Cassandra started to speak with relief, but he cut her short with, "Damn it, Cassandra, that isn't the reason and you know it. I don't have to marry you to make Benjie mine because he is. I could adopt him legally without going through the strain of ... I'm sorry, angel, I didn't mean to snap at you," he apologised, changing his tone. "I want to marry you because I love you."

Cassandra thought what a thrill those words would have given her in the past. Now all she could feel was a sense of entrapment and panic.

224

"You're still sick," she told him as calmly as she could. "Why don't you shelve all this until you're better?"

"I don't want to wait," he said stubbornly. "It might be too late."

"Too late? What do you mean?"

"Listen, Cassandra, what I'm proposing is not wholly selfish. I know I'm a cripple and a washout and cannot offer you much. I also know your feelings for me have changed. But you did love me once and it's for the sake of that love I ask you, no, beg you to indulge me. What do you have to lose? If you cannot do it for me, do it for our son. I have no other child and God knows I don't intend to have any," he added in a monotone.

For some time, he seemed lost in a world of his own: a world full of pain and anguish which reminded Cassandra vividly of the man she once knew and loved. But before she could get carried away, another image, equally lovable and more inexorable, thrust itself before her, successfully breaking the spell.

"It could mean all the difference to Benjie's future both materially and psychologically," Raymond pursued.

"No, Ray," Cassandra cried, jumping down from the bed. "You don't understand. I cannot marry you."

"I understand very well, Cassandra. You too don't want to be tied to a cripple although you've been pretending to care for me," he remarked bitterly. "It's all very well to play Florence Nightingale but when it comes to the crunch, you're not any different from the others who have walked away."

"It's not like that, Ray," Cassandra cried, touched. "Of course I care for you but..."

"But what?"

"I need more time to think about it," she said, agitatedly pacing up and down.

"There's nothing to think about if you love me. Do you?"

"Don't let me say things I'd regret afterwards," Cassandra pleaded.

"Go ahead and say whatever you feel. I know I treated you shabbily once. It's only natural you should hold it against me but I was not myself then. But all that is in the past and if you say yes, I promise you'll never regret marrying me. I'll be a model husband to you. You'll see."

Cassandra knew him well enough to know that for some reason, he wanted to marry her badly. But Bevis' love was all that she wanted. However, she felt a twinge of pity for the man who would never be the same again and advancing towards him said, "I know how you feel, Ray, but I don't think all this excitement is good for you. Let's discuss the subject some other time when you've had time to reflect upon it properly."

"Don't patronise me, for heaven's sake, Cassandra. I'm physically, not mentally, disabled," he told her, annoyed.

"I'm sorry, I didn't mean to offend you. I simply thought that too much excitement..."

"I like the feeling of excitement. I've been too much in the doldrums. I thought you'd be happy for me," he pleaded, grasping her hand impulsively. "Please help me, Cassandra, help me to pull through. Only you can do it."

Filled with pity, Cassandra looked at him with a softened expression. At that very moment, there was a light knock on the door followed by Bevis.

"Bevis!" they both exclaimed. Cassandra's face radiated pleasure at seeing him while Raymond's took on a sardonic smile. The time spent on his back brooding had been partly devoted to comparing his rotten luck with his brother's, which inevitably gave rise to resentment of the latter.

"I'm glad you've come, Bevis," he said with a false smile. "You'll be the first to know Cassandra has agreed to be my wife." He gave her hand a gentle squeeze which, to her horror, was still imprisoned in his. She tried to pull it away but he increased the pressure without appearing to do so.

"I imagine congratulations're in order then," Bevis said without looking at Cassandra.

"You imagine right, brother," Raymond quickly put in before Cassandra could contradict him. She looked at Bevis appealingly but met with a frosty stare.

"I'll leave the two of you to make the most of this great moment. I have a busy afternoon. Catch you later," he added to nobody in particular. As his hand hovered over the handle, he paused to say over his shoulder, "Something has come up which might make it necessary for me to go out of town, Ray. I might therefore not see you for some days. But needless to say, I leave you in very good hands." He then looked at Cassandra with a contempt-filled glance before he shut the door behind him.

Cassandra, who had stood still in a kind of paralytic shock, came alive at the sound of the closing door. She wrenched her hand free and without a word was out of the room with the speed of lightning. She was just in time to see Bevis' car shooting through the hospital gate at breakneck speed. She looked for a special hire taxi and directed it to the Magna Mansions building on the main street where he had his office.

"Mr Agutamba's busy now; I'll let him know you're here as soon as he's free," the secretary told her. "What name?"

"Cassandra."

"Cassandra who?"

"Just say 'Cassandra'."

A few minutes passed in which she was joined by two clients who, fortunately, wished to see the other partner. Eventually the door opposite her opened, and a man came out followed by Bevis. At the sight of her, Bevis froze, his eyes briefly betraying the shock he felt. But he soon recovered his composure, and instructed his secretary to make another appointment for Mr Kiwuka before waving him out of the door.

"I must talk to you, Bevis," Cassandra said urgently as he headed back to his office. He halted, with his back to the room, and then swiftly swung round as if he meant to get it over there and then. But a slight sound from his secretary, the unwitting observer, apparently forced him to reconsider. He held the door open, allowing Cassandra to enter.

"Tell John I'd like a conference with him as soon as possible, Jessica," he said before closing the door.

"Bevis, please, give me a chance to explain everything," Cassandra said, standing in the middle of the book-lined room, and determinedly refusing to be intimidated.

Bevis crossed to his desk and rested his hands on its top as if for support. He did not sit down or invite her to do so.

"We have nothing to say to each other, Cassandra," he answered her harshly.

"It's not what you think, Bevis, I did not agree to marry Ray. You must believe me," she pleaded, feeling that she was losing ground.

"Really? You could have fooled me back there."

"If only you'd allow me to explain."

"No explanations are necessary, and for the record, let me state that I don't have the slightest interest in what passed between you and Ray. Now if you'll excuse me..." he busied himself sorting papers on his desk.

His secretary knocked and entered. "Mr Bindeeba'll be free in ten minutes' time."

"Good."

The secretary withdrew.

"You do mean it, don't you? It's all over between us?" Cassandra remarked dully advancing toward his desk. "You did not mean all that stuff about loving me. You were stringing me along in the true Agutamba fashion!"

"I have a serious discussion with my partner in less than ten minutes, do you mind?" he said coldly and advanced towards the door as if to show her out. But Cassandra intercepted him saying, "Yes, I mind very much, as a matter of fact. You fooled me and I don't care to be fooled. You made me believe you loved me but there can be no meaningful relationship between us without trust. I thought you were different but you're just as cold-blooded as the rest of the breed. Well, you can find yourself somebody else to pander to your ego because as far as I'm concerned, this is the last time I'll ever allow anybody to take me for a ride." Furiously she turned and marched to the door, almost colliding with somebody who was about to enter.

"Sorry. I'll come back later," a young man in a suit said, drawing back.

"No, come in, John. Miss Mutono was just leaving as you can see," Bevis said, callously denying her even the benefit of a dignified exit. The man addressed as John hesitated, taking in the situation at a glance.

"Problems?" he ventured after wrenching his glance from Cassandra's back and closing the door.

"That was my brother's fiancee," the other said briefly. "Down to business," he added resolutely, suppressing a desire to put his head down on his desk and howl like a wounded lion. The pain he felt in his heart was very real and deep. But to allow it to show would be the ultimate humiliation. He decided his hell would be a private hell. He unconsciously clamped his jaws together, his dark eyes turning as cold as a stone. "I have to go away rather suddenly," he forced himself to continue, "and I wondered whether your schedule would allow you to take on some of my most urgent cases."

After comparing notes and discussing strategies, John remarked, "This trip is kind of sudden, isn't it?" He studied his fellow lawyer, intrigued by the peep he had just had into his secret window. Somehow he found it difficult to imagine Bevis with tempests and turbulences in his life. But what did he know of the man except that he was an excellent criminal lawyer and a reasonable person to work with? Bevis was so taciturn about his private life that he knew as much about him now as when they first met five years back, which was practically nothing.

"It has," Bevis said crisply. "I hope you don't mind?"

"Not at all. It's kind of a slow season for me and anyway, most of these," he flicked the list with his finger, "are mere routine and require no special skill except this Ntambi case which has been pending. I'll shelve it again, I'm afraid because I think you should be the one to handle it."

"That's only coming up for mention," Bevis said, getting up to indicate the end of the conference. "I appreciate your cooperation John, I'll try to keep in touch."

As soon as John left, Bevis buzzed his secretary for dictation. After that, he cleared his desk, packed his briefcase, locked his cabinets and left. It was only twenty-five past five, which was pretty early for him.

* * *

228

Bevis sat in his study brooding over the afternoon's events. It was two hours since he had left his office with the intention of putting in motion preparations for his immediate departure. But somehow the energy necessary to act upon his decision was lacking. The image of Cassandra, devastatingly beautiful even in anger, would not leave him alone. His whole being had cried out to take her in his arms and reassure her. But the memory of her, radiant with happiness as she and Raymond held hands, deterred him.

But where could he go, anyway, where he would not be reminded of her? Wherever he went, she would be there, in his thoughts, mocking him for his stupidity and gullibility. What he could not understand, though, was why she had found it necessary at all to string him along. And even more puzzling was the scene in his office. If he had not seen her with his own eyes with his brother, he might have believed in her sincerity. But those same eyes which glittered with unshed tears were the same ones which had glittered with ecstasy a while back in the hospital room. 'No, she doesn't love me and never will,' he concluded.

He sat in the silent room watching as night rapidly descended over the earth, blocking out day. He made no effort to put on the light but continued to sit still, his hands clasped in his lap, meditating on life, love and women. Why do human relationships have to be complicated by emotions, he wondered. Why is love so vital without which one feels empty, incomplete? Why, why? His head throbbed with the imponderables until he was completely exhausted. It was all he could do to stop himself drowning in his own sorrow. "Life goes on," he told himself, getting up to answer May's persistent summons.

"I don't want dinner," he told her.

"What nonsense is this? Of course you want dinner unless you're going to eat out and I see no preparations to that effect. You've not had anything since you came, not even a drop of tea, and judging by that haggard face, I doubt that you had lunch either," she vociferated, facing him squarely. "A body needs to eat or else what's the point of life?"

How simple May made life sound. To her, the greatest joy in life lay in eating.

"All right, May," he acquiesced, sighing. Eating was a small part of the motions of living he would have to go through in the future. He spent the next few days trying to put his derailed life back on track and hoping that the pain he felt would one day disappear.

Chapter Fifteen

The next couple of days were the hardest Cassandra could ever remember having to endure. She could not believe that Bevis could be so stupid as to doubt the sincerity of her feelings for him. Either he was completely blinded by jealousy of his brother or he had not meant a single word of what he had said.

After a week had passed without hearing from him, Cassandra knew she would have to make the first move. She would do whatever she could to convince him of her commitment to him and win him back. The first step, she knew, was to cut the knot which still bound her to Raymond by revealing Benjie's true paternity. She knew what she was contemplating was a cruel thing to do, especially to a man who had gone through much suffering, but she did not have a choice.

The next day being Saturday, she took Benjie to Luzzi and went to the hospital in the early afternoon. Raymond was asleep and Dominic was sitting in the visitor's chair boredly turning the pages of a magazine. He cheered up immensely when he saw her.

"Hi!" he saluted, vacating the chair for her. "Long time no see, what?"

"I've been busy. How's he?" Cassandra asked, looking at the recumbent figure on the bed. He looked inordinately still although the pulley was gone. "Is his leg all right now?"

"Almost," Dominic replied. "The encasement for his spine is gone too and he can now hobble about with the aid of crutches," he added, indicating a pair in the far corner. "We keep it far from him so that he doesn't overexert himself."

"That's good news. I'm glad for him," Cassandra said with genuine pleasure. She was also thinking that it would make her task that less odious.

"It's a pity he's asleep. I would have liked to tell him how delighted I am for him before I go."

"But there's no rush, is there? He'll be awake any time now," Dominic put in quickly. "As a matter of fact, I'm wondering whether you could sit with him for a few minutes while I go out to stretch my legs."

"What's your idea of 'a few minutes', Dome?" Cassandra wanted only a few minutes with Raymond when he was awake but she didn't want to be stranded in the room until his other relatives came.

"Ten, twenty, not more than that."

"Let's fix it at exactly fifteen minutes. If you stretch it beyond that, you'll not find me here."

"Gee, Cassandra, you're tops," the young man said, loping out of the room with indecent haste.

Cassandra lifted the chair quietly and put it by the window. Before she sat down to reorganise her thoughts, she adjusted the drapes on the window to shield the room from the glare of the afternoon sun. When she turned to see whether Raymond was now protected from the sun, she found his eyes on her.

"So you've come back at long last! I knew you would."

"I'm glad you're feeling so much better," Cassandra, thrown off balance by his blind belief that she couldn't stay away from him, said the first thing that came to her.

"They tell me I'll be a new man when I leave here," he told her cynically.

"At least you'll be able to walk again."

"Yes, with a limp. I'll be referred to as that cripple," he added bitterly.

"Don't be so ungrateful, Ray. There're people who come out of accidents worse off than you. Others even die."

"Yeah, you're right. I'm glad I'm alive and I'm grateful you're willing to give me a second chance. It'll be different this time, Cassandra, I promise you."

"About that, Ray ... " Cassandra started hesitantly.

"Don't worry your head about details, Cassandra, I'll deal with them as soon as I'm out of here. Now, I want to hear about Benjie, how's he, does he remember me, ask about me? Come on, don't keep me in suspense!" By now he was half-sitting in bed, his eyes alight with eagerness.

"It's Benjie I came to talk to you about ..." Cassandra said and stopped, not sure whether she could bring herself to dim the light in his eyes, perhaps forever, by revealing the truth.

"Yes? What about Benjie? He's not sick, is he?"

"No...o...o-o. He's fine."

"Whew!" Raymond sighed with relief. "Don't ever frighten me like that

231

again, Cassandra. I'm still considered delicate, you know," he told her with a charming smile. "So, what was it about Benjie you wanted to tell me?" He watched her intently as she struggled inwardly, wondering whether to go on with her plan or wait until he was completely cured and discharged. "Cassandra?" he called her softly, putting on his most tantalising smile. "You wanted to tell me something?"

"No. I didn't," Cassandra said almost angrily and got up. She had a feeling he knew exactly what she had come to tell him and played on her susceptibilities to prevent it. But how could he know? Only she and Bevis knew the truth which neither had ever divulged to anybody else. Unless of course he had always known and had only been making believe. About to leave, she changed her mind and sat down again. "You know, Ray, that I did not promise to marry you as you've been telling everybody?" she said quietly.

"I didn't tell everybody: I only told Bevis!"

"Bevis only is plenty as far as I'm concerned because he is the man I'm going to marry," she told him and held her breath. There was utter silence from the bed. Raymond seemed to have undergone a complete change, all twisted with the ugliness of intense hatred. Cassandra half-rose from her chair, frightened.

"Do you really think Bevis loves you?"

"I know he does."

"I thought you were smart, Cassandra," he said with derisive laugh. "Can't you see why he's doing it, pretending to love you?"

"Why, in your opinion, is he doing it?" she asked him coldly.

"To have his revenge on me. Perhaps he has never told you about Belinda?" he added slyly and watched to see the effect of his words.

"Why should he tell me about your wife? You told me plenty yourself."

"Perhaps. But I didn't tell you that Bevis wanted to marry her first. She was his girlfriend, you see. But she chose me instead." He looked expectantly at her but Cassandra's face wore only a contemptuous look. "You don't believe me? Why don't you ask him?"

"I shall, soon. I'm going to see him now." She picked up her bag and started walking towards the door.

"Listen, Cassandra," he said in a harsh voice, "there's no way I'm going to allow my son to grow up calling Bevis his father. So keep that in mind when you're making your plans."

"Don't threaten me, Ray. I, not you, can prevent Benjie from growing up calling the wrong man his father," Cassandra told him, halting in the middle of the room.

"And what do you mean by that?"

"What I mean is that Benjie is Bevis' son, not yours," she told him without compassion. The little she had felt had been killed by his attack on Bevis' integrity.

"That's a lie!" he screamed, jumping out of bed. "Why, you slut!" he growled, lunging at her.

Cassandra did not know quite what happened. One minute he was moving towards her swiftly and the next lying in a heap on the floor, clutching wildly at his throat, his eyes wide and full of fear. Everything happened so fast and unexpectedly that she could do nothing at first but simply stand rooted to the spot. Then as suddenly, she rushed to him, calling his name but it was obvious he could not hear her. He was thrashing about, his breath quick and shallow.

"Please God, don't let him die," Cassandra prayed, springing to her feet and rushing for the door to get help. As she raised her hand, the door opened and Bevis walked in.

"What is it?" he asked sharply, and then seeing his brother on the floor, rushed to him with an exclamation on his lips. "Get help, Cassandra, quick."

Cassandra flew out of the room and ran to the office where a nurse on duty quickly answered her call and rushed to Raymond's room. Bevis was holding the patient on his lap as he vomited on the floor, making choking noises as he did so. Cassandra automatically noticed that Bevis' trousers were soiled but he himself seemed unaware of it as he concentrated on easing his brother's discomfort.

The nurse took one look at the patient and darted out of the room to come back shortly with two doctors and another nurse. Cassandra was unceremoniously shoved out as Raymond was being lifted back to his bed.

She waited for almost an hour on the visitors' bench near the entrance, watching the medical staff darting here and there but fearing to ask them for any news. Oh why doesn't someone come and tell me what's happening, she kept wondering , her teeth chattering as if she was cold. The waiting was extremely agonising.

"Hey, Cassandra," Dominic ambled towards her and joined her on the bench. "Why're you out here, doctor in?"

"It's Ray," Cassandra said, trying to steady her voice. "He ... collapsed."

"Gosh, it had to happen to me."

"To Ray, not to you," Cassandra snapped.

"I mean if Bevis ever finds out I had not been in the room, he'll flay me alive."

"Stop whining, Dome. Your brother is in there fighting for his life and all you can think about is what's going to happen to you!" she rebuked.

He looked taken aback by her manner. "Is it as bad as that?"

"I don't know. They've been in there for a while. What can they be doing?

233

Bevis could at least come and tell me what's happening. He knows how worried I am."

"Is he there too?" Dominic asked, his eyes roving restlessly around as if searching for an escape.

"Yes." Cassandra then briefed him on what had happened, omitting the little dispute she had had with Raymond. "Why don't you go and find out what's happening?"

A few minutes later, Bevis himself dropped down wearily beside her.

"How's he?" she asked, searching his face for signs, any signs.

"The doctors say the next few hours are going to be crucial."

"But what caused the attack?" As if I don't know, she added to herself silently.

Bevis looked at her strangely before he answered. "He had a heart attack."

"A heart attack? But ... but ... I didn't know he had a weak heart!" she exclaimed weakly. Now there was no doubt she was responsible for the crisis.

"He had no history of heart disease, if that's what you mean. But as you know, any kind of shock or excitement can bring on an attack, especially in a weakened condition like Ray's. He was diagnosed diabetic a few weeks ago which, I understand, is another risk factor for a heart attack."

"My God, I didn't know," Cassandra whispered, covering her face with her hands. "Why didn't you tell me?"

"I did not think it was necessary for you to know—at the time," he answered coldly.

Cassandra debated whether to tell him the truth about what had happened exactly but decided this was not the time.

"Dome asked me to sit with him for a while so that he could go out. Ray was asleep at the time and then woke up. The next thing I knew he was on the floor in a kind of fit. I was just trying to help him when you came."

"All right. It would be better if you went home now. I'll try to keep you informed of his progress."

"But why? You're not blaming me for the attack, are you, Bevis?"

"I'm not blaming you for anything. But I think it would be better if you stayed away for your own sake." He got up and left without another word.

Two days later, Raymond died without ever regaining consciousness. Cassandra felt shattered and weighed down with guilt. And the worst part was that she could not talk to anybody about it.

Two weeks after Raymond's funeral, which she did not attend, Cassandra flew to London at her sister's invitation.

After her return from London, Bevis suggested a meeting to talk over Raymond's will.

"You certainly took your time coming back," was his greeting. They were sitting facing each other in the lounge of the Hotel Concord.

"I didn't have much to come back to, did I?" Cassandra retorted.

"You have a child who needs you in case you've forgotten."

"I left Benjie in good hands. But I don't think we came here to discuss Benjie."

"In a way we did because as you know, he's Ray's sole heir and you and I the executors of the will."

"What?" Cassandra exclaimed, feeling an insane urge to burst into laughter. She was not surprised Ray had made Benjie his heir, but that he should have named her and Bevis executors of the will was surely carrying his sense of irony too far! "Anyway," she said in a controlled voice, "I've given the matter a lot of thought and have decided, that on behalf of my son, who is still a minor, I cannot accept the inheritance. You're free to do with it whatever you like. Benjie cannot have it."

Bevis gave her a long, hard stare before he said, "I'm afraid you cannot do that. The estate is bequeathed to Benjie and not to you. You're just a caretaker until he's of age."

"And when he is, who do we say left it to him?"

"The opening sentence of the will makes it vastly clear... 'To my only son and heir Benjamin Mugarura...' he read aloud. You are not thinking of challenging a dead man in a paternity suit, I hope?"

"You think I'm heartless, don't you?"

"What my thoughts *are* on the matter is really not the issue here. I don't feel equal to engaging in a battle of wills with you now, Cassandra."

"Back to the will then."

"Yes, back to the will. Here's your copy, which you may wish to study at your leisure. I'll now highlight what I think is important. Before we proceed, there's something I want to say. Only you and I know that Benjie's not Ray's real son. It would, in my opinion, serve no useful purpose to make any disclosures now. My father was very much attached to Ray and his death was a big blow to him. However, the fact that Ray left a son is a consolation. I promised I would take Benjie to be installed as Ray's heir in accordance with traditions. I hope you don't have objections to that?"

"It doesn't bother me if it doesn't bother you," Cassandra answered, watching him thoughtfully.

Bevis shrugged, saying, "We've already agreed to go along with the lie, so what difference would it make now? To turn to the document, Ray did not have much to leave. The long stay in the hospital ate into his savings and forced him to sell some of his shares in the company. But after a few bequests, mainly to family members, the rest goes to Benjie. It's all there," he pointed to her copy of the will.

Cassandra glanced through the document quickly and then raised her eyes to his. "You seem to be the only member of his family he has not left anything, not even a small memento to remember him by?"

"There was no need for Ray to leave me anything. He was my brother and I shall always remember and miss him," Bevis told her coldly.

"Do you blame me for his death?"

"I beg your pardon?"

"I said that do you think I was responsible for Ray's death?"

"I heard what you said the first time," he interjected testily. "I was only wondering what I could've possibly said to make you jump to that fantastic conclusion."

"I thought ... that ... " Cassandra stammered and to her mortification, she felt a threat of tears behind her eyelids. "Excuse me," she jumped up, grabbed her bag and hurried away.

After waiting fifteen minutes more without any sign of her, Bevis gathered his papers, put them in his briefcase and left.

* * *

"No grief lasts for ever," his friend, James, told him. "Give it time."

"But time is not on my side. I don't have forever to live. I'm thirty-six now and soon I'll be regarded as an old man. I'd like to settle down now, have more kids with her," Bevis said.

"More kids?" James eagerly seized on that. He had had his suspicions about Cassandra's kid ever since the sleepwalking incident.

"She already has one kid, hasn't she?"

"Ah, yes. And so she has. You have other options you know?"

"No, I don't," Bevis said stubbornly. "Christ, I could strangle her!"

"Hey, cool it, man. Why don't you take a holiday while the courts are in recess?"

"I wish I could but I have a lot of work to do."

"And work's your antidote to moping, right?"

"Something like that."

"I wish I could be of help, like having wings to play Cupid!"

"Even without wings, talking to you always helps me to put my problems in perspective. Now let's talk about you. How're you and Jane getting along?"

"Like a house on fire. We've decided to tie the knot and you're going to be our bestman. How's that for irony? It could have been you, remember?"

"Stop looking over your shoulder, man, and be happy. You and Jane are made for each other and I'm more than happy to be of service to you both," Bevis said sincerely. But at the same time he felt a deep longing for the kind of bliss he saw on his friend's face. "Tell me more about your plans, have you set the date?"

"Only tentatively. When it's confirmed, you'll be the first to know."

* * *

Lotus International was going through its share of postwar depression and rumours of retrenchment and cutbacks were rife, undermining the morale of the staff. Wakilo had died some months back of AIDS, or so it was rumoured, and the man who had replaced him as Managing Director seemed to have come with the sole purpose of lining his pockets, regardless of whether the company went bankrupt or not.

"I hear Collin has threatened to resign. He says he can't work with Mulindwa," Marie remarked one day.

"For once I'm in total agreement with him," Cassandra commented. "It appears to me we might be witnessing the last days of LI."

"Which means our last days as salaried employees too. I'm glad you raised the subject because I've been intending to talk to you about us."

"Ass?"

"No. 'Us' as in U S," Marie spelt out. "I think it's time to make our exit too."

"Go on, Marie, I'm all ears. Where do we go, what do we do?"

"How about starting our own publishing company? Ours," she added and looked at her expectantly.

"You're kidding of course?"

"Never been more serious in my life. I think it's better to make graceful exits than wait to be shoved out of the door. Think seriously about my proposal, Cassandra."

"I don't have to think about it. It sounds quite exciting but doesn't it require a lot of money?"

"Definitely, but let's jump that hurdle when we come to it."

• "I should imagine that would be the very first one to get out of the way?"

"No. The very first stage is to agree in principle what we want to do."

"Then we come to the money? What's the use of talking about something you can't afford to do?"

"That's when we ask some expert to do a feasibility study for us."

"That's really putting the cart before the horse because feasibility study or

237

no feasibility study, the crux of the matter is still how much capital will the project require and how much of that can the two of us put up?"

"I think we might be using different words to mean the same thing. Quite seriously, this is not an off-the-cuff idea. I've been mulling over it for some time now and I know the two of us can make it work."

"Ah ... I don't know," Cassandra said skeptically. "The kind of capital needed for that kind of venture seems way beyond our means."

"Don't be a wet blanket, Cassandra, of course we can afford it. We'll borrow, cheat or steal but we'll have a go at it. Most businesses are built on credit, you know."

"Well, okay. So how do we go about hiring somebody to do the feasibility study?"

"Dan has a team of experts. I don't see why we can't ask him to help."

"I have no objection to that."

"Good."

* * *

But when the report was ready, neither could believe the magnitude, in terms of costs, of the proposed project.

"It reads like the National Budget," Marie exclaimed.

"Twenty five million shillings is ridiculous! Where can we get all this money from?" Cassandra added incredulously.

"This shows how unprepared, you girls are for this kind of venture," Dan told them condescendingly. "You're not planning a Sunday picnic for heaven's sake. You're contemplating joining the world of women entrepreneurs. From now on, you start to think and talk in terms of seven figures plus."

"But it does not change the fact that this is far beyond our means," Cassandra persisted.

"Let me see how best to put it. You cannot make money without spending money, and the more you invest the more worthwhile the endeavour," Dan told them. "Am I making sense?"

"Sure. Basically, what you are saying's that those who have shall have more, and those who don't ..." his wife was saying sarcastically when Cassandra cut her short, saying gravely, "Can we study this before we commit ourselves?"

"By all means."

***

Later Marie made a shot at persuading Cassandra to accept Dan's offer of a

238

loan. "He's not offering charity, you know. We'll be expected to pay it back in full plus interest. If we're going to do business with a modicum of success, we're going to have to be astute and seize every opportunity which comes our way."

"We could try getting the loan from the Uganda Women Finance and Credit Trust. I hear they offer favourable terms," Cassandra suggested.

"You must have heard that from one of the workers there. They offer peanuts and that, after making you sweat blood to prove that you qualify for the loan."

"In that case, I suggest we revise the proposal and reduce the principle sum to a more realistic figure. There are many non-essentials we could do away with."

"How much share capital would you be comfortable with?" Marie asked her.

"I could manage to borrow five million," Cassandra said doubtfully, wondering whether her sister's offer of financial help still held.

"I'll have to ask George," Mellinda told her when approached on the phone.

"Why?"

"Well, everything I own is now his and vice versa."

"You don't say! Are you sure George does not want to marry you for your money, Mellie?"

"That's the most unkind thing you've ever said to me, Cassandra."

"I'm sorry, Mellie, it was a joke.

"A joke in poor taste. I'll think about your request and get back to you."

Next she approached her brother. "I don't have money to throw down the drain," was Gavin's unkind response. "If you're dissatisfied with your present job, find another one. You have enough experience in the field to stand you in good stead."

"I'm well aware of what I'm worth, thank you, but how I choose to utilise it is my business," Cassandra told him coldly.

"Well, good luck to you then."

"Luck has nothing to do with it." She vowed she would make him eat his words when she had attained what she wanted without his help. She thought of approaching Bevis to allow her to borrow the money from Benjie's trust but dismissed the idea. He probably held the same view as Gavin.

At the next meeting, Dan suggested that they could reduce their share-capital by forming a limited company and inviting other people to buy shares. "You two could retain majority shares which will ensure your controlling power over the company. You could draw up a memorandum of understanding to that effect."

"It sounds reasonable if we can find people willing to risk their money," Cassandra said.

239

"You have one already... me," Dan told them magnanimously. "And I think I can sell the idea to John." John was Marie's brother and his business partner.

"I'll ask Mellie too," Cassandra promised, excited by the idea.

Mellinda readily agreed and instructed her to discuss it with Gavin.

"Have you secured your own share of the capital?" Gavin asked her.

"I'll get it, don't you worry," she told him airily.

"Well, I'm not worried because as it happens, I'm in a position to put your agony to an end."

"Really? How?"

"I can lend you the money myself," he told her affably and then waited for the effect.

"I don't understand," Cassandra remarked, puzzled. "Hardly a month ago you thought me a bad insurance risk. What has made you change your mind now?"

"Let's say I revised my opinion of your remarkable ability to succeed at whatever you set your mind on," Gavin replied brusquely. "You have the unfortunate habit of looking gift horses in the mouth, sis dear."

"I'm sorry, but I never expected you of all people ... I mean, I'm rather overwhelmed," Cassandra amended quickly. "Are you sure you want to do this – give me all the money for my share in the venture?" Cassandra quizzed with excitement.

"No. I'm not giving you the money, I'm lending it to you."

"That's what I meant."

"And I'll expect it back in a period to be agreed on between us plus some nominal interest of 2% pa."

"Yes, sir! I can't tell you how relieved I am. It's very generous of you, Gavin."

"Hey, what're brothers for?" And fools, Gavin added to himself. He had tried to dissuade Bevis from his misguided chivalry to no avail. "Cassandra has neither the experience nor the aptitude for business. This venture of her is doomed to fail," he had warned.

"I don't think chicanery is a prerequisite for the kind of business Cassandra and Marie are contemplating," Bevis had replied. "Don't forget they have the weight of a veteran business man, Kizito, behind them. I think they'll do just fine."

"I hope you don't feel sort of responsible for her, do you?" Gavin pursued. He was totally baffled by Bevis' behaviour. "It's not as if she was Raymond's widow," he added tentatively.

"You're reading too much into a simple gesture, Gavin," Bevis coolly told him. "Cassandra wants to start a business and I have the means to help her do so. It's as simple as that."

"Well then, why the secrecy? Why don't you go to her and say, 'Hey, chum, I'm your guardian angel who has been sent from heaven to bestow upon you a largesse', because that's what you are, in effect, doing?"

"Let it go, pal," Bevis advised and Gavin acted upon his instructions with a clear conscience.

After the groundwork was laid, and everything for launching the new publishing company, **NEW AGE PUBLISHERS**, was in place, Cassandra and Marie adjudged it the right time to tender their resignations from Lotus International. Not long after that, the firm came crashing down like a pack of cards. This was to turn out to be of advantage to the emerging young company as a number of good manuscripts found their way there. But in the meantime, the two young and inexperienced entrepreneurs had numerous teething problems to battle with.

Marie was designated the Director of **NAP** and Cassandra the Chief Editor. But although Marie's interest had initially been as ardent as Cassandra's, it gradually started to wane when her husband was appointed a Cabinet Minister in the new administration. She had to divide her time between the business and her increasing social duties.

The person, therefore, who wielded the greatest control over the business, shaping it and giving it the legacy of efficiency and reliability, was Cassandra.

Chapter Sixteen

"Good morning, crew," Cassandra greeted as she swept through the front room of **NAP** without stopping.

"Good morning, Mrs Agutamba," the three occupants replied in unison, their eyes reflecting varied emotions as they followed her elegant figure to the inner office.

"When I grow old, I want to look just like that," Nabunnya, the youngest of the three, said with open envy.

"You call her old?" Dorcas, the Office Manager and personal secretary to the two executives, remarked, scandalised. She was of indeterminate age and often tried to pass herself off as a young woman. "She can't be more than thirty," she added, referring to Cassandra.

"That's ancient as far as I'm concerned," the nineteen-year-old insisted.

"Don't worry, Nabu, in ten years or so, you too'll have the world at your feet just like her," Dorcas consoled her.

"Ten years! But that's forever," Nabunnya exclaimed. "I want to get there now."

"The young are so impatient," Juma, the Marketing Manager, remarked.

"And the old are so smug," Nabunnya shot back.

"I think we can put our time to better use than bickering," Dorcas told the two as she gathered a bundle of correspondence and her dictation pad and headed for the passage leading to Cassandra's office.

Outside the mahogany door on which was emblazoned, **Chief Editor**, in black, Dorcas stopped to smoothen down her grey skirt and straighten the collar of her white blouse.

"Come in," Cassandra called when she knocked. "What do you have for me?"

242

"A couple of messages and a report."

"All right, take a seat ... shan't be long." Cassandra returned to her file, allowing Dorcas to study her discreetly. She was wearing a lilac two-piece of crimplene material. Around her neck was a tiny string of pearls with matching earrings. Her long permed hair was gathered in a chignon at the back and secured with a black ribbon with tiny silver beads. Her makeup was so expertly applied that it gave the impression of uncontrived good looks.

Some people have all the luck, Dorcas thought. She naturally envied Cassandra for being everything she could never hope to be but she did not allow it to interfere with her work or her loyalty to her employer.

"Sorry," Cassandra said, pushing the file away. "Didn't mean to keep you waiting." She skimmed through the letters Dorcas had pushed towards her before appending her signature. "I don't think I'll have time for dictation this morning," she said observing Dorcas' note book and poised pen. "I want to go through these reports before the meeting. Has Mrs Kizito come in yet?"

"No. She telephoned shortly before you came in to say she was held up and could not make it before the afternoon. She suggested rescheduling the meeting to another day in the week but I wanted to consult with you first before informing other board members."

"Umm," Cassandra grunted thoughtfully. "Did she say exactly when she would be coming in?"

"No. Only that she couldn't make it before two."

"Right. I'll give her a ring later. Now, let's see ... Wednesday would be a good day but I better talk to John and Mirembe first. I'll let you know afterwards so that you can issue a notice to that effect. What else do you have on your mind?"

Dorcas consulted her notebook. "Your brother-in-law called and left a message that he'd call on you at 12.30. I warned him you might have a lunch engagement but he said he'd risk it."

"I have, as a matter of fact, with my husband. It's our second wedding anniversary," Cassandra confided impulsively.

"Oh, congratulations, Mrs Agutamba. I hope you'll celebrate many more in future."

"Thank you, Dorcas." She tried to imagine how excited Bevis would be at her wonderful news and felt impatient with the dragging hours. She wanted to be with him, to see the thrill she felt reciprocated on his face.

They had been married for two years and yet every morning she woke up beside him seemed like a miracle. It had taken almost another tragedy, after Raymond's death, to bring them together again.

After her resignation from LI, Cassandra had had to vacate the company

243

house and find alternative accommodation. This had not been easy and once again she had accepted Gavin and Tonia's invitation to stay at Luzzi until something suitable was found. While there, it was inevitable that she and Bevis should come into constant contact.

"Have you ever thought what a handsome couple you and Cassandra would make?" Tonia whispered to Bevis one evening. He had just brought Cassandra and the children back from a Sunday evening ride. "Why don't you ask her?" went on the irrepressible Tonia, "for Benjie's sake, if not for any other reason!"

Bevis did not answer her but he raised his eyes and looked at Cassandra, who blissfully was unaware of her sister-in-law's efforts at matchmaking. Tonia, whose suggestion had been on the spur of the moment, was shocked by the naked desire in Bevis' eyes as he gazed at Cassandra. A feeling of excitement went through her and her imagination began soaring.

It was almost a year since Raymond's death and apart from the fact that Cassandra never went out with another man, there was no other evidence of grief. With a little encouragement and subtle push in the right direction, everything could turn out well, she thought dreamily.

"I must be going back now," Bevis said, getting up abruptly.

"But you said you'd wait for Gavin," she reminded him. "He should be home any minute now."

"I'll talk to Gavin tomorrow."

"Say something to make him stay for dinner," Tonia appealed to Cassandra, and then turning back to Bevis added, "You said you were having problems with your housekeeper?"

"May?" Cassandra asked, immediately alert.

"I'm not having problems with May exactly, it's her son, Byensi. He's now a major in the army and thinks the position of housekeeper too lowly for his mother."

"What does he want her to do?" Cassandra asked him.

"He wants her to go back home and look after his recently acquired property."

"So what's the problem? Finding a new housekeeper?'

"No, although that's a bridge I'll have to cross later. But the problem now is May herself. She resents being told what to do by a beardless youth, who until he ran to the bush and came back shouldering a gun, was still running to her for his meals. Her words, not mine."

"Well, that settles it then, doesn't it? May must do what she feels will make her happy."

"It's not quite that simple. Byensi thinks I'm exerting undue influence on May to stay but I've actually left the choice to her. Well, I don't want to bore you with my domestic problems and May is still very much in charge." This directly to Cassandra who understood the vagaries of May's draconian law regarding meals.

Feeling uncomfortable under his piercing stare, Cassandra turned to the children and clapped her hands to gain their attention.

"Uncle Bevis is leaving, what do you say?"

"Good-bye, Uncle Bevis," Namara and Benjie sang out while baby Lucie, of less than two years, mimed them. Bevis hugged each in turn and left.

* * *

It was after supper when the phone rang and Gavin picked it up. "Yes, James, this is Gavin." He listened for some moments, his face registering shock. "When?" He listened some more. "But he was here less than two hours ago— yes, yes how terrible!" That caught the two women's attention and they both listened intently.

"How's he? Sure, I'm on my way."

"What's happened to Bevis?" both Tonia and Cassandra demanded as soon as he replaced the receiver.

"Sit down please and I'll tell you all about it."

"Really, Gavin!" Cassandra postulated but she fell into a chair all the same, and not because her brother demanded it but because her legs could no longer support her.

"For heaven's sake, Gavin, don't keep us in suspense because you feel the occasion calls for solemnity," his wife exclaimed tartly.

"Okay. Bevis has been shot."

"What?" both exclaimed shooting up from their chairs.

"Calm down, calm down. It's not as bad as it sounds. He was wounded ... you know, just wounded."

"Where's he now?" from Cassandra.

"Who did it?" from Tonia.

"He's at home and the assailant has not been apprehended. I'm going there now and will have more information when I come back."

"I'm coming with you," Cassandra told him.

"It's rather late, Cassandra, you can see him in the morning."

"I can find my own transport if you don't want to take me."

"All right but hurry."

"I'm ready, let's go."

Dr James Mugodi was waiting for them downstairs at Kalungu. He and

Gavin knew each other from their college days but Cassandra had never met him.

"How's he?" Gavin asked anxiously.

"He's resting," the doctor said, his attention on Cassandra.

"This is my sister, Cassandra. She insisted on coming along," Gavin hurriedly performed the introductions, hoping to refocus James' wandering interest on Bevis and his condition.

"I'm mighty pleased to meet you, Cassandra, at long last. I've heard so much about you."

"Look here, man," Gavin said impatiently but James laid a firm hand on his arm and led him to a chair. Gavin dropped into it with a sigh of exasperation. Cassandra remained standing, provoking an inquiring look from the substitute host.

"May I go to him?" she asked, looking at the doctor directly.

"I don't see why not. It'd do him a world of good." He was about to follow this up with directions when Cassandra darted away.

Both men were silent, listening to the sound of her scampering steps on the stairs.

Turning to Gavin with a good-humoured expression on his face, James found the latter scowling. "Was Bevis shot and wounded or wasn't he?"

"Oh, Mr Lawyer, don't sound so intimidating. I'm not in the witness stand," James crowed. Then assuming a more serious expression, he went on, "Indeed Bevis was shot and wounded by that scandal of the housekeeper's son but fortunately, not fatally. The bullet caught him in the left arm. A few more centimetres to the right and we'd not be here telling bedtime stories."

"But why ... I mean, why did May's son try to kill him? As I recall, he, Bevis, was extraordinarily good to him?"

"Search me," James said, spreading his hands.

"How did it happen?"

"The young soldier, who I gather, is a little too fond of the bottle, had an argument with his mother earlier in the day. He left the place uttering threats and came back later, armed, to make good these threats. According to the *shamba* boy, when Bevis hooted, he ran to open for him and heard the shot just before he got to the gate. Fortunately Bevis kept his head and managed to drive in. The bullet missed his heart by only a fraction of an inch."

"Shouldn't he be in hospital?"

"He wouldn't hear of it. I managed to dislodge the bullet using local anaesthesia, dressed the wound and sent him to bed with painkillers. He should be okay in a few days."

"Has the incident been reported to the police? Attempted murder is a felony, if I may remind you."

"You don't need to remind me, Gavin. That was the first thing I wanted to do immediately after I attended to Bevis but he would not have it. In fact, he made it clear that he did not want any of this to get out. I suppose it was his housekeeper he was thinking about."

"Well, I can well believe that of him. Where's the woman herself anyway? Has she cleared off the premises yet?"

"She was a bit hysterical and I sent her to bed with a sedative. If anyone's inclined to report the incident, I think it is she. She was breathing fire."

"Don't you believe it. Blood's thicker than water. I don't think she'd have the heart. If she wants to save her master though, it would be better if she cleared off the property first thing in the morning. I'll suggest it to her if she is too thick to see it herself," Gavin added with determination. "She's staying an awful long time up there," he added, changing the subject.

"Who? Oh Cassandra. You're surely not worrying about her maiden virtue, are you?" the doctor asked, twinkling at him. "The man can barely sit up, let alone overpower a strong-willed, sensible girl like the 'exhibit'," he added, poking fun at his lawyer friend.

Completely missing the humour, Gavin said gravely, "Cassandra and Bevis don't always hit it off together, you know."

"What do you bet we go up there and find them wrapped in each other's arms metaphorically speaking, of course?"

"Do you know something I don't?" Gavin asked suspiciously.

"I wouldn't tell you even if I did. But we can now go and rescue Bevis from that tigress sister of yours."

"Cassandra is not ... " Gavin started to protest hotly when he saw a twinkle in the other's eyes. "You haven't changed much, James, have you? You still love to play the fool!"

"I think what ails our nation mainly these days is not the disease, the poverty and hunger, the unemployment, corruption and what have you. It's the fact that people've forgotten how to laugh," James told him solemnly as they ascended the staircase. "People no longer know what it is like to be happy, to play and have fun. They go about with grim faces calculating profits and losses, plotting against each other and generally conniving with the devil to turn a perfectly beautiful country, like ours, into purgatory."

"That's quite some philosophy, doctor! Let's get together sometime and talk more about it," Gavin remarked as they approached the sickroom.

* * *

Outside Bevis' bedroom, Cassandra halted and took a deep breath to steady herself before she turned the handle. Inside, the room was dimly lit by a shaded bedside lamp. But she could easily make out Bevis' form propped up by pillows on the bed. She approached cautiously and stood gazing at him while tears ran down her cheeks freely. She shuddered at the thought of what the madman almost did and made a vow to herself about what she was going to do once Bevis was out of danger. She knelt down on the carpet and took his hand in hers, prepared to wait for him to wake up.

"I had the most wonderful dream," Bevis' voice, sounding a little disembodied, startled her. "Tell me that it's real and not a dream."

"Oh, you're awake?" Cassandra said. "I almost died when I heard you had been shot."

"I think it's a dream after all," Bevis said, trying to raise himself to a halfsitting position.

"Let me help you." Cassandra expertly propped pillows behind him and gently pushed him back.

"Good, now I can look at you properly. Tell me," he asked in a more serious tone, "why my demise might have robbed you of a good night's sleep."

"Because I love you, Bevis," Cassandra replied instantly.

"Do you really, Cassandra?" He tried to lean forward but stopped halfway with an exclamation of pain.

"What's the matter? Shall I call Dr Mugodi?" Cassandra asked, alarmed.

"Don't you dare!" he growled out harshly. Beads of perspiration trembled on his forehead and his breath came out in short, sharp gasps.

"I think you need a doctor, Bevis."

"No, not yet. I want to tell you my dream."

"Afterwards, when you're not in pain," Cassandra suggested, hovering over him helplessly. "Is there anything at all I can do to help?"

"As a matter of fact there is," Bevis replied, smiling wanly. "You can kiss me and make my dream come true."

"You humbug, I should have guessed you were shamming," Cassandra reproached him, before bending to touch his lips lightly with hers.

"If I die now, I'll die the happiest man on earth," he murmured with his eyes closed.

"I think I'll call the doctor after all; you sound more delirious every minute. Perhaps you better rest now before you exhaust yourself."

"I don't mind exhausting myself into a coma because as I said, I don't want to wake up and find that I was dreaming all this, after all."

"Oh you'll wake up all right. Benjie and I need you too much to let you slip through our fingers now."

"That sounds like a proposal, is it?" he asked her.

"It's an affirmation of my feelings for you."

"Do you know, in spite of the pain and shock, I'm almost glad Byensi took a shot at me."

"Of course you don't mean that?" Cassandra expostulated.

He smiled at her gently and stretched his hand for hers, this time without mishap. "I do mean it, beautiful, because the incident has brought us together again and stirred that which has been dormant in your heart."

"That's not true. My heart has not known any rest for a long time and no one but you lay at the bottom of it."

"Tell me more about that," he requested.

"It's a long story which you'll perhaps get to hear about some day. Tonight you're weak and need to rest. Let's just limit it to rejoicing for being back together again. This time for good, I hope."

"Amen to that," Bevis echoed, his voice fading. "You now have my permission to summon the doctor," he added in a whisper and closed his eyes.

Cassandra quietly let herself out of the room and was closing the door when the two men reached the top stair, "Shh, he's asleep," she told them.

"In that case, we shall not disturb him," James said, his shrewd eyes studying her.

"I'll just take a peep if it's all the same to you," Gavin said, opening the door.

"How did you find him?" James asked Cassandra as they descended the steps. "Did you get to talk to him?"

"A little. He seemed drowsy."

"That's the drug he's been resisting. He'll now sleep until morning."

"Is he in much pain?"

"Not much more than expected in the circumstances. He lost a lot of blood and should be in hospital on a drip but we shall try to improvise here with lots of fluids. The drug'll take care of the pain and in a month or so, he can take you dancing."

"Who's going dancing?" Gavin asked, joining them.

"No one. Just a figure of speech. About tonight, you two can go home now. I'll stay the night."

"I'm staying too," Cassandra said firmly.

"Dash it, Cassandra, what for?" Gavin asked her. "It's perfectly understandable for James to stay, but you'll be in the way."

"I can make myself useful just in case May decides to leave or is unequal to playing her role. What do you think, doctor?'

"I think that firstly, you should dispense with formalities and call me James. Secondly, I think your staying is a good idea."

Gavin scowled at them both before asking his sister, "What would you like me to bring you in the morning?"

"I'll jot down what I need... Here you are."

"I'll walk you to the car," James said. "Incidentally, shouldn't we inform Emily about this?'

"I'll ring her in the morning from my office. No need to alarm her more than necessary," Gavin offered and then added awkwardly, "I hope Cassandra's foolhardy action'll not give rise to talk? I suppose you think I sound like an old hen but... ... "

"No, Gavin, I don't. I think it does you credit to be concerned about your sister's reputation. But judging from the little I've seen of her, I'd say she is the last person to give a damn. In any case, you can always demand he makes an honest woman of her, to use an old-fashioned expression, failing which you can challenge him to a duel."

"I never know when you're serious or joking, James," Gavin complained, getting into his car. As he drove away, he allowed his mind to conjure up the picture of Bevis and Cassandra together, a dashed good idea, he thought.

As things turned out, no threats were issued or duels fought by anybody to bring about the desired end. Only a simple civil ceremony five months later did it.

The two years of her marriage to Bevis had more than fulfilled her expectations of a happy union. The only cloud, on her otherwise bright horizon, was her failure to conceive again.

The doctors told them there was nothing wrong with either of them but still nothing happened. But two months before their second anniversary, Cassandra missed her period and started to feel a ray of hope. But she restrained from telling her husband until the doctor had confirmed her suspicions. But even after that, she decided she would not tell Bevis until the day of their anniversary which was today. It would be her present to him and she knew he would be overjoyed with the news.

* * *

"Did you say you're pregnant, Cassandra?" Bevis whispered hoarsely. Cassandra looked at him with alarm as the thought that there might be hereditary heart disease in the family flashed through her mind.

"Are you all right, darling?" she asked anxiously. Before he answered, Bevis took a large handkerchief and mopped his face.

"About what you said, are you sure?" he asked, still breathing fas.

"Of course I'm sure. I confirmed it with the doctor two weeks ago."

"And you did not tell me?"

"I wanted the news to be my anniversary present to you. Don't you want this baby?"

"Dearest, you know I want us to have more babies. I've been wanting it ever since we got married as you know, but we were both convinced it would never be. That's why the news of your pregnancy almost knocked me senseless."

"Take it easy, sweetheart, perhaps I shouldn't have sprung it on you like this."

"Cassandra, this means more to me than you'll ever know. I feel like a man once more, like I could never disappoint you again."

"But you've never disappointed me, Bevis!" Cassandra cried. "You've more than fulfilled my highest expectations. It was not your fault that it took me so long to conceive."

"I thought it was my fault. I thought I was barren," Bevis told her gravely.

"How could you think that when we already have Benjie?" He did not answer but looked at her strangely. "Oh no!" she cried with a horrified look. "Surely you did not think Benjie was Ray's child after all, did you?"

He nodded dumbly. "I'm a fool all right but what else could I think?"

"You could have come to me with your fears, confided in me."

"I wanted to but I did not have the guts."

"It's my fault. I shouldn't have gone on and on about it. I had no idea you were tormenting yourself like that. Please forgive me."

"Right now, there's nothing I wouldn't forgive you, including murder. You've just restored my life to me in its entirety, you see."

"You did that once for me, so why shouldn't I return the favour? Besides, seeing a smile like that on your face again is worth everything I could ever wish for."

"Oh what a lovely thing to hear you say! Now I want you here, in my arms, telling me that you love me."

"I love you, dear husband; very much. You know that, don't you?" she said, falling into his inviting arms.

"I do now, yes, I do, dearest. It's been a long road to travel but I believe I've finally made it home, thanks to your unfailing love."

"I think it's more to your perseverance. A less resolute person would have given up on me long ago. But you didn't."

"No, I didn't because I knew that without you, sweet Cassandra, my life would not be complete. Only you could make me feel like this, good and absolutely whole."

"Oh Bevis!" was all Cassandra could say.